# Ignited

# laurie wetzel

ISBN 13: 978-1-63489-002-1
eISBN: 978-1-63489-001-4

LCCN: 2015944820
Printed in the United States of America
First Printing: 2015
19   18   17   16   15          5   4   3   2   1

Cover and Interior design by Tiffany Daniels

Wise Ink Creative Publishing
837 Glenwood Avenue
Minneapolis, MN 55405
wiseinkpub.com

To order, visit www.itascabooks.com or call 1-800-901-3480.
Reseller discounts available.

*For my dad, Lawrence Dean Burger,*
*and my dear friends Anne Walsh and Duane Comnick.*
*Though you've gone too soon, memories of you live on.*

# CHAPTER 1

# Maddy

I'M DATING AN ANGEL.

Up until yesterday, I thought they didn't exist. Now I'm falling in love with one.

Considering the insane events that have happened in the last five days—especially the last twenty-four hours—I shouldn't be focusing on what MJ is. I am, though.

Whether or not I believed in them, angel references are everywhere. They appear in books, movies, and TV, wearing anything from white togas to trench coats. Their image has been made into figurines and appears on jewelry and even clothes. They're a symbol of hope that billions of people all over the world have accepted. Some people pray to them daily, assured in their beliefs; others do it in times of desperation, when all hope seems lost. So many people have prayed for a miracle—prayed for proof that someone is listening.

Why then was I chosen over all of them?

I glance over at MJ lying beside me on Hiniker Bridge. He's staring at the clouds with his head resting on his arms. It's easy to forget what he is. His short brown hair is messy as if only his fingers have touched it, his hazel eyes suck me in no matter how far apart we are, and his smile shines brighter than high beams on the darkest night. He wears plain white shirts and dark jeans, and somehow on him they look better than a designer outfit—not that I wouldn't mind seeing him in one. The only thing keeping him from being perfect is the silence coming from his chest.

My heart stutters, pounding out the truth I can't ignore. MJ is dead.

He is dead and I am not.

A sigh unintentionally leaves my lips.

MJ rolls to face me. "What is it?"

I offer a weak smile. "Nothing."

He reaches out, taking my hand. A buzzing jolt of energy—his essence—courses through my body, searching for any clues as to what upset me. He frowns, not liking whatever he found.

"No more secrets, remember?"

All morning we've been sharing small details of our lives, making good on the promise we made yesterday. MJ's asked me about school, hobbies, and music. I've asked about places he's traveled and what foods he'd like to try now that he can taste again. As nice as it is to have time like this—where everything is calm—we're both deflecting.

He's distracting me from thinking about yesterday—the worst day of my life. I'm avoiding anything even remotely related to his angelic side. But we can't avoid it forever. At some point, we'll have to talk about it if I want to have a true relationship with him.

I take a deep breath. Talking to MJ has always been easier than talking to anyone else, but it's still uncomfortable baring my thoughts to him. He could pop the barrier I put between the world and myself as if it were no more than a bubble. I'm not sure I want him to—at least not yet.

As I release my held breath, I prepare myself for answers I'll probably never be ready to hear. "Why don't you have a halo, white gown, or wings?"

He snorts and then releases my hand, running his fingers through his hair. "That does look pretty on church windows and on top of Christmas trees, doesn't it?"

I blush and nod, hoping I haven't just insulted him.

His lips twitch, fighting a grin. "The halo is a myth. They were used in literature and art dating back to the first century to signify a holy being. It represents our light, and by that I mean good versus evil. The white gown and wings are true, though."

I expected the gown to be true, seeing as Elizabeth wore one, but not the wings. Where are hers? Where are MJ's? Every image I've seen of angel wings flows through my mind. There are so many, and they're all so different, each pair beautiful in its own way. I'm sure MJ's would be amazing.

"So where are your wings?" My stomach winds into knots, and my heart quickens. This is it. If I see them, there's no turning back—no way to unsee them. As scary as it is, I want this. I want to prove to us both that I can handle this.

His eyes darken, and he frowns. Even though we're right next to each other, it suddenly feels as if many miles separate us. "Hidden."

"Can I see them?"

"No."

His words are like an earthquake shaking my foundation. "Why not?"

"It's against the rules for angels and demons to unglamour them. And while I'm breaking many rules lately, that's one I have to keep. If an angel like me, a Protector, were to unglamour his or her wings, it would send a pulse through the air that calls to our kind—almost like a battle cry or call to arms in war. We don't need that kind of attention right now. I nearly lost you yesterday—I won't let that happen again."

My eyes clamp shut in defense as I'm bombarded with images from yesterday. The dead old woman in the bathtub ... My sister, Hannah, tied to a chair ... Justin's ludicrous toast to me and my abilities ... Learning he and MJ are dead ... Witnessing MJ's death from hundreds of years ago from inside Elizabeth's magic fountain ... Ben's death ...

Ben.

My hands still feel covered in blood from trying to save him. The pain in his eyes as he begged me to forgive him will haunt me forever.

As horrifying as all that is, one piece from yesterday can still destroy everything—the Binding Agreement. The final moments of my time in Justin's house are a blur. The evil contract that binds my soul to Justin for eternity was on the wall. The feather pen, filled with my blood, was less than an inch from touching it. One drop on the parchment was all he needed to seal the deal. One drop, and he'd own my soul for eternity.

I don't know if any of my blood touched the contract before MJ arrived. I don't know if Justin owns me. If he does, he could show up at any moment and take me away.

I know that's why MJ won't leave me alone. I'm glad, though. Eternity with Justin would be worse than Hell.

My lip quivers. Instantly, MJ is beside me, wrapping his arms around me as he pulls us into a seated position. I snuggle into his chest as his essence enters me again. It fills the ever-present hole in my heart and reduces my fear.

I didn't know relationships could be like this—feel this good. A single touch from him dissolves my problems until they're so small they no longer seem like problems at all. Even without his essence, I know his touch would comfort me and bring me strength. It means he's here for me, ready and waiting for me to let him in. Me, I'm working on it.

"Hey," he whispers. "I'm right here. Let me help you."

I sigh and bury my head farther into his chest. His arms tighten around me, and he places a kiss in my hair. A pulse of his essence ripples through me from my head to my toes.

"Please," MJ begs. "After everything you've been through, the last thing I want is to make things harder for you, but we have to figure out how to stop your emotions from manifesting into the environment. While I will be forever grateful that your storm led me to you last night, things could have been a lot worse if other beings were in town."

I turn in his arms and peek up at him, not understanding what he meant. "Why?"

"Your storm wasn't natural—just like the clouds you've created now. There is a charge in the air, almost like waves of energy, pulsing around you—anxiously waiting to see what you require next. It's not strong enough for mortals to detect. Immortals, though, would seek out the source, just as I did last night. They can use your own ability to find you. We've been lucky so far, but luck doesn't last forever."

I peek up at the sky. Dark storm clouds cover every inch. The lowest ones swirl above us, threatening to swoop down and swallow us.

Justin's words come back to haunt me: *It was supposed to be a mild October, yet it's been cloudy and raining off and on since the night you met me. Your fears have blocked out the sun.*

I glare at the darkened sky, hating that it reflects the emotions battling inside me. It's as if I have my own Bat Signal in the sky. Except mine isn't cool. Mine says, "Hey, all you angels and demons—here's the girl you're looking for. Come and get her."

"I don't know how to turn it off," I say. "I don't even know if it's possible. Am I just supposed to walk around on autopilot, unaffected by the world around me just so the sky stays blue?"

MJ lifts my chin, forcing me to meet his gaze. I melt a little, seeing the softness that exists only for me.

"I didn't mean that. What you can do"—he looks at the sky—"it's nothing I've ever seen before. But we'll figure it out. Together. And it will be easier if you talk to me."

Together. I like the sound of that. I take a deep breath and rest back against MJ.

"I was thinking about the contract."

He stiffens. "I will never let him—or anyone else—take you from me. You, Maddy, are my heart. You're my everything."

"If it's signed, there's nothing you can do."

"There is one thing."

Hope sparks in my heart, growing stronger with each beat. "What?"

IGNITED

"Do you know what demons do when a good man goes to war?"

"No."

"They run."

"Are you saying you'd start a war for me?" I joke.

"The war began long before either of us was born. For you, I'd do what my side has longed for and what the other side has feared. I'd fight."

I gasp and pull back, staring into his hazel eyes. There isn't a trace of humor or fear in them. He would go to war for me.

A battle rages inside me—one side protesting with handmade antiviolence signs, the other side gearing up to fight alongside him. I've never meant that much to someone before. It's oddly comforting. The battle inside quiets as both sides are suddenly united by one common thread: MJ.

He tilts his head up. "There now. That's better."

I follow his gaze to the once-again-clear sky.

Surprisingly, that was easy. But it was only easy because he makes the bad things seem manageable.

"When your emotions are bearing down on you and affecting the environment," he begins, "try distracting yourself with feelings that match what the weather is supposed to be doing. Like camouflage. I know it's not a perfect solution, but it'll work for the time being."

I stare at the pristine shade of robin's-egg blue that only exists on perfect days. The hope I found moments ago—the hope he created—becomes so large, it feels as if it will burst out of me at any moment. This could work. Maybe not forever, but it's a decent start.

MJ hugs me. My heart, once again whole, quickens. My stomach dips. My arms tingle, and I wrap them around him, wishing this moment would never end.

"If you're up for it, there's another one of your abilities I'd like to work on today."

Last night when we talked about my "abilities," I hadn't grasped what it meant. I was still so raw from everything that had happened. Even today, it's hard to think about my abilities—and even harder to hear him talk about them. I want him to see *me*, not some girl who does all these strange, crazy things.

My gaze roams his face, trying to dissect his thoughts. A slight smile rests on his lips, but his eyes are wide and bright. Emotions are new to him. He isn't good at hiding them. Whatever he wants to do, he's eager or excited about it.

I stand and move to the railing, looking out at the pond. The sky reflects off the glassy surface. The bright sun that appeared moments ago is now hidden behind clouds again. The reflection dissipates as a small flock of geese swim through it. On shore, fallen leaves crunch as animals scurry about. Their lives are simple—eat and sleep. Mine used to be simple too. But even after everything that has happened, do I want to go back to that? I don't know.

MJ moves beside me. "What did I—"

"Nothing."

"We both know that's not true. Tell me. Please."

Lying would be easier. It always has been. Then we could go on with our day, pretending nothing is wrong. But lies build until one day there is a hole in our relationship the size of the Grand Canyon, with me standing alone on one side, and MJ standing alone on the other. That's what happened with my family and friends. I don't want that to happen with us. It *can't* happen to us.

I turn and meet his gaze. "It's just, twenty-four hours ago I was mostly normal."

I stop. Saying it out loud makes it so much more real than in my head. I'm not normal. So what am I? Tears line my eyes, my heart races, and my lip quivers as I try to fight my emotions long enough to tell him how I feel.

"Now I'm this *thing* that has all these abilit—"

"Don't," he says, his face flinching as if in pain. "Don't ever talk like that again. Do you have any idea of the depth of my emotions for you? And then to hear you say such awful things about yourself ... These abilities don't define you. Only you can do that. All they do is show the rest of the world something I knew the moment I saw you."

"What's that?"

"That you, Maddy Page, are unique. On your gorgeous outside, you appear just as helpless as any other mortal, but you're not. It's a trick. Smoke and mirrors. You're stronger than many of the angels and demons I've come across. And that is a good thing. Because what you do to me—what you make me feel—is a gift of the utmost importance, and it needs to be protected. You have the potential to change everything. When you do, there will finally be peace for all beings Father created. But until that day, your safety is in danger. Which is why we need to do everything we can to figure out how your abilities work. Once you understand them, you can utilize them to their fullest extent."

I swallow the lump in my throat that grew as he spoke. I hadn't thought beyond today, let alone me *changing the world*.

"What if I don't want my abilities? What if I just want to be normal?"

A deep ridge forms between his brows as he stares at me. The pond quiets until only the sound of my breath can be heard. The way he spoke about me changing the world frightened me, but in his eyes I saw a spark of how greatly he wanted it.

"MJ, I'm sor—"

"No. It's my fault. I got ahead of myself. I'm used to having abilities. You're not. They're an enormous responsibility. Many angels have chosen to be reborn so they could return to a life without them. I was about to join them, until I met you. You don't have the option to be reborn, to give up your abilities. Your abilities can be wonderful, or they can cause great devastation. We can't be careless with them. I'll help you gain control over them so you can choose to use them or not use them. Either way, I support you."

"Thank you."

A weak smile forms on his lips. And with that, I know how deeply he's hurting. I didn't mean to hurt him or squash his hopes. I didn't know he had hopes for my abilities. He's obviously given them more thought than I have. He's not freaked out—that has to be a good sign, right? And he did say they could be wonderful. His being able to feel is a good thing. So is his being able to taste food. And I like it when we touch and I bring our souls to the bridge. Maybe, with control, my other abilities could be good too? But whether I gain control of them or not, his vision of me changing the world will never come true. I'm no superhero. Their fight is not mine. I'll leave that to him.

Hoping to fix the damage I've done and ease the mood between us, I move away from the railing and smile. "All right. I'm ready. What do you want to work on?"

"Are you sure?" He tilts his head, thinking back to all the other times he's done that.

I nod.

His smile widens. "When we touched and you brought our souls here, were you specifically thinking about the bridge, or did we come here by some other power?"

"I was thinking about the bridge."

"Good."

As he weaves his fingers with mine, I feel his softness for a moment, right before his essence enters me.

"If you thought of something else—another real place or perhaps even a 'place' you saw in a dream—do you think you could send us there too?"

"Maybe. I'm not really sure."

His hazel eyes brighten, and he grins. "That's better than a no. So let's try it."

"Try what?"

"Try sending us into one of your dreams."

I take a step back. Some dreams are safe for him to see. Others—the ones that are Elizabeth's memories—are not. They belong to her, not me, so sharing them doesn't feel right. And that's if I can even do this in the first place.

"What sort of dream do you mean?" I ask, trying to keep calm. "Mortifying ones of school? Nonsense ones with purple monsters and unicorns? Or something inspired by movies and books?"

"None of the above. I'm interested in a particular *recent* dream."

My heart skips a beat, hoping he won't ask to see Elizabeth's dreams, but what else can it be? I told him about them yesterday at school. Of course he would want to know more. "W-what one is that?"

"The one you had yesterday while you were unconscious. I need to know how you saw my death."

# CHAPTER 2

# MJ

**M**ADDY'S BEAUTIFUL MOUTH FALLS AS SHE GASPS. "I–I don't know if I can."

"Try. That's all I'm asking."

"No, it's not. You don't *know* what you're asking. That dream ... it's different. I can't—I can't explain it. It's just—"

Tears line her eyes. Moisture fills the air around us, ready and waiting to fall as rain the moment that teardrop breaks free. I will *not* be the reason behind her pain. I pull her into me, wrapping my arms around her.

"Hey. It's okay. You don't have to explain. I know you were unconscious and had no control over anything that happened to you. I just wanted to understand what you saw and how you saw it. We don't need to try it. It's fine. Nothing is more important to me than you."

For several moments, she's silent in my arms. But her emotions are so chaotic, my essence can barely keep up. Just as swiftly, though, her emotions settle inside her and calmness fills the air around us. She's made her decision.

We're done for the day. I'm not disappointed or upset by this. I will never force her to do anything she doesn't want to do. I respect her choice.

"If we do this," she begins, "and it does work, what then?"

I arch a brow, caught off guard by her question. Does this mean she's considering it? I choose my next words carefully, not wanting to sway her one way or the other. "We could practice—work on strengthening this ability—"

"No. I mean, what will *you* do if this works and you relive that day all over again?"

My mouth opens, but nothing comes out. Her words sink in, leaving their mark on my soul. I've battled millions of demons and secretly fought against the leader of the Fallen. Not once did anyone worry for *me*. Of course she would.

Me, I hadn't thought it through that far. If she could somehow recreate that day and make it feel just as real as her bridge does … I don't know what I'd do. It's not something I can predict, having never experienced or even contemplated something like this before. Any other dream or any other day wouldn't matter as much, but this is different—just as she said. It's the day I failed everyone.

I take an unnecessary breath to push back my thoughts before I say, "I've spent my afterlife trying to atone for the mistakes I made that day. Perhaps seeing it from an outsider's perspective, I could put my own personal 'demons' to rest."

She leans back, and I'm once again lost in the deep green forest of her eyes. "Okay. I'll try. But I can't guarantee it will work."

Gently, I place my hand on her cheek—my essence strengthens inside her. I search out her doubts, trying to give her the reassurance she needs. Instead I find her heart racing and her muscles tightening. Even though I can't read her mind, I don't need to. I've been matching her emotions to the thoughts she's shared, trying to put them together so I can figure her out and not be so clueless. She isn't doubting herself. She's afraid.

"It's okay," I say. "If it works, we'll be together. And besides, we know how this works, right? One touch sends us there. The next one sends us back. You'll be safe. I'll be fine. I promise."

Her eyes narrow, searching me as she mulls it over for a moment. Then she nods. "Okay."

I nod back. "Would it help you concentrate on sending us if I described the scene to you?"

She shudders. "No. I doubt I'll ever forget it. I'll try to bring us to the part where you met the Village Girl—"

"Lifa. And what do you mean, 'try'?"

"This is different than the bridge. The bridge is a real, physical place. This was a dream—a nightmare of a dream—that doesn't really exist. Not anymore. Plus, getting there is only part of the problem. There was a lot going on in the village. I wouldn't want us to land in a pile of rubble or in a fire or in front of people. I don't even know if they can see us."

"It was a dream, Maddy. A vision. It may have felt real, but it wasn't. There's nothing to fear by going back into it. Dreams can't hurt you."

She huffs and shakes her head in disbelief.

"Do you think I would willingly put you at risk?"

For a moment, I think she's going to argue, then she bites her lip and turns away. I close the small gap between us, wrapping my arms around her. My essence feeds off the excitement building inside her. Within a second, it returns to me. The outside world falls away, and I'm once again lost in the dense forest of her emerald-green eyes. I lean down. Her warm breath kisses my lips—mine are dry, itching to touch hers.

"You can do this, Maddy. I believe in you."

Her eyes widen, and then she shuts them.

DARKNESS DESCENDS ON ME—MY BODY TWISTS AND tightens as if it were being sent through a clothes wringer. Suddenly the feelings vanish. The darkness fades, and I open my eyes. Thick black smoke covers the sky. Screams echo on the wind, which carries the scent I've tried to forget. The smell is my people burning.

I reach for my sword and feel nothing but the coarse fabric of my jeans.

"MJ!" a voice cries out. I follow the sound to my Maddy crouching behind a broken wooden cart fifteen feet in front of me.

I'm torn between rushing to her and rushing to help my people. There is nothing I can do for them, though. They all died. This is just a recreation existing in an alternate plane, like the version of the bridge she sends us to, but it's more lifelike than any dream.

Maddy waves her hand, motioning for me to come to her. If I don't, it's just a matter of time before she comes to me. Besides, her cart offers more protection, even though it looks as if it might fall apart at any moment. I rush to her side, taking care not to touch her.

"We didn't stay together," she says.

I think back to all the times she's taken us to the bridge. No matter what our original position was, it would be different when we arrived on the bridge. We could be standing, sitting, or lying down. The distance between us could be anywhere from a few inches to several feet. The only thing that remained consistent was that we were never touching there.

"Maybe that's just how it works," I reply. "Or maybe that will change once you can control it more."

A thud sounds on the other side of the cart. Maddy crawls underneath the cart, but it isn't stable. The front end is smashed, and the left wheel is barely hanging on. It could collapse and crush her.

I take a breath, reminding myself this is a dream, and dreams can't hurt her, then I follow her under the cart.

A woman lays on the ground with her foot caught on a human bone—what's left of one of the villagers. Her dress is tattered and torn, and her face is hidden behind dirty golden locks. But still, I know who it is. *Lifa.*

All at once, I'm lost in a forgotten memory.

NIKOLAS STRUGGLED, HIS BACK TO ME, TRYING TO FREE HIS sword from his scabbard. Seizing the opportunity, I stepped behind him and raised my sword to his neck, pressing the blade below his chin.

"Gaze upon your destiny. With this sword I will cleave your lying, maggot mouth from your swine head!" I roared. The corners of my mouth twitched upward, ready to celebrate besting him yet again, but I fought the urge.

For a moment, he was as still as a night with no moon. Silence from him was a victory in and of itself. Before I could mock him more, he thrust his head back into my nose. The snap echoed through the woods. I let out a curse as he broke free.

He raised his sword—now free from its leather prison—and stared down the blade at me. "If I were destined to meet my maker by the end of a sword, it would not be held by a carrion-eater like you."

I wiped my arm across my face and winced from the pain. "There is no shame in admitting defeat, Nikolas," I said. "Bow out now, while you still can."

He smiled, defiance shining through his blue eyes as he circled me. "And swear fealty to you, Magnus? Wild beasts will feast on my entrails long before that happens."

The sound of horse hooves came from behind him. Moments later, an old gray mare with a ratted mane exited the woods pulling a cart. The cart had two passengers—a farmer and his daughter. Nikolas's eyes widened, then he sheathed his sword and set about fixing his tunic and hair.

I smirked and straightened, then got to work inspecting the damage done to my face. For the moment our fight was no more. Seeing the love of his life—as he called her—always took the fight out of him.

She glanced at Nikolas, then tucked a strand of blonde hair behind her ear and smiled. He stood there like a buffoon as they passed.

I sighed, then moved to stand beside him. "Have you spoken to her yet?" I asked.

He shook his head. "She is perfection. I cannot lay claim to her hand in marriage no more than I can ask for the throne."

"She is a farmer's daughter, not a princess."

"But that is the life she deserves. The most I could ever be is a warrior like our fathers."

"So be a warrior. Save the kingdom with me. Her father would not refuse a hero."

"Help me make that happen, Magnus, and I *will* swear fealty to you. I will be in your debt, in this life and the next. She is worth it."

THE MEMORY FADES, AND I'M ONCE AGAIN LYING BESIDE Maddy in the dirt under a cart on the day I died. Her breath stills as we hear a voice—my voice—speaking to Lifa.

"I don't get it," Maddy says. "I can't understand them now."

"You could in the dream?"

"Yes. Everyone was speaking English. Now they're not."

My brows furrow, further plagued by the mysterious woman I love. "What you're hearing is my native language. I've spoken a little bit of it to you."

"Why was it English last time?"

"I don't know."

I glance over at her, and she's watching on, wide-eyed, absorbing it all. She doesn't understand the significance or the events that led to this tragic day.

I lean in and whisper, "My best friend, Nikolas, was in love with Lifa. When we heard news of Sigurdsson and his men raiding her village, Nikolas raced here to find her. I told my warriors to save the citizens and kill our enemies while I searched for Nikolas. Instead I found her."

Strangers' voices stem from around the corner, and I watch on as my dream-self pulls Lifa to her feet and runs up the dirt path to the field. But I know there is no salvation up the hill. In a few minutes, it will all be over. I'll die, and she'll be sentenced to a short, miserable life. The leader of the Fallen will win again.

I don't want to see it again. This is harder than I expected. But I need to see where I went wrong. I need to see if there was anything I could have done differently that day to save her. I move to follow them, but then the strangers' voices around the corner change into raucous laughter as a man hollers out in pain—calling them carrion eaters. I know that voice.

Shortly after I died and arrived in Immortal City, I was reunited with Nikolas. He wouldn't tell me about his death, and I didn't press him. We had been at war. He died in battle. It was all I needed to know back then, though I always carried the weight of failing him.

If Lifa and I had stayed a few seconds longer, we would have heard him. We would have found him, and I would have reunited them. I wish I could somehow control Maddy's dream and choose what I want it to show me. Then I could discover at last what had happened to Nikolas. But I know I can see only what Maddy saw. And because Maddy and I are still here in the village and not following my dream-self and Lifa up the hill, I assume that means the dream will end in a moment.

But then Nikolas cries out, and the sound echoes inside me, shattering my control.

I rush out from underneath the cart toward Nikolas. In the back of my mind, I know I shouldn't be seeing this—Maddy didn't see this in her dream—but I can't focus on that. I maybe have seconds before this ends. I have to get to him. I have to know what happened.

Around the corner three men surround something on the ground. They move in a circle, kicking and spitting on their prey. Between their legs, I catch glimpses of Nikolas's bloody, beaten face. He is dying right in front of me. I have to save him. Even if it isn't real.

Searching for anything to use as a weapon, I find a splintered piece of wood. It's over three feet long and heavy, though it fits in my grasp. It may not kill them, but it will knock at least one of them out.

My hands tighten around my impromptu weapon as I march upon my enemies. Nikolas cries out again as they kick him. I should have been here to help him.

I'm here now.

I stop behind the largest one and pull back, aiming for his head. I swing forward, but the moment before I connect, someone touches my arm.

NIKOLAS, HIS KILLERS, AND THE RAVAGED VILLAGE DISAPpear. Suddenly I'm on my back, staring up at Maddy on Hiniker Bridge.

# CHAPTER 3

# Maddy

"WHAT WERE YOU THINKING, MJ?" I DEMAND AS thunder crashes, echoing through the pond.

"How could you do that?" he shouts, jumping to his feet and pacing before me. "He was right there! I could have saved him!"

"*Saved* him?"

I stop and stare at him. His hands twist into his hair as he crouches down on the bridge, muttering something I can't hear. A tear rolls down his cheek. I knew it would be hard for him to see that dream, but I didn't expect it to be *this* bad. And I didn't expect him to try to interfere. When he rushed at those men, I panicked. I knew the chunk of wood would pass through that man's head as if it were a hand through vapor, but I didn't want MJ to see that. I didn't want him to feel helpless.

"MJ, that wasn't real, remember? I know it felt like it was, but it wasn't." I reach for him, but he pulls away.

"Yes, it was! I don't know how, but it was."

"MJ, be reasonable. You're letting emotions blind you to the truth. What I did—where I sent us—was just like all the times I sent us to that other bridge."

"And what was that? What do you *think* you do?"

I pause, caught off guard by both his question and the venom in his voice. I know he's upset by what he saw— he's not really mad at me. But it still hurts. I only did what he asked, and I didn't expect it to work. So how did it work? How did I take us there? What *is* my ability?

"The other bridge," I begin, digging for the right words to help him understand, "is like this safe space where I know nothing bad will ever happen. And now that I know a bit about how it works, I know it'll always be there whenever I need it, no matter what. And even though I don't fully understand it, I'm not sure I want to. Because what if I find out my ability isn't this 'great gift' you think it is? That would make that place, that ability—and *me*— bad. I'm not bad, MJ. So I know that dream place where I sent us … it was fine."

He shakes his head. "It wasn't."

"What was it then, huh? Where did we go?"

"Back."

"Back? What do you mean?"

He mutters something. I can't quite catch it, but it sounds like "home."

Back home.

"MJ, you can't honestly think—"

"Why were people not speaking English, then?" His head snaps up, and he stares at me with wild eyes. "And it should have ended once we didn't go up the hill. We should have only seen and heard what you did yesterday in the original dream. But it was different. Why was it different, Maddy?"

He stares at me, watching and waiting for me to answer. But I can't. I don't have answers for any of his questions. But now that he's asked them, I want to know the answers too.

All I did was concentrate on the memory of what I experienced inside Elizabeth's fountain so I could recreate it as a "place" and send us there. But what *was* that? He's right—how could we have seen and felt things I didn't know about?

"MJ, what did I—"

A twig snaps across the pond, and we both turn toward it. MJ steps in front of me, shielding me—his pain and our fight momentarily forgotten. I move out and stand beside him as I search the trees, trying to see what made the sound. I find nothing.

But it was loud, louder than any animal typically found here. Someone's watching us. Is it a human? Angel? Demon?

"Who's there?" I whisper.

MJ doesn't move as he stares at the empty space. I move closer to MJ, placing my hand on his arm, desperate to feel his essence and be reassured that we're together. He flinches as his essence rushes in, but instead of lingering to reassure me, it zips back to him.

"Are we okay?" I whisper again.

His stance loosens, and he turns to me. The pain in his eyes is gone, but with his furrowed brows, I know he's still worried. "It's nothing."

I glance back at the woods, still not finding anything. "Are you sure?"

"Positive. If it were a mortal, I'd hear his or her heartbeat. If it were an angel, demon, or any other paranormal entity, I'd sense its essence. There is nothing there but animals. We're okay."

I stare at the trees, not trusting my eyes. Nothing is there. I can see that, and after what MJ just said, I believe him. But why am I still afraid?

I hug myself and find my answer. It's not the trees, and it's not from the noise. It's what *isn't* happening—MJ's not touching me. His essence isn't coursing through my veins and reducing my fear. Even when I touched him a moment ago, his essence didn't linger.

Why?

Why is he being so different?

A dark thought sparks in my mind, and even though I know it's ridiculous and insecure, I can't shake it. Am I the cause of his strange behavior?

I reach for his hand again. He pulls away as if I might burn him. Thunder rumbles, shaking the bridge, as a fear worse than even the ones I felt at Justin's house creeps over me.

"You're afraid to touch me."

"No, I'm not," he quickly says.

"You are. How could you not be? We know I can use this … ability only when you're touching me, and I'm better now at making sure I don't send us anywhere when we do. But now … you have no idea what's going to happen when we touch."

He frowns and his eyes soften. "I'm not afraid to touch you, Maddy. Nor am I afraid of that ability—any of your abilities. You shouldn't be either."

He reaches for me, and this time *I* step back. "You're sure?"

"If I weren't sure, would I do this?"

His strong arms wrap around me. For a moment, our eyes meet. Mine are wide, shocked by his sudden change and unsure of what he's going to do next. His eyes are alight with a hint of mischief. He smirks. Then he bends to kiss me.

My insides clench as I hold my breath—hoping I'm not imagining this. But then all the dark pockets of fear and worry that have twisted inside me all morning dissipate as MJ's essence works to unravel them. And with all my troubles gone, I'm able to focus on what's right in front of me—MJ.

I close my eyes, eager to see what wonderfully strange things will happen the moment our lips touch now that I'm fully healed.

The air around us stills. The sounds from the water and animals disappear. It's as if nature is curious about the effects an immortal kissing a … well, whatever I am … will have on its delicate balance.

Our lips meet.

The softness and tenderness of his lips cause all thoughts to disappear. His essence pulses from me to him, uniting us again, which only deepens the kiss.

My heart races as my stomach quivers. Everything is fine now. We're fine.

A warm glow fills me. It drives me, making me want more. More of MJ, more of the closeness, more of the heat.

His essence builds, stretching and filling all of me. It grows until it seeps through my skin, causing it to tingle, and my hairs stand on end. It isn't painful. It's … exhilarating.

I take a breath, breathing in MJ's nature-inspired scent. It's perfect. Like fresh cut grass with fragrant flowers. The air has that crisp, clean smell to it—the scent that comes after a thunderstorm.

I reach up, grabbing fistfuls of his hair to hold him closer. The wind picks up, howling in my ears as it swirls around us, caressing my skin with a heated breeze reminding me of the warmest days of summer.

MJ holds me tighter, gripping me to him as the heat and wind intensify. Beads of sweat drip down my neck, and my hair whips around us. In the back of my mind, I know something is happening around us, but I don't care. I don't want to stop kissing him.

Ever.

Bright light dances through my closed eyes. It calls to me—begging me to look. I try to resist, but I'm losing the battle. It's stronger than me. Stronger than MJ.

I peek, and the sight causes me to end our kiss.

Flames blend with water and dance in a cyclone that begins in the pond, then reaches up to the sky. MJ and I are centered within it, surrounded by a strange, silver bubble, just as we were last night.

MJ's body stills against mine, and I hear him suck in his breath, but I can't look away from the flames. They're so close. All I'd have to do is let go of him and reach out in any direction and I'd touch it. We should be burning, but we're not. Why aren't we? The air isn't even choking me as it did last night.

His essence slows, causing the silver glow around us to shrink until it snaps back through me and into him. We both stumble, but MJ manages to keep us away from the flames.

The fire suddenly extinguishes, leaving behind only the water that had been caught up in it. The water is suspended in the air for a moment, no longer spinning, then it plummets from the sky, sending waves crashing along the muddy shore and up onto the bridge, soaking our shoes.

MJ and I break away. Around us are scorch marks on the bridge. They look like parentheses where the flames blazed outside his bubble before extending out over the water.

"What was that?" I ask in breathless wonder.

"I-I don't know." His voice is tense as he looks between me, the burn marks, and the now-choppy water. Tight lines appear by his mouth and forehead—he's trying to rein in his emotions.

If he doesn't want me to see his reaction, it can't be good. Is he worried? Nervous? Afraid? That's it, isn't it? Whatever just happened, he's never experienced it before.

The sounds of nature resume, but at a fraction of the volume prior to our kiss. Nature is giving us a wide berth.

Giving me a wide berth.

It's afraid of me too.

Dark clouds claim the sky once more, and even though I know how to remove them now, I just … can't.

A twig snaps again across the pond, in the same area as before. MJ squints at the trees as I move closer to him. My skin tingles, and I get the sensation that someone's watching us. It's not the first time I've felt that, and with everything that's been happening lately, I'm sure it won't be the last.

"Someone's over there, right?" I ask.

He stares a few seconds longer before shaking his head. "No. Come on. It's time to go home."

His fingers lace with mine, and he pulls me out of the blackened markings. As we walk toward my house, I look back at the woods, trying in vain to see someone. Just as before, I see nothing, but the feeling of being watched is still there.

I had that feeling the day I met MJ, and I was right then. He had been watching me. He was in the Veil of Shadows, though, so I wouldn't see him. Is that what this person is doing? If so, MJ would know someone is there. Am I wrong, or is MJ lying?

# CHAPTER 4

# MJ

USIC BLARES FROM THE BATHROOM, AND THE scent of fruit drifts through the air as Maddy showers. She wasn't keen on the idea at first, but her body needs to relax after testing her abilities. At least that was the excuse I used. I don't like lying to her, but I need a few minutes of privacy—and after the situation at the park, we're not separating again. Even being in different rooms has me anxious.

The powers she wields shouldn't be possible. I've had Charges that had an ability, but never multiple. They were always simple ones like psychic visions or minor telekinesis.

Maddy's are powerful and made even more dangerous by her inability to control them and her lack of knowledge of them. Given time, we can control the majority of them.

However, the one I'm most concerned about is whatever happened when we kissed. I felt it building inside her. My essence fought to tame it—to keep us both from losing control—but I have no control when I'm kissing her. Everything inside me is heightened. It's overwhelming. It must be why my Mark—the shield each Protector places around the essence of the Charge—was suddenly visible outside of the Veil of Shadows. But Maddy is not my Charge. How did I Mark her, and why did the Mark come back to me when we stopped kissing? She still needed to be protected from the flames.

The water the flame tornado scooped up from the pond may have kept the heat down, but it still could have hurt her. I didn't know how we were going to get out of there. I was relieved when it vanished. But for all the danger we were in, Maddy wasn't frightened. I couldn't believe it as she just watched on with a sense of wonder, in awe of what we'd done—she'd done.

The easiest way to handle it is to not kiss her again. But even thinking it, I know neither of us can resist. So what sparked that reaction in her? And how was she able to manipulate two elements—fire and water—without recognizing she was responsible for it?

I listen for her heartbeat again, finding solace in the calming rhythm. She's safe. I clear my mind and reach out for Alexander using Cerebrallink.

*MJ,* he says once our minds have connected.

*Did you find anyone at the park?* I ask.

*No. The woods were empty. The spirit is gone. Do you think it's the same one you've encountered before?*

The day I met Maddy, a spirit tried to shield her from me in the park. Maybe this same spirit made that sound in the woods at the bridge. The spirit is still unknown, but I believe it's part of a group of four supernatural beings supposedly working together to protect Maddy. The only confirmed member is Maddy's Guardian, posing as the substitute math teacher Ms. Morgan. A suspected member is

Duane, the Shadowwalker posing as Maddy's uncle. I have no leads on the fourth member.

Considering none of them helped save Maddy from the demon last night, they're done being a part of her life. I will hunt them all down and send them to Hell. I need to keep her safe and hidden.

Thunder rolls through the air. I check on Maddy again, listening to her elevated, but still normal, heart rate. I move to the bathroom door and peek inside. The shower curtain is closed, though I can hear the water as it hits her skin. No one else is in here. She's safe.

I shut the door and link back to Alexander. *I'm not sure if it's the same spirit. I didn't sense an essence, but I* knew *someone was there. I don't understand how that's possible.*

*I have a thought,* Alexander says, *but you're not going to like it.*

I don't like the majority of the situation we're in. *Out with it,* I reply.

He's silent for a moment, which only increases my anxiety. *I don't think it was the spirit—it had an essence. I think it was one of the Fallen.*

My body stiffens. Hairs stand on my neck. *That's not possible,* I say, though I don't know if the lie is for me or him.

The Fallen's essences are guarded so we cannot detect when they are on Mortal Ground. I already know the Acquisitioner is after her, but that doesn't mean Death, the Gatekeeper, and the Ferryman aren't too. Maddy could change everything about the afterlife. If the others know about her, I have to assume she makes them nervous.

Though if that being *were* a member of the Fallen, it would have either killed her or taken her by now.

*You're probably right,* Alexander says, drawing me from my thoughts. *It's probably not possible. Speaking of the impossible, any ideas on the fire tornado?*

I groan. *You saw it?*

*I'd wager half the state saw it, not to mention Immortal City.*

I sigh and run my fingers through my hair, desperate for control. I must contain this. I must protect her. *Come here. Bring the others too. We need to talk.*

A moment later, Alexander appears near the window in Maddy's room. His jeans are covered in dirt, and his shirt has several burrs stuck to it. As grateful as I am for his help, I don't need evidence of his presence sprinkled on Maddy's floor.

I wave my hand at him, removing the traces of his search through the woods.

He looks down at his now-clean clothes and shrugs.

"Thank you," says a female voice near Maddy's bed.

I turn. Tension builds inside as I gaze at the two women standing before me.

Tamitha brushes strands of her long brown hair behind her shoulder and then motions to Alexander, smiling. "We were all in the woods, yet he was the only one covered in dirt."

"That's his norm," Sissy, the redheaded angel beside her, scoffs. Her light brown eyes land on me, taking me all in.

I trained her—all of them—but now I'm different. Even from here, I can sense their unease. Maddy ... takes some getting used to. If they're not ready yet, I'm not letting them come near her. I couldn't admit it to her last night, mostly because I didn't want to admit it to myself, but Justin was right. My kind could kill her.

The first and most important rule is to keep our identity a secret. If mortals knew the truth of the afterlife, their life on earth would lose its value. People would take as many irresponsible risks as they pleased, then they'd die and be reborn as if it were no more than pressing restart on a video game. To protect our existence, we were given the ability to compel mortals. Both angels and demons use it every day. It's the one rule everyone abides by.

Maddy can't be compelled, and she can shield her thoughts from us—both violate rule one. I've told my team this, but hearing about her and actually experiencing her are different.

*I called you here,* I begin, speaking to their minds so Maddy will not hear, *to discuss recent events. We already had the odds stacked against us in regards to protecting Maddy, but things have changed again—and not for the better.*

They stiffen, and Alexander frowns. *Is this about the tornado? I was joking—mostly. And anyway, we can—*

*No.* My head pounds as a headache forms. I close my eyes and pinch the bridge of my nose, trying to soothe it. After a moment, I give up, dropping my arm to my side. *I mean, the tornado is troubling too. But before the flame tornado, I was testing one of Maddy's abilities. When we touch, sometimes she sends our souls someplace, while our bodies remain in the original location. She's always sent us to the bridge until today.*

*Where did you go?* Tamitha asks, stepping closer.

Emotions sway inside me, rolling like the waves of the ocean, and I am no more than a drifter clinging to a life raft. For a moment, I consider not telling them, but I'm in over my head.

*I asked her to send us to what can best be described as a dream—a nightmare, really. She did, but it wasn't a recreation or an alternate plane. It was real.*

Alexander places his hand on my shoulder, sending the reassurance I needed. *What are you saying, MJ?*

*Maddy sent us back in time to the day I died.*

The truth clings to the air, silencing the room. I didn't want to believe it either. I tried to find another explanation, but there isn't one.

They all step back. Then their voices start shouting in my head, blending in a cacophony of shock and disbelief. I rub my temples, trying to drown them out. After this reaction, I'm glad I downplayed the tornado.

Thunder rips through the air, rocking the house. I check on Maddy again, listening to her quickened heart. If I search the room again, I might catch her in a vulnerable state now that the shower is off. Instead I listen for other sounds in the room—anything to shed a light on what's upset her. I hear nothing other than music, her racing heart, and ragged breathing. The demons she's facing are her own. Is she realizing what this morning means too?

I want to go to her—comfort her. It won't take away her pain, but it seems to help her. However, I can't while the other Protectors are here.

After several moments, the thunder and other angels calm. So do I.

*MJ*, Alexander says, *have you considered that perhaps this is why the Acquisitioner is after her?*

My shoulders slump, fearing the truth of his words. The Binding Agreement—the contract the Influencer had—

was created by the Acquisitioner. He drafts all contracts in Hell—mainly Binding Agreements, which he uses to collect souls for the Devil. So why did he write that contract for the Influencer to use with Maddy, and what does the Acquisitioner get out of it? More than likely, as Alexander suggested, he's after Maddy for himself.

I've already lost too much to him. I won't lose her too.

*He's right,* Sissy says. *With access to that kind of ability, the Acquisitioner could travel to any fixed point in time and change it. History could be rewritten. Everything is in jeopardy, including us. He could stop the creation of the Protectors. He could even go back and prevent the Fall. This ability is too dangerous—not to mention the other abilities Maddy seems to have. We cannot allow her to fall into his hands.*

She cannot fall into *any* of the Fallen's hands.

*So you'll help me with her?* I ask.

Hope grows as they agree. Sharing her isn't ideal—I had hoped to protect her myself. But I can't do it on my own—not until the situation is resolved with the Influencer and the Acquisitioner. With my team on board, we might protect Maddy. She needs to meet them, though. That way they can help protect her.

*Give me an hour to get her ready. Meet us at the park across the street.*

*You're doing the right thing, MJ,* Sissy says.

*We'll clean out the park,* Tamitha adds. *Just in case there are any more incidents like at the bridge.*

I nod, and they take their leave. This will work. I have to believe it. The only problem left is getting Maddy to go along with it.

# CHAPTER 5

# Maddy

STEAMING HOT WATER RAINS DOWN ON ME FROM THE shower head while Blake Shelton blares from my iPod. I had cranked up the volume, hoping it would help keep my mind quiet. It's not working.

My mind is too full of the park and everything that happened there.

I touch my lips, thinking back to the kiss. It was wonderful. I could spend the rest of my life kissing him—and I hope to. But what caused the tornado? It didn't happen last night when we kissed. The difference today is me—I'm healed. So did I do it, then? Is it some unknown, uncontrollable ability?

It was actually kind of pretty the way the flames and water merged. But MJ was freaked out by it. I guess there was some danger—it did get a lot hotter once that silver bubble disappeared. I think the bubble must be a part of MJ—his angelic side. At least I hope it didn't come from me—I have enough new abilities as it is, and I barely understand them.

MJ had it all wrong about where—or should I say *when*—I sent us. I did the exact same thing as I do when I send us to the bridge. I don't know what I do, but I do know it's not what he's thinking. I didn't send us back to his home … in the *past*.

Thinking about abilities and angels has me longing again for simpler days. Days where I could laugh with my friends and not worry about anything.

Images of my time with Ben suddenly play on a loop. The ache in my heart grows, knowing I'm to blame for his death. But that isn't all I'm guilty for; I see that now. Ben was so kind and patient with me, but I took him for granted. I didn't know what love was, and I never gave it a chance. Ben deserved so much more than I gave him. He deserved love. He deserved to be happy. Now he'll never have that. I still can't believe he's gone.

I press my palms to my eyes to hold in the tears. I will not cry. MJ will know if I do. It's not fair. Ben died because of me, but if I mourn him, I'll hurt MJ. No matter what I do, someone I care about suffers.

MJ's lingering essence stirs within me, trying to dispel my anger, pain, and frustration, but there's too much. His essence falters and then fades away, leaving me hollow. I grind my teeth and try to calm the storm brewing inside me.

Thunder rumbles outside.

It's a reminder that nothing is private anymore. My emotions are broadcasted on a massive scale. This is worse than angels and demons hearing my thoughts. I feel exposed, as if my heart and soul were bared for everyone to see.

I need to call Ben's mom. She deserves to know. But what do I say? How do I explain what happened to him? She can't know a demon killed him.

MJ will have to help me with that. But he can't help me with everything from yesterday. He can't help me forget it.

I fought—*hard*. MJ was surprised I held Justin off as long as I did. Now that I know he's a demon, I am too.

There's one thing about yesterday that I haven't told MJ. The kiss. I hated it. It was the most confusing kiss I've ever had. I expected Justin to be aggressive and slobbery, like kissing a rabid dog. But he wasn't. The kiss was slow, delicate, yet full of his sick and twisted emotions for me. And even though it was against my will, it still feels like a betrayal.

There was a bubble then too—a blue one—surrounding us. I'd nearly forgotten that, with everything that's happened. So who was responsible for that one—me or Justin? And why was Justin's blue and MJ's silver? Do I somehow make the colors different? Or do they?

A new song comes on. After only a few guitar chords, goose bumps pepper my skin. It's Marilyn Manson's version of "Sweet Dreams."

Justin's song.

I don't have this song on my iPod.

With shaking hands, I turn the shower off and reach for my towel. I wrap it around me and step out, coming face-to-face with Justin.

# CHAPTER 6

# Justin

OUR SONG BLARES FROM MADS'S IPOD. SHE STANDS there, mouth hung open, dripping wet from her shower, wearing nothing but a towel.

Her wall is down. She's exposed. Vulnerable. It's real and honest. This is her true self.

And dammit if I don't find her all the more attractive for it.

I stood by in the Veil of Shadows as *he* slept beside her, comforted her, trained her, fought with her, and even kissed her. They almost caught me twice, with the damn twigs snapping, but I eluded him and the Protectors he sent. How could he be so careless to tell others about her?

I've managed to keep my feelings in check. It's why I thought I was ready to face her—I didn't think I'd be distracted by the emotions that stir whenever I'm with her. Leave it to her to mess up my plans again. This was my first chance to get her alone. I could have waited until she was dressed, but this is more fun.

I won't do anything yet. I will never hurt her again. I'm only trying to make sense of what the Acquisitioner

said about Mads having a weakness. That weakness—
whatever it may be—is the key to getting her to sign
the Binding Agreement, condemning her soul to the
Acquisitioner and me.

When I tried to compel her last night so she would sign
the contract, it almost worked. I could feel her letting go of
her resistance. But then that damn spirit came back. I cast
it out of my house again, but it was too late. It distracted
Mads long enough for her to break my hold.

I'm glad it didn't work, then. The Acquisitioner tricked
me. There will be no traveling or happily ever after for
me and Mads. With Mads's abilities at his command, the
Acquisitioner will be the next ruler of Hell. We'll spend
eternity in misery. It's what has to be done, though. With
her soul unclaimed, it's the only way she'll stay safe.

I wish I could take her and run. Right now. It would be
perfect. No one can sense her essence without physically
touching her. The *Protector* won't be able to find her, as he
can with all other mortals. He can't even sense me from
the next damn room, thanks to the ring the Acquisitioner
gave me last night. The ring is an occultum—an object
enhanced to hide a being's essence. Only members of the
Fallen are allowed to wear them. Until now, that is.

Thunder booms, shaking the house.

Mads shakes her head and steps back toward the wall.
She's cornered.

My hands twitch, tempted to reach for her and make
my fantasy a reality.

The only thing that could ruin my plan to steal her
away is Mads's ability to affect the weather. It could give
away our location, just as it did last night. I must find a
way to keep that from happening.

The one time she didn't affect the weather was when she was unconscious. It was the only real peace and privacy we had. When I'm ready to make my next move, I could keep her sedated, just enough to make her suggestible and to keep the weather in check. It's not great, but it's good enough to be plan B.

Her breathing increases as the shock wears off. A moment later, a terrified shriek escapes from that perfect, tempting mouth, and I know my time is up. I summon the Veil of Shadows and continue observing her, in hopes of finding something much harder to find than a needle in a haystack. I'm searching for the flaw in my Aphrodite.

# CHAPTER 7

# MJ

A BLOOD-CURDLING SCREAM COMES FROM THE OTHER side of the bathroom door. I burst through it, frantically searching the room.

My hollow chest tightens when I see the empty shower. Then my panic lessens as I spot Maddy crouched on the floor beside the shower. Her eyes are wide—frozen with fear on a spot behind me. I glance over my shoulder expecting to see whatever frightened her, but I find nothing.

My gaze returns to her. She's sopping wet and shivering—still not looking away from that spot. I doubt she's even aware I'm here.

I wave my hand in front of her iPod, turning the blaring music off. She doesn't react. I swallow a lump in my throat, then bend down in front of her.

"Maddy," I whisper, taking care not to startle her.

Still, she doesn't move or blink.

"Maddy," I repeat a little louder.

I reach out to touch her knee but hesitate, fearing she might send us somewhere again. It's not the first time I've been leery about touching her, and I doubt it will be the last. But if she's going to send herself someplace, I'd rather it be me who goes with her.

I take a breath while gently placing my hand on her knee.

She's freezing. My essence enters her, racing through her body, slowing her heart, controlling her breath, and eliminating pockets of terror.

She blinks and says, "Justin."

Instantly, I whip back around, expecting to see him. Other than us, the bathroom is empty.

I take a moment to settle myself, then shake my head. She must be reliving some terrible memory from last night—the unspeakable things Justin did to her. But he's not here. He never was. I would have felt him long before he entered this house. I release my breath and return to her.

"There's no one here but us, Maddy. You're safe." My hand returns to her knee, and this time my essence works on warming her to stop her shivering.

"No," she says. "He was right there. I *saw* him."

Agony tears me apart inside. The things she shared of her time in that house were horrific. If I had done my job and not left her alone after school, he wouldn't have gotten her. Everything she suffered through that night was my fault. I want nothing more than to make her forget what he did—forget him completely—but it's the one thing I can't do.

"He wasn't here, Maddy. I'm sure of it."

Finally her eyes leave that spot and fix on mine. They suck me in, searching for reassurance. "You're wrong," she declares. "He was right there. I *know* it. He put his song on my iPod."

That's it—the song from the card she received Monday morning and the one the students kept whistling under the Influencer's control. The song randomly came on and triggered her panic attack.

I sit, pulling her into an embrace. She watches as I wave my hand again in the direction of her iPod, this time erasing the song from its database.

"There," I say. "The song is gone now. He must have put it on there several days ago in hopes of frightening you. I'm sorry. I didn't think to check for it."

"It doesn't matter when he put it on there. He turned it on just now, knowing what it would do to me, and then he just stood there, watching my reaction."

My hand rubs soothing circles on her back. No matter what I say, she's going to argue. She's headstrong and doesn't trust easily.

"What you went through yesterday," I begin, "was traumatic. Everything came at you so fast, your mind didn't have time to process it. What you just saw was … an aftershock—like with an earthquake. But Justin wasn't really here. He couldn't have been."

"How?" she demands. "How can you know that? You weren't here."

"I know his essence now. If he comes within fifty miles of Mankato, I'll know and I'll take you someplace safe. He won't get you. I promise."

"So, that was … what? A hallucination?"

"Yes."

Her bottom lip quivers. "I'm not crazy."

"No. You're a *mortal*—a remarkable one, facing a situation you were never meant to face. You need time to heal, Maddy."

"You're sure he wasn't really here?"

I smile, trying to convey how confident I am. "Positive."

She nods, seeming to finally accept my answer, then relaxes against me. A moment later, though, she straightens and stares at me.

"What did you mean when you said the song is gone now?"

"I removed the song from your iPod."

"Why?"

I tilt my head as I stare down at her. My essence picks up inside her, feeling frustration and rage building, though I don't know why. "Because it upset you."

"Is that how you handle everything—you just make something vanish? Songs, memories—who knows what else?"

"Yes, which is why it aggravates me so much that I can't remove your pain."

For a moment, I suspect she's going to continue arguing. Then she just shakes her head as she drops back against me. She's silent for a while.

"Justin will make *me* vanish soon," she finally says, a strange numbness in her voice.

I flinch, then hold her tighter. "No, he won't. I told you earlier, I will *never* let him touch you again."

"My blood may be on that contract. He said he'd hurt everyone who's ever met me if I didn't honor it. Sooner or later, he'll return to collect me. And if my blood didn't touch it, then he'll return to make me sign it. Don't you see, MJ? No matter what, my soul belongs to—"

Rage rips through me. It takes everything to keep from shaking. "You don't belong to him! You don't belong *to* anyone." I take a deep breath as the rage simmers. "But I hope you'd agree that you belong *with* me."

Slowly, a smile spreads across her lips. I want to kiss them, but considering what happened with the kiss at the bridge, I can't.

"How do you do it?" she whispers.

"Do what?"

"Know the right thing to say and do to keep me from falling apart?"

Since day one, I've been fumbling my way through each moment with her, utterly useless without my abilities. But as I gaze down at her, I see she means it. Her smile is brighter now—her fear is gone.

Her eyes shine with pride, happiness, and ... something else. Something I've yet to see in her eyes but I've seen in millions of mortals' eyes before.

Love.

Could it be? Does she love me?

Suddenly, my chest clenches in pain, then it releases. A thump echoes through me. Then another and another as my heart beats again.

Careful not to make it stop, I reach for her hand and place it over my now-beating heart.

Her eyes widen.

"This is what you do to me, Maddy. My heart *beats* for you. Only you. You bring life back to me with your smile, your light, your compassion ... I mean it when I say you are my everything. No one—not Justin or anyone else—will come between us ever again."

Tears pool in her eyes as she continues to feel my beating heart. If those tears fell, my heart would break.

Silence fills my chest once more. She frowns and pulls her hand back.

"I know—it doesn't last long," I say. "But it's okay. The important thing is that my heart has beat several times since meeting you. Each time, the number of beats increases. I just … I just want to show you how much you mean to me." I pause to gaze at her. "Are you all right?"

She nods.

I stand and take a deep breath. "Good. Given what you've been through lately, I hate to add more stress … but I'm afraid it cannot be avoided."

Her brows furrow. "What are you talking about?"

"I've been speaking with the Protectors who helped me last night. They're ready to meet you. I know we've had an eventful day already, and I don't want you to overdo it. But when it comes to your safety, I'm not taking any chances. We need them."

She stands, clutching her towel so hard her knuckles are white.

For the first time since entering this room, I notice the state of her undress. I turn away, not wanting to take advantage of the situation. Still, heat builds inside me as my mind becomes overrun with thoughts of what I did see.

She's gorgeous—inside and out. I just wish she could see it. As brave and bold as she is, she's cautious when it comes to herself. She's placed a barrier around her heart that rivals Fort Knox. Others have tried to break down her wall only to fail. I am no better than them, yet she's slowly lowering her defenses for me. She trusts me—whether or not she knows it yet. Her trust is a gift, and I'm not about to lose it.

I turn toward her again and move closer, holding my eyes only on hers. "Please. If not for you, then meet them for me. Having them here will give me comfort, knowing you're safe. Plus, they can take over watching Amber, leaving me free to be with you."

Her head nods once. "Okay."

"Remember," I say, "you're safe." Then I leave the bathroom.

# CHAPTER 8
## Maddy

**M**J'S RIGHT—JUSTIN WASN'T REALLY THERE. I understand that now. I'm safe. I have to move past what Justin did to me and focus on the good things.

Like MJ. *His heart was beating.* That shouldn't be possible. But I felt it. And he said it was because of me. I want to know when else it's happened—see if I can figure out what I did to spur that in him. It's a miracle, and miracles always turn out well. They have to.

After dressing, I open the door to my room, letting MJ know he can come back in. He was waiting in the hallway. I told him to go downstairs and watch TV, but he didn't want to. Ever since we got home from the bridge, he's been hovering over me like crazy. It's sort of annoying, though I also sort of don't mind—not after everything that's happened in the last twenty-four hours. But I wish he'd tell me why. Now more than ever, I suspect he was lying at the bridge—someone *was* watching us.

MJ sits on my desk chair, watching as I fuss with my bed, trying to buy some time. I'm usually not this nervous about meeting new people, but my emotions are all over the place. Plus, they're not exactly "people."

Adding to my nerves is the unnatural silence in the house. I miss my family. I want to make good on the promise I made to myself yesterday to show them how much they mean to me.

"MJ, where's my family?"

"I sent them out for the day after I compelled them."

I flinch, then hope he didn't see it. I was glad last night when he told me others were coming to compel the town and that he would compel my family so no one would remember Justin. I didn't want my family especially to remember the awful things he made them do. But today … it just feels wrong to take away someone's memories—even the bad ones.

When I notice MJ isn't talking, I stop messing with my bed and glance over my shoulder at him.

"You and I need to discuss a few things before they return," he says. "We'll do that after you meet my team."

I hold back a shudder. I'm already anxious for the upcoming meeting with his "team," and now I'm also anxious about what he needs to talk to me about before I can see my family.

Suddenly he's standing beside me, taking my hand. His essence rushes in, familiar with the space.

"Their memories of the last few days no longer match yours," he explains. "But don't worry. We'll discuss how to handle that later."

I give him a weak smile. Not wanting to think about how we'll *handle* my memories not matching the rest of the town's, I say, "Tell me about them—the Protectors. I assume you've told them about me, so it's only fair."

He sits on my bed, then tugs on my hand for me to join him. My stomach dips. Even though we spent the whole night together, it's different now. I was still recovering and in shock; now I'm fully aware of him.

My gaze falls to his lips, and my mind flashes back to our kiss on the bridge. My lips are dry and my skin tingles, longing to be in his arms again.

We're alone.

If we kissed here ... what would happen?

On the bridge, I was lost in his essence—lost in him. The fire distracted me. Without it, who knows how far the kiss would have gone.

I blush, then sit beside MJ.

His knuckles graze my heated cheeks. My stomach rolls, and I fight the urge to kiss him.

"What do you want to know?" he asks.

I take a breath to calm myself. "I don't know. What are they like? How long have you known them? Why are they here over all the other Protectors you know?"

He smiles. "Tamitha is the newest Protector in the group. She joined us three years ago. Her mortal life was very structured and organized—every detail planned out. That stayed with her, and it's proven useful on many assignments.

"Sissy spent most of her mortal life caring for others. She became a Protector during the First World War. She's undoubtedly the smartest woman I know.

"Alexander has been with me for over two centuries. He died protecting his town and has since gone on to help me protect millions of people. He's my confidant. He helped me many times in the last week with you—including last night—and he's very eager to meet you. He wants to thank you for changing my mind about being reborn."

He smiles again, waiting for my reply, but all I can think about is how long he's known them. I've been avoiding thinking about MJ's past life. I'm not sure I want to know the exact number of years he's existed. He looks somewhere between seventeen and twenty, but his soul is much older. Having seen the barbaric men who killed him and the living conditions in the village, I would guess he lived before even Shakespeare, but I'm not sure …

Being that people can be reborn, technically all souls could be as old as his, if not older—including mine. Because he's an angel, MJ just gets the advantage of retaining many lifetimes of memories. And he uses that knowledge to save people. That should count for something.

"When did you—" I can't say "die." That would definitely make this weirder. "When did you become a Protector?"

His smile falls, and he turns away, staring out the window. "I'll tell you that when we have more time. Right now, my team is waiting, which I believe is the real reason you're stalling."

I sigh and look away.

Not even a second later, he's kneeling in front of me. His hand strokes my cheek, tilting my head so I can't hide from him. "Do you think I would ever put you at risk?"

"No …"

I pause, trying to find the right words to describe how I feel. Angel or not, he can't save me from everything. We learned that the hard way yesterday.

"Not if you had a choice," I continue. "But I think you're stuck now. You need help. And if you think this is a good idea, then I trust you."

We stare at each other in silence. I want him to tell me I'm right, but he doesn't. Instead his face shifts, displaying whatever emotions are rippling inside him. When his emotions settle, my jaw clenches as I recognize the look on his face—it's one I do often enough. His face is taut, and humor has left his eyes. Whatever he's thinking, he won't hear any arguments against it.

"Don't forget—you're not just any mortal. You stopped me when I made the worst mistake of my life and tried to attack you. You fought off an abnormally skilled demon and saved your sister. As horrified as I am that you had to do that, I'm also glad you can defend yourself. Trust your gut out there with my team. If anything doesn't feel right to you, squeeze my hand and I'll take you to safety."

His words are meant to comfort me, but they don't. It sounds as if he too thinks things could go bad there.

"Come on," he whispers. Mischief fills his eyes as he smirks. "Don't make me *dare* you."

Our first date flashes through my mind, and I try my best not to grin. "You wouldn't."

"Why not? I'm on a winning streak."

"You won once. That's not a streak."

"I wasn't just talking about bowling."

Confused, I lean back.

He leans in, running his nose along mine.

My entire body tingles. If I weren't sitting down, I would have collapsed to the floor.

"I won you," he whispers, and I feel his words on my lips.

"Haven't you figured out that I'm unlucky?" I ask, barely recognizing the breathless voice that comes out of me.

"Luck has nothing to do with it, Maddy. You are a courageous, selfless, brilliant, cunning, gorgeous woman.

I thank Father every day for the choices I've made that led me to you. When I say I 'won' you, I don't mean you're some prize or trophy. I mean I feel as if I won the test of a lifetime, and the gift of having you in my life is my reward. You are my true salvation."

"MJ, I—" I'm at a loss for words. I'm not … what he said. But telling him that would do nothing but start another fight. Instead I say, "Let's go meet your friends."

WE HOLD HANDS ON THE WAY TO THE PARK ACROSS THE street. After all the heavy discussions we've had this morning, the farther we get from my house, the lighter I feel. By the time we reach the corner, my mind is clear.

I swing our joined hands as I hop over the curb. I like holding hands with MJ. My skin tingles, butterflies nervously flutter in my belly, and I can't stop the smile spreading across my face. I feel giddy and excited. That's surprising, knowing what I'm about to do. But I suppose meeting your boyfriend's friends is supposed to be nerve-racking. Take away the fact that these friends might *kill* me, and this is something most couples deal with in the beginning.

As his essence increases inside me, I get the feeling he isn't holding my hand just because he likes to. He's monitoring my emotions and trying to keep me calm. I'm smiling, and the sun is shining. So far, I think I'm doing well.

We round the curve in the parking lot and stop as three people materialize where Ben and MJ fought on Monday.

They're all dressed similarly to MJ in jeans and white shirts. On the right is a slender woman. She's the shortest of the group, though she still has three inches on me. She has olive skin, the most dazzling chestnut eyes I've ever seen, and perfect wavy brown hair. Not a single strand is out of place even with the light breeze.

Next to her is a guy with spiked brown hair, calm brown eyes, and a timid but friendly smile. He must be Alexander. He's stocky, more muscular than MJ, but looks more like a teddy bear than a brute.

The last one has me fighting an urge to step back. She's gorgeous like the other two, with pale skin, brown eyes, and curly auburn hair. She's smiling, but it seems forced. It's not the smile, though, that makes me wary. It's her eyes.

While Alexander and the brunette angel alternate between staring at me and MJ, she's fixated on our joined hands. As if she's waiting for the exact moment MJ lets go.

Before I can panic, a burst of heated energy flows into me. It rushes up into my heart, filling the space easily, as if it's always belonged there. Then it spreads to the rest of me. My senses sharpen as muscles all over my body tighten and twitch with excitement.

I've felt this before—when I've perceived a danger of some sort. This, whatever it is, makes me feel *whole*. It helped me defend myself against Justin, Ben, and even MJ. And just as I did those times, I find a desire growing.

A desire for the angel to attack me so I can fight her.

The new energy searches out MJ's essence, pulling it away from every place it's lingering inside me. Then, without warning, the new energy forces MJ's essence out of me.

"Ouch, Maddy." MJ pulls his hand away from me and shakes it. "What did you just do?"

I want to tell him *I* didn't do it, but before I can answer him, a flash of red moves in the corner of my eye. I turn. The redhead's running at me.

Time slows as MJ dashes in front of me using his angelic speed, but this time I can see ripples in the air behind him.

The other two Protectors follow the redhead— rushing at me.

I think back to my lessons with Duane, trying to pick a fighting stance to defend this type of attack. I know nothing may work against an angel, but I have to try.

But suddenly my body moves on its own—shifting and bending until I'm standing at an angle with one hand held back ready to attack, the other outstretched, waiting to block her.

Bright light flashes in the sky as thunder crashes. The ground rumbles underneath me, causing all the Protectors to halt in their tracks.

They turn to me.

The three new Protectors' faces range from apprehensive to shocked to furious. MJ's furious too, his eyes that frightening shade of red that belongs to demons. The redhead betrayed him. She betrayed his trust. She *hurt* my MJ.

The energy inside me changes from a buzzing excitement to fury.

A ripping noise, louder than all other sounds, echoes through the air as if thick fabric were torn in two. Jagged lines cut through the pavement, stretching from one end of the parking lot to the other.

The redness leaves MJ's eyes, and his jaw drops.

The ground shakes with such force that it takes everything I've got to stay upright. Once it settles, I look back at MJ, only to find a seven-foot gap separating us.

MJ and the redhead glare at each other for a moment, then they each race toward me.

My hands rise again in defense, acting again on their own. Heat builds in my palms, growing so fast it feels as if they're immersed in flames, though I feel no pain. My hands lift to the sky. A moment later, massive flames burst out of the ground.

My left hand slices through the air. The fire follows the movement, swirling around me. Just as on the bridge, I'm encased in a flame tornado. This time, without MJ and his protective bubble, I feel the heat. It feels and smells wonderful. As if I'm sitting beside a bonfire. It's familiar, for some reason reminding me of ... *home*.

I may not know what's happening, and I don't want to be separated from MJ, but I'm glad for this. I'm glad I—or this unknown source of energy—saved myself from the angry angel.

Once she's gone, and MJ and I are safe, I'll figure out what—or who—is overtaking me. I need to know how to control this. Until then, I'm not taking my eyes off my MJ.

# CHAPTER 9

# MJ

ALEXANDER HOLDS ME IN AN IRON GRIP AS I FIGHT to get to Maddy. The flames are blocking her, swirling around her, and reaching up past the clouds. I can't get to her, but neither can Sissy.

Somehow Maddy knew Sissy was going to attack her, but she wasn't afraid. As brave as she is, though, I know this isn't her. Someone or something is inside her. *She's possessed.* That's the only explanation to why her emerald eyes turned red.

Through the flames, I can see the toll on her. The enraged, defensive stance is gone. Now her body sags, as if she's struggling against something. It's either the heat of the flames or whoever is controlling her. Regardless, I'm on the outside, powerless to help.

"Dammit," I shout. "I said let me go! That's an order."

"No," Alexander grits, tightening his grip. "Not until you come to your senses and stop trying to run into whatever the hell that is."

"Do you know what this is?" Tamitha asks, moving beside us.

"Were you aware she possessed this kind of power?" Sissy asks, now standing on my other side. "It's remarkable."

From the corner of my eye, I see her gazing in wonder at what Maddy has done. I tried to tell her—tried to explain to them all—what Maddy could do, but experiencing the raw power of her abilities is indescribable. So many emotions stir inside me during times like this. The strongest are awe and fear. But my fear is *for* Maddy. Never *of* Maddy. She is my everything.

And Sissy nearly took her from me.

"Get out of my sight!" I snap. "How dare you betray me!"

"Betray you? I was doing as you instructed."

I tear my gaze from Maddy and glare at Sissy. "I called you here to help protect her, not kill her!"

Her ringlets bounce as she shakes her head. "No. You agreed that her ability is too dangerous to fall into the hands of the Acquisitioner."

"That doesn't mean *kill* her!"

She tilts her head to the side, frowning. "Yes, it does."

My fists clench—the hand that held Maddy's throbs from the force of my essence being shoved back into me. I don't know how the demon did that, but I'll find out.

I turn my attention back to Maddy. Sweat drips down her skin.

"She is innocent," I say. "We protect the innocent. If you cannot do that, leave now, before I do something I might regret."

Sissy leaves without another word.

"Please, MJ," Tamitha begs. "We misunderstood what you meant by this meeting. I'm sorry. I will help you protect her. Whatever has hold of her, it's hurting her. You'll need help when this is done."

Suddenly, Maddy becomes unsteady. Her left side moves close, much too close, to the flames. I lunge, but Tamitha joins Alexander in holding me back—keeping me from rescuing Maddy.

"Please," I cry out. "Let me help her!"

"We will once the flames are gone," Alexander says.

"Look up, MJ," Tamitha says. "The flames are only fifteen feet high now. They'll be gone soon. She'll need you. We'll stay to guard you from both sides and to repair the scene. There's no way this went unnoticed."

Pain lashes through my silent heart, wanting to get to her, but knowing they're right. "Hold on, Maddy," I say as the flames continue to lower. "It's almost over."

"And then what?" Alexander asks.

"Then I save her," I say.

"What about the demon?"

"I'll send whoever that is back to Hell."

"Coincidences, MJ," Alexander says and gives me a pointed look.

I tug against him. "This isn't the time for puzzles. She needs help!"

"You're thinking with your heart, not with your head! She's possessed by a demon who can manipulate fire. It's not the first time we've come across this, is it?"

I grimace, not wanting to follow the trail he's creating.

"What are you saying?" Tamitha asks.

"Either two demons can do the impossible," Alexander begins, "or Maddy's possessed by the very killer MJ's here to stop."

"No," Tamitha whispers in shock.

She says something to Alexander, but I don't hear it. My attention is on the flames as they dip below Maddy's head, finally allowing me to see her beautiful face. Her hair is matted, and beads of sweat drip down her flushed skin. The redness has left her eyes, but she looks wrung out—as if she could collapse at any moment.

I want to leap over the flames and take her away, but Alexander's words are sinking in. The chances of two demons harboring such power are miniscule. Yet despite the odds, I'm hoping it's true. Maddy already has too many similarities to my case for my comfort level. If this is the serial killer demon, did I lead him to her, just as her uncle predicted?

I wait and watch in horror—feeling helpless—as inch by painstakingly slow inch the flames lower and Maddy continues to waver. If she falls now, she'll fall into the flames and possibly down into the unknown depths of the cracked concrete.

Finally, the flames extinguish. Alexander and Tamitha release me. I leap over just in time to catch her as she falls.

"Maddy, wake up," I beg. "Look at me, please."

She doesn't.

"What's wrong with her?" Alexander asks, now standing beside me.

"Please tell me she's okay," Tamitha says, her voice cracking with fear and sadness. She sucks in her breath, overcome by the new emotions awakening inside her. "It's true, then. She *does* make us feel. It's remarkable. Tell me you can fix her!"

I follow my essence as it flows through Maddy, verifying a heartbeat and brain activity. Then I scan the rest of her, looking for clues about what just occurred. I find no information.

I find nothing at all.

There's no trace of anything left inside her.

Dread fills me. I hold her limp body closer. "She's alive, but I can't sense her essence or feel any emotions. When she sleeps and when I healed her last night, I could feel something from her. There's nothing now. Her soul is gone."

"The demon can do that?" Tamitha asks.

"No, but Maddy can, remember? That's how she travels to alternate planes and through time. Maybe that's what happened."

The more I think about it, the harder I wish for that to be the answer. I hope her soul is gone because she herself sent it somewhere, of her own power. I want to—have to—believe she's fighting back for control.

I don't want her soul to be in some unknown place with a demon. I don't want her to be anywhere with a demon, alone, facing Father only knows what. But this is her ability, and she controls it. All she has to do is get the bastard to touch her again, and the touch will send her back. It might bring him back too, which I want. That way I can hurt him for hurting her.

"Find him," I say as I run my fingers through her sweat-soaked hair. "Find him, then come back to me. *I dare you*. You can't leave. We only just found each other. I love you."

I place a kiss on her forehead, then lift and carry her vacant body back to her house so she can rest and recover in peace.

# CHAPTER 10

# Maddy

I CRY OUT AS I HIT THE GROUND HARD. I TAKE IN A DEEP breath—then almost choke on how hot and dry the air is. It makes me feel as if my blood were boiling. Even the ground feels like hot coals.

I pry my eyes open, then clamp them shut again, overwhelmed by brightness. I blink and try to focus.

Leaning over me is a face in a porcelain mask. It's a woman. Red eyes stare at me. Demon eyes.

I bolt up to my feet, staggering as I distance myself from her. I stand there, face-to-face with a demon, waiting and watching for her to attack me. She straightens, but doesn't advance on me.

I stare at her, taking her in. I feel her eyes on me, doing the same.

She's my height and size, though her brown hair is longer, stopping near her elbows. She's wearing a short, robin's-egg blue dress. Her fingernails are painted red, and on her right hand is a black, heart-shaped ring. With the demon eyes and strange mask, it makes her look like a frightening doll.

My hands clench at my sides, trying to calm myself. I notice her hands doing the same.

I stop.

She stops.

My eyes narrow as I stare at her mask. She does the same, glaring back.

She's mimicking me.

The longer I stare at her, the less frightening she becomes. I don't trust her—she's a demon and she can easily kill me. But she hasn't done it yet.

I count to ten in my head, giving myself courage to break the staring contest and figure out where I am.

I look around.

Chandeliers hang from a ceiling far out of view, illuminating the massive space. A huge bar is next to a sitting area with leather couches and a TV. The walls and floor are black stone, and flowing through it are glowing red veins that give off nearly the same heat as the fire tornado. A massive stone table sits in the centermost point in the room. For as large as it is, it's strange that there are only two chairs.

A lone archway stretches across the far sidewall, while the largest fireplace I've ever seen rests on the right sidewall. The fireplace is so big I could walk right into it. Near the fireplace is a ginormous desk made of red stone. The edges are marked with intricate carvings, but I can't see what they are from here. Behind the desk are unending rows of glass shelves, filled with multicolored files.

Nothing in this space matches the size of this female demon. Whoever—or whatever—lives with her, I don't want to meet it.

Suddenly without warning, the demon grabs hold of my arm. Her essence rushes in. It instantly fills the hole in my heart, making me feel whole again, then in less than a second, it travels throughout my entire body.

The unbearable heat of this place suddenly feels comfortable against my skin. Did she do this, and if so, why?

I stare into her crimson eyes, wondering once again whether she'll hurt me, but she just stands there, letting her essence flow through me.

It feels … good. Powerful. Familiar. It's the same exact feeling that came over me in the park as that redheaded angel rushed me. The energy I felt belongs to this demon—it's *her* essence. It controlled me. And I just let it, never even bothering to figure out what it was.

But I liked it. It helped me control my fears at Justin's house last night, right before I stabbed him … And it's how and why I fought against Ben when he attacked me … It's helped in my dreams and with MJ … And countless other times over the past few weeks. It all started the night I met Justin.

If it weren't for her, not only would I have lost all those battles, but I also never would have made it out of Justin's party that first night. She's what made me run away.

MJ and Justin made it sound as if I were invincible, and this just proved them wrong.

Oh my God.

I pull my arm back. She tightens her grip.

"You are not supposed to be here," she says in a soft soprano voice.

"Where am I?"

Her essence surges inside me, projecting images of her, this room, and fire. Lots and lots of fire. In my mind, I see people burning. Their screams fill me—rattling my bones and eclipsing every happy memory. I heard these screams when I was inside Damien in my dreams. I heard them again the day MJ died. These people are being tortured.

A tear slides down my cheek. I want to unsee everything she showed me.

This is Hell.

"Well, no—*this* is just a room," she replies as if she had heard my thoughts, even though that's not possible. "Beyond that door, though"—she points to a mammoth set of doors near the bar—"is a world you are not meant to see."

I step back, but she moves with me. "Why did you bring me here?"

"It was not my intent, though I am glad for it."

If her essence even inadvertently brought me here, why haven't I gone back now that we've touched? That's how it works with MJ and Justin: one touch sends us to another place, the second touch sends us home. She's still touching me. *Why* is she still touching me?

She drops her hand and turns away.

That's twice now. She replied to my unspoken words a moment ago and just now removed her hand when I questioned it in my mind. The words I've heard many times with Damien and MJ drift through my mind: *there's no such thing as coincidence*. So how can she read my thoughts if MJ and Justin—

"Because I am not like them, so I am not bound by their rules."

I clench my fists again as my mind reels. "Rules or no rules—you have no right to my private thoughts. And you sure as hell don't have the right to overtake my body. Stay out of my head and stay out of me."

"I cannot do that. It is imperative you survive, no matter the costs."

My fingers run through my hair as I struggle to make sense of this. It is *imperative* I survive? Imperative to whom? Me? Or her?

"I'm glad it's so damn important to *you* that I stay alive! So why aren't you helping *more*, then? All you've done is hijacked my body for a few minutes here and there."

She huffs. "I saved your life on multiple occasions."

I roll my eyes and huff right back. "You *used* me to fight, then you just abandoned me and left me to pick up the pieces alone."

She flinches. "I did not mean to cause you pain. For that, I am deeply sorry. I wish circumstances were different and I did not have to go to such extremes to save you—"

"You didn't *save* me."

She's silent for a moment then says, "What about your dream Sunday night? It was my voice that urged you to continue through the snow when you had all but given up. And again when I told you to go to the blanket inside the cabin and rest. In fact, you would not have even entered the cabin had I not opened the door for you."

I shake my head, hating that she's right. Between Justin and now her, I feel as if my control is slipping. Every time I thought I was brave and held my own against them … it was all her.

I hug myself, trying to keep from falling to pieces in front of a demon.

She moves closer, reaching out to touch me, and for a moment I want her to. I want to feel her essence inside me again, giving me strength.

Her hand falls back to her side and I cringe, feeling even more alone. Somehow, I suspect she feels that way too.

"It was not all me," she admits. "Mostly I tap into strengths and abilities you already possess. MJ is right—you will change everything."

MJ's name echoes inside me. My heart stutters. The force of those extra beats sends a charge through me. It shoves down my insecurities and ignites a fire in me.

I'm *done*.

I'm done being a pawn in their game.

I'm done being her puppet.

I'm done being kept in the dark.

I stand tall, dropping my hands, refusing to let her intimidate me. I won't give her total control anymore.

"How did you create the fire in the park?" I ask.

She steps back, eyes widening.

I advance on her, refusing to stop until I know *everything*. "How did you split the ground? Justin doesn't have that kind of power. How can you do all this? What *are* you?"

"I—I created a wall of fire to separate you from the angels. It was inspired by your own show this morning on the bridge. The rest was all you. As I said, I merely tap into what you already have. Your power is truly magnificent. You could do great things—" She pauses and shakes her head. "If only you were able to control it."

I turn away from her.

"I'm working on it," I snap, surprised by how much her comment bothers me. I want to control my abilities. Even if it's just so I never use them again.

"You cannot control them," she says. "Not on your own. Your abilities are tied into your emotions, and right now you cannot control them. Kissing brings flames of passion. Heartache could flood the world. Anger, especially over someone you love being hurt, rips apart the earth. The angel is lucky I intervened. She may not have survived your wrath."

I struggle to rein in my reaction. I can control myself. She's a demon, and I can't trust anything she says—no matter how much I think she's right.

"You must see something," she says suddenly, turning away and moving to the sitting area. She sits on the love seat and motions for me to sit on the black leather couch beside it.

I consider refusing, but I doubt it would do any good.

As I sit, the demon picks up the remote and turns on the TV.

Something inside me snaps as it shows *my bedroom*.

I'm lying motionless on my bed. MJ is beside me. Alexander and the brunette angel are with him.

I watch MJ lightly kiss my forehead. "Please come back to me," he says. He turns to Alexander, panic in his eyes. "Get me another cold rag. She's burning up."

"What is this?" I whisper.

"This is you. Streaming live, I guess you could say."

My mind is torn, trying to decide what is more unreal: where I am or what she's saying. It's all just … too much. Slowly, my emotions shrivel up, replaced by empty numbness.

She mutes the TV. "I have—we have—watched you grow, every day, from here," she begins. "I admit it is strange having you here now, actually seeing you and speaking with you. I am—what do you call it— star struck."

I feel her eyes on me again, but I can't react. Every moment of my life has been ... broadcasted, live, in Hell. For a *demon*.

I turn my head, letting my hair hide my face from the demon. My gaze lands on the bar, and I'm reminded that she doesn't live here alone. Whoever—or whatever—owns this massive room, watches me too ...

The numbness shatters. My stomach churns. An overwhelming sense of violation creeps over me. This is so much worse than when MJ and Justin watch me from the Veil of Shadows.

"Up until recently," she says in my silence, "you lived a very boring life, which fooled us into thinking we had succeeded. For this reason, we were not watching as closely as we should have been this month."

"Succeeded with what?" I hear myself ask.

"Concealing you from angels and demons. After Thursday, however, we started watching constantly. Whenever I saw you were in trouble, I alerted my master—"

"Who's that?" I whisper, though I don't want to know.

She stands and steps closer to me. "Someone like me— someone helping you. He sends me to you. I enter you, not unlike how you enter others in your dreams and visions. But it only works for a few minutes. It is rather draining to my strength, and it takes about a day to recuperate. I helped you fight against Justin, but I was not able to hold

on once he hit you. All I could do was watch from here"—
she points to the TV—"as you fought bravely for your life."

I look up, catching her gaze.

Her eyes lighten, and I get the feeling she's smiling
behind her mask. "You are so strong, Maddy."

Unsure of what to say, I nod.

She sits beside me on the couch. She leans over even as
I lean back. "Watching you has many benefits." She leans
in farther and whispers, "I know what happened in the
last moments at Justin's house."

I freeze. Fear and anxiousness battle inside me as
I stare at the demon who knows whether or not Justin
owns my soul.

"The contract is protected by a spell, guarding it
against Protectors," she says. "It vanished when MJ
arrived. The drop of your blood that clung to the end of
the pen fell to the floor. It never hit the contract."

"Justin doesn't own my soul?" I whisper, testing
the words.

"Not yet."

Tears of joy fill my eyes. I look up at the demon, and
for the first time, I'm glad for her presence. Justin does not
own me. This feeling won't last forever—I know he won't
give up. But for now, I don't care. Let him come. Let him
come and just *try* to hurt me again. With MJ's and this
demon's help, Justin will know what it's like to feel fear.

Then I pause. As grateful as I am to know this, I can't
help but wonder why she's telling me now.

"More beings are becoming aware of you," she replies
to my unspoken thoughts. "I will do what I can to help you
fight them."

She turns her head to the TV. MJ is still leaning over me. My heart breaks at the lines of worry etched on his face.

"You cannot stay here," she says. "It is time I send you back."

I close my eyes and let out the breath I seem to have been holding since waking up here.

She picks up the remote and presses another button. The TV now makes a whooshing noise as the image on the screen rolls like waves on the ocean.

"I admit, our Time Keeper is not as fancy as that fountain," she says, "but it works just the same."

Elizabeth's fountain?

She's going to push me into the TV. No.

"When I send you in, you should return to your own body."

"*Should*?" I take a few steps back toward the bar. My breath quickens.

"It has never been done before."

She grabs my arm. Her essence hums to life inside me, pushing down my fears and replacing them with excitement.

Yes. I find myself smiling. Not only do I get to try this Time Keeper out, but I get to go back to MJ.

"Listen," she says as her red eyes look me over. "I wish I did not have to do this to you, but I cannot take any chances."

I start to ask, "Do what?" but her essence picks up and a fog swirls inside my head. Each swirl sends a pulse of energy through my body that vibrates as a piano string does long after the note is played. It's hard to think. Fuzzy. I'm floating, and the only thing keeping me tethered is her.

"You cannot tell MJ about me yet," she says in a soothing voice. "When MJ asks, tell him you do not know where you went. It was dark and hard to see, but you found the demon that took hold of you. You touched him. That sent you home and sent him back to the City of the Damned."

"City of the Damned," I repeat, floating even more.

She looks deeper into my eyes. "MJ needs to worry about others coming for you—soon they will. You must ensure that no one else learns of you. No matter what, you can never tell anyone you were adopted. Everything will be ruined if someone discovers who you truly are."

I nod. Even through the fog, I know she's right.

"There are a few dreams left for you to see. Tell MJ about them. Tell him you spoke with Elizabeth, but do not say her name. With your connection to the dreams broken, things will get a lot worse for you. Stay strong and trust MJ. Do that, and you could save many lives."

She hugs me, holding me close. "Good-bye, Maddy. I will see you again, soon."

She shoves me. I fall, but nothing stops me.

I keep falling.

# CHAPTER 11

# MJ

I STARE INTO HER EMERALD EYES, DISBELIEVING WHAT I'm seeing.

She's back.

An hour ago, she left me and I had no idea how or by whom. I held her, keeping my essence inside her. But no matter how hard I tried, I felt nothing from her—even when her skin turned red with the fever I couldn't break. All I could do was watch.

It was as if the nightmare of yesterday never ended. But today was worse. Yesterday I couldn't find her. Today I was with her—I was *right there*—but I still couldn't protect her. Even my team was no help. Despite all my immortal abilities, I wasn't enough to keep her safe.

As I carried her limp body home, I prayed to Father, asking him to guide her back to me—begging him to let her be okay. I wasn't sure if it would work, having never prayed before. Because I'm a Protector, praying isn't necessary. But I had to try—I had to do something. Even though Father has no idea who Maddy is, he would have to take note of one of his angels praying.

Her body shivers.

I move my hands to her hair, brushing it from her face as my essence picks up inside her—searching for her needs. Her heart is racing, and her body is twisted with fear. I calm them, giving her space to breathe.

"Oh, Maddy ... I'm so glad you're awake. What happened?"

She blinks, and her brows narrow in confusion. "I–I'm back? Is this real?"

I nod, taken aback by her questions. What did the demon do to her?

She looks up and lets out a relieved breath. Then suddenly she slams into me, wrapping her arms around me.

I hold her closer as my own fear—that I'd never see her again—settles.

"Where were you?" I whisper into her hair.

She clings to me even harder. "I don't know. I'm cold."

She's not. Her skin shimmers with sweat, which is only a sign of the fire I can now feel inside her. Still, I cannot deny her what she wants.

"Tamitha," I call, but she's already next to me with a blanket. She throws it over Maddy, knowing I need to keep my hands on Maddy so my essence can continue flowing.

Slowly, I lower her and rest beside her on the bed. She stares into my eyes, and I get the feeling she still doesn't believe she's here with me. I reach up and stroke her cheek.

"Please, Maddy, tell me anything you remember."

After a moment, she says, "I don't know where I went. It was dark and hard to see, but I found the demon that took hold of me. I touched him. That sent me home and sent him back to the City of the Damned."

My head whips up as I look at Tamitha and Alexander. The alarm in their eyes must mirror my own.

Mortals don't know the name of that place. I've never said it around Maddy. We rarely say it even amongst ourselves. That place is an abomination—a constant reminder of our darkest day. Perhaps the Influencer said it yesterday, and Maddy's just repeating it now. I'd rather it be from him than this new demon.

Only those in league with the Fallen refer to Hell by that name.

My essence picks up inside Maddy, making sure she came back alone. She did.

"Tell me about the demon," I say. "Tell me what you remember about him so I can find him."

She shakes her head. "I don't remember him."

I frown and tilt my head. She touched the demon. She has to remember something.

There's no reason for her to protect him from me, yet she is. My essence picks up inside her, trying to figure this out. When my essence returns to me, my worry grows. I found nothing. I know the demon didn't compel Maddy—she's resistant to that ability. And she isn't afraid, so that means the demon didn't force her to lie under threats.

"The demon from yesterday must have told this other demon about her," Tamitha says.

"Yes," Alexander agrees. "What are the odds she would be attacked by two demons two days in a row? They're connected."

Maddy shudders. "Justin—he's still coming for me."

"Maddy," I begin. Sorrow fills me. As much as I want to know why she's covering for a demon, there are more pressing matters—her needs. "He won't hurt you again. I promise. I don't give a damn what that contract says."

"I didn't sign it."

I can only blink.

"The contract wasn't signed. He doesn't own me."

My body sags, freed of the weight the contract held over Maddy, over me, over us. I would have fought for her, but I know the odds of winning wouldn't have been in our favor. I was terrified of losing her. Even now, I'm not foolish enough to believe we're safe, but without the contract, at least we have a chance at a life together.

Then my joy suddenly fades. "Did the demon tell you this? How do you know?" I ask. I want to believe her, but I don't trust the source.

Her eyes dim as she searches for what should be an easy answer. "I ... I don't know. I just do."

It's all the proof I need.

"It doesn't matter how I know," she continues. "You just can't tell anyone else about me. It's only a matter of time before more beings come for me. We need to be ready."

Whether I trust this new demon's word, I know this much is true—more will come for her. They outnumber us twenty to one. Even if I keep her identity contained to our small team, at most she'll stay a secret for a month. All my immortal gifts are meaningless if they cannot keep her safe.

"I will do whatever it takes to keep you a secret," I say. *"Þú ert minn hvatvetna. Minn ást. Minn líf. Minn Maddy."*

I meant every word. She is my everything. My love. My life. My Maddy.

I look down at her with emotions I can't even describe. *"Ek ann þér,"* I say softly.

Curious green eyes meet mine. If she knew what those words meant, she would pull even farther away from me. She's afraid of love. She doesn't accept it from anyone and never gives it back. She isn't ready to know how I feel about her just yet. But still I have to say it. I have to say the three words that terrify her.

I love you.

I hold her closer to me and kiss her forehead, breathing in her fruit-and-nature scent. "You're safe now, *minn hvatvetna*," I say, tucking her hair behind her ear. "You're home."

At the word "home," she unravels. Raindrops pelt the house.

I wrap my arms around her again, holding her close. Tamitha and Alexander leave the room, though they're still on guard. Sissy has been with Amber since she left the park. Not knowing what we're up against has us all on high alert.

I lay with Maddy, soothing her as best I can.

This is the second demon that attacked her in less than a week. The first one tried to own her soul with a contract he shouldn't have had access to in the first place. What is this one after? Who is he? Why can't she remember him? How was he able to possess her? And the fire, the cracked concrete, the destruction, the power—was that him?

Or Maddy?

# CHAPTER 12

## Justin

**M**Y FIST HOVERS IN FRONT OF THE MOUNTAINOUS door, listening to the sound of my knock echo inside it. We're supposed to tremble and feel inferior before it, but this time I don't. There's a reason so many people fear desperate men—we fear nothing but that which we are about to lose.

The echoes fade into silence. This wasn't what I expected. I know he doesn't sit in his chambers all day. But she's in danger, and he's the only one who can help her.

"Please," I beg, pounding again. "If you don't answer … if you don't let me in … then our deal is over. She won't survive long enough for me to find her weakness."

My head hangs, fighting against thoughts of what the world would be like without her. Losing her would be like losing the sun. My world would be forever dark.

A throat clears behind me.

I whip around. Towering over me in a black hooded cloak is the Acquisitioner. But unlike the other times, this time I don't drop my gaze. I can't. My mission is too important—she's too important—for me to be submissive.

"I did not think I could be surprised by your kind. But here you are, waiting *outside* my chambers this time," he says, referring to my breaking and entering last night. "You are fortunate that my plans require complete secrecy. Otherwise, I would hand you to my sister to remind you of your place, demon. With your emotions restored, you would fold on the first Trial."

My body convulses, remembering all too well the pleasure his sister, the Gatekeeper, takes from inflicting pain both during the Trials and privately in her chambers.

"Move," he commands. "This had better be worth my time."

I nod and stand to the side as the doors open. Silently I follow him inside. This time, I keep my eyes down, not wanting to upset him further. Holding my tongue and treating him—any of them—with respect is hard, even though it has been beaten into me. But with Mads's life on the line, I have no choice.

He takes his time, making himself at home behind his enormous desk, though he doesn't lower his cloak. It isn't surprising. Other than the Gatekeeper's, I've never seen any of the Fallen's faces. She hardly ever wears a cloak, whereas the others hardly ever take them off. Not that I'd ever *want* to look upon the faces of the Acquisitioner, the Ferryman, or Death.

I met all of the Fallen except the Acquisitioner the first day I came here. Death greeted me when I took my last breath. He stood over eight feet tall, wearing nothing but a black cloak. His hood was pulled so far forward that only darkness existed where his face should have been. Without a word, he took me into the Great Divide. I didn't fully understand what had happened to me until we arrived in

Immortal City for the reading of my file—my judgment. When my fate was set, Death met me again and transported me to Hell, where the Ferryman took over.

Like his brother, he stood silent in his cloak as he guided hundreds of ferries across the Styx. When we made it to shore, monsters more grotesque than anything I'd seen in movies and TV led us through the Gates of Hell. Every direction I looked was more horrifying than the last. But then they stopped us, and there, standing amidst twin pyres, was a woman dressed in black leather and stiletto boots.

She was the embodiment of every fantasy I'd yet to have. The way the leather clung to her body … it was as if she weren't wearing anything at all. Plum lips were curved in a secretive smile, and her onyx eyes could cut you to shreds the instant they were on you. She put every female rock star, every centerfold, to shame. But she wasn't a rock star or a pinup girl. She was the Gatekeeper, and she was there to make my life a literal hell.

The Acquisitioner lets out a long exhale. "State your business, demon, before my patience runs out."

Memories of my past fade away as Mads reclaims her place as my primary thought. "Another demon found her today, sir."

He sits up, leaning over his desk and placing a cloaked hand inside the darkness of his hood, where I assume his chin is. "Where is she now?"

"Resting with the Protector, sir."

"With him and not you?"

I grimace. If there's anything I hate more than the sight of her in *his* arms, it's having it thrown in my face.

"Good," he says, listening to my thoughts. "You have proper motivation."

"He hasn't left her side since last night, and now there are other Protectors helping him. I can't get close enough to her to discover her weakness. We're running out of time. Can't you just tell me—"

"Consider yourself lucky I even told you she *has* a weakness. Is this all you came to tell me, or was there a point to your visit?"

Mads's face flashes in my mind. I take a deep breath and vow to do whatever it takes to save her. Then I straighten and stare straight into his red eyes.

"I've come for a weapon. One that can protect her from the untold numbers of angels and demons who will come for her. Even when the contract is signed, the other side will still try to take her from me—from you."

"Angels and demons cannot be killed. You are on a fool's errand."

"What about the weapon you used on the Nephil—"

Before I can finish, my body is raised in the air, my extremities pulled to their limits, just as last night.

He shoves out of his chair so fast it falls behind him. He leans over his desk resting his weight on his massive hands. "How do you know of that?" he booms. He pulls tighter, forcing me to answer.

"Past lives," I spit out.

He loosens the tension.

"I've been recalling as many past lives as I can," I continue. "I remember the purge of the Nephilim. You were charged with their destruction, having sired most of them."

His fingers flex on the desk, digging into the stone, and his body convulses underneath his cloak. "You remember too much, demon."

The purge of the Nephilim nearly ended the human race. Born of lust or rape, the spawns of the Archangels were rotten, unholy creatures. It didn't matter which side of the fight their immortal fathers fell on—the Nephilim were all the same. They had the abilities of their Archangel fathers, but lacked the ability to control them.

Heavenly Father put an end to them, commanding the Acquisitioner to destroy them all. It took almost a century. After that, Heavenly Father decreed the Archangels of both sides shall no longer mate with mortals. The Devil agreed. As added insurance, Heavenly Father made it so that no child shall ever again be created from a union between an immortal and a mortal.

His shoulders sag, no doubt listening to my thoughts again.

After a moment, he releases me, and I collapse to the stone ground. He turns and walks down the rows of files. I stretch my arms and legs, trying to appease the ache in them. As I watch the Acquisitioner walk away from me, a startling revelation dawns on me.

He reacted with surprise.

He reacted with anger.

He reacted with guilt and sadness.

He can *feel*.

Can only he feel, or can all of the Fallen? All of the Archangels? Is this why he's after Mads?

A moment later, he reappears holding a lone object wrapped in a dirty cloth. He places the package on the desk and motions for me to open it.

The object is about a foot and a half long, and no wider than my hand. I arch a brow, doubting this is what purged thousands of Nephilim. After a breath, I grab the cloth. It's old. Far older than anything created in this century. Carefully, I unravel it.

Once the weapon is revealed, I stare down at it—in awe. It's a blade made of bone. The handle is wrapped in what looks like leather. I suspect it's as old as the blade itself, though it's remarkably intact. The back of the blade has an almost elegant curve, though the instrument is anything but. Chipped teeth and jagged grooves cover the edge—worn down from the many souls it has slain.

"This is Requiem Aeternam. Angel, demon, mortal—the blade does not care what blood it sheds."

Pressure eases in my chest. Finally, I will be able to protect her.

I reach down to grab the blade, but the Acquisitioner blocks me, placing his hand in front of the blade.

He stares at me, searching for something deep down inside me.

"Know this, demon," he warns, "whoever you strike with this blade shall cease to exist. Can you live with that kind of weight on your soul?"

I place my hands on his desk, near the blade as it rests on that ancient cloth. I feel the power—his power and the power of the blade—rush up through my palms before I stare into his red eyes.

"I would obliterate billions of souls in order to save hers."

His hood moves in a small nod. "Then it is yours. Do not let any of her blood touch it. The next time we meet, I expect the contract to be signed. It should not be a problem

with how determined you are to keep her safe." He glares
at me a moment longer, then pushes off the desk. "You are
dismissed."

I grab the blade and rush out of his office before I make
the mistake of thinking. As I tuck the blade inside my
coat, a tension loosens from my body. I won't use it on MJ.
Though my hatred of him spans many centuries, he doesn't
deserve the blade.

I will use it on whoever possessed her at the
park, though.

The Acquisitioner's doors close behind me. Before
anyone can notice me outside his chambers, I summon the
Great Divide and leave Hell.

No matter what happens now, I will keep her safe.

# CHAPTER 13
## Maddy

MJ'S FUSSING OVER ME EVEN MORE NOW. HE MADE a huge lunch, and now I'm sitting on his lap in the living room. He keeps asking if I'm okay, even though his essence is constantly checking too. I keep telling him I'm fine even though I'm anything but.

And I keep thinking I'm getting better at this—at accepting the whole Heaven and Hell package that comes with MJ. But I'm not. My knowledge of him and his world is equivalent to an ant hill sitting on Mount Everest; I will never be able to take it all in. I'm not sure I want to.

His essence has been battling with my fears. I tried to push them all down—hide them away from him—but there are too many.

I don't like lying to MJ about where I went. It creates knots in my stomach. Even though I want to undo the lies, the words won't come. She forced me to lie to him. I think she compelled me, even though no one else can compel me.

I should hate her. She's given me more than enough reasons to. But … I can't. It's not because of all the good things she's done for me in the past. Or the things she'll do in the future. It's just that despite all the wrong things … I miss being connected with her.

MJ whispers something in my ear again. I think it's Norwegian. I don't know what it means, but from the tender way he says it and the kisses and nuzzles afterward, I think it's a nickname. Something like "my baby" or "my sweetie"—but better. More from the heart. Something similar to what he said last night—that I am at the very center of his heart.

He rarely talks of his previous life. And from the expressions on his teammates' faces, I don't think they've ever heard him use his native language. I like that he says it for me.

Alexander and Tamitha seem nice, now that they've had a real chance to introduce themselves. They're sitting on the love seat making faces at each other—trying out their new emotions.

I guess I'm not the only one adjusting to new things.

Suddenly MJ, Tamitha, and Alexander turn their heads toward the kitchen. A half breath later, Tamitha and Alexander disappear.

My heart races as my head snaps toward the kitchen too.

The door in the kitchen opens, and laughter fills the house as my family returns from shopping—an "idea" MJ gave them to get them out of the house while I was recuperating from the incident at the park. I hear Hannah run upstairs and my parents putting away some groceries.

Even though it's great they're home and happy, I feel nervous again.

During lunch, MJ told me my family's memories of the past few days have all been altered. Mine haven't. If I say something they don't remember, then they'll question me in their minds. They may even question their own memories. Guardian Angels monitor people after demonic attacks to make sure the new memories stay intact. If they suspect someone remembers the truth, MJ said the Perfugae will be brought back to investigate.

I stiffen at the thought. MJ said the Perfugae were Archangels that fell from Heaven after Lucifer. But when they saw how horrible life in Hell was, they tried to return to Heaven. They were turned away. Then they tried to return to Hell, but Lucifer shunned them too. Every day since, they've tried to make amends with and win favor from both sides. Their penance is to prevent mortals from discovering the existence of angels and demons.

MJ erased my family's memories to keep the Perfugae away from them—really, to keep them away from me. I think they're the same beings Justin was afraid of last night. I can't do something stupid and mess this up. I have to go along with their new memories.

I wish I could have these last days back with my family. Even though many horrible things happened, there were many good things too. I finally started connecting with them. I even told Hannah I loved her. Now that memory is gone for her. I hate it.

I'd never said that out loud before. I'd never said it out loud to any of them. Even just thinking the words felt like a lie for some reason. They've been my family for almost seventeen years, and I love them. But I still can't bring myself to say those words again.

Deep down, I think a part of me has always suspected I'm different from my family. And now I realize I'm not just different from them. I'm different from everyone. It's not just about being adopted anymore. All sorts of normal people are adopted. But me, I'm … some sort of an emotionally unstable, supernatural time bomb. I'm different. I'm not normal.

I shake my head. It doesn't matter.

I won't let it matter.

"Oh, there you two are," Mom says as she enters the living room. "Did you kids have a nice—"

Mom stops midsentence, eyes wide. Coming in right behind her, Dad takes one look, then sucks in a breath so fast, he breaks into a fit of coughing. Mom slaps his back while her eyes stay glued to my face.

I stare back at them in complete confusion—until it finally dawns on me.

I'm still sitting in MJ's lap, his arms still wrapped around me.

If I hadn't almost died several times recently, I would wish for death now.

MJ quickly lifts me and sets me on the couch, then jumps up to help Dad—not understanding that his lap and the fact that I was in it is what spurred my dad to choke.

I was never serious with Ben. We didn't hold hands. We rarely kissed. And I never sat in his lap—even when we were alone. MJ might as well have rented a billboard that said "WE'RE DATING—IT'S SERIOUS!" in big neon letters and placed it in the front yard.

Dad recovers. His face is blank, but the brow above his green eye is arched. It's a look I know well. He's too polite to voice his opinion in front of MJ, but he has something to say about this. I'm sure we'll have a family meeting later. I hope I can convince MJ and the other angels to give me some actual privacy for it and not just be watching from the Veil of Shadows.

But then I realize the masked demon and her master will be watching too. Nothing is private anymore …

My worlds collide. The lines between reality and fantasy have crossed over so many times lately that I can barely distinguish between the two. Here they are—my family—unknowingly interacting with an angel. And he's pretending to be mortal while he interacts with the people he believes are my birth parents because I haven't—and now can't—tell him the truth.

The only thing I know for sure at this moment is that I love them all, regardless of who or what they are.

Incredibly, my knees don't wobble as I stand and join the three of them. They're all silent, unsure of what to say. Mom and Dad look at me expectantly.

I can't tell them he's an angel. And I can't tell them that snuggling up with him on the couch made me feel better after I've been through Hell—literally. Not unless I want them to think I'm on drugs. But I have to say something.

I open my mouth and hope words will spill out on their own. "Umm … MJ's from Norway," I say, then shrug.

"I see," Dad says.

"Oh," Mom adds. "So you're a foreign exchange student?"

They both turn to MJ, and I nod my head, hoping he'll play along.

"Yes," MJ says.

I release my breath.

"Oh, well … isn't that neat," Mom says.

Awkwardness drips off the walls, oozing over me as I shift from foot to foot.

"It's a wonderful opportunity," MJ says. "And although I've heard it can be difficult to adjust to a new culture, Maddy has been a wonderful help while I acclimate. You've raised a remarkable daughter. You should be very proud."

Dad and Mom smile.

"That she is," Dad says, relaxing a bit. "Have you eaten yet, kiddo?" he asks me, wrapping an arm around Mom.

"Not since lunch."

"Good," Dad says. "How's dinner out sound? MJ, you're welcome to join us too."

"That'd be great," MJ says. He squeezes my hand. "I've never been on a double date before."

I stand there, gaping at MJ, hoping he didn't just call eating with me and my parents a double date. Maybe I just imagined it. But I glance at my parents, and they're gaping at him too. He really said it.

I rub my neck, trying to ease the tension in me and the room. "When did you want to eat?" I finally ask, smiling as if this weren't the most mortifying moment ever.

For a moment, my parents don't reply. Then Dad says, "We'll leave in twenty minutes."

Thankfully they leave the room, but not before casting one last glance back at MJ and me.

I take a deep breath, turn to MJ, and say, "Yeah. Next time your 'angel sense' is tingling about my parents coming, make sure we're not doing anything more than holding hands. And please don't say stuff about dating and whatnot in front of them either. Okay? I don't want to get 'the Talk.'"

He tilts his head.

I rub my brow and sigh. "There's this whole speech parents give when they think their kid is in a serious relationship, and I don't need to deal with that. And for the record, no one goes on a double date with their parents. Ew. Double dates are with friends."

His own brows furrow as he nods. "What's this speech about? Parents are very wise, and yours love you a great deal. You should listen to them."

I can't even look at him. The only thing more embarrassing than having the Talk with my parents would be talking about the Talk with MJ.

Thanks to my half semester of health class last year, I already know what I need to do to stay off the latest "teen mom" show—not that I considered doing any of that, then or now. But MJ hasn't had health class. Depending on how long it's been since he dated, relationships and … intimacy … could be way different.

"If you really want to know, use my computer to look up the phrase 'the birds and the bees' while I get ready for dinner. But just know that I'm not ready to have that sort of relationship with you. Okay?"

MJ's eyes widen, and he takes a step back. His cheeks flush. "I'm familiar with that reference. I came across it while doing research into you last weekend."

"What sort of research would have led you to that topic?"

"Well …" He pauses, running a hand behind his neck. "I was brushing up on my knowledge of a particular skill set I hadn't utilized as a Protector before. That phrase was in several books I read."

A laugh sounds, and Alexander suddenly reappears. He clamps a hand down on MJ's shoulder. "What this bumbling fool is trying to say is that he's a dummy when it comes to dating you. In fact—"

"Shouldn't you be in the Veil of Shadows?" MJ interrupts. A red hue flows up his neck and face.

Alexander just laughs some more. "You and I both know Maddy's parents are in their bedroom and can't hear me." He gives MJ a playful shove. "As I was saying, he's a dummy, and I have proof: *Dating for Dummies* was the book he was reading when I found him in the Immortal City library."

MJ looks away as his head and shoulders slump. Alexander chuckles, then disappears with a wink.

MJ's embarrassed. That's incredibly sweet. Not wanting him to suffer any longer, I change the subject. "Heaven has a library?"

"Yes," he admits, though he doesn't look up.

"When were you there?"

"Sunday," he mutters.

Now it makes sense. He truly didn't know what he was doing on our date that day, but he tried for me. He didn't even know my name then.

I throw my arms around him and kiss his cheek. He gasps and stumbles backward.

"Thank you," I say.

Before he can say anything back, I leave the room to get ready for dinner.

# CHAPTER 14

# MJ

Sex.

That's what Maddy's parents want to discuss with her, thanks to her being in my lap when they walked in. Part of me wants to compel them to forget it. But if I went around erasing every embarrassing moment just to make things easier for us, then I'd be no better than a demon.

Her parents are thinking about it now upstairs, trying to decide how involved Maddy and I are and how detailed they need to be when they talk with her. They figured they would be having the Talk—as everyone keeps calling it—with Hannah before Maddy. Hannah has always been more aware of boys.

Unknown to Maddy, her father had words with Ben about their relationship. He wanted to know why a twenty-one-year-old in his last year of college would be so interested in a sixteen-year-old girl in high school. (It's fortunate he doesn't know how old I am.)

Ben told him there are people in the world destined for greatness, and he could tell the minute he saw Maddy that she's one of them. He said he didn't know where their relationship would go; that was up to her. She was in control, and he was okay with it.

Ben had no idea how right he was. I like him a little bit more for that—which makes me feel even worse for what happened to him. I should have done more to protect him from the demon. But I was so focused on saving Maddy, I neglected to consider what would happen to him or the emotional toll it would have on Maddy.

His death and her pain are on me.

In the driveway, Maddy and I hold hands as we head to my truck so I can drive us to the restaurant.

Maddy stops and stares at her family heading for their car. My essence inside her is suddenly pulled apart: half of her is eager to spend more time with me, the other half wishes to be with her family. As much as I want to be alone with her, I will not make her chose between me and her family. Especially considering that if things get worse, I'll have no choice but to take her from them to protect her.

I hope if that day comes, she'll forgive me.

"Actually," I say and nod toward their car, "I don't know where we're going, so why don't we ride with your family instead?"

She looks up at me, eyes beaming with joy. It nearly breaks my heart seeing the happiness such a small act can bring to her.

We squeeze into the backseat with Hannah. Maddy intentionally bumps into her sister. They both grin.

"Mom!" Hannah whines. "Maddy's touching me!"

Both Hannah and Maddy giggle as their mother turns around to roll her eyes and shake her head at them. From the car's side mirror, I can see her crack a smile as she turns forward again.

Maddy's dad pulls the car out of the driveway. His mind and her mom's are filled with happy memories of Maddy and Hannah in their youth. I squeeze Maddy's hand, sending more essence into her to keep this light-hearted moment going.

She smiles at me so brightly, her eyes shine with a light I've only seen a few times before.

That familiar thump echoes inside me as my heart beats again. I count eight beats before Maddy turns back to talk with her sister.

I can see the love she has for them. But I can also see the pain it causes her—and I'm at a loss about why. I don't understand how she can be this full of life, love, and compassion yet have said only a few days ago that she was never going to fall in love.

Maddy's father looks back at us in the rearview mirror.

To her parents, I'm trouble. I'm the reason for her disappearance and disobedience on Sunday. But they also realize Maddy has formed a deep attachment to me and that she's changing in good ways. It reminds them of who she used to be, before that camping trip with the Shadowwalker.

Unlike everyone else, they aren't curious about what took place during that trip, when everything changed for Maddy. I can tell they know the truth behind it all, but I can't access it. The Shadowwalker put a block in their minds to keep it secret. It's a strong block—stronger than it should be. Like the demon who took her on Tuesday, the Shadowwalker must have heightened powers too.

Her father sighs then returns his eyes to the road. As happy as her parents are to have her returning to her old self, they fear our relationship will burn bright and fast, then rapidly extinguish. They worry about the effect that would have on her.

They're wrong, though. I would never hurt her. I plan on spending eternity with her. Even with the threat of demons, I'm not going to rush this.

Maddy rests her head on my shoulder, spurring such foreign reactions in me. It's impossible to breathe without inhaling the fruit scent of her shampoo and conditioner, laced with her own scents of sunshine, summer air, and spring rain.

But there's a new scent I hadn't smelled on her before today. Now she smells of fire. Just a hint of it, but it's exotic, and it makes me want to kiss her to see if I taste it on her lips.

In comfortable silence, I allow my mind to rest and listen to whatever her parents have on the radio. It's a news station, and the announcer is talking about the upcoming election and predictions of who will win their districts. We seldom pay attention to mortal politics, but I hear a name I know—James Atwood.

Instantly, Maddy's stomach tightens, and an over-whelming heat fills her. I cringe against the pain and send more of my essence to reduce it. Just as quickly, though, the heat vanishes.

I stare at her. Her eyes are wide, and she's panting. She tries her best to not draw the others' attention. Luckily,

Hannah's texting a friend and their parents are talking about their plans for the weekend.

"What happened?" I whisper.

"I don't know," she whispers back. "Something just feels weird—I'm not sure what it is."

I hold my breath as my essence searches every inch of her. How could Maddy have a reaction like that when she heard Atwood's name? This has to be a coincidence. In the back of my mind, though, I can hear Alexander's "there are no coincidences" speech. I clench my jaw and search her harder, willing myself to find any other explanation, no matter how implausible, that proves Alexander wrong.

My essence returns and dread fills me. There's no physical or emotional reason for her reaction. It wasn't a coincidence. It was triggered by something that has me more worried than any other demon or angel. It was triggered by Maddy herself.

James Atwood, the politician the radio mentioned, has a daughter, and she's the next target for the demon serial killer.

Her eyes search mine, full of questions. From her expression, I can tell she has no idea who Atwood is or why she reacted to his name. Very few psychics understand how their ability works and even fewer can control it. Whether this happened via psychic power or some other ability, all Maddy knows is the panic that suddenly flooded her.

Needing answers and fearing the worst, I reach out to Gary, the Protector assigned to the Atwood case.

*Sir,* he says once we're connected.

Not wanting to mention Maddy in any way, I use a cover story. *I've been in contact with a psychic who believes your Charge may be in imminent danger.*

Even though Gary doesn't have emotions yet, I feel his senses sharpen. *I am watching her from the Veil of Shadows now.*

*She's safe?* I ask.

*For now, though it would help if I had more information about the psychic's premonition.*

*The psychic is new to her abilities,* I reply. *If I hear more, I'll contact you. Until then, stay close to her.*

We disconnect.

Knowing the Atwood girl is alive, I decide not to burden Maddy with the details and possible explanations. After everything she's been through, she needs a night of peace and normalcy—even if it means I have to keep the truth from her. Tomorrow, I'll tell her what happened, and we can discuss her reaction at length.

But tonight, I'm going to do everything in my power to keep her happy.

"Relax," I whisper, smiling and squeezing her hand. "There's nothing to worry about."

She glances at her family, still engrossed in their own conversations. Then her eyes narrow in disbelief at me. "You're sure?"

I nod.

"But what just happened? You didn't feel anything—another essence or whatever?"

I pull her into me, hugging her as best I can in the backseat. "No. You're probably just nervous for dinner. I'm nervous too. But I'm glad I get to spend the evening with you."

Inside, I can feel her struggling to let go of her fears and trust my words. As difficult as it is to sit by and feel her go through this, I know it would be so much worse if I hadn't lied to Maddy. Protecting her from the truth has spared her unnecessary stress. I push her remaining fears down, letting her find the peace she needs. After a moment, her inner conflict settles, and she rests her head on my shoulder.

Her father pulls into the parking lot of the restaurant.

Maddy sits up and gives me a small smile. Through my essence, I feel her stomach clinch. I know she isn't sick. I believe this is what the dating books refer to as "butterflies." She's had them many times around me, and it's supposed to be a good thing.

I never dated in my mortal life—not that we "dated" much back then. Most marriages were arranged. I should have been married; I was at the age when most men already were. But I was fighting in the war, as was my father.

I'm glad that I can experience it all now for the first time with Maddy. Even though we're from different times, she's my soulmate.

Times like this, when she's so humanly vulnerable, I find my love for her growing even stronger. Normally she's sealed off, but every now and then she lowers the drawbridge and I see a glimpse of what I feel inside her.

I raise our joined hands and place a kiss on the soft skin of her knuckles.

Her father clears his throat, and I look to see him raising a brow at her hand in mine. His expression might show only mild annoyance, but his mind is screaming at me. She means the world to me, but it's clear she means the world to him too.

With the extra flutter Maddy's heart does whenever she's near her father, I have a feeling his approval is a big deal to her. Somehow, I will impress this man. I could compel him, of course, but I don't want to. This is something most mortal men must face, and I want to experience this as they would.

I lower her hand, though I don't let go of it, and exit the car. Two demons have taken her from me in the last two days. From now on, I'm only letting her go when absolutely necessary.

# CHAPTER 15
## Maddy

AFTER DINNER, MJ AND I WALK ALONG THE WATER-front behind the restaurant. We stop at the end of a dock to watch the sun set over Lake Washington. Red, blue, pink, and orange swirl in the sky and reflect off the choppy lake surface. This has been another perfect night.

There's a chill in the air, but thanks to MJ's essence, I don't have goose bumps on my skin. I'm so comfortable. I feel as if it's the end of August, even though Halloween and my seventeenth birthday are nine days away.

Hannah's skipping rocks by the boat landing with a friend who's here with her family as well. My parents are on the patio behind MJ and me, trying to hide the fact that they're watching us. Not that it matters. They're just another set of eyes watching and waiting for something to happen. At least the intention behind *their* spying is honor-able—they're doing it because they love me.

I'm still glad for this moment. Even with my family nearby, this moment feels like a date.

"You're incredible, MJ," I say as the last speck of sunlight disappears and dusk settles over the water. "With everything that's happening to me, I should be barely hanging on. But because of you, I get moments of peace when I forget all that and I can just be me. I … thank you."

I should have said, *I love you*. The words were right there on the tip of my tongue, but I couldn't say them.

I know he loves me and that saying it back wouldn't scare him away, but he and I are on a tightrope. We still face many challenges. His role as a Protector, angels and demons, my unknown abilities, and our secrets are lying below in the darkness, waiting for the moment when we lose our balance. If I tell him how I feel, it'll make me vulnerable—and I can't be that right now.

His arms tighten around me, and he rubs his chin in my hair. "I promise that someday soon, moments like this will happen all the time. These are the moments you deserve. I hope you'll never tire of them because I'll never tire of holding you like this."

I slowly exhale as I relax even farther into him. I can't wait for that day.

MJ grabs his phone from his pocket, opening it up to a music app. Sam Smith's newest love song starts. MJ sticks his phone back in his pocket. My heart quickens, unsure of where this is going.

He lifts my wrists, placing them over his shoulders. Then he wraps his arms around my waist, pulling me into his hardened body. Fire erupts inside as he turns us in a small circle, dancing on the dock.

I smile and rest my head against his silent chest to hide my blushing. Silly, romantic MJ. If this were any other guy, I would feel stupid—especially knowing we're being watched. With MJ, I don't care. It feels … right. I want to do this every day.

We sway in the small space of the dock, careful not to slip off. The butterflies, his essence, and the fire are all present, but they're moving with the beat too. They're in control, making it even easier to flow along with the rhythm. I wish this song would never end.

"There's a dance at your school on Friday next week," MJ says.

I peek up at him only to find him staring out over the water.

"I know that's Halloween and your birthday," he continues, "so if you have plans, I understand. But I'd like to accompany you."

I've been looking forward to this dance since school began. I love Halloween, not just because it's my birthday, but also because I can be whoever I want to be for the night. When I put on that perfect dress and mask, my fears, abilities, and pain will all disappear. For one night, I will allow myself to drop my guard and believe in the fairy tale of happily ever after. MJ and I will dance. We'll kiss. And somehow, we'll fall more in love with each other.

The thought of spending that night with him has me holding in a squeal. It will be the best night of my life, even if the whole school will be there too.

Then dread fills me and darkness claims my perfect night. "What about Amber?"

MJ promised to tell me about her case once I was healed, but so far he hasn't mentioned it.

"Amber will be there, as will many others. She isn't my main concern. You are."

"MJ—" I grimace. I can't believe I'm going to turn him down because of her, but I have to. "She needs to be your main concern. A demon is trying to kill her, remember?"

"Maddy, while it's true some unknown demon is after Amber, that won't always be the case. As I told you last night, other Protectors have been assigned to watch over the remaining targets. My team is protecting Amber. We're close to catching him. Any one of the Protectors could find the demon and stop him before he comes to Mankato."

Varied emotions swirl inside me. I wish there were something I could do to help Amber, but I don't think there is. My abilities are too unpredictable—not that I want to use them, anyway.

"You, however, will *always* need protecting," MJ continues. "I hope to be the one to keep you safe."

I stop our dance. I hadn't thought about that. I should have, though. Even if one day I manage to control my emotions and most of my abilities, there will still be factors I can never control. I cannot control who can and cannot hear my thoughts and compel me. I cannot control what happens when an angel or demon touches me. And I cannot control, nor do I understand, how I make them feel emotions again.

Word is spreading about me. I highly doubt beings will just leave me alone. So this is my future, then? Always being watched? Always in danger? Never allowed to just be normal? Never allowed to be a girl in love with a boy?

I don't want that. Even if it means walking away from who I was and embracing whatever I am now.

I may not be able to help Amber, but I *can* help myself. I am not one of MJ's Charges, and I will not let him treat me as such. I have abilities and power even he doesn't have. That none of them have.

My fingers brush the stubble along his jaw, trying to soothe him for what I'm about to say.

"I don't need protecting, MJ. But I do want *you*. Not the Protector. I want the guy who's tearing down my walls, scraping away all the layers of lies I built up, and uncovering the real me. You know me better than I even know myself sometimes. That should scare me, but it doesn't."

I stop and take a breath.

"I trust you, MJ. Not because of what you are. It's because of what you *do*. Somehow you're getting me to do things I once thought were reserved for foolish saps and love-struck idiots. Like watching sunsets and sunrises, holding hands, and dancing on a dock to music from a phone."

He laughs, then his face turns serious when he sees I'm not kidding.

"As much as I like doing these things with you, there is one thing I won't do, and that's become some helpless, weak girl who stands around waiting to be rescued. That's not me. So when the time comes and someone or something tries to come after me, I hope you'll fight by my side instead of fighting for me."

He strokes my cheek with his knuckles—returning the calming gesture. A frown rests on his lips while sadness pours out from his hazel eyes.

"You barely survived the demon last night ..." he begins.

I try to turn away, but he stops me, holding his gaze steady on me until I meet it.

"Another demon took you today. What about the next one? Or the one after that? You have many abilities, Maddy. But you *don't* have the ability to send them to Hell. I do. How many more times do you think I can see you get hurt because I couldn't protect you?"

"MJ, I—"

"It hurts"—he closes his eyes and grimaces—"so much, knowing I could have prevented all your suffering." His eyes open, and he stares down at me.

My heart clenches. I have to fight the desire to hug him and tell him anything he wants to hear, just so I never have to see that much pain in his eyes. But I can't. I won't.

"Maddy, I *know* how strong you are. I do. I know you can fight and protect yourself. But if I let you fight," MJ continues, "if I willingly put you in harm's way, any bruise, scratch, cut, or worse injury will be on me. I could lose you, and it would be my fault. I can't survive that. I can't exist without you. So *no*. I won't let you risk your life just to prove a point that doesn't even need proving in the first place. Not to me. And if any other supernatural beings wanted proof, all they'd have to do is look at the markings on your arm."

He lets go, turns the music off, then sits on the edge of the dock, dangling his feet over the water.

My mind reels. I knew he was affected by what happened to me, but I didn't know he blamed himself. I see it now. He's been so attentive, so cautious, so … clingy. It will only get worse if more things keep happening to me.

He's not to blame for any of it. Not yet. But if he refuses to help me, refuses to support me and give me the tools I need to defend myself, then any future bruise, scratch, cut, or worse injury will *truly* be on him.

"Why did you become a warrior, MJ?" I ask, gazing at the stars peeking out behind the clouds—*my* clouds.

He twists and looks up at me. For a moment I fear he won't answer. Then he says, "We'd been at war long before even my father was born. He was a warrior, as was his father and his father, and so on for generations."

"So you had to follow in their footsteps?"

"No. I could have done other things. But I didn't want to. I knew the enemy would one day come and try to destroy everything I valued. So I chose to pick up a sword and fight."

I hug myself, then meet his gaze. "We're at war now, MJ."

"No," he says, standing. "This is different."

"You're right. Because this time the enemy is threatening to destroy everything *I* value. And I'm here, begging you to help me fight, and you're refusing. You're putting me in a hole—just like Lifa."

## CHAPTER 16

# Maddy

MJ IS SILENT THE ENTIRE RIDE HOME. I KNOW I upset him, and maybe I did go too far by bringing up Lifa. But I had to make him see that there's protecting me and then there's sheltering me, and sheltering will do more harm than good.

Mom, Dad, and Hannah go inside as MJ and I awkwardly linger in the driveway, looking at each other but saying nothing.

Suddenly he huffs and shakes his head. "I'd say goodnight, but that's a bit ridiculous."

My eyes narrow, not understanding.

"We both know I'm just going into the Veil of Shadows." He smirks.

In that moment, I know our fight is over. It doesn't mean either one of us has let the point go. But it does mean we don't want to be mad at each other anymore.

He hugs me, resting his chin on my head. "Once I'm confident everyone else is going to bed, I'll come out of the Veil."

I smile and say, "Bedtime can't come soon enough."

I head upstairs and get ready for bed. Before too long, a knock sounds on my door. I open it. "Hey, Dad. What's up?"

"Can I come in for a minute, kiddo?" He smiles, but it's not as big as usual.

Oh, God. Please don't give me the Talk.

"Umm … sure," I say as he enters.

Dad sits on my bed and motions for me to join him. I don't want to hear this. I'll forever connect this horrid moment to my bed. Maybe that's Dad's plan. If MJ and I do come to a point in our relationship where we're on—or in—my bed together in *that way*, I'll remember the Talk and everything will be ruined.

I suck in a breath, remembering that MJ is most likely in here, watching on and listening in from the Veil of Shadows. His team is probably here too. And the masked demon and her master have cushioned seats in Hell to watch this mortifying moment. I hope Dad doesn't say anything too embarrassing.

It feels as if forty-pound weights are attached to my feet as I trudge over and sit. I stare at my carpet, unable to look Dad in the eyes.

For years, I thought he was the one who gave me my green eyes because he has one green eye and the other is blue. Reality is, I have no idea where my green eyes come from. I don't know anything about my birth parents. I want to find them now. I want to know why they gave me up.

Suddenly I wonder if my birth parents had abilities too. Maybe they gave me up to hide me. Protect me. That could explain why they loved me enough to name me.

But what if they're dead, like Amber's birth parents? Maybe they're in Heaven waiting for me?

Or maybe none of the above is right. They could just be a-holes.

"We never did finish our conversation from Monday when I took you to school," Dad says.

I glance at him, caught off guard by the subject. In the car on Monday, I thought I had disappointed him and that I'd lost his love. I'm glad he still remembers that moment. He told me he loved me. And for the first time ever, I truly believed him.

Dad's usually the strong, silent type. He's very observant. He tried to talk to me about MJ then, and I avoided it. But it doesn't look like I'm getting out of it tonight.

He's silent for a moment while I draw circles in the carpet with my toes. Finally he snorts. "Parenting is a hard gig, Maddy. I love you, but you don't always make it easy."

Guilt swirls inside me for all the horrible things I've said and done. I want to show him how much I've changed and how much I love him, but I can't. I can't act too different too quickly, or the Guardian Angels will summon the Perfugae. I have to still stay behind the huge wall I built up to shut my family out, even though it crumbled to dust this week.

"Every man who has a daughter dreads the day she starts dating."

I cringe. Here it comes.

"I got lucky. I got you for a daughter."

"I'm not lucky," I mumble and turn away.

He clutches my chin, turning me back to him. His blue and green eyes shine.

"As MJ said earlier, you're remarkable. I've known it all along, even if you've hid yourself away for a bit. But I can see that greatness coming back. It's in your eyes, your smile. Your whole body radiates with positivity. I've missed seeing you like this. I know MJ is the reason behind it. I'll forever be in his debt for accomplishing in just a few short days what I failed to do in three years."

I want to throw myself into his arms and tell him that I'm sorry and that I love him, but I'm too stunned to move.

"You're a great judge of character, kiddo. If you think this MJ is worthy of you, then I trust you. It's obvious that he means a great deal to you. All I ask is that you enjoy the moment and don't be in such a rush to grow up. I love you, Maddy." He places his arm around my shoulders, and I lean into his embrace.

"Me too, Daddy," I whisper into his shirt. But again, they're not the words I should be saying.

He wraps his other arm around me, holding me tighter in a full-on Dad-bear-hug I've missed so much. His breath is shaky as he exhales. Before I'm ready, our hug ends and he stands.

Right before he opens the door, he turns and says, "If your mother asks, tell her we had the Talk and you agreed not to 'round the bases' with MJ. I like him, so I'd prefer to not shoot him."

I turn pink and nod as Dad leaves, knowing I got off way easy.

I close my eyes and flop back onto my bed. The mattress dips on my right side. I smile, knowing MJ's lying down beside me.

A burst of energy rushes through me at my wrist as he touches me. My arm tingles as his hand slides up it.

"How are you?" he asks. His essence fills me, and I know he's checking my emotions, even though he won't know the reasons behind whatever he finds.

"Better, now that you're here."

"Hmm," he mutters as his hand stills.

I roll over and face him. His lips are tight and his brows are pulled together.

"What's wrong?"

"Maddy, if I couldn't stay the whole night, would you be okay? Tamitha and Alexander would be here, so you wouldn't be alone. But there are a few things I need to take care of."

My mouth pops open, stunned at the thought of him leaving. A second later, I'm pissed at myself.

A few hours ago, I stood in front of him, devastated by his unwillingness to see me as more than one of his Charges. And here, at the first chance to prove to him—to prove to us both—that I can handle myself, I cave.

I take a deep breath and try again. "I've gone nearly seventeen years without you, so yes. I'll be fine," I reply.

I'll be fine, I repeat to myself. And if something does happen, Tamitha and Alexander are here, and the masked demon is watching too. Between them and myself, it should be enough.

"I'm sure you're right. I should be back before school."

"What are you going to do?" I ask, trying to sound more curious than heartbroken.

"I'm going up to Immortal City. I was summoned to explain a few things that occurred today," he continues.

I'm sure he's referring to my mile-high fire-tornados. "Everything's okay, right?"

"Of course," he says. "Plus, I need to pick up some clothes, I'm nearly out."

I hadn't thought about how he gets clothes. But I suppose he doesn't really have a home here. Should I clear out room in my dresser for him—or would that be weird? When do couples start leaving things such as clothes and other personal effects at each other's places? Do couples our age even do that? I need to ask my friends about this.

But those are normal problems for a normal relationship. Normal couples don't spend Wednesday night talking about making a run to Heaven.

It's strange to hear him talk about going to Heaven as if it were no big deal. I wonder if I've ever come across any other angels or demons before. Although, given what effect I have on them, I suppose I'd remember such a meeting if it had happened.

As I try to absorb that the afterlife has a come-and-go-as-you-please policy for certain beings, I suddenly realize it changes everything I've ever thought about death. It's no longer an end. MJ, his team, and even Justin have merely continued their lives in new ways. And it's the same for everyone else who has died.

Ben.

"Before you leave," I begin, my voice unsure, "I'd like to ask you something first. If—if that's okay."

Relief flashes in his eyes, and I get the feeling he doesn't *want* to leave.

"You are my priority. Ask me whatever you'd like."

I swallow the lump of fear and nerves in my throat. "I don't want to take advantage of your work … or the position you have there … or get us into more trou—"

"Maddy. Whatever it is, you can tell me."

I close my eyes and take a deep breath. "While you're up there, I'd like you to find Ben."

When he doesn't answer, I open my eyes. His mouth is pressed together in a thin line.

I stroke his cheek, trying to make him understand. "I just … I feel like if I knew he was in Heaven, safe and happy, that it wouldn't hurt as much."

He places a hand over mine. "I can't promise he'll be there. Everyone's journey is different, and sometimes it takes longer to cross over, but I will look for him."

"Thank you. When you find him, could you ask him to forgive me?"

"For what?"

"For getting him killed."

In a move so fast it makes my head spin, MJ shifts us around so we're kneeling on the bed facing each other. His hands are on the sides of my face while my arms dangle at my sides.

"You have *nothing* to feel guilty about," he says. "Justin killed him. *Not you.* Please don't think like that. It pains me to hear you say that."

MJ's eyes intensify, as if he could will me to agree with him. But he can't will me, and I can't agree. I'm not going to lie about this.

"Just ask him. Please."

He pulls me into him and kisses my forehead—sending more of his essence pulsing through me. I become a tangled mess of butterflies, tightened muscles, and a racing heart. After a few seconds, I wrap my arms around him.

"Just hurry back to me. We still have a lot of things to discuss."

His lips leave my forehead, and he rests his chin in my hair. "Get some rest. I'll come back as soon as I can."

I want more than a kiss on my head. I want a kiss with flames bursting and an uncontrollable sense of raw passion and emotions that sends my head spinning. So what if it might start my room on fire? Damn the consequences.

I lift my hands away from his back to run my fingers through his smooth hair. My hands find only air.

I open my eyes.

He's gone.

# CHAPTER 17

# MJ

*S*he's fine, TAMITHA'S VOICE SOUNDS IN MY HEAD AS we communicate via Cerebrallink. *She turned the lights off, and she's going to sleep.*

I halt on the busy, mist-covered pathway made of clouds in Immortal City. A few Protectors and Guardians mutter as they have to move to avoid hitting me.

My body tightens and twists with fear. Maddy is sleeping. I forgot to warn Tamitha and Alexander about Maddy's dreams.

*I'm coming back,* I say. *I was stupid to think I could leave her.*

*Seriously, MJ? You just got there. You must see the Council. You can't ignore a summons.*

*I know,* I reply, *but there's something I forgot to tell you about her.*

*MJ,* Alexander says, joining in on the conversation. *You left us a seven-page list of dos and don'ts, even though you'll only be separated for a few hours. Maddy's nearly an adult, and she has some pretty kick-ass abilities. Relax. We got this.*

Alexander doesn't get it. Maddy doesn't get it. It's true she handled herself remarkably well against the demons yesterday and today, but she shouldn't have had to face them. She's not *supposed* to.

I've battled demons for over eight hundred years. I'm not perfect, even though many think I am. They don't know about the women I've tried to protect in secret—and failed. But Maddy means more to me than Lifa and her descendants. If I lost Maddy … I can't even fathom what that would be like.

*Just do me a favor and monitor her dreams,* I say. *They're … unusual.*

*Unusual how?* Tamitha asks.

I rub the back of my neck and stare up at the pristine blue sky, letting out a long exhale.

*She's psychic.*

*Dude!* Alexander yells. *I'm pretty sure the "she's psychic" card should have been revealed sooner.*

Seeing as it's impossible to keep my emotions in check while discussing Maddy, I move away from the main street so I don't draw more attention to myself. I duck between buildings shaped to resemble Buckingham Palace and the White House.

*Look, I only found out about her being a psychic yesterday morning. She and I haven't had a chance to discuss exactly what it all entails, but I do know she communicates with a dead woman while she sleeps. She also moves around and talks during them, so monitor what she says and does. I need to uncover who this woman is so I can track her down and see what she knows.*

*How can she have all these abilities?* Tamitha asks.

I lean against the White House, letting it support me. *Maybe the woman from her dreams can answer your question, Tamitha, because I sure can't.*

*Well, I guess that explains why she accepted our existence so easily,* Alexander says. *She's no stranger to the paranormal. And for the record, I'm adding "she dreams about a dead chick" into the WTF pile.*

I shake my head. He might be right about this being why Maddy has handled things so well in the last few weeks. Learning about angels and demons—part of me still worries her mind could snap like a typical mortal's would. But Maddy is not typical. Still, I'd never forgive myself if she ended up in a mental institution.

*I'll be back as soon as I can.*

*MJ,* Tamitha says, *try to relax.*

Our conversation ends, but it did little to reduce my angst. Here I am, feeling as if a chunk of my soul is missing, and she's simply falling asleep. I'm an immortal, yet somehow, she's the stronger one of us.

In order to face the Archangels, I must remove all traces of Maddy from my thoughts. Their abilities are stronger than ours. Whenever we are near them, they don't just hear our thoughts, they can access whatever they want in our minds. Because of this, they stay in their home, located high above the city. They've rarely left it since I agreed to be the first Protector in 1185, one year after my death.

During the first year of my afterlife, I watched over Lifa. I tried to keep her safe not just for myself, but for Nikolas too.

The Acquisitioner was behind it all—my death, Nikolas's death, my family's, and eventually Lifa's. Demons were creating wars, using religion as the driving force behind it. The Acquisitioner convinced Sverre Sigurdsson that it was God's will he rule Norway.

During the civil war, he made Sigurdsson believe he was the long-lost son of King Sigurd Munn, which gave Sverre claim to the throne. He told Sigurdsson that marrying Lifa would help him gain support from the people. I don't see how—Sigurdsson's supporters murdered most of the kingdom and her whole village.

Lifa gave birth to twins before dying—a boy with Sigurdsson's red hair and brown eyes and a girl with Lifa's blond hair and green eyes.

When she died, Nikolas blamed me for it. He chose to be reborn rather than stay in Immortal City with me. Her death was what made me see that even in the afterlife, I would forever be a warrior.

In secret, I watched over the daughter. I thought if I could protect her, it would be as if I'd saved Lifa. She grew up, married, and had children of her own. I thought she was safe, but one day while I was on an assignment, she was killed. The Acquisitioner was behind it as well.

A vicious cycle began, and it lasted eight centuries. Through the line of Lifa's descendants, somehow one daughter always matched Lifa's traits. That was who I focused on, and that was who the Acquisitioner killed whenever I was away protecting some other mortal.

He never did the killing himself, so he wouldn't get caught breaking the rules. Still, I knew it was him. In all, thirty descendants died by his hands. Thirty chances to get it right and have vindication for failing Lifa and Nikolas—only to fail all thirty times.

The line is now broken. He killed the last descendant and her mother, along with 319 others, on the girl's wedding night. She'd just graduated high school. She hadn't had a child yet. The bastard even kept her soul, not allowing her to join Lifa and find peace in Immortal City.

Now, he's after Maddy.

What does he want her for? It must be something substantial if he's violating so many rules and drafting a Binding Agreement for an Influencer. Does the Acquisitioner know what Maddy is capable of? For my own sanity, I have to hope Justin was smart enough not to reveal everything she can do.

To give myself some time to bury my thoughts, I return to the streets and head to the Supplementum for weapons. All buildings are pearly white, and the interior walls absorb the continuous sunlight to illuminate the inside. The only way to tell them apart is by the shape. The Supplementum is currently the Tower of Pisa.

Hundreds of Protectors come and go from here to pick up various supplies to handle demons. Fire is the obvious first choice. But convincing demons to hold still long enough to set them on fire and send them back to Hell proves difficult.

As I head for the back workshop, I pass an angel stationed at the front counter. His feathers rustle as he looks up to tell me not to go back there, but upon seeing it's me, he nods and allows me to pass. Even though my wings are concealed, I outrank him, and he knows it. He's a standard angel—an angel who never leaves Heaven until the day he's reborn.

With millions of angels coming and going, the Council wanted an easy way to differentiate between the different types. There's a dress code. All angels who do not appear on Mortal Ground wear white robes. Standard angels have plain white rope bands at the waist, Guardians' bands are bronze, and the Archangels' are gold. Protectors wear whatever fits our assignment, though we do wear robes with silver accents when we're here for longer periods of time.

The Archangels took it another step further in the late thirteenth century when they began dipping our wings. Archangels' wings have gold tips. Protectors' are silver tipped. The Guardians' are bronze. The wings of standard angels have not been enhanced, so they are plain white. The colors of our wings and robe accents were chosen to match the Mark we place on the souls of mortals under Immortal City's care.

Demons and the Fallen, the five Archangels of Hell, have blackened wings. Hell's Archangels did manage to maintain the heavenly sheen on their wings. All other demons' wings are matte with color-coated tips to signify which of the twelve Castes they belong to.

The wings of a Perfugae, however, match their traitorous souls. They're limp, gray, full of holes, missing all their feathers, and overall useless—a rather fitting resemblance to their owners. They cannot be hidden, so they wear gray cloaks when they are on Mortal Ground to shield themselves.

At the end of the hall is a set of swinging glass doors. All the tools we use to defend mortals from demons are created on the other side of those doors. I pass through them into Immortal City's workshop.

Several angels with plain wings glance up from their workstations, while others remain focused on their tasks.

I ignore them all. They're the grunts. Only one angel here can *create*. He's whom I must speak with.

The clang of metal on metal comes from the far corner of the room. I follow it, nearly tripping over a silver-tipped axe, then I stop beside a long table near a large kiln. The table is filled with nearly twenty items, ranging from a scythe to a pen.

John stands at the table with his back to me. His massive arms hammer on a blaze-orange sword, and his slick black hair flops in the aftershocks of the movement. It's been a while since we used such archaic weapons.

I clear my throat, and his hammer hesitates in the air for a moment, then he continues banging.

"Give me a second," he says. "I need to finish this."

He bangs the blade twice more with his hammer, then drops it in a vat of pure light. A ring of light bursts through the space, hitting me right in the gut.

All at once, everything is calm. My fears and worries are gone. Everything will turn out as it should, for that is Father's will, and I am but an extension of him.

John pulls the blade out of the vat. The ring of light retracts, yet the sensations it stirred inside me remain. I don't need to ask what that was. I know it well. It's the essence of Immortal City. New Protectors carry some in a vial around their necks to help battle darkness. It's where the term "liquid courage" began.

He moves his goggles into his hair, then smiles as he wipes his hands on his leather apron. "MJ! Great to see you, sir."

He hands the sword to me—it's now polished silver. I grip the hilt. I'm used to one-handed blades, but this has space to accommodate both hands.

"Take a swing," he says.

I back up, and as I slice through the air, the edges of the blade become emblazed in fire.

"Whoa."

"I call it Gladius Mulciber."

"The Sword of Fire," I mutter in astonishment, staring at the flames radiating off the sword. He's finally done it. For four hundred years, he's wanted to control fire, like his predecessor Hephaestus. Control over an element is not something that can be taught; it has to be earned.

"Demons won't stand a chance against her," John says. "One hit, and their soul is vanquished permanently. There are no more free rides to the basement with this puppy."

We've created many weapons over the years to battle demons. When we win, they're sent back to Hell. When they win, we return here. It's pointless, but that's how it's always been. But this sword blazing in my hands changes everything.

"Why would we create something that's sole purpose is to destroy?" I ask, staring at the blade in a new light. "That's not who we are."

"You have to fight fire with fire."

I stare at him, not understanding. Then a sick suspicion grows.

"Do you mean they possess a weapon capable of destroying *us*?"

"Yes."

The flat tone of his voice is at odds with the seriousness of his message. I hand him back the sword, wanting to rid myself of such darkness. At the changing of hands, the flames extinguish.

I've always liked John. We lose most of ourselves when we cross over, but some things remain. John has maintained his fascination with creations. I've always thought his inventions were brilliant. But this—

"Maximus!" he suddenly shouts.

I look up only to find him focused behind me.

"It's up, down, left, *then* right," he shouts to an angel holding a cross we use for exorcisms.

The angel nods, then properly blesses the cross.

John raises a brow and shakes his head. "Can you believe what they send me? How can an angel not know how to make the Sign of the Cross? Can you imagine what would have happened had that cross gone out to the shop?"

"It would—"

"It would have been a catastrophe!" he shouts, throwing his arms in the air. "Not to mention the damage it would have done to my reputation."

He glares once more at the offending angel, then his eyes fall on the table beside me. He smiles, warmth filling his brown eyes again.

"Look at this." He grabs a multi-tool pocketknife and holds it out for me. "Careful," he says as I reach for it. "Take a step back and brace yourself. Make sure none of your fingers are over the top."

My stomach flutters and I grin as I carefully take the two-inch gadget, holding it by the base.

"Okay. Now pull them out—one at a time."

I do as he says, opening each full-sized component. Out come a broadsword, a battle-ax, a mace, a katana, a scythe, a set of five daggers, a set of six throwing stars, a rifle, a crossbow with an integrated magazine—and a pen.

They're all the items I had seen laying on the table when I walked up.

"How did you do this?" I ask.

"I used the same concept as the Veil of Shadows to conceal the weapons so they can be easily transported and readily available whenever a Protector needs them."

"But a pen?" I ask, not understanding how that could be a weapon.

"Very useful." He nods. "Excellent for note-taking, and in a pinch, you can stab someone with it. A jab in the eye tends to do the most damage, but with enough force, any area of the body would be affected."

"As great as this is, we don't fight mortals, so we have no use for their weapons."

"Look at the markings on each weapon."

"The markings?" As soon as I ask, I notice the etching in the blade of the scythe: a simple equilateral triangle. Taking care not to cut John or myself, I twist the arsenal of weapons and notice the same symbol on all of them, as well as on the handle of the pocketknife. The symbol means fire.

"You mean to tell me all of these weapons are infused with the power of fire?"

"Yes. Once they are detached and held by a Protector, the weapons will harness the Immortal Flames, just as the sword had earlier."

I inhale sharply. This is worse than I feared.

He holds out his hand, and after a moment, I hand back the travel-friendly arsenal. He tucks each weapon back inside its protective case, then sets it back on the table.

"It's a prototype," he begins, "but I think it'll be effective once it goes into production."

"Production? You're making more? Why?"

"The Council asked me to increase weapon production as well as to come up with new weapons. It's no secret there has been a rise in demonic activity over the past seventeen years. Demons are grouping together, expanding beyond the twelve Castes. Aside from Lucifer, all members of the Fallen are making more frequent trips to Mortal Ground. They're organizing and planning."

"Planning for what?"

"War."

The moment I became a Protector, the Council warned me that this day would come. The Archangels survived the Holy War, so they know what they're talking about. After centuries of nothing but minor battles, I'd come to the conclusion that it wasn't true and history wasn't going to repeat itself.

But demons are working together now. They're sharing their knowledge and expanding their abilities. War is coming. Of all the years to finally strike, they had to pick the one when I stand to lose everything.

My chest tightens at the thought of Maddy and the upcoming war. My reasons for being here are even more justified. I glance over my shoulder at the other angels. They're tinkering at their stations, though I'm sure they're listening. I sigh, then move closer to John.

"I don't wish to take advantage of our relationship," I begin, "but if I asked you to make something for me—off the books—would you do it?"

I had planned on him making this so I could give it to her next Friday, but I can't wait any longer. Now it's not just for my own peace of mind. Now it's necessary for her safety.

He hesitates, leaning his head to the side and fixing his gaze on my face. His index finger taps his thin lips.

*What do you require?* he asks, using Cerebrallink.

I hand him my bag of Segrego Stones, then respond in the same manner to ensure no one overhears.

*A gift for someone of high importance.*

He's silent while I use Cerebrallink to launch into a detailed description of her birthday present. When I finish, he stares at me—brows narrowed, lips pursed, scowling.

He shouldn't feel emotions, but somehow I think I've angered him. Has Maddy's ability affected all beings, whether they have contact with her or not? If so … we're in big trouble.

"Look, John," I say out loud, "forget I said anything. I'll figure something else out."

He smiles. "It worked! You thought I was angry, didn't you? I've been waiting for someone to request a secret project. I admit I hoped it would be you, the Original Protector, but I didn't think it would actually happen."

A sense of relief floods me. "So why the theatrics?" I ask.

"Oh, that! Don't tell anyone," he says, leaning closer, "but I altered my Time Keeper to pick up something called 'television.' I've been studying facial expressions and practicing them in case I'm called upon to go down there. A favorite show of mine is about a spy named Bond. Mostly he's an ordinary spy, except he works with a man named Q, who creates ingenious weapons that help him battle evil and save the world."

"So that's where you've been getting your inspiration?"

"Every artist needs a muse. When do you need this by?"

"Could you have it ready today?"

"I think so."

"Fantastic. Let me know when it's ready. I have to stop at the Vestimentum for more clothes before meeting with the Council."

We shake hands, and I leave him so he can make the only thing I can think of to help keep Maddy safe.

# CHAPTER 18

# Justin

THE MOMENT MJ LEAVES, I STAND BESIDE MADS'S BED in the Veil of Shadows. I'm glad he left.

He should have took her and run after what happened at the park. I wanted to. I thought going to the Acquisitioner would solve everything. For as much as he wants that contract signed, I thought for sure he'd just tell me her weakness so I can stop wasting time, have her sign, and *know* she's safe. But he didn't seem to care.

No one does.

It doesn't matter, though. I'll protect her on my own—without the Acquisitioner's help—if I have to. I will find out who the demon was, and I'll make sure he never touches her again.

When she came back, she was different. Her confidence wavered. She's looking to MJ for her source of strength, asking his permission to defend herself, though I don't know why. She's always looked to herself. I admired that about her.

Even now, he's affecting her. She's tossing and turning, struggling to find rest. She tossed and turned a little bit back when I used to watch her sleep, but not to this extent. With all the things she's experienced in the last week, it's no wonder she can't sleep. He should be here, comforting her and helping her process this. Instead he's rushing off to heed the call of the *others*. He's made them his priority and left Mads in the hands of two pathetic excuses for Protectors.

I should take Mads just to teach him a lesson.

But instead, I'll stay here, by her side, watching over her and keeping her safe.

It takes several hours for her to fall asleep. Now that she's not moving, I slide in beside her.

Something's wrong.

The air around her is fifty degrees cooler. She's freezing. If I help her, I'll have to step out of the Veil. They'll know I'm here. While seeing the expression on their smug faces would be enjoyable, it wouldn't help me figure out her weakness.

I'm close. Whatever the answer is, it's simple. Right on the tip of my finger. I'm sure I'll figure it out tomorrow. But first, I need to stop whatever is happening to Mads.

As much as I hate to admit this, MJ needs to return.

I purposely cause the bed to squeak, and the two Protectors jump from their positions near the window and door. A half second later, they're beside the bed watching as Mads's breath turns to ice.

Come on, you idiots. Call for MJ. It's obvious she needs help.

If they don't summon him in five seconds, I'm gonna use the Requiem Aeternam on them. Then I'll take her. I swear.

I move to stand behind the large male. Five, four …

# CHAPTER 19

## Maddy

A CHILLY WIND BLOWS OVER ME. ALEXANDER AND Tamitha must have opened a window. But when I open my eyes, I'm facing a red door.

I know this door.

I'm standing on the wooden porch of Elizabeth's cabin. It's a dream.

My feet and calves tingle with a burning sensation. Everything below my knees is buried in snow. I shiver in my pj's, and a puff of condensed vapor appears as I exhale. Having already had a dream like this, I know I'll be cold and miserable when I wake up.

This sucks.

At least I'm already on her porch, so I won't get as cold as last time, when I had to trudge all that way through the snow. I know I can warm myself up by the fireplace while they talk so I won't wake up with hypothermia.

Should I knock or let myself in? Seeing as I can't interact with them, I guess I should let myself in. It feels impolite, but I don't want to get frostbite.

My arm shakes as I reach for the doorknob. I grab it, but I can't make it turn. It's not locked; it just won't move. I can't open the door.

Oh no.

The masked demon opened the door last time. Why hasn't she done it now? If she's watching me, she knows I need her help.

But then I remember what she said about how draining it is to help me. She already helped me today in the park— she doesn't have the strength to help me so soon after. I'm *truly* on my own here.

Maybe I can pass through the door like a ghost. I'm not *physically* here. I know my body is in my bed. Here, I'm just my subconscious or soul or something.

I take a deep breath and race for the door.

I collide with it. The all-too-real force of the hit sends pain rippling through me. My freezing fingers rub my forehead, where I hit the door the hardest. Now I'm cold and I have a headache.

I can't turn the knob, and I can't go through the door. Am I just stuck out here, then?

The wind howls, whipping frozen flakes up my back. I shiver, and my teeth rattle together. What's the point of this dream if I can't even open the damn door?

No.

I'm not powerless. I don't need anyone's help. I can figure this out myself.

I take another deep breath and cough. My insides hurt as if they were already beginning to crystalize.

Come on, handle. Turn, dang it! I can do this. It's just a door. A door inside some sort of crazy dream-memory I don't have any control over.

I whimper as fear sets in. I don't want to find out what happens if I die here.

Please open the door, Elizabeth. Walk outside for something so I can slip in. My fingers are turning blue.

I pound on the door, but it doesn't make a sound.

"P-please open the d-d-door!"

A crunch sounds behind me, then an immense heat consumes me. It's so hot it steals my breath away. But it's such a welcome relief to the bitter cold.

My muscles, bones, blood, and skin all feel energized. I feel strong, powerful, in control. I relax and let the feelings continue to coat over me. Without even thinking, I give them complete control.

I PAUSE ON OUR DOORSTEP, TAKING A MOMENT TO SILENCE the screams inside my head. Even here, at my sanctuary, they follow me, trying to taint the goodness I have found.

Trepidation claims my barren soul. Only she could instill such a foreign sensation inside me. It has been far too long since I have seen my Elizabeth. It is the cruelest form of torture to tear myself from her side, but I cannot risk anyone discovering her. She must be kept safe. She matters more to me than my own existence.

The door opens, and I enter our home. Every time I come here, she has made an adjustment to the décor. If I could risk coming up here more often to help her, I would, but some of my siblings are becoming suspicious of my actions.

"Damien!" Elizabeth's face illuminates with a smile as she rushes toward me. She is the only one who has ever been excited to see me. Words cannot express the joy that fills me each time I see the happiness my presence brings her.

My body aches to embrace her and be overcome by the soothing, ecstatic, affectionate feelings that stem from her contact.

Our lips join, giving me exactly what I crave.

WITH THEIR KISS, I'M FINALLY ABLE TO SEPARATE FROM Damien.

It took seeing Elizabeth through his eyes for me to realize what happened. I've never connected with someone's mind right away like that. I typically have to choose to enter someone's body and accept his or her thoughts. But Damien entered *me*. I felt warmth and power, and I didn't care what caused the feelings. I just … gave in. I caved and became exactly what I don't want to be anymore. I became a puppet.

Why was it different this time?

Maybe a small part of me knew it was Damien even before I connected to him. The heat and powerful feelings should have been a big enough clue. And those dark thoughts about the screams torturing him—the screams most likely belonged to the souls trapped in Hell.

Demons.

I need to remember that they're demons and that they did something to deserve being sent there. Even the masked demon is there for a reason.

Suddenly I glance at Damien, taking in his all-too-familiar black eyes. Damien is a demon too.

I should have pieced it together last night when I learned what Justin is. But I was just so overwhelmed by everything. Now that I know the truth about Damien, it's even more ridiculous that Elizabeth expects me to trust him.

I don't know if he's an Influencer like Justin or if he's … whatever the masked demon is. I don't really want to find out. What I do want to know, though, is how he can love Elizabeth. Demons and angels can't feel emotions unless they come across me, yet Damien cares and loves Elizabeth in his own way. So are MJ and Justin wrong—are there others out there who can make angels and demons feel? And if so, is Elizabeth one of them? Or is something else responsible for giving Damien emotions?

One way or another, Damien really does care for her, and he wants her to be safe. If she does make him feel, that means he would go back to an emotionless existence if he were to lose her.

That's how he feels about her, yet he still killed her. *He's a demon.*

I should have detached from him sooner, but being inside Damien this time was so much more enticing than the previous time. My body craved the intensity of his emotions and physical power. I felt invincible. Even now, my body itches to move closer to him. To reach out and touch him so his essence can fill me again.

For all the times I've felt MJ's essence, I should be used to it, but I'm not. I yearn for his touch. The rush of energy that flows through my veins as soon as we're connected makes me feel better.

But Damien's essence is different. It has all the same feelings as MJ's essence, but with Damien's, they're more intense. More powerful. It's weird because he's a demon and I know I shouldn't feel this way, but it goes beyond feeling. It's *knowing*. I know I'm strong and not even close to utilizing my full potential, even though I don't know what my full potential is yet. Once I do know, I *will* be able to protect myself against all of them.

"Are you feeling well?" Damien asks, stroking Elizabeth's pale face. "Your cheeks are less rosy than the previous time I was here."

She smiles, but it's forced. "I'm fine. The winters are a little harsher than I expected. As soon as winter is over, I'm sure I'll be all right."

This is all new. A new dream. New is good. New means answers.

Damien takes her hand, and he leads her into the living room. They sit on the oak couch with the fluffy red pillows. It looks comfy, but I can't sit down. I'm still bursting with Damien's essence.

"I am sorry things are not progressing as quickly as I had hoped," Damien says. "Leaving the family business is more difficult than I anticipated. Know that I am doing everything in my power to get out so I can be with you permanently. If I could offer you more details, I would. However, the nature of my work would upset you."

As great as his essence makes me feel, I still don't trust him. He's a demon. They're evil, deceitful murderers.

Damien *stole* her away from her family and then just left her here, alone. Every time she's thought of her family, he's compelled her to forget them. Why did he take her? Why did he bring her here? And why does he only visit instead of staying with her?

I glare at him, watching on as he caresses her cheek. As much as I don't want to, I can't deny the fact that he's telling her the truth about being unable to discuss what he does for work. It doesn't change what he did to her, though.

Elizabeth places her hand on his cheek, staring deep into his eyes. "I want to know everything about you," she says. "But I want you to tell me when you're ready. I trust you. I know you're doing what you can, and someday soon we can have the life we want. I miss you when you're gone, but I know you're only gone because you don't have any other choice right now. You're the best thing that has ever happened to me, and I will wait for you. However long you need."

And people call *me* naïve. Damien is gone for months at a time, and Elizabeth has no idea when or if he'll come back. She just stays here, waiting around for him to grace her with his presence whenever it's convenient for him. He's turned her into his pet.

They stare at each other for a moment, then he kisses her with such passion that I blush and turn away.

"I have something for you," he says. A nervous smile is on his lips as he reaches behind him. Suddenly a black square box is in his hands. He holds it out for her and says, "Happy birthday, Elizabeth."

Her birthday. I glance around the space for a calendar to show me the date, but I don't see one.

Her mouth falls open. It widens as he opens the box, revealing a diamond necklace. In the center is a blue stone.

Elizabeth recovers from her shock and frowns. "Everything I have is from you. You didn't need to do this."

"Needing and wanting are two different things. I wanted to get you something special. When I was on my last errand for my father, I saw this and thought of you."

She turns away. "I can't accept this. I can't let you spend this much money on me."

Pain flashes in his eyes. She hurt him.

Suddenly I think of my family. I've never liked getting gifts. Gifts show someone you care about them—love them. When I found out I was adopted, I refused their gifts—refused their love. I've hurt everyone who loves me.

Damien stares at Elizabeth's back in silence for a while, then he softly says, "You love my gift, Elizabeth. You will wear it every day."

Suddenly, she turns back around, smiling. "Thank you. I love your gift."

It's such an immediate change, I can't help but wonder if Damien compelled her to accept it. The times he's done that before have been—in his eyes—for her protection. But this is just a necklace.

Damien closes his eyes for a moment. When they reopen, they seem lighter, even though they're still black.

"Now for your next gift," he says. He whistles, and out of nowhere a huge dog appears beside him. It's black with red eyes. Its face is scrunched, like a bull dog's. It's the ugliest dog I've ever seen.

Elizabeth stands and steps away. "Damien, I—"

He stands and closes the distance between them. "You are lonely, Elizabeth. That is my doing. This dog, she is here to watch over you and keep you company while I am gone."

Elizabeth stares at the dog, clearly not thrilled. I don't blame her.

Damien exhales, and that same sadness fills his eyes as he turns Elizabeth to face him.

"This is my dog," Damien says in a smooth voice. "And I am leaving her here to keep you safe. This is a good thing, Elizabeth. You are happy to have my dog."

"I am happy to have your dog," she repeats.

I stiffen. That's it—he's compelling her again. It sickens me.

"What is her name?" Elizabeth asks.

"She does not have a name. We do not name objects where I come from."

My fists clench. That was cruel—even for a demon. I can't stand watching this any longer. I race over and wave my hand between their faces, wanting to end the connection. But it doesn't work. This is a memory. I can't affect it.

Damien leans back and Elizabeth blinks, coming out of the fog.

She smiles at the dog, then at Damien. "Thank you, Damien. It will be nice having her here."

He smiles, then wraps his arms around her, embracing her.

I huff and turn away, hating how easily he toys with her. I don't care what his reasons are—this isn't right.

Elizabeth giggles, and I turn back to see Elizabeth in his arms.

They stare at each other with such love, tenderness, and desire, it makes everything that took place just moments ago no longer seem real.

"Say the word, and we'll stop," he says. "This is your choice, Elizabeth."

She blushes, then says, "I want this. I wanted it since the night we met."

They exchange another nervous look while I stand there, wondering what they're talking about.

He carries her down the hall. I begin to follow but stop when it becomes blatantly obvious where they're going and what they intend to do.

I stand in the hallway staring at the bedroom door. Even though I know they can't see, hear, or feel me, I want to stop them. It's not just because I need more information or that's he's a demon, but because I can't help but wonder if Damien compelled her to sleep with him. For her sake, I hope he didn't. Plus, if that's all he wanted, he could have compelled her to sleep with him the night they met.

No. He loves her too much to do that. Maybe that's what he meant when he said it was her choice. I hope so.

I shiver, recalling Justin's party and how he tried to compel me to sleep with him too. Thank God it didn't work.

Is that what demons do—take away a woman's right to say no? If so, it's rape. I don't care how *they* see it. It's wrong, and it needs to stop.

I can't take this. I need to wake up. Before, Elizabeth chose when to end the dreams. But that changed when the dreams broke. I think back, trying to remember what has woken me up the past couple nights. Sunday night I felt Damien's essence. Monday night I connected Damien to MJ. Now that Elizabeth's not in control of the dreams, maybe I need to experience something really shocking inside it in order to wake up.

A loud squeak comes from the bedroom, followed by murmured noises of mutual enjoyment.

I grimace.

I'm sure if I go into the bedroom, I will see something shocking. Perhaps that might get me out of here. But I don't want to do that. That's a very private, intimate moment. And while they won't know I'm watching, I'd know. I know how it feels to have your privacy violated, and I can't do that to someone else. There has got to be a way for me to control these dreams.

Maybe with Damien's essence still in me, I can wake up on my own. Even though I haven't mastered my abilities, I'm probably capable of things I don't even know about yet.

I bounce up and down, shaking my arms to reduce my nervous energy so I can relax. That will work. Relaxing brought me here; relaxing can get me out.

Elizabeth's green walls turn black as my eyelids drop.

I imagine I'm home. I take a few deep breaths to center myself.

I can wake up. I'm strong enough to wake myself up. I'm in control. I have power over myself. I can do this on my own. I'm home.

Please work …

## CHAPTER 20

# MJ

*How is it going?* I ASK TAMITHA AND ALEXANDER using Cerebrallink. I tap Maddy's present, which is tucked safely in my pocket, while I wait for their response. Maybe I do worry too much, but given everything Maddy and I have gone through, and how important she is to me, how could I not?

Neither of them reply.

I move off the main street so I don't draw attention to my panic.

*What's wrong?* I ask.

Still nothing.

My world stops as fear builds inside me, overwhelming me, nearly bringing me to my knees. Of course the demons were waiting for me to leave her.

I sprint out of Immortal City and leap off the clouds, entering the Great Divide. I have no idea what I'll be walking into when I land in Maddy's bedroom, but I don't care. I'll destroy whatever is trying to take her from me.

As my journey ends, Alexander and Tamitha jump up from their positions beside Maddy's bed and shift into defensive crouches. They sigh when they see it's just me. Tamitha returns to her previous position—kneeling beside the bed—while Alexander steps closer to me.

"Jeez, MJ," Alexander whispers. "You could have given me a heart attack—you know, if I wasn't dead already."

"Why didn't you answer? I thought something happened."

"Sorry," Alexander replies. "We heard you. We just didn't know what to say. I know you warned us, but we didn't expect this."

"Expect what?"

Tamitha turns to face me. She frowns. "You didn't tell us her dreams were this bad."

Again my world comes to an abrupt halt. Fear grips me so tightly, I feel as if I can't breathe—even though I don't physically need to.

I move and sit beside Maddy. She's trembling. Her breath is so cold I can see it, and her skin is turning blue.

I reach out to touch her and fix whatever this is.

"Don't," Tamitha says. "She could be having a vision. You know the risks of waking a psychic."

"So I'm just supposed to sit here and watch her freeze to death?"

"No," Alexander says, throwing another blanket on her. "If it gets worse, wake her. Right now, though, I agree with Tamitha. Besides, you're the one who taught us the rules for dealing with mortals who have a sixth sense. She'll wake up once she's seen whatever she's meant to see."

"I never should have left her."

I run my fingers through my hair, yanking it in hopes of feeling something other than helplessness. I know pulling a mortal out of a vision can be detrimental to his or her mental stability. I never had an issue following the rules before. But I wasn't in love with the other psychics.

I release my breath and watch over *minn ást* as she battles another unknown force on her own.

"How did it go with the Council?" Tamitha asks.

"I haven't met with them yet."

Maddy lifts a shaking arm, reaching for something invisible to us, and turns her hand.

Puffs of frozen air appear faster from her blue lips as she coughs.

"This has got to be the strangest thing I've ever seen," Alexander says, sitting on the opposite side of the bed near Tamitha.

I lay down beside her, trying to imagine what she's seeing. I think she's trying to turn a knob or a handle of some sort.

"Whatever you do, don't tell her about this when she wakes. She doesn't need to know the three of us watched on as she dealt with whatever this is."

They nod.

Maddy drops her arm, then her body spasms. She grunts and rubs her forehead. When she pulls her hand away, a red welt appears on her pale skin.

I leap from the bed and pace beside it. "Tell me this isn't possible. Tell me that injuries in her dreams can't actually harm her physically too."

"I … I don't know," Tamitha whispers.

My hands clench in an effort to control my overwhelming need to touch her and get her the hell out of there.

I've heard that psychics have a higher chance of also being empaths, or highly sensitive people. Some feel emotionally connected to the vision spirits or beings. Their minds are often tricked into believing that whatever is happening inside the vision is also happening to their physical bodies outside the vision. Whether Maddy is an empath or not, there's a physical mark on her body from something that hit her head in the vision.

I can't protect her from something I can't see. We haven't even been together a week, and everything keeps trying to take her from me.

Maddy shivers, and her teeth chatter. She raises her fists and furiously pounds in the air. "P-please open the d-d-door!"

At the sound of her freezing, panic-filled voice, I crumble to the bed beside her. I don't know if she can hear me. I don't care, though. I have to do something.

"You're not *there*, Maddy," I say. "You're home in your bed. Come back to me. Please, Father, help her come back to me."

She stops moving, sucks in a huge breath, and does … nothing.

"That's it. I'm getting her out of there."

I reach out to touch her pale, freezing skin, but Tamitha grabs my hand and stops me.

"Look," she says, pointing to Maddy.

I follow her gaze, and remarkably, Maddy is no longer shaking. Her breathing seems to be at a more normal rate, and it's no longer frozen puffs. Her skin is even returning to light ivory.

"Oh, thank Father," I say and release a ragged breath.

Tamitha and Alexander let out relieved sighs as well.

Maddy smiles as her arms open wide then shrink slightly, as if she's hugging the air. Then she tilts her head, her lips pucker, and—

I turn away, not wanting to watch on as she kisses some unseen entity. Clearly, she has no control over what happens inside her dreams. But I want to know who the—

"I thought you said she dreams of a woman?" Alexander asks. "I know this is the twenty-first century and equality is finally coming closer to its intended definition, but I didn't see *this* coming."

"There's a man too," I grumble.

I remember him from her friend Kelli's mind. Kelli envisioned him as the classic hero who swoops in and rescues the dream woman. Maddy doesn't know Kelli sketches him. She has notebooks full of him, especially his eyes. She loves to draw his captivating black eyes.

"Oh, dammit!"

"What?" Tamitha and Alexander ask together.

I whip around back to Maddy. Other than a sly smile on her face and a slightly accelerated heart rate, she's resting peacefully.

"I've been so consumed by the woman that I missed it."

"Missed what?" Alexander asks.

"The guy she's dreamed of since she was a baby is a demon."

For a moment, the room is silent as we continue to watch over Maddy.

"Do you think … he knows about her?" Alexander asks.

"I don't know. Maddy always believed the woman controlled the dreams. Maybe it's true. If so, maybe she's trying to warn Maddy of him."

"Do we know what he looks like or anything about what type of demon he is?" Alexander asks. "Anything that might help us find him?"

If I weren't so overwhelmed, I'd smile. He barely knows Maddy, yet he's ready to face another demon to help me keep her safe.

"His name is Damien," I reply. "That's all I got from reading Maddy's friend's mind."

"Well, a name is more than you had when we first looked into Maddy."

"You're right. I can find him. Then I can figure out just how much he knows about her."

"No, go talk to the Council first," Tamitha says. "They're not known for their patience. Then when you're back, Alexander can help you find the demon. If we don't get a handle on this situation, we will be up to our elbows in demons by the weekend."

I look back at Maddy, now sleeping peacefully. Tamitha's right. I do have to go. But it's so hard to leave Maddy with so many things left unknown.

"Promise me you'll answer if I call?"

"Yes," Tamitha says.

"Or if the vision changes more?"

"Yes," she says as she shoos me away from the bed.

"Okay. I'll go. Just tell her that—"

"She knows."

"We all do," Alexander adds.

I cast one more glance at Maddy and then, incredibly, I find the strength to leave her and return to Immortal City.

# CHAPTER 21

## MJ

THE KALEIDOSCOPE ENDS AS I EXIT THE GREAT DIVIDE. I stumble, and my jaw drops as I take in the shocking scene. The misty path is empty—no one is waiting to cross over into Immortal City.

My body tenses. I look to Thaddeus, who guards the gates, for an explanation. But not only is he not standing at his post, the Gates are closed. In all my years, this has never happened.

Suddenly a bright silhouette appears before the gates. I shield my eyes for a moment, waiting for it to dim before I lower my arm.

As I blink, a figure begins to take shape. Massive wings span nearly twenty feet. Golden armor, over his white robe, glistens in the ever-shining sunlight. He's clutching a shield in one hand and a sword in the other.

He's an Archangel, and he's ready for war.

I take a moment to clear my mind and unglamour my wings. I adjust my footing to account for the weight. My feathers rustle in the breeze. It's been a while since I set them free.

My wings bend to a relaxed position. The tips touch the ground, though they're nowhere near as impressive as the ones before me.

The Archangel's wings retract as he walks toward me. He towers over me—reaching beyond eight feet tall. His skin, a golden tan, defines his muscles. He has bright blue eyes and wavy light brown hair. He is the Archangel Michael.

I'm not used to seeing him outside his home, let alone on the other side of the Gates. Even though I'm still disturbed by the sight before me, I wait for him to speak.

"What news do you bear from Mortal Ground?" he asks.

I straighten and keep my mind clear. Whatever is going on here, it isn't good. My response will either calm him— or start the war.

"It has not already begun?" he asks, hearing my thoughts. He shifts, losing some of his edge.

"No. Why would you think it had?"

He stares at me. From the intrusion I feel in my mind, I'm confident he's searching for something hidden in my memory.

He pulls back, then his battle gear disappears, leaving him in just his robe. He clasps his hand in front of him and begins walking along the border between Immortal City and the Great Divide. I follow.

"I summoned you six mortal hours ago," he begins. "I felt your presence in Immortal City shortly after, but you did not come to the summons at the Basilica Trascendentium. Instead you went to the Supplementum, Vestimentum—"

"Forgive me. I was low on supplies and clothes. I thought it wise to collect them before meeting with you."

"That I can understand. What troubles me is what occurred after."

I look at him, unsure of what he's talking about. His face is serene, giving no hints.

"Millions of angels watched you run through the heart of Immortal City and leap into the Great Divide."

I can picture in my head how it must have looked to everyone. At first I'm sure they were startled to see an angel do such a thing. Then once they realized it was me, they probably assumed the worst.

Michael murmurs an agreement and bows his head. "So you see my confusion, then, when you returned with a peaceful, albeit worried, mind."

"I apologize," I say, though it is not enough. "I did fear that my team was under attack, but it proved to be a false alarm."

"Immortal City will be glad to hear it."

The atmosphere calms, and tension in my body loosens. We walk in silence.

"Since we are not in fact at war and your Charge is being tended to," he finally says, "I trust you are now able to answer your summons."

"Yes," I reply. "Of course."

We circle back toward the Gates.

"We have heard troubling things from your area," he begins, "and we thought it best to confer with you before seeking further action."

"Further action" means calling on the Perfugae. I do my best to control my reaction to the news. Knowing he's reading my mind, I play a slideshow of images in my head that I want him to know about.

"The town has many troubling details," I reply. "The most pressing matter is that the town has a Trifecta, though it is not recorded on any of the Trifecta catalogs. If a lesser-trained Protector had been sent there, I fear the result could have been catastrophic."

He stops walking and turns to face me. "How does the fire that reached the sky factor into this?"

I do not lie. "I have yet to discover how that happened."

"Is that why you have called in for reinforcements? From our understanding of your case, your Charge is not in any imminent threat. Unless the demon were to alter its plans, of course."

Not seeing any way around it, I say, "I have placed my Charge in the hands of my team while I look into these matters. While the town indeed has a Trifecta, I have encountered only one spirit and one demon, when there should be hundreds. Also, there were many inconsistencies in my Charge's file about the town and townsfolk, which, when combined, leads me to believe an entity, or a group of entities, has somehow gone to extreme measures to hide the town even from us."

He strokes his chin while his eyes look over the Divide. "The demon you mentioned," he says. "Do you believe it is trying to control the town?"

"The Influencer managed to control a large portion of the town," I begin. "But I suspect he is a scapegoat for someone more powerful."

"We have heard of this Influencer from Protector Andrew, who was assigned to Benjamin Wolters—"

"Has his file been read?"

He falls silent, and his gaze flashes to mine.

The mention of Ben caught me off guard. If his file's been read, that would mean he's here somewhere—unless he chose to be reborn already. Finding him is exactly what I need to help—

I immediately stop my train of thought, not wanting him to hear it.

His brow narrows; suspicion fills his eyes as I feel his intrusion in my mind again.

After a moment, he resumes walking.

"His file has not been read," Michael replies.

"Did Protector Andrew say how the Influencer killed Ben?"

"You know as well as anyone that Influencers cannot kill. They can influence one mortal to kill another, but it is up to the mortal to follow the suggestion."

"These were not suggestions!" I shout.

His eyes widen.

I take a moment to calm myself. "I apologize, but his actions will ripple through all of us. He did not *influence* Ben or the elderly woman. He *compelled* them to kill themselves."

"Compulsion cannot be used in that manner," he scolds. "You should know better."

"Be that as it may, he still managed it."

Michael strokes his chin, fixing his blue eyes on me. I feel him digging through my mind. "Do you have proof to support your claim?"

I lean toward him. "No. Not yet. But I would like your permission to look into the matter further."

"You did not ask permission when you called on the other Protectors," he says. "Why are you now?"

I consider my next words carefully, not wanting to upset him further, but knowing it will anyway. "It is my fear that a member of the Fallen may be responsible for the Influencer's boost in abilities."

Michael clenches his fists and breathes so hard his nostrils flare.

I try to conceal my own surprise as I watch him. Like all angels, he should have no emotions. That's what we've been told. Yet he's been reacting in a way he never has before. Is he faking it, as John had earlier? Or have the Archangels lied to us the whole time?

Michael calms himself, then he leans toward me. "Tread carefully," he warns. "The Fallen are forbidden from aiding demons. Violating that treaty is an act of war."

My body tightens, reacting to the threat of war, yet in his eyes I see a glimmer of excitement.

He wants a war.

"Will you grant me permission to look into it or not?"

Instead of answering, he remains quiet. He's so still that, if I didn't know better, I'd swear he was a statue. More than likely, he's communicating with his brothers— Gabriel and Raphael.

Time is meaningless here, so I have no idea how long I've walked with him. I can't tell him to hurry up. Still, the silence is driving me crazy.

I shift, and he blinks. He meets my gaze, and I suspect he's reading my mind to see why I disturbed him. I think about the killer. I think about Amber. I think about all the troubling things I've shared with him and my own displeasure that I have no answers for him.

"Is this why you have gone against protocol and erased the memories belonging to the Page family instead of allowing it to be done by the Perfugae?" he asks.

I had a feeling this question would come up, so I've already rehearsed my answer. "Their minds were altered by the Influencer. Because I suspect the Fallen may be involved, I thought it best to handle the Page family myself."

He stares at me a moment longer before turning away. We're now back at the Pearly Gates. They're still closed. We're still the only souls on this side.

"Do you require further assistance?" he asks, his tone short.

"Does this mean you're granting me permission to look into the Fallen?"

He takes a moment to answer. "If you do this, you will report your findings to us immediately. Do you understand?"

"Yes," I reply, grateful for his approval.

"Then it is done," he says. "Go with peace, Protector MJ."

The Gates open, and he walks toward them.

"Will you send the Perfugae back in?" I call after him, holding my breath.

"You appear to have the situation under control," he says.

He walks away with his head bowed.

I turn back to the Great Divide, ready to return to Maddy.

I'll have to be more cautious next time. The last thing anyone needs is Michael and the other Archangels to come to Mortal Ground. If that happened, we'd be doomed.

# CHAPTER 22

# Maddy

I SMILE AT THE GLOW-IN-THE-DARK STARS DECORATING the ceiling. I'm home. I did it. Granted, it was only possible because Damien's essence was still lingering inside me, but it's still a big step forward in understanding my abilities. I don't need to be touching an angel or a demon to send myself somewhere else—I just need to "borrow" their essence.

"Maddy?" Tamitha asks, her tone cautious.

Disappointment fills me. If she's here, that means MJ isn't. I roll over toward her. "Yes."

"Ar-are you well?"

I take a moment to be sure. While I no longer feel Damien's essence inside me, it doesn't matter. I feel refreshed. Energized. But best of all, I'm not cold.

"I feel great," I reply. "Why?"

"I'm just ... being thorough," Tamitha says. "MJ has never given me an assignment this important. I don't want to fail him."

"I'm not an assignment," I snap.

"Right," she says, bobbing her head. "Of course you're not. You're so much more than that. You're the one who's going to change everything."

I look away.

"I should stop talking now," she says. "We have a big day ahead of us, and I'm keeping you from getting ready."

"Ready for what?" I grumble. "School doesn't start for three hours."

"I know. But you have an itinerary—which you're now running behind schedule on. So … get up! Shake a leg! Put some pep in your step!"

"What itinerary?" I ask, sitting up.

"MJ was very specific." She pulls a long piece of paper out of thin air.

I shiver, thinking of Justin and the Binding Agreement.

Instantly, she's in front of me, worrying over me as Mom used to do before I completely pushed her away.

"Are you feeling okay? Can I get you anything? I can call for Alexander—he's just in the park ensuring it's safe for you."

"I'm fine," I reply, leaning back. She fusses worse than MJ.

Worry lines deepen on her face.

"That paper is from MJ?" I ask.

After a moment, she straightens and smiles, although her brown eyes still look as if they're scanning me.

"Yes," she replies. "In case he wasn't back when you woke, he wanted us to wake you up at five, take you for a run, let you watch the sunrise, then feed you breakfast. If MJ is still not back, then we need to explain how school is going to work in his absence."

I snort. "You're serious?"

"Quite. As is MJ, so quit wasting time, and let's go."

"What do you need to 'explain' about school?"

"I'll tell you after breakfast. Which we'll be late for too if you don't hurry up."

I glare at her as I grab my running clothes—which she already had sitting out—and go in the bathroom. I take a few minutes longer than necessary. I'm not trying to screw up her plans, but from the sounds of it, this will be the only opportunity I get on my own until MJ is home.

As much as I love seeing MJ, I'm used to being alone. Dad's either working, practicing his guitar, or gone with the band. Mom's busy with her cooking classes, and whenever she publishes a new cookbook, she goes on many radio and TV shows to promote it. On the weekends, she goes with Dad to his concerts. Hannah's gone from sunup to sundown just about every day. I don't think she likes being alone.

The idea of someone dictating how I spend my time is less than appealing. But it's not really Tamitha's fault. She's just doing as she's told. I will be discussing this with MJ when he comes back.

"Can't we just walk side by side?" I ask Alexander, ignoring his outstretched hand. He glances at Tamitha, and she shakes her head.

Alexander is leaning on MJ's truck, which he drove here to school. Amber is behind him, popping bubbles with her gum while tapping the toes of her kitten-heeled shoes on the pavement. Tamitha is across from us, alternating between looking at her watch, then me—her nonverbal way of reminding me about the schedule.

"No," Alexander says. "Everyone else will see me as MJ, so we have to hold hands. It's what you would do if he were here. Just … don't send us anywhere, please."

My arms tighten farther around me. "He told you about that?"

"In order for me to protect you while he was gone, he had to."

My frown deepens, knowing he's right. Still, I wish MJ had told me he was sharing such details with Alexander and Tamitha. What else has he told them? My abilities already make me feel like a freak; I don't need everyone else thinking I am one too.

He moves his hand closer, waiting for me to agree.

"Look," I say, "I know this is stupid, but MJ is the first guy I've actually enjoyed doing this kind of stuff with. So it feels like"—I pause, trying to find the right words—"it feels like I'm devaluing our relationship by faking it with you."

"Prude," Amber says.

"Shut up," Alexander and I reply in unison.

Alexander's quick snap at Amber reminds me of MJ's intolerance for Amber's personality. I fight back a grin.

"Maddy," Alexander softly says. "This goes beyond your relationship with MJ. So many dark things took place here at school. But even in the shadow of the demon's influence, your entire class took note of the way you interacted with MJ on Monday and Tuesday. The demon was erased from their minds, but you two weren't. Your friends are waiting in the lobby—I can hear their thoughts from here.

They're anxious to see how your relationship has blossomed in the last two days."

"My friends?"

As my gaze rests on the school, a knot builds inside me. The last time I saw them, they were all compelled by Justin. He made them question our friendships. He made them turn their backs on me. And I made it easy for him because I had taken my friends for granted all these years.

I'm no prize. They are. Each of them has a unique light. Luke and Mason are adventurous and always quick to joke around. Shawn is smart and humble. Jake, Kayla, and Maggie—the triplets—are quiet, kind souls. Kelli is fiercely loyal and not afraid to be herself. Just being with them makes me feel balanced.

"They're all inside, waiting for you," Alexander says. "Waiting for us—with me as MJ. Seeing you walk through the doors holding MJ's hand will make them happy. Only the five of us here will know it's me and not him. And MJ, of course, as this was his idea."

Five of us. Alexander, Tamitha, Amber, and I make four. I flinch as I realize Sissy is the fifth. I should have known—she's part of the team protecting Amber. But I'm still nervous—unsure of how close she is or what she could be doing without my knowledge.

MJ trusts Alexander, I remind myself. So as long as I'm connected to him, Sissy shouldn't be able to do anything to me.

"Okay," I say. I put out my hand and close my eyes, waiting for him to grab it.

"You're really against this, aren't you?" he asks.

"I'm sure MJ will be touched," says a female voice behind me.

I turn, and there stands Sissy.

My heart rate spikes, and my lungs crave more oxygen than I can give them. I can't speak.

"While he may have eternity to wait on you," Sissy continues, "the rest of the world does not. Do you have any idea how much we're risking by lying to the Council to hide you?"

I shake my head. "What's the Council? Are they like the Perfugae?"

Sissy chuckles. "The Council is—"

"Sissy, don't," Alexander warns.

"No," she protests. "MJ may be fine with the consequences, but I'm not."

"What consequences?" I ask, hating that MJ has once again left me in the dark.

"The Council is the Archangels. For lying to them, we'd be discharged forever. We won't even be allowed to be Guardians. We'd either be stuck up there as standard angels, or we'd have to be reborn. And no matter how good we are or how many people we help with our future lives, we can never again be Protectors." She narrows her eyes at me. "So either play your part and pretend that Alexander is MJ or go home. I became a Protector to save mortals from demons. You are a threat not only to mortals, but to us as well. I did not sign on to babysit someone whose entire *mortal beginning* is in question."

Heat courses through my veins. What the heck does she mean my "mortal beginning is in question"? But there's more to my anger than just Sissy. How dare MJ keep all that from me? Did he even give the others a choice in coming to help me?

"I didn't ask to be born," I say through my gritted teeth. "And *I* sure as hell didn't ask for your help. As far as I'm concerned, you can leave."

A gust of wind suddenly kicks up and knocks Sissy off balance.

Alexander and Tamitha take defensive stances around me.

Amber's mouth pops open.

I smile. The wind—I think I know what that means. Elizabeth must be okay. She's still with me. Sissy's comment must have really upset her.

Sissy regains her footing, then takes a step away from me. Her eyes are wide with confusion. "What did you just do?"

I stare at her, not understanding her question.

Tamitha and Alexander straighten and face me. Alexander takes a tentative step toward me.

"Maddy," he says. "I know you can't control your abilities, but I'd like to know what you did or what we did"— he nods toward Sissy—"to spur that reaction from you."

If Elizabeth will be doing things like that, I won't be able to hide her for long. I'll protect her name, as the masked demon told me to, but I can't keep lying.

"I didn't do that," I start. "You guys aren't the only supernatural beings watching out for me. That wind is a friend. She helped me at Justin's house too. Apparently she didn't like the way Sissy talked to me."

Tamitha and Sissy gape, but Alexander appears unaffected. "This wind," he says, "it's the same one from the park the day you met MJ, isn't it?"

"You know about that too?"

He nods. "MJ followed it. It's a spirit, but the trail went cold. So who is she, and how do you know she's a friend?"

I can't believe this. MJ tells Alexander everything and yet he barely tells me a thing. Elizabeth showed me MJ's death. Justin told me about my abilities. Other than revealing that he's an angel—after I knew he died—MJ hasn't been forthcoming about anything. I should have learned all of that from him. But I didn't. So much for his "no more secrets" promise.

"I'm not saying another word about her until I talk to MJ. For now, we can either go home or we can continue with his stupid plan of acting like everything is normal."

Alexander rubs his neck and looks away. "My orders are to take you to school. Sorry, Maddy."

I huff and grab his hand. A warm, tingly sensation rushes into my palm. His essence. It spreads through the bones, muscles, and veins in my hand, but stops when it reaches my wrist and begins pooling.

And pooling.

And pooling.

I look at our joined hands, expecting to see mine swelling from the pressure building, but then the built-up essence releases back into Alexander. It's as if his essence met a wall, and even though it tried to break through, it couldn't.

I'm glad his essence didn't go farther. I don't need him knowing just how miserable I feel. The slate storm clouds stretching the sky above us do a fine job of showing that, anyway.

# CHAPTER 23

## Justin

I SHOULD'VE JUST USED THE BLADE ON THAT PROTECTOR instead of pushing her. She deserved it for saying that shit.

Mads's mortal status isn't in question. She's human. The real question is, what gave her all her abilities? Mortals typically gain supernatural abilities from a supernatural event. Whatever Mads lived through, it had to have been big. Maybe if I find out how she gained her abilities, I can figure out how to control her.

I look around Maddy's bedroom and sigh. Even though I've combed her home several times before, I'm going to do it again. From a previous search through her parents' minds, I discovered that the first big events in Mads's life are missing from their memories—someone compelled them to forget it all. They can't recall the pregnancy, her birth, or the first three weeks of her life. They—and I— have no idea what happened during that time.

The thought of something hurting Mads when she was an infant is appalling. We don't mess with those who can't fight back. Even the vilest demons honor that principle.

So then who was stupid enough to go after Mads when she was a baby—and why?

I move from room to room, searching through files and pictures, trying to find anything useful. In the basement, I stop and stare at her father's guitar. It's an Ibanez SR505 five-string bass. It has a beautiful mahogany finish. My fingers itch to touch it.

I pick it up, and my left fingers take their places along the frets while my right hand strums along the strings. The vibration of the chords fills me, calling out to a part of me I thought I lost with my last mortal death.

The basement of Mads's house is gone, and in its place is the memory of the dank, grungy shithole of Mike's garage.

THE WALLS AND FLOOR RATTLED FROM THE COMBINATION of the nonstop pounding from Mike's drums, the kick-ass strumming on Paul's lead guitar, and my wicked fingering on bass. Eric belted out the ending lyrics, and the song faded into silence.

My fingers shook as my heart still raced with the fast rhythm of the song. Music was my one true passion. It awakened me from my numb state. I lost myself in it. For however long the guitar was in my hand, I could forget all the crap that existed in my life. It only got better with the blended harmony of the drums, lead guitar, and vocals. This was my calling. I needed it more than ever.

We were on the verge of something big—I could feel it. We won the talent show the previous month, and now we were playing prom. There was talk of us doing some parties. Every gig counted. Eventually we wanted to move on to dive bars, and hopefully we'd catch a break and get a recording contract. Each practice got us one step closer to high-paying gigs and having enough money to get the hell out of here.

I looked at the rest of the guys. All of them had eyes wide, like deer in headlights.

My lips curved into a huge grin.

"Go ahead—say it," Paul said.

I shrugged and held my hands up in mock confusion. "Say what?"

"You know what," he said.

My smile widened. "*I told you* we could do it."

"Yeah, yeah," Mike said from behind his drums. "Don't be a dick about it. Besides, it cost me ten sticks to finally nail it." For proof, he held up another busted drumstick.

"We haven't nailed it," Eric said. "We made it through one time without messing up. Prom is in three weeks, and this song is insane."

"Come on, guys," I groaned. "Opening prom playing the Beastie Boys' 'Fight for Your Right' is going to be killer. I'm telling you, gigs are gonna roll in. Let's do it again."

Mike cleared his throat. "It's getting late."

I looked out the garage door. The treetops blazed orange, reflecting the sun setting behind the garage. I hadn't realized it was so late. I knew I was going to catch hell for this, but that was nothing new.

"Tomorrow then." I take off my guitar and hastily put it back in its case.

I waved good-bye to the guys and started walking toward home.

"Wait up!" Paul called as he ran after me.

I slowed my pace and waited for him. Normally we'd leave the garage together, but in my haste to get home, I forgot.

"So, Sara asked about you today," he said.

I shrugged.

"Her friend Kate thinks you're hot, and Sara wants me to set up a double date for us all."

I shook my head. "I need to focus on the music now." We both knew it was a lie.

It's just too soon after Mom.

"Come on," he begged. "If you say yes, Sara will *thank me*, if you know what I mean." He laughed and jabbed me in the ribs.

I grinned, but my happiness quickly faded. "As much as I hate to cock-block you, I don't have time to waste on a girl like Kate. She's not my type."

"Dude. She's hot and easy! What more do you want?"

I glanced at him, debating on whether I should tell him. I took a deep breath.

"I want the kind of girl who makes me want to be a better version of myself. Not because she asked me to change, but because I want to. If I'm lucky enough for her to fall for me, I won't just sit back and take it for granted. I'll surprise her. Make her fall more in love with me every day because she's worth the effort and because I'd be devastated without her. She'll know exactly how deeply I love her. She'll be there during the good times and when shit gets really bad. And incredibly, she'll love me even more for it."

He whistled. "Dang. Who is she?"

"Who's who?"

"This girl you're in love with."

"I haven't met her yet. But when I do, I'll move Heaven and Earth to keep her happy and safe."

I'll do what Dad failed to do.

I PUT MADS'S FATHER'S GUITAR BACK AND BURY THE FEELings my past conjured up. Knowing I won't be able to find answers here, I leave Mankato.

Moments later I step out of the Veil of Shadows in Atlanta, Georgia, the town where Mads was born, determined to find a way to keep her safe.

I'll do what MJ's failing to do.

# CHAPTER 24

## Maddy

THE LOBBY IS PACKED WITH STUDENTS CHATTING about the flooding in the school's basement—the cover story MJ used after erasing their minds and keeping them home yesterday.

Before the door closes behind Alexander and me, I'm blindsided by a mop of blonde hair. Arms covered in a black Jon Bon Jovi hoodie wrap around my waist, constricting like a snake.

"I missed you so much," Kelli squeals.

In her mind, we've been apart only since Monday afternoon. We go longer than that every weekend, but she's never been this animated about the separation. But after Justin brainwashed her and I faced the thought of never seeing her again, I'm glad for the hug.

"Missed you too," I say, wrapping my free arm around her back.

One by one, I hug all my friends, and although we've rarely done that, it feels good—as if they've forgiven me for putting them in a peril they no longer remember.

A bit of the unease in my stomach disappears, and I don't feel the need to force my smile—it's just there.

Hand in hand, Alexander and I walk the halls between all my morning classes with Kelli glued to my other side. She keeps beaming at me and wiggling her eyebrows whenever she thinks he's not looking. As weird as this is, I could get used to this ... with the real MJ, I mean.

AFTER FOURTH PERIOD, I PULL ALEXANDER INTO A NOOK created by two fire doors. Kelli keeps walking, but not before giving me two enthusiastic thumbs up—which Alexander sees.

"What's wrong?" he whispers.

"I was wondering if I could eat alone with my friends today."

"No. That wouldn't be a good idea."

"Why? There are a little over a thousand people here, so it's not like I'd really be alone. Even if MJ were here I'd ask for this."

"You would?"

"Yes. I mean, don't get me wrong: I'm falling for him—hard—and I enjoy being with him. But I don't want to get swallowed up by it. After everything that happened, I don't want my friends to feel like I'm choosing him over them. They're important to me too. Even though they don't know it, I nearly lost them the other day."

He sighs. "I get it. But I'm not supposed to leave you until MJ returns."

I let out an exasperated breath. "How long will he be gone?"

"I don't know. For the most part, time doesn't exist up there—at least not as you know it. He's speaking with the Council, and we're not allowed to disturb him unless there's an emergency. He'll contact us when he's able."

"Why did they summon him?"

"It's not my place to ask."

This time I suck in a deep breath as I recall what Sissy said in the parking lot about the Council. "Is he in trouble?"

"Relax, Maddy. MJ can handle himself. Besides, he's in Immortal City. What sort of trouble do you think could come from such a place?"

"The Perfugae. The Devil. Whoever gave Justin added abilities and the rights to my sou—"

"He doesn't have the rights to your soul," Alexander interrupts. "No matter what happens, MJ and I will not let Justin, or anyone else, take you again."

"You're just like MJ—you don't get it. You can't promise any of that! Justin won't stop after one failed attempt."

Alexander's eyes narrow as he reaches out to hold my arm. "How do you know? Have you *seen* something with your psychic abilities?"

My mouth drops, and I pull away. "He told you that too?"

Alexander's eyes snap shut as he groans.

I slide back deeper into the nook, a tightness building in my chest. It increases, scraping along my insides and tearing away all the safety, security, and hope that was bridging the gap between the girl I once was and the mystery I've become. All that's left is emptiness.

"I'm sorry," he says. "He didn't want us to say anything. Not until he had a chance to talk to you about it."

*Us.* So the others know too.

"It's fine," I reply dully. "It had to come out sooner or later. But for the record, I'm not psychic. I just have these … dreams. And if I had dreamed about Justin returning and forcing me to sign that contract, it would be too late—he'd own me by now." A violent shudder ripples through me at the frightening thought that he could do that.

"What do you mean? How do you know you're not psychic?"

"I don't know how I know—I just *know*," I lie. Elizabeth told me. But I can't tell him that.

He stares at me. His eyes soften as the seconds on the clock behind him tick their incessant tocks continuing to mark each long moment since I last saw MJ and the over-whelming amount of unknown time that exists until I can see him again.

Emotions are rippling inside me. I'm trying *so hard* to play my part today, but between the "itinerary," the erased memories, this charade with Alexander as MJ, and finding out more of MJ's secrets, it's nearly too much to bear.

And the one thing that will help me is the one thing I can't have right now: MJ. Which only confuses me more. A big part of me is so upset with him, yet a bigger part of me just wants him here so we can work it out. Together. That's how hard I've fallen for him.

But what I do have now is my friends. They can keep my head treading above water.

"Please, can I eat with my friends?" I beg. "You could be in the Veil. I don't care. I need them. To them, I'm just Maddy, not some freak with—"

"You're not a *freak*, Maddy."

He stands there, willing me to believe him. He's so much like MJ that it makes our separation all the more painful.

"Please," I repeat.

"All right."

A huge portion of dread leaves me, and in its place moves a feeling I haven't felt for a few days—normalcy. When I'm with my friends, there will be no talk of angels, demons, Heaven or Hell, my abilities, or any other topic that's suffocating me. For the next hour, I can be the old me.

I beam up at Alexander, and he reels just as MJ does when I'm this happy. I roll my eyes and tug him out of the corner before heading off on my own to rejoin the rest of my peers.

I grab lunch from the cafeteria, then head to our spot beside the entrance door. My friends wave and shift over for me.

"Where's Norway?" Kelli asks, looking around for "MJ."

"I wanted to have you guys all to myself."

"Good—"

"Because we all—"

"Wanted to talk to you," Jake, Kayla, and Maggie say in their usual triplet way.

Seeing how connected these siblings are makes me miss Hannah, even though we just had breakfast together. She's here, though, eating lunch in the cafeteria with her friends.

"*Mahd-dee*," Luke says in a strange accented voice, "you got some 'splainin' to do!"

I tilt my head and gaze across our oval-shaped group at him. I've heard that accent and saying before. "Ricky Ricardo? From *I Love Lucy*?"

He flashes me a grin. "I knew you would get it."

When Dad has weekends off, he watches old movies and TV shows. *Lucy* is one of his favorites. Luke knows of the show because of a project we did last year on Latin American actors.

"So ... " Mason says, his hand gesturing in the air in a "carry on" motion.

"So what?" I ask.

Shawn pushes his glasses up his nose and then looks over at me. "You left school Monday with MJ practically begging for your attention, and now you two are the new 'it' couple. What happened between then and now?"

My friends stare, smiling, waiting for me to fill them in on all the juicy details of my last two days with MJ. They assume my days were spent with MJ, happily falling for him as we created fun memories. They think that because the real events were so horrible, they had to be erased from their memories.

My own memories stream forward, and I resist the urge to shudder. A tingling sensation builds in my shoulder as an angel's essence pools there. I'm not sure which one of them it is. As comforting as it is to know I'm not alone, it's also a reminder of how drastically my life has changed.

There must be something I can tell them. "MJ and I spent most of Tuesday and Wednesday together. It was ... nice."

"Nice?" Kelli asks. "You can do better than that."

Kayla and Maggie nod in agreement.

"Okay. We went for a run, hung out, and talked for-ever. I like him. Okay?"

Kelli bumps into my shoulder. "Why, Maddy, I do declare you're in love," she exclaims in her best southern belle imitation.

I flush. How does she know?

Kayla and Maggie sigh and lean on each other.

"Well, good," Luke says. "But tomorrow, bring him to lunch."

"Yeah," Mason adds. "We need to see if he's good enough for our Maddy."

*Our Maddy.*

The words drift in, wrapping themselves around the mass of fear and worry about my friendships with them. The mass reduces until it shrinks away.

"Thanks, guys," I reply.

I grin, feeling lighter. For the moment, they're fine. We're fine. I'm glad I got to do this. I missed this—our friendship. Plus, I needed to see they were all back to themselves after everything Justin did to them.

The fear of losing them is quiet—for now. It's not gone. It will never be gone. Not after seeing how easily Justin used them to hurt me. It's a mistake I won't make twice.

# CHAPTER 25

# Maddy

I WAVE GOOD-BYE TO MY FRIENDS AS ALEXANDER, Amber, and I walk out to the parking lot. Alexander places his hand on the small of my back. I stop walking. My stomach flutters at the intimate contact. Then everything inside me stills, waiting to see how this point of contact will react.

His essence flows in and again hits a wall. I frown and notice him do the same.

"Come on," he says, guiding me to the stairs, his hand still on my back.

Even though we barely agreed to hold hands this morning, throughout the day Alexander has progressed to touching my arm, resting his arm on my shoulder, and now touching my back. He's not being a jerk or trying to hit on me. I think he's just conducting an experiment, and I'm his guinea pig. Perhaps he's checking to see if my body reacts the same way everywhere. So far it has.

I've touched five supernatural beings prior to Alexander: MJ, Damien (though thankfully only in my dreams), Elizabeth, Justin, and the masked demon.

Alexander's essence is the first to react this way. Is it him? Or me? From the deep lines of concentration on his forehead, I'm guessing he's puzzled by it as well. So it must be me.

I walk to the back door of the truck, but Alexander stops me. "You can have shotgun, Maddy."

"What about Amber?" I glance over at her.

"I have better things to do than waste my evening with you," she snaps.

Sissy steps out from the Veil. I move closer to Alexander.

"Alexander. Maddy." She nods to us and uses a surprisingly polite tone. "Come along, Amber." She touches Amber's arm, and a moment later they're gone.

"Where did they go?"

"You only have to be together during school hours," Alexander replies. "Unless you feel like joining her on a date with Tom?"

"Uh, no thanks." Up until MJ's arrival, Tom and Amber were usually swapping spit every chance they got. I wonder if MJ is the reason they don't do that anymore.

Alexander closes his eyes and tilts his head to the sky. His expression relaxes, as if years of stress and worry vanished from him. For a moment I'm envious.

"What are you doing?"

He lowers his gaze and smiles so joyously his brown eyes shine. "Come on. I have a surprise for you."

"What?"

"Get in the truck. I promise you'll like it."

"I don't like surprises. Just tell me what it is." I cross my arms and try to glare at him. But it's so hard not to smile with the excitement radiating off him.

"Did you know I used to be a cowboy, Maddy?"

His question has me dropping the charade. "No," I say, smiling at the thought.

"I was a sheriff—a lawman, as we were called back then—and I was great at it. People learned real quick not to test me. Now, I like you, so I would prefer to do this the easy way, but it's your choice. I've been ordered to take you somewhere but to not reveal the location—"

"Wait, when were you 'ordered' this?"

"Just now."

"By who?"

"MJ."

"How?"

He cracks his knuckles and grins. "In the words of Tamitha, we have a schedule to keep, and we're running late. Get in the truck, or I will *put* you in it. Nicely, I mean. I'm sure the remaining students loitering about will enjoy the show."

"Okay. Jeez," I say, opening my door.

Inside, the butterflies awaken. If MJ communicated with Alexander, that means he isn't home yet, but he's okay.

ALEXANDER PULLS UP ALONGSIDE THE CURB BY THE JOG-ging path that leads to Hiniker Bridge.

"I had fun today," he says. "Though I know it was awkward for you, it was still great getting to know you better."

I lean back into my door and stare at him. He's frowning, and a little indent in his chin mirrors the curve of his lips. "Why does it sound like you're saying good-bye?"

"Getting a soft spot for me, eh?"

I pause. As strange as it may seem, I have actually enjoyed some of our time together. He's funny and easy to be around.

"Well … you didn't try to kill me yesterday. I suppose that was nice of you," I joke.

"Right. Sissy is truly sorry about that. But just so there are no secrets between us, I was pushing MJ to kill you when he met you. I'm glad he didn't listen."

I snort. "Me too."

"You're going to be fine, Maddy."

Again, this sounds like a good-bye. I look down the jogging path that leads to my safe haven. It looks different now—no longer inviting. The barren branches that curve over the path rustle in the breeze, looking as if they're hands waiting to reach out and trap me. Hold me prisoner forever. Alone. He's going to just leave me here. By myself. I don't want him to go.

"I thought you couldn't leave me alone," I whisper.

I squeeze my hands between my knees so he can't see them shake. Heat builds between them from the friction, making them slick with sweat. The cab of the truck darkens. I don't have to look outside to know the sky just changed to a grayish-black color.

He sighs and places a hand on my arm. "I know something happened to make you lose faith in people. I'm sorry that happened. I wish you would put your trust in me, though I realize you've only known me a day. MJ, however, you've known a little while longer. Actions always speak clearer than words, and I think you know he would never let any harm come to you, so long as he could help it. One day I hope you'll feel the same toward me. Tamitha and Sissy too. We're all stumped when it comes to you, but we're going to do everything we can to keep you safe."

"Abandoning me here, alone, isn't safe," I say, my voice barely audible.

He smiles a little. "After everything I just said, do you really think I would bring you to your favorite place just to abandon you?"

I stare at him, taking in the gentle tone and the softness in his eyes. I was right yesterday—he is more teddy bear than brute. Even though I barely know him, I trust that he means what he says—he will do all he can to keep me safe.

A bit of my fear lessens.

"I—I guess not."

"Unlike you, I happen to like surprises—what I can recall of them, anyway. And I like the anticipation leading up to the reveal. So, with that in mind, get out of MJ's truck so I can do all kinds of reckless, stupid stuff with it before I have to return it to him. Please."

I shake my head and laugh. "Okay."

When I open my door, Tamitha stands beside it. Is this the surprise? If so, it's not a very good one.

"Alexander is taking me to do something called 'mudding.' Have a good night!" she says.

I stare at her, first noting the ear-to-ear grin on her face, then her straw cowboy hat, flowery dress, and brown leather boots.

"Wait. Are you two going on a *date*?"

"What'd you think we're gonna do with our free time now that we can feel?" Alexander asks. "Sit around and talk about our feelings? Nope. We've got a lot of living to catch up on, and time is a-wasting. Giddy on up here, Tamitha."

"Don't wait up," she sings as she climbs in and sits in the center seat next to him.

"So what's my surprise?" I ask, still unsure.

Tamitha presses her lips together and then runs her fingers over them, zipping her mouth shut.

Alexander shakes his head and laughs some more. "It's all about the anticipation, remember?"

I wave as they drive off. They seem like a cute couple. It gives me hope for my relationship with MJ. In this life and the next.

As the truck fades out of view, I turn and there stands MJ.

Every high and low of the day suddenly vanishes.

I sprint toward him, desperate to erase the distance between us. He does the same. In less than a second, his arms wrap around me, hugging me and lifting my feet off the pavement. His essence—the essence my body has craved all day—rushes into my body, filling me instantly, having memorized the space.

Even though this is exactly where I want to be—and I'm ridiculously happy—I have a strong desire to cry. I missed him so much.

My heart rate lowers and my breathing slows as my body finally catches up to my head in realization that everything is perfect now.

He lowers me so my feet touch down, and he places kiss after kiss in my hair. Each one sends a shockwave through me, strengthening his essence inside me.

Hand in hand we walk to the center of the bridge, and he turns to face me. We stand like this for I don't know how long, drinking in the sight of each other. If this were all we did for the rest of the day, I would be more than okay with it.

"Could you take us to the bridge?" he asks.

"We are at the bridge," I reply breathlessly.

"No." He lightly taps my temple. "The one in your mind. I spent two-thirds of the day apart from you, and I'd like to make up the time."

I hug him harder. "Not right now. I can't touch you there. I just want to be in your arms—I've missed you way too much."

He grins and motions for us to sit along the back railing. When we do, he shifts so he's behind me with his arms wrapped around me. I link my hands over his and rest my head on his shoulder.

"How's your day been?" he asks.

"Long."

He chuckles. "Me too. I've missed you."

My heart flutters, and my smile widens. "Good."

"What did you do today?"

"My day was quite busy, thanks to your 'itinerary.'"

His body tenses around me.

I kiss the back of his hand to lighten the blow. "To be honest, I was a bit ticked about it. But now that you're back, I'm so happy to see you that I don't care."

He mirrors me by placing a kiss on my hand. "If I had been here today, those were all the things I would have done with you. I didn't want you to miss out on anything simply because I was unavoidably detained."

I hadn't thought of it like that. Leave it to him to be thoughtful and sweet.

I tug on his arms, making him hug me even harder. "How did it go up there?" I pause. "Did you find Ben?"

He's silent. I can guess his answer.

I thought MJ would find him. I wanted him to—even though I dreaded the idea. I assumed Ben would tell him how much he hated me and blamed me for his death. But this—this is worse. Where is he, then? Ben's life ended miserably, and now his afterlife is just as miserable. He deserves peace.

I try to put on a brave face. But in the reflection in the water, I can see storm clouds swirling above us. The traitorous sky reveals the truth.

"I will find him," MJ says. "I promise."

I change the subject. "What happened with the Council? They aren't going to punish you, are they?"

MJ sighs and places another kiss in my hair. "It went as well as could be expected. I met with Michael. He and his two brothers make up the surviving Heavenly Archangels. He knew about some things that took place here, and I filled in some gaps. I have their blessing to remain here, as does my team, so you can relax. They aren't going to punish anyone."

"Oh. What did he say about me?"

"Nothing. I'm keeping you a secret for as long as possible. I can't promise we can keep this quiet forever, especially considering he asked about the fire tornados. But for now, we'll take it one day at a time."

My chest constricts as fear pounds into me. "He saw the tornadoes?" MJ is trying so hard to protect me, and my own abilities are working against us.

"Heard of them."

"We can't kiss, then, can we?"

laurie wetzel          185

He huffs. "The hell we can't. We'll be careful and take it slow so we can figure out what stirs that reaction in you."

"But what about your future, and the others', if the Council finds out you hid me from them? Sissy says you could be banished."

He stiffens. "It won't happen."

"But what if it does?"

"Then we'll deal with it. End of story. She shouldn't have told you that."

I twist and lean back to see his face. "You're right. *You* should have told me about this. You should have told me about a lot of things."

He frowns and turns away.

I grab his chin and turn him back to me.

"It's not fair to ask the others to risk their futures for me."

"They knew what they were signing up for," he says. "Besides, there's one aspect of Heaven you're forgetting about."

"What's that?"

He smiles, though it doesn't reach his eyes. "They're pretty big on forgiveness."

# CHAPTER 26

## MJ

I HOLD MADDY FOR NEARLY AN HOUR BEFORE SHE'S ready to bring us to the bridge in her mind. Unsure of how long we'll be gone, I'm compelling the area. If anyone were to come to the bridge, they wouldn't notice our motionless bodies. They'd just move around us, as if we were a puddle, and not think anything of it.

"All done," I say when the compulsion is complete, then I kiss her temple.

My essence inside her buzzes, feeling her excitement. She closes her eyes, and I do the same. A moment later, my body twists and contorts as my soul is pulled from it.

I reopen my eyes. It worked. I'm lying on the bridge—the one in her mind. Maddy rests beside me, though a safe distance away so we don't accidentally touch.

Curved above and below us are black markings identical to the ones on the bridge we just left.

Even though we've been here many times before, it's different now that I know more about this ability of hers. Coming to the bridge feels different than our time traveling yesterday—less intense. Also, I can still feel how my body is back on the real bridge, whereas I could not feel it yesterday. Those two differences lead me to believe we're not time traveling now. If it's possible, I think this space exists in an alternate realm—similar to the Veil of Shadows. Whatever this is, Maddy can take us here and time travel, all with just my essence inside her.

I wonder if she would use her ability to take me into another dream—one with Damien. Then I could see what Damien and the woman look like. It would help me find them.

No. These abilities shouldn't be taken lightly, yet I'm doing just that, making requests for her to send us here and there as if she were my own personal teleportation device. It's reckless. I won't ask her to time travel, not until I know more about it.

But I can't resist coming here. I need to be with her as long as possible, and here we can just *be*.

It's summer here again. The sky is so clear it rivals the view from Immortal City. Birds, bees, frogs, and even a family of deer across the pond all move to the speed unique to this place. Everything here is controlled by Maddy, though I don't think she's figured that out yet.

At some point, I'll have to tell her what she can do with this ability—that she can travel through time and alternate planes. But once she knows the full truth, I fear she won't want to do this again, and I'm not sure I'm ready to give this place up.

When she's excited and happy, this place is bright and magical. It steals my breath away, just as she does. When she's sad, there's a darkness. But even then, it's so beautiful that I'm torn between marveling at the view and consoling her.

But there are selfish reasons too for not wanting to give this place up. There are no angels, demons, or other entities here that can steal her away from me. I don't have to be on constant alert. Back on the real Hiniker Bridge, it was unnerving when we heard those twigs snap the other morning and I couldn't find the source. I still don't know who or what was there. But here, I can truly relax and enjoy being with her. It's nice to have a place like this—a place where I can't fail her.

If it's possible … I think this place is a reflection of her soul. She told me what it looked like with Justin—bleak and empty. If that's true, it's imperative I keep him from her. She burns far too brightly to let him extinguish her.

He, and other demons, inspired her birthday gift. I'm nervous about giving it to her. I learned through her family's memories that Maddy doesn't enjoy receiving gifts. It's always been that way, but whatever happened between her and the Shadowwalker three years ago amplified everything. Ever since, she wants nothing from anyone. Her parents stopped trying with gifts. Now they put money into an account for when she turns eighteen. For some reason, they fear she'll leave and never look back when that day comes.

I tried to find out why they think that, but so many things about Maddy are sealed off in their memories. Most are just tiny fragments sprinkled here and there. And the pregnancy, birth, and first three weeks of her life are completely missing. They don't even have any photos in the house. A very powerful demon covered it up well. Whatever exists behind the black curtains are the keys to everything.

There are two ways to restore someone's memories. You can find the being that compelled the person and have the being undo it. Or you can kill the person. Since I'm not going to kill her family, I'm adding this demon to my ever-expanding list of immortal beings to track down.

That's why my gift to Maddy is so important. With it, no demon will ever get close to her again. I just have to find the right time to give it to her.

Her chest slowly deflates as a content sigh leaves her lips. Despite the risks, coming here is exactly what she needed. Her ankles are crossed, and her right arm is behind her head. Her eyes are wide, absorbing everything and becoming a brighter green as more and more stress leaves her. There's a slight, relaxed curve to her lips. I miss those lips.

"If I wanted to try something here—" I pause when she looks at me.

My body leans forward on instinct, as if pulled by her gaze. With my essence having been inside her so often, it's as if it automatically responds to her desires even before my mind recognizes what they are.

"I want to kiss you," I blurt.

I meant to say it better—in a more romantic way—but that would have taken too long. Right now, I just *need* her.

The light, warmth, and happiness that held her expression vanish in an instant. Clouds roll in, and a rustling sound echoes around us as wind shakes the trees.

"I want to," she whispers. "Really, I do. I just … want a day free of trouble. I just got you back. I don't want them *summoning* you again."

Sharp pain ripples through my stomach as if it'd been kicked.

She's afraid to kiss me.

The last thing I want to do is hurt her. I take a moment to breathe and calm the hurt before explaining further.

"That's what I want to test out. I think our time here ends when my essence connects with you—not just when we touch. If I held my essence back, then maybe we could touch and not leave."

"You can do that?" Her gaze is wide and pleading.

I feel the same way. It's been too long since we've kissed.

"I don't know. I've never tried."

"Is that what happened with Alexander today?"

Alexander told me of the trouble he'd experienced in getting his essence to flow through Maddy.

"I'm not sure why you reacted differently to him, but a part of me is glad for it. I like that only my essence works that way."

She turns away, and the clouds darken further.

It takes only a moment to decipher what it means. "Justin's essence works similar to mine, doesn't it?"

She nods, barely.

"I'm sorry," I whisper. "I'm sorry you had to go through that. I wish more than anything you didn't have to remember him. But that's all he is now, just a distant, bad memory. You and I together is the future."

Slowly, I move my hand toward hers. She stiffens, bracing herself for our touch.

As the space between our hands decreases, I focus on holding back my essence—fighting against what comes naturally to me. When I feel the soft, silky skin of her hand, my body tingles as my essence rushes to the source of contact, but I stop it.

It's not easy. Having my essence inside her body is like nothing I could ever begin to describe. It's the first time I've ever felt truly alive. And no matter what, I will never get enough. But somehow, I have to find the will to hold myself back while we're here.

After five seconds, my confidence grows. I move from touching her with just the tip of a finger, to my whole hand. It's easier to hold back now. I could spend the rest of my life touching her like this. There's a tingling in my palm as it glides over the smooth texture of her skin. These sensations have always been overshadowed by all the things my essence detected inside her.

She doesn't move.

I can hear and feel her heart rate increasing. Her chest rises and falls at a quickening pace too. I think she's excited, but I don't know. I move forward to see how far we can push this before I break.

I hold her gaze as I lean in, slowly closing the space between our lips. Her breath blows on mine, and a deep rumble sounds inside me. A moment later, our lips meet. Just as I did when I touched her hand, I battle against my basic instinct and instead focus on her. On the soft wetness of her lips as they mold to mine. On the way her entire body relaxes, craving this moment since the last time our lips touched.

A soft moan escapes her, and it ripples through me. An overwhelming need to be closer to her consumes me. My arms curl around her, gripping her back and pressing her into me. I need to feel her in this new way. Her skin is so soft, softer than anything that existed in my previous life.

Her hands move to my hair. She yanks hard in her drive to pull me closer too. My body tightens in shock, but not even a second later it's replaced by exquisite bliss. She needs me as badly as I need her.

I don't care if we set fire to the whole world—I will never go this long without kissing her again.

I find the strength to break away from her tender lips to kiss and nibble her neck. She pants to catch her breath, pushing her chest farther into me.

"So beautiful," I say as I rub my nose along her jaw-line, inhaling her scent that reminds me of summer.

She shivers.

And before my mind can stop it, my essence rushes in to warm her.

I still feel her body against mine, but it's not the same. Her back is to me. I'm once again holding her on Hiniker Bridge—the real bridge. Our souls have returned to our bodies.

# CHAPTER 27

# Maddy

I turn in MJ's arms. "That was—" I have to stop as I struggle to catch my breath.

He frowns and looks away. "I'm sorry. I got carried away."

I sit up on my knees, placing my hands on his cheeks, forcing him to look at me.

"Don't you *dare* apologize for kissing me like that! Look around, MJ." I sweep a hand behind me. "Everything is fine. *We are fine.* We kissed. And it was intense and beautiful and … perfect. Nothing took that moment away from us. It worked."

I shift closer to him, moving my hands behind his head to play with his hair. Muscles clench deep in my belly, and I bite my lip.

His eyes darken.

"I can kiss you," I say, breathless. "And you can kiss me. Nothing can stop us from being together."

He leans into me—our foreheads touch. His fingertips brush along my cheekbones, and that's all I feel. His essence doesn't enter me. His touch moves into my hair.

I close my eyes and just absorb the feel of his calloused fingers trailing down my neck and arms before stopping at my waist. Every spot he touches feels as if it were on fire. I want more of him.

I tilt my neck to bring my lips to his, but I don't find them.

In the distance, I hear voices, but they're muffled. They're chanting or yelling, like at a sporting event, but I can't make it out. All at once, the sensations from MJ's touch leave me.

I open my eyes.

MJ's gone.

Hiniker Bridge has been transformed into a small white room. To the left is a sitting area with plush brown couches and a privacy screen that's maybe used for dressing. On the right, a mirror and vanity covers the length of the room.

I've been in rooms like this before. In the summer, the whole family comes along when Dad's band opens for somebody really famous. I'm backstage at an event of some sort, though I don't understand how.

The voices grow louder. They're excited. There must be a huge crowd out there.

I don't care about them or this room. I want to go back to MJ. I was just about to kiss him.

I go to wrap my arms around myself, but they won't move. *Nothing* will move.

Suddenly, without my control, my body walks to the mirror. My stomach tightens when I focus on the reflection.

It's me—but not. Blonde highlights streak through my hair. My lips are fuller, and I have pink lipstick. My nose is different too—thinner with a sharp point.

I think I'm dreaming, only not about myself but instead about someone who looks a lot like me. Did MJ put me to sleep again? He must have, but why? The masked demon said there were a few more dreams to see of Elizabeth, so maybe this is one of hers.

A knock sounds to my right. Maybe that's Elizabeth? A voice says, "Come in."

If I hadn't been watching the mirror, I wouldn't have known that voice came from me. It's higher and a bit snooty. But then again, it matches the navy dress and pearls I'm wearing.

A woman with curly blonde hair enters, closing the door behind her. Disappointment fills me—it's not Elizabeth. So who is she and where am I?

The new woman is in a navy skirt and matching blazer with a white blouse. I have no idea who she is, but with the way her brown eyes are watching me, she knows me.

She walks up to me with a sway I've only ever seen people do on TV. She hugs me lightly, then lets go and grabs my hands.

"I know you don't want to be here," she says with a weak smile, "but this night is important to your father."

*How do you know my dad?* I try to ask, but my own voice won't cooperate.

Instead, my only response is a huff that could rival one of Amber's.

"Once the election is over," the woman continues, "you can see Chris as often as you'd like. Until then, we all have to make sacrifices."

"I know—an Atwood win is a win for us all," the snooty voice belonging to this body says with a sigh.

The woman smiles, and the warmth of it pulls me in. "That's right, sweetie. They need us on stage in five minutes. I'll give you a moment to prepare. I love you, Lauren." She leaves.

Now I feel slightly better. I think I know what's going on. I'm somehow dreaming about Lauren—a girl who looks similar to me. The Atwood name sounds familiar too, though I can't remember how I know it. Now if I could just figure out *how* I got here and *why* …

All of a sudden there are loud popping sounds behind me. Lauren spins around in time to see the vanity lights explode.

Heated glass shards fly everywhere. Lauren leaps behind the privacy screen. Her heart races as she kneels on all fours. She turns to the vanity, but it has disappeared behind flames.

Memories of Justin's house resurface. I can't do this. Not again. I won't survive it.

Lauren runs to the door, but it won't open. She coughs, gasping for air as she pounds on the door. My own throat burns too. I have to get out of here.

I try to use her body as the masked demon has used mine—hoping that between her and I, we'll have the strength to open the door. The handle turns, but the door won't budge. Not even a tiny bit. I can't help her.

It's just a dream, I remind myself. This isn't real. But I can't make myself believe the words. I don't know what this is, but it feels real. Realer than any time I've been inside Elizabeth and Lifa. Real or not, Lauren is going to die here. If I can't get myself out, I'll die too.

Guilt fills me as I decide to leave this place on my own, just as I did this morning. I close my eyes and try to block out her panic. I remind myself I'm actually on the bridge with MJ. I can do this. I need to do this. Please … let this work.

I open my eyes. I'm facing the damn door.

It didn't work. I don't have any essence inside me.

I'm trapped here.

With the intense heat, beads of sweat slide down her skin, making her dress cling to her body.

"Someone help!" she screams. I echo her, crying out for help, even though no one can hear me.

Voices sound on the outside of the door. She and I cough out relieved cries.

We're saved.

"Open the door, Lauren!" someone shouts.

Again she grabs the handle—I try to help her. Again it doesn't budge.

"I can't!" she screams back, then breaks into another fit of coughs.

The door vibrates as if something hit it. The people on the other side are trying to break it down.

A smell I've become far too familiar with coats the air. Sharp, searing agony stems from her feet and calves. I feel it in mine too.

Flames climb up her skin.

We're burning.

A blood-curdling scream escapes her lips. I'm not sure if it belongs to her, me, or both of us.

I close my eyes, trying to fight against the panic consuming me. It's no use. The pain is too great.

I'm going to die here, and I don't even know where *here* is.

*Maddy!* MJ's horrified voice echoes in my mind. *Maddy, wake up!*

His fear shreds me. I need to get back to him.

*Please, Maddy,* he begs.

As flames ravage more of Lauren's body, I allow his voice to coat me. It seeks out the last memory I have of us together.

We were about to kiss on Hiniker Bridge. I was safe. I *need* to go back there.

The room calms—the sounds distant, the pain fading. There is nothing but … bliss. Somehow I recognize it as death. It calls to me, welcoming me with open arms—embracing me as if I truly belong. It's peaceful, but I can't give in.

I hold even harder to the memory of MJ until it becomes so real I can almost reach out and touch it.

I do, and everything disappears.

## CHAPTER 28

# MJ

"It's been five minutes," Alexander says over Maddy's terrified screams. He and Tamitha grip harder to her legs as she fights something we can't see. "Whatever this is," he says, "she can't take much more."

I kiss her tear-and-rain-soaked temple as I send more of my essence into her mind, trying to pull her from wherever she is. "Maddy! Maddy, wake up!"

Her body stills in my arms, and I feel a change inside her. She's back.

"That's it, *minn ást*. Find your way home to me."

Her tears and screams continue, but they're different this time. Before, her heart raced and she pounded and clawed at the air as if she were trying to escape from wherever she was. Now her body curls in on itself in pain.

I push more of my essence into her, desperate to know if this is a vision, if she time traveled, or if a demon took her again. My essence scatters, pulled apart in so many directions by her needs, making it difficult for me to follow it.

When it returns to me, my knees buckle from the sensations terrorizing my feet and calves. My flesh feels as if it were burning from my body.

Tamitha and Alexander look from me to Maddy, then to each other.

"Give her to me," Alexander says, trying to take Maddy from my arms.

I can't respond. If I open my mouth, the scream I'm holding will escape. Instead I hold her closer, knowing this excruciating sense of fear, pain, and hopelessness is coming from her. If Alexander takes her, I won't feel this anymore. But as badly as I want to be free of the pain, I can't allow her to go through this alone.

Through the pain, I suddenly remember the bruise on Maddy's forehead during last night's vision. That means there could be bruising or damage on her legs to match the pain I'm feeling. I can't bring myself to check, though. It hurts too much to move.

*What is it?* Tamitha asks using Cerebrallink.

*Legs,* I utter. It's all I can risk for fear I might scream even through Cerebrallink.

"Check his legs," Tamitha says to Alexander.

"No!" I growl through my locked jaw. I fight with all I have to hold back my cries.

They don't understand. Every second they waste, Maddy's suffering grows. Alexander looks at me, his face gripped with fear. He's never seen one of us in pain before. When we fight the demons, we get injured. Sometimes even badly enough that we have to return to Heaven to recharge. But we never feel any pain or sensation.

My body is burning. Every nerve ending is in an agonizing torment. But still, Maddy is the one truly suffering.

I stare at Alexander, then drop my gaze to her legs, hoping he understands my message.

He kneels down beside her and rolls back the hem of her jeans. He and Tamitha gasp while a muffled moan sounds in my throat. Her legs are charred, blackened to a point where I fear they might crumble to ash with the slightest touch.

Even though it hurts, I push all my essence into her legs, repairing the damage. After a moment of hesitation, Tamitha and Alexander gently place their hands on her legs and feet. As they feel their first taste of pain in this life, they fight their own desires to scream.

As we struggle through our shared pain, our combined essences work to repair the layers of damage on her lower body. Their essences still won't move beyond where they are touching her. I don't understand why. I also don't understand why it's taking three of us to heal her. I've healed countless mortals by myself. I should be able to repair this damage immediately and end her suffering, but I can't—just as I couldn't two nights ago.

She clings harder to me, digging her nails into my shoulder and bicep. Blood runs down my arm, but I ignore it and keep my focus on her.

Slowly we soothe the burning sensation. Maddy stops screaming. Our own pain lessens.

Maddy stares up at me—her eyes wide with fear and confusion. Then she turns, buries her head in my lap, and falls to pieces. Heavy rain bursts from the clouds, instantly soaking us all. Violent sobs shake her body.

As more of her cells and tissues regenerate, I split my essence and send half of it through the rest of her body to calm her down. There's still so much fear inside her. I need to know what she went through, but I know she's not ready.

I break up every pocket of fear I can find. Her heart slows. Her sobs lessen. The rain turns into a light drizzle.

She looks up, and those emerald eyes hit me again. Everything she's been through in the last week flashes through my mind. I stare down at her in awe.

I push her wet hair from her face. "You're so brave, Maddy. I'm so sorry I couldn't protect you from this."

Her lips tremble.

Tears well up inside me. I lean down and kiss her forehead so she won't see one fall.

*MJ,* Tamitha says in my mind.

I sit up and turn my attention to her. She's still seated on one side of Maddy's legs while Alexander is seated on the other side.

*I think the worst is over,* she says.

She glances at Maddy's legs, and my eyes follow. Her legs are a pink hue, as if sunburned. That's the only visual evidence of what she went through.

*You can let go,* I tell Tamitha, knowing that's what she's indirectly asking.

Her body slumps as she lets out a relieved sigh. Cautiously she removes her hands and essence from Maddy.

I stare down at Maddy, watching for any sign of the pain returning. She just stares up at me. I don't think she's even aware that Tamitha and Alexander are here.

Alexander shifts. I look at him and nod, giving him the okay.

*Are you sure?* he asks.

No, I'm not sure, but I don't want him or anyone to know. Instead I sit there watching Maddy yet again, praying I'm not making a mistake. It took all three of us to heal her and soothe the pain. She didn't react when Tamitha pulled away, but will my essence be enough on its own if Alexander pulls away too?

His essence withdraws. Maddy doesn't react.

My fingers run through her damp hair as I hold her, protecting her as best I can. I need answers.

"Please tell me what happened to you. Tell me so I can fix it."

She coughs, and the raspy sound fills me with anger—anger at whoever or whatever did this to her.

Tamitha hands her a bottle of water. Maddy's eyes close as she takes a few sips. When her eyes reopen, they're distant and unfocused.

"I—I don't know what happened," she says weakly.

I send more of my essence to her throat to ease the ache. She takes another breath and doesn't wince this time.

"I was with you and then I wasn't," she says, looking at me. Her voice sounds stronger this time, but it's still not her angelic tone. "I was backstage at what I first thought was a show of my dad's, but when I looked in the mirror, my reflection was different. It was me, but it wasn't. I don't know how else to explain it. A lady came in, and she called me Lauren."

I stiffen.

It's a coincidence. That's all.

Her lip trembles as she clamps her eyes shut for a moment. "The woman said something about an election and an Atwood win, then she left … and the room started on f-fire." She trembles even more. "Lauren couldn't get out. I felt the fire consuming me. I couldn't wake up. I felt her slipping, giving in to death. And it was so peaceful.

Then I heard you." She stops and stares so deeply into my eyes, it's as if she were seeing into my heart. "I didn't want to leave you."

I nearly lost her—again. I hold her closer, kissing her hair and allowing myself a moment to let her words sink in.

I push back my feelings in order to focus on discovering how and why she was taken. Then I catch Alexander's gaze.

*Was this a vision?* he asks.

*I'm not sure.*

*I've said it before: there's no such thing as coincidence.*

I let out a ragged breath. *Go find Protector Gary and see if his Charge is safe. Take Tamitha with you.*

*I can stay,* Tamitha offers.

After what we went through, I know they need time to process it. We all do.

*No, stay together,* I tell them both. *I don't know what you'll find when you get there.*

They nod. A moment later, they're gone.

# CHAPTER 29

## Maddy

EVEN THOUGH THE PAIN OF THE BURNS IS GONE, I don't want to let go of MJ. I pull his arms tighter around me. He shifts, making the boards of Hiniker Bridge groan.

I glance around, waiting for Alexander and Tamitha to reappear at the noise, but they don't. They must have left.

I turn back into MJ, still raw with confusion. He makes it better. Focusing on his essence continuously looping around my insides reminds me I'm with him. I'm safe.

"I wanted to wait …" he begins.

I look up into his hazel eyes. They're hooded, concealing most of their brilliance, as he frowns.

"I wanted to let things settle down. I didn't want to push you. But I need to know about your visions. I need to know how and why this happens," he says, pointing to my now-healed legs. "And I need to know how to keep you from getting hurt like this."

I take a deep breath, preparing myself. Incredibly, I'm not nervous as I was when I told Kelli about the dreams. No matter what, I know MJ will accept me and still love me. I won't tell him all the secrets—not when he's still keeping things from me. But I trust him with this.

"For as long as I can remember, I've dreamed of a fairy-tale romance between two people known as the Dream Girl and the Dark Prince …"

I tell him about the dreams. I tell him how they work and that I'm not psychic. And I tell him how the dreams have changed now that the connection to Elizabeth—though I don't say her name—is broken. I grip his hand harder when I tell him I met the Dream Girl and that she helped me at Justin's house.

"You mean you dreamed of her, right?" He gazes deeper into me as he wills me to say yes, but I can't.

"No. It was real. She somehow brought me to her while my body was with Justin."

His eyes clamp shut, and the veins in his neck extend as he tightens his jaw. After a few controlled breaths, he opens his eyes. There is a coldness to them now—as if he's pulled away from me.

I wish he'd stop reacting whenever I mention what took place at Justin's house. I know he blames himself, but he shouldn't.

"Were you here at the bridge?" MJ asks. His voice feels a million miles away. I have to bring him back to me.

"No. She said it was a version of Heaven, and from the perfect sky and clouded ground, I believed her. I think she wanted to tell me what you and Justin were, but she couldn't. So instead, she showed me your death."

"What do you mean she showed it to you? You said you dreamed about my death."

I turn away, not wanting to see his expression as he uncovers this lie. But then I turn back to him and meet his eyes. I'm done lying to him.

"She has this fountain—she called it a Time Keeper. On the surface of the water were images of you and Lifa. She put me in the fountain, and when I came out of it, I was inside Lifa. That's how I saw your death. I wanted to explain all this to you … I just didn't know how. Calling it a dream seemed simpler at the time."

"What else did she do to you?" he snaps.

I don't believe he's mad at me—at least I hope not. I think his anger lies with Elizabeth. To him, she's just another unknown being in a long list of beings he wants to protect me from. But she's not like the others. She's good, and I need to make him see that.

"When I woke up, I was back at Justin's house, but I could feel her with me. She helped me before you got there. If it weren't for her, I would've signed the contract the first time Justin tried."

The horrible, painful memory plagues me. What little safety I felt here with MJ is sucked out of me, and all that's left is an icy chill.

A burst of frozen air escapes my lips as I take in the changing scene around us. Frost creeps along the pond, shriveling everything it touches with its icy claws.

MJ's essence furiously battles the bitter cold inside me. Slowly, warmth builds inside me, and slowly the pond returns to normal.

MJ caresses my cheek. "Can you promise me something, Maddy?"

"What?"

"Don't use your ability to go to other places anymore—not even the bridge. Not until we understand it better."

"Why?"

"Just promise me, please."

I stare at him, seeing the distance in his eyes. Something scared him. Was it the frost, the vision of Lauren, or is there more to it? Whatever it is, I want to put his mind at ease. "Okay," I reply. "I'll try not to use my ability."

"Thank you," he says. Then his brows furrow. "If this Dream Girl is responsible for sending you dreams and showing you my death, how and why did you see Lauren?"

I frown, still haunted by what happened. "I don't think the Dream Girl had anything to do with that. Her memories are meant to help me—build trust between us by showing me the truth. But what I experienced with Lauren … there was nothing good about it."

"If this was a vision, then how in the world did it burn your legs like that?"

My frown deepens, knowing this will upset him further. "Since my dreams with the Dream Girl have broken, any time something bad happens in a vision, it happens to me too."

His eyes widen. "Tell me there's a way to stop you from dreaming. Please."

"The Dream Girl is trying to stop the dreams. She says there are only a few left, though."

"I don't care. I can't stand seeing you get hurt like this, Maddy. It's crushing me."

My heart twists in agony, hating what these visions do to both of us. What I see and feel is horrible, but MJ is forced to sit by and watch me go through it. He feels the pain when he heals me—including my emotional aftermath. I wish I could stop these dreams, but I can't. I have no control over them, just as I no longer have control over a lot of things.

"I'll find a way," he says. "I promise."

I meet his gaze and offer a weak smile, knowing he can't.

"Has the Dream Girl helped you other times?" he asks.

"Yes."

"When?"

"The day I met you."

His eyes drift as he thinks back to that day. Suddenly his eyes brighten.

"She created the windstorm, didn't she?"

I nod.

He pauses. "Do you trust her?"

"I don't fully trust anyone, MJ."

He looks away, but not before I see his eyes dim. He knows that includes him.

"I'm sorry if that hurts," I say, "but I want to be honest with you. Regardless of how I feel about you, we met *six days* ago. We can't expect to know everything about each other in that amount of time. Certain pieces of ourselves are still in the dark for one reason or another. Besides, if we did know everything about each other, what would we talk about for the rest of our lives?"

Suddenly, he grins, his arms curling around me, holding me closer to his chest. "There's plenty to do when we run out of things to talk about ..."

In a blur, MJ pulls me to my feet, then kisses me. Just as earlier, he holds his essence back, but that's where the similarities end. His lips move furiously against mine. He's always been so gentle, but this … this is a rough, needy, desperate kind of kiss that makes my toes curl.

He bends me backward, curving over me. His tongue slides into my mouth. I just … give in to the bliss. I feel him *everywhere*—his body pressed against mine and his hands exploring my back.

My heart pounds. He must feel it against him. Heat consumes me, but I want to be devoured by *this* blaze.

My hands move into his hair, curling, yanking, desperate to find some way to pull him closer. It's no longer a question of want. I *need* him. I need him more than I need sunlight, water, air.

This amazing, powerful, sensual kiss is my new addiction. Whatever I did to make him kiss me like this, I want to do it over and over and over again.

Our kiss ends, and I snuggle closer, knowing our time here won't last forever. His essence resumes flowing through me. My mind quiets, and a content smile crosses my face. I don't know if he removed all my troubles or just shoved them into places out of reach, but for the moment, I don't care.

"Thank you for everything today," I say. "I'm sure healing me wasn't easy—nor was hearing the truth about my dreams. I don't know what I'd do without you."

"You'll never have to find out. I'm never letting you go."

"After everything that's happened lately, I don't want you to."

"Good. There are millions of angels like me and only one of you."

My heart flutters, and again I'm in awe of how easy and *right* it feels to be with him. Despite our secrets and despite our differences, we keep coming back to moments like this—where everything is perfect. And it only exists because we're together.

No matter what happens next, no matter who tries to take me from him, I have to keep fighting. I have to fight for myself. For him. For us. I will not let anything take this from me.

With all the positivity flowing through me, I want the conversation to stay light and airy. I want to joke around, as we did when we went bowling. MJ was more human than I've seen him any other time we've been together. Maybe a bit of his mortal personality was coming through. I want to know more about *MJ* instead of Protector MJ.

"Hmm … " I begin. "A million MJs. I like the sound of that."

I feel his cheek move against the top of my head. "I don't know." His voice lightens, and I suspect he's smiling. "I'm not sure I could share you, even with someone extremely good-looking."

I snort.

"I hope that was in reaction to my possessiveness and not a critique of my looks."

"Actually, it *was* about your looks. Specifically that 'extremely good-looking' is an inadequate modifier."

"Well, then. Someone's been paying attention in English class."

"Hardly. My friends all say you're 'hot,' but that's not good enough. I've been trying to come up with something better."

"And what have you come up with?"

"I've found many words that I thought were perfect, then I'd see you again and realize they didn't fit. I finally

212    IGNITED

came to the conclusion that since you aren't technically mortal, no mortal word would ever work for you. It was a very freeing realization. Plus, why rack my brains for words to describe you when it's way more fun to just sit back and admire the pretty?"

"The *pretty*?"

I throw my arms around his neck. "My pretty."

"Um, let's not call me that around Alexander. That would make for a very long eternity."

I smirk, liking how they tease each other. "Deal. Where is he, anyway? And Tamitha?"

He tenses against me, and his essence flowing through me suddenly jerks. "I'm not sure. Hang on."

MJ pulls back his essence and lets me go. I lean against the railing, watching him. His eyes are closed, and his face is relaxed.

"What are you doing?" I ask.

"I'm reaching out to Alexander."

"What does that mean?"

The corners of his mouth twitch as he fights a smile. "I'm using something we call Cerebrallink to search out his essence and communicate with him."

So they can communicate nonverbally with each other? Maybe that explains how Damien talked to Elizabeth in her mind. And this must have been what Alexander was doing in the parking lot after school before my "surprise."

All of a sudden, MJ stiffens as if a jolt of electricity went through him. He opens his eyes, and they're darker. A ridge appears between his brows.

I reach out for him, placing my hand on his arm. "MJ, what's wrong? What did Alexander say?"

He frowns before placing a swift kiss on my forehead. "Let's get you home. Your parents will be making dinner soon."

I cross my arms. "Tell me what he said," I demand.

He rubs his neck and meets my gaze. We stay there, silently staring at each other.

Then he says, "The demon serial killer claimed another victim today."

# CHAPTER 30
# Maddy

SEEING MJ SO UPSET HAS ME ACHING TO COMFORT him. I place my hand in his, and silently we walk back to my house.

When we turn the corner of my block, we both freeze on the sidewalk. In front of my house sit two black Suburbans.

Duane.

MJ's essence flows faster through our joined hands. He knows me well enough to soothe me even before my body can react to something upsetting like this. Still, essence or no essence, I'm consumed with figuring out why Uncle Duane would be here.

Apparently MJ is thinking the same thing. His eyes narrow, fixating on the vehicles.

The last time MJ and Duane were together, Duane told him to stay away from me. MJ listened for as long as either of us could stand, which was less than a day.

Duane has always been very protective of me, but it was more than that. He knows about MJ and Justin somehow. He also knows MJ is working the same serial killer case he and his FBI team are working. I believe that case is the reason behind his warning to MJ. I just hope Duane doesn't know the full extent of it—that the killer is actually a demon.

And I know there's no way in hell I'll let Duane send MJ or the other angels away.

"Come on," I say, tugging his arm. "Let's get this over with."

He pulls back, stopping me with ease. His free hand caresses my cheek, and I lean into his touch.

"I think I should be in the Veil of Shadows. At least until we figure out why he's here."

I picture walking into the house to face everything alone. It would certainly prevent a testosterone showdown between Duane and MJ and their differing opinions on my safety.

But I don't *want* to go in there alone. I'm not afraid, but I am nervous. I'm about to do something I've never done before. I'm introducing my boyfriend to my extended family. It's a huge step for me. The other night at dinner, my parents got a glimpse of how serious we are. But introducing him to Duane as more than my friend is on a whole other level. An it's-a-good-thing-he's-already-dead-'cuz-Duane-might-kill-him level.

I wrap my free arm around his waist and rest my head on his chest, right where his silent heart sits.

"You're coming with me, MJ. You're in my life now, and I'm not ashamed of that. Sooner or later, Duane will find out about us, and I'd rather it come from us. This way, he'll know just how important you are to me."

"Maddy, I don't know if—"

"You're mine. No one can send you away from me ever again, and that includes my family."

I reach up, stroking his cheek as he did mine.

His eyes close, and I hear a sound like the kind Hannah makes when she takes that first bite of her favorite triple-chocolate-brownie ice cream. When his eyes reopen, there is this look to them, as if he wants to kiss me or do something *else*. My stomach flips while muscles clench all over my body.

"I don't want anything to take you from me either," he says in a throaty voice. He stares down at me, then the pain and fear return to his eyes.

I know what he's feeling. The fear I felt when Duane first sent MJ away was crippling, and I barely knew MJ then. What MJ is going through is worse. I've been taken from him three times now. I can't imagine how helpless he feels. And now Duane is here, and neither of us knows why.

I throw my arms tighter around him, wanting to erase the space between us. "I'm sorry, MJ. I wish I could stop what's happening to me and stay with you always."

He inhales sharply at my words, then smiles and leans back. "I have something for you."

Before I can speak, one of his hands falls away from my back. A moment later, it curls around my right wrist, attaching something thin and cool.

I pull my wrist closer, inspecting the foreign object. It's a bracelet with multicolored stones that reflect the evening sunlight. There are twelve of them, each one a different shape and color. They're birthstones. Topaz, emerald, ruby, sapphire—and my heart stops at the sight of the clear gem.

"These are fake, right?"

He shakes his head.

All of the stones are huge. They're bigger than any-thing in my mother's jewelry collection, and she's been married forever. They're almost as big as the stones on the necklace Damien gave Elizabeth. The biggest is a flawless, brilliantly clear diamond.

"I know your birthday isn't for another week, but I want to give this to you now. I had this created for you while I was in Immortal City."

Not only are the stones real, but they're from *Heaven*.

"A-are there a lot of these up … there?"

"No. Yours is the only one in existence."

"Why?" I ask. "Why are you giving me this?"

"I want to give it to you before something else happens."

He smiles, but there's something behind his expression. It's that same fear I saw in his eyes a moment ago. I can't help but think there's more to this gift than he's telling me.

I stare down at the bracelet. It's heavy, as if it were pushing my arm to the sidewalk. It's heavy with the weight of what it means to him, me, us, my family, and the world.

Walking into the house holding his hand was going to be a huge step. But this—accepting and wearing such an elaborate, priceless gift from him? This goes beyond dating and getting to know each other. This makes it *real*. Finite. And not just to me, but the world too. I'm not ready for this, to be so far committed in our relationship that I'm now wearing one-of-a-kind jewelry from Heaven.

I haven't even said "I love you" yet.

"Do you like it?" he asks.

I hate it, but I can't tell him that. I hate how confused it makes me. I hate that it would hurt him if I told him the truth. And I hate that it represents the one thing I can't give him—love.

Everything about this damn bracelet screams out how much he loves me. Yet I can't show him or even say those three little words. This bracelet is nothing but a physical reminder that I don't deserve him.

"MJ …" I say. "I don't know if I'm ready for this. It's too fast. Too soon. I—I can't." I shake my head. "You have to just give me more time."

"Please wear it," he begs. "Do it for me."

Muscles tighten all over my body and my stomach rolls, threatening to vomit. I feel his eyes on me. He isn't touching me, and that's a blessing. That way he won't know how truly terrified I am of the priceless white-gold-and-gemstone bracelet. Terrified of all it symbolizes.

A sudden gust of wind blows stray hairs in my face, disrupting my trance-like stare at my now-unfamiliar wrist. With great effort, I look up. The sky is a wall of gray. Power lines whip through the air, enslaved to a turbulent storm. Trees groan as the wind bends them so far over, their branches touch the ground. Shingles flap on rooftops, as if clinging to the houses for dear life.

I turn to MJ, but he looks away, turning his face into the wind. He knows what this is—this is my storm. And it speaks louder than words.

I close my eyes and concentrate on my breathing. I focus on silencing the fear that caused this storm inside and out. I shove those overwhelming emotions down into a place so dark even MJ won't run across them when we touch.

When I reopen my eyes, the breeze is gone, trees are still. No sound other than my breath can be heard. It's as if the world stopped. MJ still won't meet my eyes.

laurie wetzel

I don't want to hurt MJ. But I can't accept this. I need more time to figure out a way to give it back without breaking his heart.

I grab his hand, start walking toward the house, and prepare to meet our next challenge—together.

# CHAPTER 31

# MJ

I THOUGHT SHE WAS GOING TO CREATE ANOTHER tornado—the wind was strong enough. Animals scurried for cover. Trees groaned, helpless as the wind bent them to its liking. Then just as quickly as it started, the world fell silent.

It's mystifying and frightening that she holds this much power, especially because it's effortless for her. If she keeps doing things like this, Mankato will be swarming with enemies from both sides in a matter of days. Like it or not, she needs to wear the Segrego bracelet—it's our only warning against a demon attack.

Without saying a word, we walk up to her house. Maddy's emotions are just as quiet as the space around us. She's buried them. I know I gave her some tips about what to do when her emotions affect the weather. But I never meant for her to use those tips to hide her emotions from me.

We need to talk. So much has happened, and she can't keep it all inside. But there isn't time right now. Once we deal with the Shadowwalker, I'll figure out a way to get her to open up—before it becomes too much for her.

Right before I open the door, I take a breath—readying myself to face the Shadowwalker. As I exhale, we step inside. Laughter and a mouthwatering aroma of meat and spices greet us. My stomach rumbles, wanting to taste whatever it is, but I ignore it.

I hear his voice in the living room speaking to Maddy's father. We step into the room. He and five other FBI agents—three men and two women—are sitting with Maddy's father.

"Shouldn't be long," he's saying to her father. "A few weeks at the—Maddy! I was wondering where you were." He smiles, but it falls as he notices me beside her and her hand in mine.

Her father blinks, looking momentarily confused. I glare at the Shadowwalker, knowing he just compelled Maddy's father.

"You remember MJ," she says.

"I thought he left," he says through his clenched jaw.

"I didn't," I reply.

"They're dating," Maddy's father says.

Maddy leans into me, hiding her blushing cheeks. The Shadowwalker's gaze deepens, and I move closer to her on instinct. He rises from the couch where he's been reclining.

But before he can say or do anything else, Maddy's mother announces that dinner is ready.

HER MOTHER COOKED A POT ROAST. I CAN SEE WHY SHE teaches cooking classes and has written so many cookbooks. I don't think I've ever tasted anything so spectacular in my life. But as delicious as it is, it's hard to enjoy it after the news we were told. The Shadowwalker and his FBI team are here in Mankato because they're on a case—my case. They've asked Maddy's parents if they can stay with them, using "budget cuts" as an excuse. Her parents "agreed."

So now he's here, in her house, until the demon is caught.

He's sitting beside Maddy at the dinner table, reminiscing about all the fun they've had together. As great as it is to see her smiling again, I want to stab him with my fork and make it look like an accident.

I look over and catch his eye.

*I'm surprised to see you here, MJ,* he says in my mind.

*Likewise,* I bite back. *And if you're planning to tell me to stay away from her, don't waste your breath.*

*I don't like repeating myself,* he says. *Besides, you seem to be well on your own way out.*

*Explain,* I snap.

*I couldn't help notice Maddy's new accessory,* he says. *Specifically that she can't stop fidgeting with it.*

I gaze at her wrist. Her left hand tugs and twists at the bracelet.

*What's your point?* I ask him.

*It means she hates it and you won't be my problem for too much longer.*

I scoff, then grab Maddy's hand. It's partly to tick him off, but I admit it's also to stop her from touching the bracelet. Just as before, my essence finds her emotions quiet.

I understand his reasons for wanting to protect her. But after the time he spent with me in Immortal City, he should know I'm the best hope he's got.

*I'm not the enemy here,* I tell him.

*You're risking her life every second you're together,* he says. *So yes, you are.*

*And you're not?*

He glares at me. *You have no idea what I've done to keep her safe.*

*Enlighten me, then,* I demand. Then I decide to push it even further. *What have you, Ms. Morgan, and the other two members of your little group done for her?*

He stiffens. *How do you know about that?*

*I'm not saying another word until you prove that you and your little band of supernatural misfits aren't a danger to her.*

He slams his glass on the table, causing everyone to look at him. He makes a pitiful excuse about it slipping out of his hand. I smirk. I may not be able to get rid of him yet, but at least I can piss him off.

As everyone else returns to their dinner conversation, he lashes out at me. *How many demons have you come in contact with since you've been here? Or entities or lost souls? You know as well as I do that this place should be swarming with the paranormal, thanks to the Trifecta. But there's nothing.*

I'm unable to hide my surprise. *You're why this place is vacant?*

*Every so often, someone shows up, but we send them packing before they learn about her.*

Regardless of how I feel toward him, I'm grateful to hear this. It may be the only reason she stayed hidden this long. Still, I can't allow him to continue thinking he's done a perfect job.

*Yeah, well, there's one being you missed.*

*We tried to keep you from—*

*Not me!* I shout in his mind. *You missed an Influencer. Didn't Ms. Morgan tell you?*

He shakes his head. *You're bluffing.*

*Am I? Aren't you curious about why the Perfugae was here yesterday? Or why Maddy's ex, Ben, has gone missing? Or better yet, have you noticed the two Featherling markings on Maddy's right arm?*

His gaze drops to her arm, and he grimaces. Guilt floods his face as he realizes he didn't protect her.

*The Influencer tried to make her sign a Binding Agreement,* I say.

He snaps back into his chair. His guilt is instantly replaced by fury. With our connection, I can sense confusion and even betrayal.

It's becoming clear to me that he does truly care for Maddy. As for the motives driving the other members of his little group, it seems now I'm not the only one with doubts. This could work to my advantage. I could use Duane to find the other members of his group. When it comes to protecting Maddy, I will do whatever is necessary. Maybe he will too.

*Is she safe?* he asks.

*For now,* I reply. *Her blood didn't touch it. But the only way she'll remain safe is if you all stay the hell out of the way. As I said, I'm not going anywhere. Now you know a fraction of why.*

AFTER DINNER, I HELP CLEAR THE TABLE, ALONG WITH two ex-military FBI agents. They didn't identify themselves as such, but it's in their constantly roaming eyes and crew-cut hairstyles. Plus, their minds are very organized. Brian, the taller of the two, even has his drill sergeant's voice still in his mind, barking out his thoughts.

I search the minds of the three agents who are still in the dining room chatting with Maddy's parents. The male is the computer specialist. The brunette female is highly intelligent. The blonde female has a knack for reading people. She was with the Shadowwalker Sunday night while the other agents were out searching for Maddy.

As I'm loading the last plate into the dishwasher, Maddy comes up behind me. She's frowning, which makes her bottom lip stick out.

My essence pulses inside me, begging for me to touch her so it can ease whatever is troubling her. I take her hand in mine. Instantly my essence rushes in, finding fear and anxiousness. I'm not pleased to find them again so soon, but at least I found something this time.

"What's wrong?" I ask.

"Nothing," she says, rubbing the bracelet again. She opens her mouth, and words spill out in a jumble. "Duane wants to talk with me downstairs. I know how you feel about him, and I don't want to upset you … But at the same time, he's my uncle. It feels really strange to think I'd have to check with someone just to talk to him. I just wanted—"

I pull her to me, hugging her as I send more of my essence to calm her nerves. She shouldn't have to deal with this—she has too much on her plate as it is. The Shadowwalker is my problem. To her, he's family. She can't handle knowing the truth about him yet.

Somehow I'll have to make a truce with the Shadowwalker. Just until things settle down with Maddy.

Then I'll tell her the truth and let her decide what to do about it.

"If you're asking my permission to talk to your uncle," I begin, "you don't need it."

"No. That wasn't what I was trying to say." She pauses, chewing her lip for a moment. Then she stares up at me. She presses her lips firmly together. Her emerald eyes are darker—fiery. Whatever she's going to say next, she's set her mind on it.

"I'm asking you not to listen."

I step back, speechless by her request. She's right—I planned on listening from the Veil of Shadows. It's not that I don't trust her or that I want to invade her privacy. It's that I've nearly lost her three times now and I'm not sure if either of us would survive a fourth.

As greatly as I want to protect her, I can't bring myself to tell her no—not when she's looking at me like that. And I can't lie to her either—I can't go into the Veil if I say I won't. The only option is to honor her wishes.

I tuck a strand of hair behind her ear. "You have my word. I won't listen."

The Shadowwalker comes into the kitchen and looks expectantly at Maddy. She kisses my cheek, then follows him over to the basement door.

I link to him. *Don't tell her what you are. She isn't ready for that. I'm trusting you here. Break that, and I will end you.*

He opens the door. The guilt is back in his eyes. After a moment, he gives me a curt nod. They head downstairs together.

# CHAPTER 32
## Maddy

THE BASEMENT IS MOSTLY DAD'S AREA FOR HIS MUSIC— other than when Mom does laundry. Autographed memorabilia from acts the band opened for cover the walls. His bass guitar sits in a stand beside the theater system, which houses all his music equipment for practicing.

Duane and I sit at opposite ends of the plaid couch. He's a germophobe. Although it's never bothered me before, right now I wish I could hug him to let him know just how much I care for him.

Suitcases and boxes belonging to Duane and his agents are scattered everywhere. When Mom and Dad said he and the team would be staying here, I hoped it would be just for the night. But now I doubt it.

"So why are you really here?" I ask. It comes out harsher than I want, but after today, I just don't have the patience to tiptoe.

He smirks. It's the first time he's shown any expression other than sadness since midway through dinner.

"Didn't buy the budget cuts story?"

I chuckle. "Not a chance. So ..."

His smirk vanishes. His intelligent, brown eyes rake me over.

"All right," he says. "Tell me the difference between a mass murder and a serial killer."

The words flow off my tongue, having memorized them. "A mass murder kills a lot of people, usually at one time. A serial killer kills at least three people, but with some time in between the victims."

He's drilled the definitions into my head so often, I remember it better than my locker combination. Each camping trip, he brings along several files and makes me profile them. The better I do, the easier he will go on me the next day during training. After all the years, I've gotten the hang of it now.

"Good," he says. "When we talked on Saturday, do you remember me mentioning my current case?"

I sit up straighter. His case is MJ's case. When we talked that morning, he warned me to be cautious of strangers.

"I remember. What about it?"

"I think in this situation, it would be easier if I showed you." He stands and waits for me to do the same. "There's something in the guest room you need to see."

He heads for the room, but I don't follow.

"Wait," I say.

He stills, his back to me. "What?"

"There's something I need to ask. You know things— things about MJ. How?"

Silence is his only reply. My head swirls, trying to understand why he's hesitating. He's always told me the truth—never sheltered me from anything. Whatever it is, it must be huge.

He finally turns, staring at the carpet.

Dread pools in my stomach.

Then he looks up, tears threatening to spill. "I'm dead, Maddy."

Suddenly I feel as if I've been transplanted to another country. I know he just said something to me, but his words won't register. They're foreign.

"Shut up." The words force out with my exhale. "Just … shut up. You're not … you can't be. I *know* you. I—"

"I died during the Second World War," he interrupts. "I was given the option to join the Protectors. I still had some fight left in me, so I agreed."

I back away, shaking my head and plugging my ears like a child. Duane waits, watching me. I know the look on his face. It's the same look he wore when he told me I was adopted.

He's telling the truth.

*He's the same as MJ.* MJ knew, the whole time, and he kept it from me.

I slowly remove my hands from my ears as tears slide down my cheeks.

"Protecting people came naturally," Duane continues. "It didn't take long before I received my first solo assignment. My Charge was a few years older than you. She was being tormented by a Marer—a demon who communicates with its victims through nightmares. It tortured her with images of her family and friends dying. Every time she closed her eyes, she saw them."

He frowns. "She was losing her grip on reality and considering taking her life. I banished the demon to the City of the Damned, but I couldn't bring myself to return to Immortal City as I was ordered.

"My mortal upbringing was still fresh in my mind, and I wanted to look after her. I could—and did—compel her mind to forget what happened to her. But you can't compel a heart. The pain of continually watching her loved ones die, even if in dreams, left its mark on her. I feared what she would do in my absence. So I stayed until she was well. During that time, she fell in love with me."

Inside, I feel as if every memory, every experience, is being sliced into a million pieces. I'm too numb to feel the pain, but I know I'm bleeding.

"She talked of marriage and having a family. Marriage is one thing, but a family—that was something I couldn't fake, even if I wanted to."

He pauses long enough so I look at him. He meets my gaze.

"Angels and demons can't have families. We're dead, and dead things can't make life. Not anymore, at least."

Thunder rumbles and my legs wobble, threatening to give out. This goes beyond Duane. This is about *me*. I may be young and new to relationships, but I've always known I want to be a mother someday. I've known that I want to give my child the love my birth parents never gave me.

But no matter what kind of future I may have with MJ, he can't give me that.

"Do you want me to stop?" Duane asks.

I take a deep breath—burying my pain—then shake my head. As difficult as it is, I may not have another chance to hear the truth.

"I left her—my Charge—and tried to return to Immortal City. I couldn't. I had disobeyed my orders by staying here too long. I was an outcast, with an automatic sentence to the City of the Damned if caught. And they're especially cruel to former angels down there."

I fight a shudder, remembering the screams of torture I've heard.

"I went into hiding, drifting along for many years. Occasionally I came across others who were stuck here like me. They showed me how to stay hidden from both sides. I've been fairly successful … until this week. But I want you to know something, Maddy. I will gladly take on any risk, including challenging my former leader"—he glances up the stairs—"to protect you."

I turn, thinking it means someone is coming downstairs. The door is closed. I let out a relieved breath. I was worried it was MJ.

My heart flinches as suddenly the pieces fall into place. Duane was a Protector.

MJ was Duane's leader.

I think back to every interaction between them. MJ wasn't uncomfortable or afraid of him because he was my uncle and an FBI agent. MJ *hates* him because he's an outcast angel.

After another minute of silence, Duane continues. "I tried to make the most of my life as an outcast. I eventually decided to date again as a way to blend in. I kept low-key jobs and moved every couple of years. That changed when I met you."

I turn away, not wanting to look at him.

"I'd been dating your aunt Deb for a few months when you came into my life," he says. "I heard your cries even before the doorbell rang. I got to the door first, but the street was empty. And there you were, crying in the rain on Dean and Marie's steps. I picked you up, and instantly I knew you weren't a normal baby. A flood of emotions rushed into me, nearly bringing me to my knees. Everything I'd forgotten, everything I'd lost, came back. I tried to figure out why, but none of my abilities worked—"

"I know about my *abilities*," I cut in.

I hug myself, rubbing my arms, and I feel something cold on my wrist. I look down at the rainbow-gem bracelet. As upset as I am to learn—again—that MJ has kept information from me, I suddenly wish he were here. I don't want to face this alone.

"I had to keep you close," Duane says. "I planted thoughts in Dean's and Marie's minds of adopting you. I actually didn't need to do much—they loved you the moment they held you. I married Deb so I could stay close to you—watch over you. I even got a job with the FBI to make sure you stayed off everyone's radar."

I keep my head turned, but I ask, "Whose radar?"

"Mortals' and immortals'. As I said, everyone's."

"So am I supposed to thank you, then?"

"You don't owe me anything, Maddy. We only want to keep you safe."

At that, I turn. "Who's 'we'?"

His eye twitches. "There are others."

"Who?" I press.

He looks away. "I'm sorry, Maddy. But that's something I cannot tell you."

"So you're keeping me in the dark too? But I guess you always have, haven't you?"

"I didn't want to keep my secret from you," he says. "But when you were a baby, you felt my essence, just as you do now with MJ. You were addicted to it for a while. I knew one day you'd be old enough to ask why a hug or touch from me was different than one from someone else. That's why I hid behind the lie of being a germophobe all these years—so I wouldn't ever touch you again."

Hundreds of responses gather on my tongue, fighting to be said. I want to lash out at him. I want to demand he leave the house, leave my family, and never return. But it would be a waste. He wouldn't leave.

I stare into his once-familiar brown eyes. "I *trusted* you."

"Everything I've done was to protect you." He shakes his head. "Despite my best efforts, though, it wasn't enough. I should have stopped him. The others should have told me he was here."

I feel a strange desire to laugh. After all that, he stills wants to act like an uncle who's concerned about his niece's boyfriend.

"MJ's good. He won't hurt—"

"I mean the demon responsible for the markings on your arm."

My left hand moves, covering them. Still the memories creep back. No matter what I do or how much time passes, there will always be a part of me that never escaped that house. "It wasn't your fault."

"It was. But it's one mistake I will not make again. Which brings me back to the original reason for our discussion." He nods to the guest bedroom. "Come with me."

I take a step back.

His frown deepens. "You have nothing to fear from me, Maddy."

I hold myself tighter as he walks into the bedroom. I glance at the stairs. Somewhere up there, MJ is waiting for me. We've already been apart for so long today. But every time we are, I discover more and more information MJ hasn't told me.

My gaze turns to the guest bedroom door. In that room lies secrets about Duane, about MJ, about Justin. Perhaps even about me. I'm not sure I'm ready to hear them, but I don't think I have a choice now.

Knowing MJ kept the truth about Duane from me has me questioning everything. And like it or not, Duane is the only one who won't protect me from the truth.

I have to go in there.

# CHAPTER 33

# MJ

THE INSTANT MADDY GOES DOWN TO THE BASEMENT with *him*, I walk outside and contact Alexander.

*Are you and Tamitha able to return?*

He doesn't answer, though I know we're connected.

*Alexander, answer—*

*I'm here,* he softly replies.

My chest tightens. Something is wrong. I've felt it nagging in my bones. I'm not sure what it is, but I know it's about Maddy.

*Are you able to report?* I ask.

*Yes. Upon arriving—*

*No,* I interrupt. *Come here and do it. Send Tamitha to relieve Sissy.*

*Understood.*

Giving the report through Cerebrallink would be easier. But I need Alexander here in case my worst fears are confirmed.

The sky darkens.

I stand on the sidewalk and clear my mind, listening for Maddy's heartbeat. It's beating at a slightly faster rate.

I know her rhythms well enough to understand she's upset over something.

I clench my jaw, hating that she asked me not to listen. I want to. Badly. But I will respect her wishes so long as the Shadowwalker doesn't endanger her further.

Alexander appears before me—shoulders sagging, staring at the ground.

"Tell me how it happened," I say. I don't normally dig into the specifics of how a demon kills, but with Maddy experiencing that vision, I need to know.

He takes a deep, shaky breath.

Because we're not living beings, we don't need to breathe as mortals do, but we mimic the motions. So for Alexander to take such a breath now, it must be a sign of how difficult his news is. It's also a sign of how much Maddy has changed us.

He looks up, his brown eyes strained and filled with emotions we're only beginning to understand.

"She was right," he whispers. "Everything Maddy said happened. The Atwood family was at the Colorado Convention Center, minutes away from Mr. Atwood speaking at the campaign rally. Lauren was in a dressing room that caught fire."

My heart sinks for the family's loss; Protector Gary, who failed; and the girls remaining on the demon's list. But mostly for Maddy and what this means for us.

"Where was Protector Gary?" I ask.

With Mr. Atwood being a political figure seen by so many mortals on a daily basis, Gary was on a strict no-contact detail. It would be too complex to compel that many memories. Instead, he protected Lauren from the Veil of Shadows. She had no knowledge of him or the danger she faced.

"He discovered a Morpher demon in the crowd and thought it might be the killer," Alexander says. "He gave chase but lost him several miles away in a supermarket. Tamitha and I arrived just as he returned."

Morpher demons are ranked highest in the Caste. There aren't many of them, but they tend to be the most deadly. Instead of possessing someone, they alter their essence, body, and voice to become that person. The impersonations can even fool Guardians. Mortals in powerful positions are common targets for them. They kill their targets—it's difficult to con people into thinking you're John Doe when the real John Doe could walk right into the same room. It's very possible that Mr. Atwood would have been killed tonight had it not been for this tragic event.

A raindrop lands on my arm, then another on my forehead. I'm torn between running to the basement to wipe away her tears and remaining here with Alexander to learn about her vision.

"There's more," Alexander says.

I stare at the sky, waiting for it to burst open and unleash her pain, but it doesn't. The sprinkles stop. Whatever they're discussing, she can handle it.

I turn back to him and decide to stay, giving Maddy the space she needs.

"We searched the room and found the fire's point of origin, but we couldn't determine what ignited the blaze. It's as if the room just burst into flames."

"So the fire was designed to kill Lauren."

"Yes. About that … according to the witness statements, the accident happened at the exact time Maddy was in the vision."

"What are you saying?"

"Maddy was inside Lauren when she died."

My knees shake. I decide to lower myself to a crouch before I collapse outright.

Thunder rumbles around us. Other than checking for her heartbeat, I do nothing.

I can't go to her. I'm not ready to hide my fears.

"Is she okay?" he asks, looking up at the sky.

My shoulders lift in a defeated shrug. Given her reactions, I can guess what's happening.

"He's telling her about himself." My voice is flat. Despondent. Dead.

It's one thing I forbade him to do, so of course he would do it. And now she knows I hid *this* from her too. How could I tell her, though? It's not my truth to tell. More importantly, I knew it would break her heart.

How many times must I watch her suffer before I break?

"Do you mean he's telling her he's a Shadowwalker? Is that wise?" Alexander asks.

"It'll shatter her trust in him—and maybe what little trust she has in me."

He sighs, then I feel his hand on my shoulder. "I'm sorry."

I huff. "Maddy nearly burned to death inside a vision of a victim of the demon serial killer. Something like this is refreshing. I can fix this. With time, she *will* trust me again. I just need to find a way to guarantee we get that time."

"I'll help. Tamitha and Sissy will too."

We watch the sky in silence as more of her tears fall as rain and her fears echo out in thunder. Just when I think it's over and she's okay, it starts up again.

"This cannot all be from him revealing himself," I say, voicing my thoughts. "What else is he telling her?"

"Whatever it is," Alexander says, "I'll help you with that too. I've been itching to send him to Hell."

I grin and stand beside him. "Me too."

Alexander quiets for a moment, then says, "Everything keeps circling around to Maddy. We need to figure out why."

I look at him, feeling lighter as hope fills me. With their help, I can protect her. "I don't know where to start."

"Simple. We start with what we know. We start with the demon called Damien."

# CHAPTER 34

# Maddy

ONCE I STEP INTO THE ROOM IN THE BASEMENT WITH Duane, all breath leaves me. The gray walls are hidden behind massive whiteboards littered with photos and notes in black marker. I count twelve boards in all, and they are grouped in various sets.

This must be his case about the serial killer—whom I now assume he knows full well is a demon.

I move closer to the first one. Some pictures show a horrible car accident. Other photos are happy snapshots of a family—who I assume were the accident victims. Most of the photos, though, are of one victim, a teenage girl. She was a pretty brunette with light green eyes. From the snapshots, I see she played the violin, went to science fairs, and ran track.

"That's Melany Zimmerman," Duane says. "She died in a motor-vehicle accident near Seattle, Washington. Her family's car was struck by a minivan in January, resulting in the death of four people."

I'm immediately confused. Car accidents aren't linked to serial killers.

He moves to the next board. The photos cause my stomach to flip. There's a burned-down building, and many bodies are charred. The snapshots again focus on one subject: a green-eyed brunette who was into lacrosse, played drums, and had awards for creative writing.

"This is Krystle Abermann. She died in a fire at Seattle Grace Hospital along with eighty-two other people. That occurred in March."

Two accidents, both in Seattle, but this one had a massive death toll.

He moves to the third board. My stomach tightens further at more pictures of fire victims. Again, one person has the most snapshots—a green-eyed, brunette female active in sports, music, and academics.

It's obvious these girls are the killer's preferred target, though many other people die along with them.

"This is Kali Fredrickson," Duane says, interrupting my thoughts. "She and eight other victims died in a fire at a Georgia foster home in May."

"Georgia?" I ask as a flag goes up in my mind. Serial killers tend to be creatures of habit. Almost all of them follow some pattern, whether it's weapon, kill zone, dumping ground, whatever. This guy kills by both car accidents and fires, doesn't seem to care how many innocent victims die along with the target, and now he's jumping states. Aside from the pattern of the main victims, it doesn't even seem like the same killer.

"Now you see what I'm up against."

He shuffles to the next set of three, which looks nearly identical to the previous set. Maybe there is a pattern after all.

"This is Jamie Miller. Her family's vehicle was involved in a ten-car pileup in Arkansas. A total of twenty-nine people died on the scene."

My head is a whirl, trying to sort out the connections.

I follow him to the fifth board, suppressing the urge to either cry or puke.

"This is Linsey Cooper. Her home in Oklahoma caught fire during a party, claiming the lives of sixteen people. That was July."

A tear slides down my cheek as we move to the sixth board. So many people suffered at the hands of this monster.

"This is Brandy Kline. She and her boyfriend were killed in Louisiana in September when their bonfire some-how got out of control."

My feet feel heavy as we move to the seventh board, which is in the last set of two. This board is different. There are snapshots of only one person.

"This is Heather Waters. She was involved in a hit-and-run in Texas last week. She's what led to us making the connections. A deputy working the case noticed how similar she was to his deceased niece, Linsey Cooper from Oklahoma. He searched for other victims matching them, found all these cases, then called us.

"The car crashes had been previously written off as accidents. And the fires had been ruled as arson, even though the investigators couldn't pinpoint the source or the person or persons responsible. Those methods are atypical of serial killers. They're too impersonal. If not for Deputy Cooper, we never would have made the connection."

I take a moment to calm down enough to talk. This case, these boards—this is different than the files he's shown me over the years. Seeing everything displayed like this … it's realer. I can almost hear their screams.

He moves to the next board. The moment I see the first photo, I close my eyes and turn away. My knees are instantly weak, and I struggle to stand as he says what I already know.

"This is Lauren Atwood. She died in a fire this afternoon at her father's campaign rally."

I know. I was inside her when she died.

My knees give, and I crumble to the floor. Lauren, like all the others, was a green-eyed, brunette teenager.

My body trembles, and thunder rumbles outside. Immediately I realize I need to get a grip on my reactions, or MJ will hear the thunder and rush down here. I need to know more.

It takes several deep breaths to calm my nerves enough to silence the sky and several more to stop the shaking. When I open my eyes again, Duane's kneeling before me. He doesn't say a word. His sharp brown eyes watch me.

I look past him, over his shoulder to the south-facing wall. There are four more boards. Those boards have snapshots and surveillance-type photos but no sickening crime scene images. Maybe they are potential targets.

"Have you noticed the killer's pattern yet?" Duane asks. "Car crash. Fire. Fire. Car crash. Fire. Fire. Car crash. Fire." He points to board nine. "The next victim will undoubtedly die by fire."

My body convulses and my calves burn, remembering Lauren's death.

I scan these final four boards; the last causes another jolt of pain to rush through me. It's Amber.

Only three girls now sit between Amber and a demon.

"What else aren't you telling me about this demon?" I ask, my voice quietly escaping my mouth.

"You're a smart girl, Madison." He nods. "It is a demon. MJ must have told you that's why he's in town to protect Amber."

Now I understand: Duane warned MJ to stay away from me because the demon coming for Amber might mix us up and kill me by mistake.

My insides are being squeezed by fear. It's hard to breathe. MJ knows the demon has killed all these girls—plus countless other people in the wake. How could he keep *so much* from me?

"Each of these girls was born on the same day," Duane says in my silence. "Do you want to guess what day?"

I shrug—but my breath races.

"They all turn seventeen on Halloween." Still kneeling in front of me, he leans in closer. "But their records aren't very accurate, so it's hard to be sure if the date is correct. That tends to be the case with *adoptions*."

I look at the photos again. Their faces morph into mine with our identical features. And we're all adopted. We have the same birthdate. The same talents. It's as if we were the same person.

I could be girl number thirteen.

Then I remember what Amber said in the office Tuesday about her parents.

I barely recognize my voice as I ask, "What happened to their birth parents?"

He lets out a long exhale. "The birth parents of all twelve girls died the day the girls were born."

My heart stutters. If all their parents are dead, are mine too?

"Do you know"—I pause, taking a breath—"about my birth parents?"

He doesn't answer. He's staring down at me with pain in his eyes.

He knows.

"Please, tell me."

He crouches down, placing a hand on my shoulder. His essence rushes in, trying to comfort me. But how can it? His touch is that of a stranger.

"I will tell you. But I must warn you—it will be difficult to hear."

My insides quiver. With everything he's ever told me, he's never offered a caution before. Not even before showing me the most graphic crime photos.

It must mean my birth parents met some tragic end. I don't want to know that. I'd rather imagine they were happy somewhere, living a great life—even if it were without me. But still, I *have* to know. Their death will be the first and only thing I know about them.

I take a moment to silence my emotions and prepare myself. Once everything calms, I meet his gaze and nod.

He stands, taking his essence with him, then moves to stand beside the first board belonging to Melany Zimmerman.

Duane looks at me carefully. "Did MJ tell you why the demon is targeting these specific girls?" He says it slowly, gauging my response.

I barely register my head shaking in reply.

"Perhaps that means he just didn't want to scare you," he says. "But hopefully, it means MJ—and everyone in Immortal City—hasn't made the connection."

"I don't want to know about a connection. Or MJ's case. I want to know about my birth parents."

"Just listen, Maddy. Seventeen years ago, on Halloween, there was a report of a motor-vehicle accident where a woman lost control of her minivan on Mount Rainier and crashed into the side of a jeep. Sound familiar?"

He taps Melany's photo, hinting at the connection.

My throat tightens, already nervous about where he's going with this.

"Both vehicles burst into flames. By the time rescue workers arrived, there was nothing left but charred remains. The driver of the minivan was identified, but the other wasn't. Next to the scene, the police found a newborn baby girl. She was somehow born shortly after the accident, before the woman driving the jeep died and before anyone came across the accident. The mother was still in the vehicle, though. No one could figure out how the baby was beside the wreckage. The baby was taken to Seattle Grace and surprisingly found to be in perfect condition. Seattle Grace is the same hospital Krystle died in this year," he says as he moves to Krystle's photo.

I try to swallow but can't.

"The day after the baby arrived, a fire started in the hospital nursery. It claimed the lives of thirty people, including an unknown baby girl. That was November first. November third, you showed up on Marie and Dean's doorstep in Georgia. They called the police and child services. The police searched multiple databases for any missing baby reports, but they came up empty. After a quick stay at the hospital, you were placed in a foster home."

The dots are starting to connect, but I don't want them to. I want him to stop talking.

He moves on to Kali's photos. "The foster home caught fire November twenty-first, the day Dean and Marie adopted you. Thirteen people perished—four ladies who ran it, and the remaining nine were children. According to the police report, one of the deceased was a three-week-old baby girl. The house was rebuilt, but it caught fire again this year, killing Kali and eight others."

He waits for me.

My fingers rub on my jeans, wiping away the sweat. Then I let out a breath.

"I'm the baby, aren't I?"

He frowns. His brown eyes fill with despair.

I know what he's going to say.

I should have died in the fire at the foster home.

I should have died in the fire at the hospital.

I should have died in the car crash—either before or after I was born.

*Born ...*

I sob into my shoulder as it suddenly hits me. My birth mother is dead. She was the unknown driver of the jeep.

"I'm sorry, Maddy."

Pain tears through my heart, shredding it to pieces. A loud moan comes from outside, as if the wind is grieving the loss too.

"What about my father?"

"He is dead too, though I don't know the specifics."

My nails dig into my palms as I tighten my fists. I try to focus on the physical pain to block out all emotions.

"The others in my group found you," he softly says, "and together we've kept you hidden from the world."

The room blurs as tears well up. "Why? Why did you do all this for me and not them? I'm just girl thirteen."

Duane looks at me with an intensity I've never seen. "You are not 'girl thirteen.' The demon is hunting *you*, Maddy. You are the real target."

I clamp my eyes shut and lean my head into my shoulder, trying not to make a sound. Trying to keep it together so MJ won't rush down here. I push it all someplace far and deep—but there's just so much. I don't know how much longer I can hold it back.

He places a hand on my shoulder, sending his essence into me again. I stare at his hand. He could have walked away in the beginning—gone on living as he had. Instead he changed his whole life, just to keep me safe.

He lets go, taking his essence with him, and moves back to the boards lining the wall. "We moved you around a lot in the beginning as a precaution."

I grimace, thinking about everything he and these "others" have done and everything my family has endured—for me.

He continues down the line, stopping at each photo. "You lived in Georgia, then Arkansas, Oklahoma, Louisiana, Texas, Colorado." He points to girls three through eight. "Then Illinois, Wisconsin, Nebraska," he continues, pointing to the three girls between Lauren and Amber. "The girls lived in your old houses."

"How is that possible?" I ask. "How could an adopted girl who looks exactly like me, with the same exact birthday and talents, just happen to live in each of my old houses?"

Duane doesn't blink. "Sacrifices had to be made to protect you."

*Sacrifices …*

I don't blink either, but it's because I'm too shocked. "Are you saying you put them in my old homes knowing it would get them killed?"

He crouches in front of me again. "I knew it was a possibility, yes. I didn't like it, but the others assured me it was necessary to keep you safe. And now that the demon is hunting you, I agree with them."

I lean away from him. "How could you say that? How could you *even* think that?"

"We needed decoys to give us time to hide you from the demon. I have a feeling that if he kills all twelve girls and realizes none of them are you, he will rip apart the earth looking for you. And in turn, we would rip apart the earth to keep you safe."

"No," I say, shaking my head. "This is crazy."

"So is a girl who restores emotions in the dead and whose emotions affect the weather."

My jaw drops. "You know about that too?"

"Maddy, Georgia nearly flooded the few weeks you lived there. Of course I noticed. I made sure no one else did, though."

"So even as a baby, I was a freak."

"You're not a freak, Maddy. You're gifted. Powerful. And I believe that's why the demon wants you."

Thunder rumbles again. The walls vibrate from the force. I try to contain my emotions, but the battle … it's too much. I stare at the bedroom doorway, waiting for MJ to race through it. He doesn't. Where is he?

My abilities—the abilities I never wanted—are a curse.

I raise my eyes, trying to stop my tears, but all I see are their faces—the faces of the girls dying for me. The bodies.

I close my eyes. The darkness—I see it. I see the car crash that killed my mother. Was that even an "accident"? Was her death my fault?

I begin to stand, shaking from the pressure building inside me. My head turns from side to side, looking for escape as if I were a caged animal.

"Where are you going, Maddy?"

"I—can't—be—here," I say through my pain and guilt.

"I can take you someplace else." He reaches for me.

I twitch, not wanting him to touch me. I don't want to feel his essence. I don't want to be reminded of his lies.

Only one thing can help me now. MJ. His arms are exactly where I want to be. I need to tell him everything.

I take a step to leave the room.

Duane moves in front of me, blocking me. He knows exactly where I'm headed and why.

"If you won't let me help you, fine. But MJ can't either."

"Yes, he can." I look for a way around him.

"No, he can't, Maddy. Listen. Everything we've done, everything they've sacrificed"—he points to the boards—"has been to keep you a secret. Keep you safe."

"I didn't ask you to do this. I don't want you to."

"This was set in motion the day you were found. When Dean and Marie adopted you, one of the 'others' I mentioned earlier posed as the case worker. He gave them a social security card and birth certificate for you. They're listed as your parents. He led them to believe that was all they would ever need. You were theirs, and no mortals would ever question it. In case any supernatural beings were to ever question it, he erased your parents' memories of adopting you, only allowing them to discuss it with you when no one else was around. He of course never filed any adoption paperwork with the government. As far as the government knows, you are not adopted. That's why you're not on the FBI's list as a potential target."

My head spins. The only reason the demon—and MJ—doesn't know who I am is because some supernatural being didn't file my adoption paperwork.

Duane's eyes bore into me. "Under no circumstances are you to tell MJ, or anyone else, you're adopted."

"I can't lie to him. It's his case. He needs to know. It can help him save the remaining gi—"

"You tell him, and it's *over*," Duane says with finality. "The demon will find you and kill you. Is that what you want?"

I hug myself. All I want is MJ. My feet shift.

"Plans are being made to get you out of here," Duane says. "That's why I'm really here, to keep you safe while the others finish preparing. It could be a day or a month—I'm not sure. But know this: if you tell *anyone* you're adopted or even hint at it, I will pull you out of here right then. You will never see your adoptive family—or MJ—again."

My eyes are wide.

"It's not a threat, Maddy," he says. "It's a promise because you must be protected." He sighs and moves to the side.

I take off.

I run from that room.

I run from him.

I run from the hundreds of innocent people dying for me.

I bound up the stairs, through the kitchen, and out the garage door in one flash. I come face to face with MJ. And when I see that tender way he looks at me—when I see the love I don't deserve—I run from him too.

Duane's right. MJ can never know the truth. If he knew that monster was killing everyone for me, he'd never forgive me.

# CHAPTER 35
## Maddy

I RUN BAREFOOT DOWN THE STREET, FIGHTING TO CATCH my breath and keep the darkness away. MJ and Alexander chase after me, but I don't stop until I've reached Hiniker Bridge.

The weight of my guilt catches up to me as I tumble to my knees. My body shakes as I heave uncontrollably over the water.

Everyone is dying because of me. Melany, Krystle, Kali, Jamie, Linsey, Brandy, Heather, and Lauren's deaths are all on my hands. Plus the 136 people who happened to be near them. There are four other girls on the list, including Amber. How many people will die with them?

But even before the girls, people were dying for me. My birth mother and the other woman from the car crash on Mount Rainier. The thirty-one people in the Seattle hospital nursery fire. The twelve people from the foster home in Georgia. Were those fires accidents, or were they *sacrifices* too?

I doubt all twelve girls' parents died randomly that same night either. All twenty-four of them are my fault.

My father too—though I don't know how he died.

And Ben … he's my fault too.

That's 217 people who have already died, and I can't even fathom how many more.

My stomach and throat burn. My body shakes. In my head, a voice from the darkness calls: *Monster. Murderer.* And I know it's true. That's why a demon is hunting me down. Evil recognizes evil.

I clamp my eyes shut, but all I see is them dying. I hear them screaming out in pain. I feel it. I feel their terror.

I press my palms over my eyes, trying to stop the tears.

Someone bends down beside me. I can tell from the way my skin begs to lean into him that it's MJ.

"Maddy," he says, his voice tender and sweet. "I'm sorry."

He's *sorry*.

His words echo inside me, circling around and around. But no matter how many revolutions they do, nothing changes. His words can't fix this, and they can't bring anyone back.

He reaches out to touch me—to take away my pain.

I flinch and lean closer to the railing. "Don't touch me. I don't trust myself not to send us somewhere. There's just … too much."

He retracts but only for a second. "Please, Maddy. Let me help you."

Again his voice is soft and sweet. It shouldn't be. If he knew what I'm responsible for, he would be repulsed by me.

The faces I saw and names I know flash in my mind.

"What are their names?" I hear myself ask.

"Whose names?"

He has the nerve to still keep me in the dark? I take a deep, raspy breath then turn to him.

That crease I like so much rests between his brows. Wide hazel eyes scan my face while his hands linger just shy of touching me. If he touches me, he'll take away my pain.

I don't deserve that, just as I don't deserve him.

"The three remaining targets between Lauren and Amber," I say. "Duane showed me the targets, but he didn't say their names."

His body shakes. His eyes shift to scarlet. "He told you *that*?"

In a flash, MJ's gone. In another flash, I hear him to my right.

"No! Let me go!"

I look over. Alexander is trying to hold MJ back as he struggles to break free.

"I *warned* him! He had *no right* to tell her!"

"I know," Alexander says, keeping his voice firm but calm. "But fighting him—"

Thunder booms and lightning streaks across the sky.

"Don't you dare touch Duane!" I shout with more conviction than I feel.

MJ stills, and even Alexander's head whips around to me.

Slowly, with more grace than I should have right now, I stand. I glare at MJ.

I count to three, letting my emotions calm just enough so I can be heard over the grumbles from the clouds above. Even after everything Duane said and did, I can't let MJ hurt him. Duane told me horrible things—things he knew I wouldn't like and would hurt me. He risked our relationship and told me the truth. But he gave me that respect and had that faith in me.

My eyes narrow even more. MJ promised no more secrets. Yet every day, I discover more he's keeping from me.

"You may not *like* that Duane told me, but I don't care. *You* should have told me. Instead you keep me in the dark about *everything*. I am so sick and tired of being drip-fed information from you—"

"Come on!" MJ shouts. "You do the exact same thing to me, and you know it."

I shake my head. "It's not the same. I haven't told you everything because it's either not my secret to tell or I'm not ready to talk about it. But you don't tell me things because you think I can't handle it."

I brush my hair from my face, fighting the wind—my wind. "Damn it, MJ! You go on and on about how I don't trust you. How can I when you don't have faith in me?"

The crimson vanishes from his eyes. "Maddy, I …"

He takes a step toward me, but I take a step back. "Don't."

He stands there for a moment, then his face calms. "I have faith in you, Maddy. I do. But I want to do everything in my power to keep you from getting hurt physically and emotionally. This has nothing to do with me being a Protector. I'm doing this because I am your boyfriend."

My insides tighten, and I hug myself.

Every time MJ has healed me or helped settle my emotions, I thought it was just a habit for him—part of his angelic side. I never considered he was doing it as my boyfriend.

"I know I'm messing everything up. I'm new at relationships too, remember?" he says. "But I'm *trying* because we're worth it. You're worth it."

The faces of the girls and the bystanders flash in my mind. I'm not *worth* that. They're all dying in my place.

I fight back tears. I fight back everything threatening to release. Then I push it down, shove it all away.

The sky falls silent. The wind disappears.

I feel nothing.

I stare at MJ. "You should have killed me at the fountain."

His face shows shock and pain while mine still shows nothing.

MJ takes another cautious step toward me. I glare at his hands, signaling that I still don't want to be touched.

He holds back, though I know he's struggling. "I don't understand why you would think *that*—let alone say it. What happened to the woman who fought death a few hours ago because she didn't want to leave me?"

Memories of Lauren resurface. I barely escaped, but she didn't. She wasn't the one who was supposed to die. None of them were.

"If you would have killed me, things would have been different," I reply.

"What *things*? Nothing is as important to me as you."

"And that's the problem!" I shout. The wind resumes, and the thunder awakens. "You put me in front of every-thing—in front of Amber and the other girls—but you have no idea who or *what* I am. You don't know the real me. And I certainly don't know the real you."

He looks away for just a moment, then those hazel eyes suck me back in. "You think I don't know you? I've *felt* your soul, Maddy. Many times. Your dreams are my desires. Your heartbeat is my life. I fell in love with you three nights ago as I watched you sleep in my arms right here on this bridge. And when I thought I lost you to that demon, I said it. I said it in my own language, even if you didn't understand it."

I can't move. I can't blink. My heart is pounding, demanding to be heard. And those beats are crying out to know more.

"*Ek ann þér.* I love you, Maddy."

*He said it.*

MJ loves me.

He loves me enough to risk his future for me. He loves me enough to walk away from centuries of being a Protector. But most importantly, he loves me enough to do the one thing I'm terrified of doing.

He says those words.

I unclench the fists I didn't realize were balled tight. He stares down at me. The pain in his eyes has me fighting the urge to throw myself into his arms and beg him to tell me everything will be okay.

But it won't be. Not for me and not for the other girls.

"Why did you have to say it now?" I ask, sadness clinging to each word.

"What?" He takes another step closer.

My heart trembles, acknowledging the truth—not even those words can change what's happening.

"I'm sorry, MJ. I can't do this."

He falls to his knees in front of me, breathing heavily. "Please no. Maddy, I love you. Don't do this."

I close my eyes, memorizing the sound of those words from his lips, knowing it's most likely the last time I'll ever hear them.

"Do you know what I was thinking before we went into my house?" I ask.

He shakes his head.

"For the first time, I was ready to bring a guy—you— home to meet my family. I wasn't scared. Despite everything that's happened, I was happy. You do that to me. You know more about me than anyone, and I want to tell you the rest." My fists clench again. "But this whole time I've been growing closer to you, you've kept your distance. You hid the fact that a demon is hunting down and killing girls who look *just like me*."

"You didn't need to know that," he says, climbing to his feet. "You didn't need to worry."

I throw my hands in the air as the sky erupts again— unleashing my rage. "Don't you get it? I'm the—"

The words won't leave my lips. It's as if they were glued there. No matter what I do, they won't come.

Then I remember why.

The masked demon compelled me. I *can't* tell MJ the truth. Plus, Duane says he'll take me away if I speak a word of being adopted. I just got my family back. I'm not ready to lose them. Not again.

Frustrated, I turn away and grip the railing.

MJ leans on the railing beside me. "There are hundreds of girls your age who fit that description. The demon is targeting a very specific, small group of them. You aren't part of that. I *know* you're not."

"You're not only lying to me—you're lying to yourself!" That much, at least, I can say.

"I'm not lying," he says. "I don't lie to you."

I scoff. "You looked into my eyes after the vision of Lauren. You knew who she was and what it meant. And you said *nothing*. None of you did," I say, shooting my glare in Alexander's direction. "Do you have any idea what it was like to see those photos down there and learn you hid all that from me?"

He opens his mouth, but I hold up my hand.

"No. I don't want to hear your excuses. I don't want to see you tonight—and I don't mean you can just watch me from the Veil of Shadows. I'm so done with all of this. I need normal right now."

Immediately I scowl at my own words. Normal is the one thing I can't be. I've never been normal, never will be. I realize that now more than ever.

"If you don't want me near you, I won't press it," he says, obviously struggling. "But I can't leave you alone. It isn't safe. Justin is still after you."

A maniacal laugh bursts out of me. "You still think Justin is my biggest problem?" I shake my head, wishing that were true. Justin may be evil and dangerous, but the monster that's hunting me makes Justin seem like nothing more than a nuisance.

"Fine," I say and shrug. "Send someone to watch me if you must. But have them stay hidden. As far as I'm concerned, you're all liars."

I walk past them, thankful neither one tries to stop me. So many emotions burst inside me I fear I might explode. I'm panting, trying to calm down, but it's no use.

As I reach the path, I hear them following behind me again. I bite my cheeks, trying to ignore them.

How long was he going to wait before telling me everything he knows about this demon and the targets? Were they all going to act as if nothing changed after Lauren? Just keep me in the dark?

If I had known … if I had figured it out sooner, maybe I could have stopped it.

I'm strong. I survived Justin, and with some training, I can survive this demon as well.

I stop and hear them stop too. I whip around to face them. They're maybe five feet away, though MJ is ahead of Alexander by just a few steps.

"I know why you don't like Duane," I begin. "He told me that too. But I want you to remember something. If it weren't for him and his support over the years, I never would have made it out of Justin's house. Duane has spent two weeks every summer teaching me how to protect myself. Because of him, I was able to break free from my restraints and get Hannah free from hers."

I raise my hand and point at him. "All *you've* done is taught me to be a coward. Do you want me to die? Do you want Justin to force me to sign that contract? Do you want me to be helpless just so you can come save me and fight my battles? Cause that's all your actions are showing so far."

He stands there silent while the sky echoes my frustrations.

I look up, focusing on the flashes of lightning and roars of thunder, synchronizing my breathing to them. Slowly, I tame them. But like my emotions, they're not gone.

"How could you think that?" he asks so quietly I can barely hear him. "I … You're everything to me. Everything I do is to keep you safe. I'm nothing without you."

I know he means it. It's in his voice, in his eyes filling with tears, and in his body that leans toward me—trying to close the distance that's never existed between us before now.

Can I be without him? Can I save those girls—and myself—on my own? I don't know. But if he refuses to help me, then I have to try on my own. I owe the girls that much—and more.

"I'm going home," I tell him. "Hopefully, tomorrow you'll come to your senses and start telling me the things I need to know."

"Maddy, please," he begs, stepping toward me.

I can't let him touch me. He can't know just how much he's hurt me and how unstable I am.

He reaches out for me. My eyes widen and my heart pounds.

"*No!*" I scream, releasing everything I've tried to hold back.

The sky erupts in deafening crashes of thunder and blinding flashes of lightning. The ground shakes. I'm thrown onto my side.

I lay in the grass, unable to hear anything but a high-pitched whining in my ears. I sit up enough to see a giant oak now across the path—right where MJ stood.

I call out for him, but with the ringing I can't tell if I'm whispering or yelling.

And I don't hear a reply.

I can't breathe. Please let him be okay. I may be angry and hurt, but I still love him.

I crawl to the fallen tree and grab onto a branch to pull myself up. As I clear the trunk, I see them.

MJ and Alexander are on their backs looking at the tree. With the way Alexander's hands are gripping MJ's shirt, I think he pulled him out of the way.

I scan over MJ, breathing again when I see he's unharmed. Alexander is fine too.

Their eyes shift to me. They both stare with creased brows and slack jaws. Alexander, I think, is in shock.

MJ's expression is similar, but there's something more to it. He shakes his head, slowly at first, then it gains speed.

He stands, but he's shaky. He takes a step back.

With that simple movement, the world falls out from underneath me.

He's afraid of me.

He looks at the tree, then at me. I follow his wide eyes, tracing the fallen tree back to where its splintered stump sits on the other side of the creek. It's blackened by something.

Lightning.

I did this. I snapped the tree, which fell where MJ stood.

I tried to hurt him.

# CHAPTER 36

## Maddy

MY HAND SHAKES AS I PLACE MJ'S BRACELET ON MY dresser, knowing we're over. I want to take it all back, but I can't. He will never forget what I said and what I tried to do.

Even though I'd worn the bracelet for only three hours, my bare wrist looks foreign without the jeweled symbol of his love.

It's stupid how gutted I feel. I should be scared or angry or bawling my eyes out while listening to Adele, but there's nothing. I'm numb. I have no desire to do anything.

Everything was perfect before MJ gave me the brace-let—or as perfect as it could be for us. Now everything is in shambles. This can't be happening. It doesn't feel real. This feels as if I were dreaming about some other version of me.

I shake my head. There *are* other versions of me. Twelve of them. And eight of them have been murdered. They died for me. And instead of vindicating them, I'm whining about breaking up with my otherworldly boy-friend I've dated for about two days.

Those girls should be my focus. I need to dedicate my time, strength, and energy to saving the four girls remaining. Duane and the "others" may be willing to sacrifice them, but I'm not.

I'm not *that* evil.

Someone knocks on my door.

Not trusting my voice, I walk over and slowly open it.

Duane stands in the hallway—one hand resting at his side, the other scratching his head.

I tense.

My mind races through everything I said with MJ, hoping Duane isn't going to take me away already.

"I'm sorry, Maddy. I know you need some time alone, but some detectives are here to speak with you. Now that you know what I am, I could send them away, if you wish."

My pain is shoved aside. He isn't here for that. I'm okay. But wait—what detectives?

"Why do detectives want to talk to me?"

He grimaces. "They're investigating Ben's 'disappearance.'"

I stumble, catching myself on the dresser next to the door. "What do I say to them? A demon killed Ben. Tons of people saw them together."

"Remember, the detectives and everyone else believe Ben is simply missing. Justin has been removed from everyone's minds. He will not come up. I'll be in the room with you. It'll be fine. I promise." He smiles, willing me to believe him.

I can't. Not yet. Not after how long he lied to me. I don't know how to believe anything anyone tells me right now.

Instead of answering, I head downstairs with him following close behind me.

Is this how it's going to be from now on—Duane monitoring my every move too?

The kitchen is packed with my parents, Duane's FBI agents, Anne in her police uniform, and two men dressed in suits who must be the detectives.

A Protector is probably in the Veil of Shadows too. Whoever MJ sent in his place.

Hell is watching too.

The gang's all here.

"Madison," Anne says.

Her face is hardened—as it usually is when she's working. But her eyes are sad. She's struggling so much more than Sunday night to distance herself personally so she can be professional.

"These are Detectives Baker and King. They've come up from Saint Petersburg, Florida. They'd like to ask you some questions, if that's okay."

I nod.

Mom leads us to the dining room. I sit between her and Dad. Under the table, they each clasp one of my hands.

That one simple motion was everything I didn't know I needed. I stare up at the light, fighting the urge to cry. Mom and Dad are here for me, no matter what. No one can take this moment from me. No matter what, right now, we're a family.

Anne sits at the head of the table. Duane takes a seat at the other end. His agents stand behind him. Detectives Baker and King sit across from me. Baker is younger and more slender than his counterpart. He holds a pen ready at a notepad.

King has to be close to retiring. From what I know of police work from Anne, I have no doubt he's seen some horrible things in his years on the force, yet he's watching me with kind eyes—much like those of an uncle.

My gaze flits to Duane, and a twinge lashes my heart. Even though he kept that huge of a secret from me, I'm not sure I can hate him. He's why I'm still alive. Everything he did—however twisted it was—was out of love for me.

Detective King clears his throat. "Madison," he begins, "could you tell us how you know Benjamin Wolters?"

I swallow, hoping my voice will steady. Mom squeezes my hand.

"He was my boyfriend."

The detectives glance at each other, then King asks, "What do you mean *was*?"

"We broke up Saturday."

King leans forward as his kind eyes brighten. "So you saw him Saturday?"

The hope in his eyes that he might, finally, have a lead to find Ben has me holding back a sob. No one will ever find him. Even in death, MJ can't find him.

"No," I say. "We broke up over the phone."

His shoulders drop as his eyes dim. "When was the last time you saw him?" he asks, his voice now flat.

"A few weeks ago—the weekend of the college homecoming."

I don't mean to lead the detectives on or give them false hope. But even though I know it's pointless, I want them to look for Ben. I don't want the world to just move on and forget about him.

Detective Baker scribbles something in his notepad while King continues, "And when did you last speak with him?"

The words Ben whispered while dying on Justin's floor haunt me. I hold back a shudder and lie. "Saturday when we broke up."

"You haven't called or texted him since?"

I shake my head, wishing I could hear his voice again.

"Are you sure?" King pushes.

"She already answered that question," Duane replies.

"Yes, but here's my problem," King says. "We have his phone records, and they show he received a call from you on Sunday that lasted five minutes."

Baker looks up from the notepad, smirking at me. They think they've caught me in a lie.

My cell was dead most of Sunday. I know I didn't talk to Ben. But am I "supposed" to remember that? Is that a part of everyone else's new memories?

"Was that from my cell or the home phone? And what time was the call?" I ask.

King arches a bushy brow while Baker flips back through his notepad. He rattles off our home number, then says, "And the call was at five thirty-eight in the evening."

If that's true, I was sleeping in MJ's truck then. *That* should still exist in everyone's minds.

"I didn't get home until almost midnight that evening. So it proves I didn't call him."

Anne nods knowingly at the detectives.

"Well," King says, he and Baker looking right at me, "then who did? It was a five-minute call."

Mom takes a sharp inhale. "I called him."

The detectives move their steely gazes on her. I look at her in surprise myself.

"Maddy was … well, there was an incident Sunday. The one that kept Maddy out until midnight. Earlier in the evening, I called Ben to see if he had talked with her," Mom explains.

Anne reaches over, placing a hand on Detective Baker's arm. "I told you what took place that night."

I shrink down in my chair. My head pounds, beating out a phrase over and over again—*my fault*.

Baker clicks his pen several times.

I look up to find him staring at me.

"How come you haven't asked what our investigation is about?" he asks.

My mouth opens, but nothing comes out.

"I told her Ben was missing when I went to get her from her room," Duane says. "As an FBI agent familiar with investigative questioning such as this, I figured I would give her a moment to digest the news in private."

The detectives stare at Duane, seemingly bothered by him stepping in.

"Madison," King says in a gentler tone, the kindness showing again in his eyes, "how close are you and Benjamin?"

"What do you mean?" I ask.

"You're a junior in high school. He's a college graduate. Some people might look at your relationship and think he was taking advantage of you. Did he *take advantage* of you?"

"Excuse me," Dad says. "But I think—"

"How dare you," I say to the detective, cutting Dad off. I want to reply to this myself. "Ben was an amazing boyfriend. If anything, I took advantage of him. I took him for granted. He was always there for me. Always treated me with respect. Yet I never truly let him in. And now it's too late. I can never make it right. I can never ask him to forgive me."

Tears well up. I leave the table, hugging myself as I stare out the dining room window.

"That's enough questioning," Dad says.

"I agree. She's not a suspect," Duane adds. "She answered your questions, and now it's time you leave."

Mom walks over and places her hand on my shoulder. I rest my head on it.

"Don't give up hope, honey. They'll find him."

I nod only because she expects me to.

"She's right," Detective King says as he stands. "We're closing in. We found his car in Atlanta, Georgia, this morning. We have people working around the clock to find him."

Anne says good-bye, then ushers the detectives out with her. Mom, Dad, Duane, and his agents linger in the dining room, but I can't. I don't want to talk to them. I *can't* talk to them. Silently, I head upstairs with their gazes following me.

I walk to my closet, not knowing why, then I look down and see my baby blanket. My mind scans through the massive amount of information I've learned today, and it lands on my birth parents.

My birth parents are dead.

They died the day I was born. Pain constricts my already broken heart. Loss and guilt ripple through me. I've hated them for so long and blamed them for so much, but none of it was their fault. They wanted me. They loved me. But they died. Did they even get to hold me?

I grab the blanket—needing a way to feel closer to them.

I curl up on my bed and wrap the blanket around me. My fingers trace along the cursive letters that spell

"Madison Rose" in the silk border, recognizing the love put into every stitch. My body shakes, but the tears won't come.

I'm sorry for the years I spent hating them. Someday, perhaps soon, I will see them and I can apologize for the horrible way I've acted. Hopefully I can save the girls and finally make them proud that I was their daughter.

# CHAPTER 37

# MJ

I STAND IN THE VEIL OF SHADOWS BESIDE TAMITHA AND Alexander, staring at my bracelet on her dresser, then at Maddy resting on her bed. I wanted to help her downstairs—comfort her through the detectives' questions—but I held back.

I thought she was just acting out of anger when she said those things at the park—Father knows I deserved it all. But taking off my bracelet says she means it. She doesn't want to be with me anymore. The Shadowwalker was right. I screwed up. I pushed too hard and broke my miracle.

"MJ," Tamitha says, "she's overwhelmed. That's all. Put yourself in her shoes. Look at everything she's had to deal with over the last week."

She's right, of course. Maddy has faced more in one week than some of us face in our entire term as Protectors.

"How do I fix this? I *need* her, Tamitha."

"I don't know," she replies.

I release a breath and move closer to Maddy. She's sweating. Restless. Are her nightmares her own, or is the

Dream Girl sending her more troubled visions? Is she inside the next victim, about to die right along with her? Even if she's not one of the targets, Maddy is somehow connected to this case with the demon serial killer.

Maddy was right. I should have told her what the vision meant right away. Maybe even warned her when she reacted to Atwood's name on the radio last night. Instead I did nothing. It should have come from me instead of *him*.

"I'm going to lose her," I say.

"No, you're not," Tamitha says, moving beside me.

"We'll make sure you don't," Alexander adds, coming up on my other side.

Maddy tosses and turns, still plagued by whatever she's seeing.

I can't watch her go through this. It's too much.

I turn to leave, then I stop. I should stay. Keep her safe.

But is that really helping her? If I hover, if I step in every time, I'm taking away chances she has to gain confidence in her abilities and herself.

I do trust her and I do have faith in her. But I don't have faith in me. I don't trust what I'd do if I ever lost her. And because of my mistakes, I might have lost her already.

As difficult as it is to admit, I'm too emotionally connected to her. In order to have any hope of solving the mystery that is the woman I love, I need time to think. Her life is a puzzle, and figuring out the pieces is the only way to keep her safe. Keep us together.

"Tamitha, if her dreams change at all ..." I begin.

Both Tamitha and Alexander look at me in surprise. There's something new in my voice. I hear it too.

"If she shows any signs of stress or pain, call me back, and I'll get her out of there."

"I will," Tamitha says. "I promise."

I hesitate a moment longer, wondering if I'm making the right choice.

Alexander puts his hand on my shoulder. "Where are we going?"

I shake my head. "I'm going alone."

"Of course you are, and I'm coming with you. It's my job—as your best friend—to help you through this."

I draw in a breath. He's right. Our relationship is far beyond professional. He's always been there for me, whether I needed him or not. Now that Maddy has restored my feelings, I see that. He is my best friend. Had I not found Maddy, I would have lost him when I was reborn. I would have lost them all.

I nod, and together we leave Maddy's room.

ASH AND SMOKE CLING TO THE AIR, AND STREETLIGHTS illuminate the burned debris that was once Justin's hideout. I hadn't meant to come here. When we left Maddy's room, I didn't really have a plan. For some reason, this is where my instincts led me.

"Good call," Alexander says, taking in our surroundings. "The Influencer is still after her. We can maybe pick up his essence and track him."

"I'm not looking for the Influencer right now," I say. "I know his essence. He hasn't been within fifty miles of her since that night."

I look around. Two people died in this house. The ground will forever be scarred with their pain. This place calls out to weak beings, like a Trifecta. They will feed off the energy created. But if I perform the ritual to cleanse this space, I could lose my best shot at finding Ben.

"We're here because Ben hasn't arrived yet."

Alexander stops and turns back to face me. "Do you think he's trapped here?"

"It's crossed my mind." I crouch down, grabbing a fistful of debris. There isn't any spiritual essence clinging to it.

"And you think finding him will fix things with Maddy?"

The dirt slips through my fingers as I stand. "No. But maybe if I find him, she'll finally let go of her guilt."

He nods. He feels the air for traces of Ben's essence. I join in, combing the area that once was the living room.

Sometimes when deaths are sudden, the deceased don't understand what happened, so they won't cross over. They'll haunt the places and people most important to them, trying to connect to them and make sense of things. When people are murdered, we often find them stuck at the scene, repeating that moment.

Whenever we stumble across lost souls, it doesn't matter if we're on a case or not; we help them. The afterlife should be about peace and acceptance, not pain and the past.

If lost souls linger on Mortal Ground too long, they become infected with mutated forms of hate, anger, and revenge. Once that happens, they're no longer granted access to Immortal City and are then cast in with the demons.

The last thing Maddy needs is for Ben to become a demon.

I sigh, knowing Ben's trail has gone cold. I want to find him for Maddy, but I don't know where else to look. If Ben isn't trapped here, the possibilities are infinite.

"This is a dead end," I say.

"You're not giving up already, are you?"

I can't find Ben. But there is another being I can perhaps find—at least on paper.

"Come on," I say.

He smiles. "Where are we going?"

"Home."

# CHAPTER 38

# Maddy

I'M SWEATING. THE HEAT FROM MY BODY SEEPS through my blankets. I toss them off, and through my closed eyes I notice it's brighter than normal.

Panic grips me. It's a fire.

Please no. Not again.

I bolt upright, coming face-to-face with the masked demon. She's on the bed, kneeling over me, staring at me with those frightening demon eyes.

I scurry back, hitting the wall.

For a moment, neither of us say anything. An odd orange glow reflects off her mask. I don't know where I am, other than in a bed. She's so close, I can't see anything but her. She's wearing a yellow dress. Her long brown hair frames her face hidden underneath that same mask. She sits with her feet tucked underneath her.

I find the courage to speak first. "What's going on? Where am I? Were you ... watching me sleep?"

"I wanted to inspect you close up," she says.

"The TV doesn't get in close enough for you?"

She shakes her head. "On screen you are untouchable. Here, you are not."

I swallow, then glance past her to determine where "here" is. I expect it's Hell, but instead it's my bedroom.

I see my dresser and nightstand. This is my bedding. The ceiling glows with my glow-in-the-dark stars. Everything is in place except … my baby blanket is missing. I dig through the blankets.

It's gone. Did she *take* it?

"Why are you in my bedroom? Get out!" I yell.

"This is not your home, Maddy," she says. "It is mine. I recreated your bedroom to learn about you by living as you do."

I look around again. The walls are the exact shade of lilac, but they're shinier. I reach out and run my hand over the wall. It's stone. I look up high above me and see that the glow I saw earlier is not my stars but a huge candelabra. Low flames run along the base of the walls and cast the orange glow. Where my door should be is a stone archway. I can see it leads into the room I was in before, the one with the TV.

It's true, then. I'm back in Hell.

I wanted one night without angels and demons, and she brings me here.

"So much has happened to you, and it is all important," she begins. "I brought your soul here rather than leave you to dream. Even though Elizabeth's memories are important too, they would not allow your mind to fully process today's events. You need to sit back, take a break, and examine things from a new angle with more objectivity— without emotions getting in the way."

She wants me to remain emotionless in the face of so much pain? I can't do that.

"You are scared," she says "You are scared that you cannot save the girls. You are scared that you will die. But mostly, you are scared of being hurt again. That is why you push MJ away every time things get rough."

My heart constricts at the mention of MJ. She's right. About everything. But there is so much more to it than that.

She scoots closer. "I understand. You are afraid there is something wrong with you. Up until today, you've always wondered if that was the real reason your birth parents ga—"

My hand covers my heart. "You can't possibly know all that."

"I have watched you all your life. Plus, I have been inside you. I have glimpsed your mind." She sits there, gazing at me. "Maddy, you must be patient. You learned of your abilities only a few days ago, and they are changing. It is impossible to master them so soon. Relax. Let MJ help you."

I shake my head. Growing up, Dad would tell me to take my time whenever I was learning something new. Be patient. I need to learn to walk before I can run. But I didn't *need* to be patient. I mastered bike riding in less time than it took him to put on and then take off my training wheels. I could play anything by Beethoven the day after learning scales on the piano. No matter what it was, I mastered it with ease.

That's why I'm so frustrated by my abilities. I can't control them. I barely understand them.

What does she know? Here I am, trying to control my abilities, but she only adds to the problem by overtaking my body and soul whenever she wants. She's yet another person who's kept the truth from me about the demon and the hundreds of people who have died as he makes his way to me.

I grind my teeth, then storm out of bed, through the archway, and into the massive room.

I stand in front of the fireplace. I'm not cold. I'm still sweating buckets, but the dance of the orange and amber flames is oddly soothing. The firelight creates shadows on the stone.

As I look at the shadows, I once again know she's right. I am letting the truth I learned today overshadow what MJ and I have together. I've been so upset about him keeping secrets from me, yet the moment I learn that truth, I immediately use it to push him away.

I feel her hand on my shoulder. Her essence flows into me, and all at once, everything feels right again.

"You have your first chance at happiness with MJ, but you are ruining it. You are letting the truth you learned today overshadow your feelings for MJ and his feelings for you."

Her words immediately bring back the flood of pain. "I don't deserve to be happy. People are being murdered. People are being killed in my name."

"They have been since you were born. The only difference now is you know about it. You have dreamed all your life of being loved. You have that now. You have always had it, actually. Not just from your adopted family and your friends, but from those of us doing everything we can to keep you alive. But MJ … he *loves* you, and I know you love him too."

"I … I don't know what to do. It feels wrong to be with him, to be happy, while they're suffering for me."

"They are dying so you can live. Do not let their sacrifices be for nothing. Love MJ—while you can. Let him help you. Work on your abilities, find your inner strength, pull back when it gets to be too much, but mostly, do not give up fighting. Ever."

Love MJ *while I can*? I sigh. I know time isn't guaranteed for us. It never has been.

I panicked last Sunday when I thought I had only a day with MJ. And it turned out to be the best day I'd ever had, even though some of it was intense. But it wasn't the end. We got a second day, and third, and they were even better.

But each day, more angels and demons learn of me. At least two beings are after my soul. Now I don't know if I'll get an hour with MJ, a day, a week, a month, or an eternity. No matter how long I'll have with him, it won't be enough.

I can't waste another second of it.

I turn to face her, pleading into her fiery eyes. "Send me home, please. I need to fix this. I need to fix us."

"Not right now," she says.

"Please, you must," I press, frantic. "I have to get back to MJ."

Her hand still on my shoulder, she sends her essence to calm me. "There will be time for that later. At the moment, MJ is off on important tasks of his own."

My head moves back in surprise. He *did* leave. Even though I asked him to leave, I never thought he'd do it. I never expected him to trust me or his team enough. Maybe I don't have much faith in him either. I should.

She removes her hand from my shoulder and walks toward the living room. "I have something to show you."

I watch her walk to the living room area, not wanting to follow her. I followed Duane into the guest room, and look how horrible that turned out.

"Yes, it was a bit overwhelming," the masked demon says, reading my thoughts. "Which is why I want to help you digest it. Come here."

She directs me to sit on the leather couch in front of the TV. She herself flops down into the loveseat, lying on it lengthwise and letting her feet dangle off the armrest. She swings her legs in a slow, almost hypnotic rhythm.

I watch her. "I sit like that too," I say, trying to show her we have something in common.

Red eyes meet mine. She tilts her head and says, "I know." Then her legs resume swinging. She grabs the remote and turns on the TV.

The screen shows me sleeping in bed—it's my physical body back in my real room at this moment. Then everything moves backward. She's rewinding my life.

She presses play, and suddenly there is MJ on the bridge, cradling my limp body against him. He bows his head, breaking down.

"What is this?" I sputter. "This isn't real!"

"It is. This is what happened to your body once your soul went into the vision of girl eight."

Without thinking, I stand in front of the TV and run my fingers across the screen, trying to soothe him.

I hadn't stopped to think about the pain he suffered while I suffered inside Lauren.

A tear falls down his cheek, and I clamp my eyes shut as my lips tremble.

Oh, MJ ... I'm so sorry.

I never should have said what I did after talking with Duane. I never should have pushed him away.

In MJ's arms, my body begins to move, pounding the air, mimicking the horror of the vision. A terrified scream sounds, coming from my body.

The demon mutes the TV, but sound or no sound, I still watch in shock. People said I moved and talked in the dreams, but seeing it happen is … there are no words.

MJ falls to his knees, his face twisting in pain and agony as he holds me. After a moment, Alexander lifts up the hem of my jeans to reveal my legs are charred.

I reel back in alarm. Did my skin actually *burn*?

"Yes. The angels healed you," she answers. "It took all three of them."

The masked demon lifts the remote and turns off the TV. I gape at the blank screen, unable yet to break away.

"These visions," she says, "are dangerous. If you cannot pull out of them, you could die inside them. You did not have visions of the other girls. Why now? It is imperative you solve this before the killer goes after girl nine. What has changed?"

Everything. Everything has changed.

## CHAPTER 39

# MJ

As we walk through the Pearly Gates, I catch the eye of Thaddeus at the gate. It appears things are back to normal.

"So where to?" Alexander asks.

I glance at Alexander, grateful he's by my side. "We're going to look for Damien."

"How? We don't have access to demon files."

"True." I stop in the middle of a street filled with angels going about their business. I gaze up the steps to the building that rises above all others. The Basilica Trascendentium. "But they do."

His eyes widen with shock. *Are you nuts?* he shouts in my mind.

I'm instantly relieved he didn't say it out loud. It keeps nearby angels from overhearing our conversation. Plus, speaking through Cerebrallink is the only way to avoid being detected by the Council, especially this close to their home.

*You want to ask the Council to help protect Maddy?* he continues. *They'd send the Perfugae after her before we'd even finished our first sentence!*

*Calm down,* I say, looking around at the angels passing by. *And remember, angels don't feel, so you better mask your expressions before you make a scene.*

He composes himself, but it takes several moments. I know it's hard to act impassive now that our emotions have been restored. In the past, we faked emotions to blend in, but up here, now we have to fake not having them. And just as in art, it's easy to spot a forgery.

*Alexander, relax. We're going to ask the Council for help, but it won't be about Maddy. I can hide my thoughts from them, and you need to as well.*

*What? How?* he asks.

*Come on. It's a long walk to the top. I'll explain on the way.*

We both unglamour our wings as we begin up the steps. Alexander's have grown since the last time I saw them. They now stop below his knees when in a state of rest.

He looks behind me, to my wingtips dragging along the ground. He whistles in amazement. *Your wings are as big as the Council's now.*

I huff. *No, they're not. Remember, the Archangels are a foot and a half taller than me.*

*Oh yeah,* he says. *It's been a while since I've seen them.*

Knowing—or at least assuming—we're a safe enough distance away to speak freely, I look Alexander carefully in the eyes.

*So, hiding your thoughts from them ...* I begin. *It's like how we compel mortals. You just have to push your memories aside and put false ones in front of them. I've been doing it since ... I started as a Protector.* I leave it at that, hoping he doesn't press for more.

He snorts, though he gives me a sideways glance. *Easy for you to say. You've had eight hundred years to perfect this technique. I need to nail it on my first try.*

He's right. And with the Council looking for any excuse to go to war, this could be the biggest mistake of my life. But I can't do this without him.

I slow my climb. *I know I'm asking a lot of you lately, but may I ask you one more thing? Pay attention to Council's reactions.*

Alexander slows even more. *What do you mean? They don't have "reactions." They have no emotions.*

*But what if they're lying?*

I bring us both to a full halt.

*I think they* do *have emotions—always have. After all, if they never had any emotions, then what started the first Holy War?*

He raises a brow before glancing over his shoulder at their home. *If you're right, MJ ... everything is going to get ugly.*

We resume walking in silence, preparing our minds for the challenge ahead.

With less than fifteen steps to go, I ask, *Ready?*

He loudly releases his breath. *If we get through this,* he says, nodding toward the entryway, *you'd also better explain* why *you've hidden your thoughts from them this long.*

I grimace. The last thing I want to be thinking about before meeting the Council is the years I spent fighting the Acquisitioner in secret. But after how badly I handled things with Maddy, I realize I need to start coming clean with the people who matter to me.

*Deal,* I say.

The Council steps outside to greet us. Raphael looks the youngest with curly blond hair and hazel eyes. But the harsh edges of his nose, brows, and jawline ensure he's taken seriously.

Gabriel's thick black hair contrasts against the pristine white building behind them. His face is stoic, taking in all with his sharp brown eyes—and giving nothing away in return.

Michael's bright blue eyes gaze between us. That same thirst for war from this morning clings to him.

Alexander falters, slowing his stride. He and most other Protectors meet with the Archangels only on rare occasions. As the leader of the Protectors, I meet with them regularly. I'm used to the brilliance that surrounds them.

They welcome me with the same handshake from my previous life.

"Welcome back, Protector MJ," Michael says. "Welcome, Protector Alexander. I presume you both have come to discuss today's developments."

I try to shut out any panic as I try to decipher what "developments" he knows about from today.

"It is curious," Raphael says, arching a brow while staring at me, "that Eight joined us so soon."

Relief swells inside me, though I keep my emotions masked. They're talking about my assignment. Lauren, victim eight, must have arrived, having her file read and judgment passed.

"Yes," I say, "the assignment is why we are here. I have a potential suspect for the killer, but I need your help before I search for him."

Alexander shuffles from foot to foot behind me. I make a small motion for him to steady, hoping they didn't catch it.

Gabriel's dark eyes narrow speculatively on us.

"You are aware we cannot step on Mortal Ground," Michael says. "Not unless the Holy War is confirmed." The undercurrent of his voice makes it clear the law is still a sore subject for him.

Before I became a Protector, the Archangels from both sides walked among mortals. They were treated as gods and enjoyed the spoils given to them. Sometimes the spoils included women. The children created—the Nephilim— were all evil and ultimately destroyed. The Archangels were forbidden to visit Mortal Ground, except in the case of the Holy War.

But at least once a century, Michael and his brothers leave to experience the changes taking place on Mortal Ground. It's supposed to be a secret mission. But like petulant children still upset over Father showing favoritism to the mortals, the Archangels leave their marks on the mortal world. Each of them has posed for famous works of art. The most recognizable and intact pieces are the *Creation of Adam* on the ceiling in the Sistine Chapel; Michael is Adam. The statue entitled *The Thinker* is Gabriel. Raphael is the statue *David*.

"I admit," Michael suddenly says, "we did not expect those pieces to be preserved for so long."

I cringe, knowing he just heard everything I thought. I called my leaders *petulant children*. "Sir, I—"

"Do not apologize, Protector MJ," he states. Then he chuckles. "Unlike your mortal companions, I am unaffected when a friend speaks the truth."

"Still, it was impolite."

"Ah yes, polite," Raphael says. "One of the many *gifts* Father gave to mortals."

Gabriel scoffs.

Their tone surprises me, but I don't comment. It's not my place to speak of the discontent between Father and the Archangels.

Alexander glances at me, arching a brow. I know he's surprised by it too.

Michael casts sharp looks at his brothers. Their tempers neutralize, becoming impassive once more.

If I don't change the subject now, our thoughts will get us in trouble.

"Please allow me to clarify," I say, trying to resume our original discussion. "We did not come for your help on Mortal Ground, but rather here."

Raphael leans his head to the side, staring at me with interest.

I take a deep breath, stealing myself to ask an unthinkable question. Please let them agree. They're my only hope.

"May we have permission to use *Od Libro Aeterna Damnatione?*"

Four beings around me gasp—Alexander included. Incredibly, I don't react. I'm sure no one has ever asked to look at the *Book of Eternal Damnation*. It lists every demon found in the twelve Castes. Because demons can't be reborn, the book spans all the way back to the beginning of man.

The Archangels compose themselves, but they don't respond. Experience says they're communicating amongst each other. If I say anything now, it won't go in my favor.

After what feels like ages, Gabriel and Michael step off to the side as Raphael steps toward us.

"Do you swear your interest in the book lies solely with your assignment?" Raphael asks.

"I do so swear."

Raphael continues to stare at me while the other two fix on Alexander. I can feel Raphael's intrusion, poking and prodding deeper into my mind.

This time, I feed him my suspicions of a demon named Damien, suggesting he may be the killer. Alexander often says there's no such thing as coincidence. If it's true, then Damien is connected to my assignment.

"Did you come by this name from your psychic?" Raphael asks, arching a brow.

Panic flares inside me, but I snuff it out as quickly as I can.

"I admit," Michael says, "the news was rather interesting when Protector Gary mentioned your psychic, considering you had not spoken of working with one when we met."

"Yes, the name Damien did come from the psychic, but her abilities are new and unpredictable," I reply, trying to remain calm. "The visions are not clear, which is why I am here, asking to look at the book. I hope this lead will enable us to prevent the death of girl nine."

Silence follows, then I feel them poking into my mind, deeper than they have ever before.

I project as much safe information as I can. No matter what, I cannot buckle under the strain. My mission is too important.

After what feels like ages, they release me.

"I grant you permission," Raphael says. "Prepare yourself, though. The book is not for the faint of heart."

He turns and motions for us to enter. As I walk by
them, I feel the weight of their suspicions like chains
around my neck.

The interior of the Basilica Trascendentium is split into
three parts. To the right and left, archways lead into other
rooms. I count eight on each side. The main area, though,
is wide open, stretching the length of the building. Toward
the back, sitting on a round stone table, is book larger than
any I have ever seen.

Alexander and I walk toward it. Somehow, even
though sunlight flows in from every angle, the book and
table are shaded. It's as if an unseen force is blocking
the light.

Alexander's stride slows, and he glances around.

*Are you sure about this, MJ?* he asks.

I don't answer. Instead I keep moving forward, hoping
it will bring me a step closer to finding answers.

I stop in front of the table. A ring of soot circles the
book. A sour smell of rot and decay clings to the air. In
such a place, the effect is staggering.

The cover is thick and black. After a deep breath,
I unlock two leather straps and open it. I expected
the pages to be frail, but they're as stiff as the day the
book was made.

Ancient Latin is scrawled across golden pages. Name
after name after name.

Immediately, I feel crushed, as if this massive book
were being dropped right upon me. There will be millions
of Damiens. I won't find him. It's hopeless.

I'm going to fail. I'm going to fail this mission. I'm
going to fail her, just as I have failed everyone. She will
die, and I will lose her forever. That will be my curse, to

spend eternity alone with the knowledge that I couldn't protect her.

Suddenly I realize what I've done. I've let my thoughts free.

I whip around, preparing for the Archangels' wrath. But they are gone.

"Are you okay?" Alexander whispers, placing a hand on my shoulder. His brown eyes search mine.

I swallow and nod. "I'm fine."

Without another word, we dive in. We sit and begin searching for the name Damien—or any variation of it, just to be safe—among the seven highest classifications of demon Castes. We rule out the lower five Castes, seeing as they aren't powerful enough to kill someone—whether with their own abilities or by third party.

The passing of time is irrelevant. I have no idea of how long it is before Alexander shuts the book, slouches back in his chair, and exhales.

"That's quite a list."

I lean back and sigh. Even ruling out the lower Castes, we still found over three hundred thousand Damiens or variants.

I *am* going to fail her.

## CHAPTER 40

# Maddy

THE MASKED DEMON SILENTLY WATCHES ME FROM HER spot on the love seat as I stand in front of the blank TV. As her legs continue to swing back and forth, I drift back through my week, looking to discover how and why I ended up inside Lauren.

It wasn't my first vision of a death. Elizabeth showed me the vision of MJ's death. That vision was much different, though. I was inside Lifa, but it was nothing like being inside Lauren—dying with her.

Before Elizabeth pushed me into the fountain—her Time Keeper—she talked about my dreams ... that they're "broken." She was so scared about that.

The memories resurface, repeating Elizabeth's words about the broken dreams: *If you aren't linked to them anymore, that means your mind is open to any one of us who knows about you. Someone else could use it to show you things, as I have. They can use it to make you do things or to find you.*

Hearing my thoughts, the masked demon eyes me. "Where's Elizabeth?" I ask. "We need her."

She shakes her head as if I've answered something incorrectly. "That is not the point to focus on."

"Yes, it is. She controls the dreams. She can fix them. I thought something happened to her after she helped me at Justin's house, but then she pushed one of MJ's team members when we were at school today. I haven't seen her since."

"That was not her."

I blink. "Then who was it?"

"Someone invested in your future. I cannot tell you more than that." Before I can even speak, she continues, "Your first assumption was closest to the truth: Elizabeth has not been heard from since helping you at the demon's house."

My heart stills. Another person I care about is missing.

"She knew the risks of helping you," the masked demon replies.

"What does that mean? Is she in danger?"

"She is dead, Maddy." I can sense a wry smile behind the mask. "She can handle whatever is being done to her."

"But what *is* being done to her? Who's doing it to her? Where's Damien? He wouldn't allow her to get—"

"Stop," she says, rising and coming over to me. She places her hands on my arms. Her essence rushes in, breaking up my worries.

"Calm down. You are our priority—Elizabeth knows that. Once you are safe, she will be also. Finding her now would not solve anything. It would only put you at a greater risk. Right now, you need to stop wasting time and figure out why you had a vision of this girl's death."

Her essence splits and rushes into my mind. Within seconds, Elizabeth's words loop again: *your mind is open to any one of us who knows about you …*

The masked demon releases me. As the words fade, my mouth slowly falls open.

That's why I had the vision of Lauren dying when I didn't with the other victims. Now that Elizabeth's Time Keeper is broken, the demon is somehow sending my soul into his victims.

He *knows* about me.

I look into the masked demon's red eyes, searching for answers.

"For nearly seventeen years, the killer could only speculate about your existence. It was not certain you were even alive. But by succeeding in sending your soul into girl eight today, the killer now knows, without a doubt, you are alive. The killer can connect with your soul. It does not know your true identity or physical whereabouts." She pauses. "Yet."

"Does this mean I'll have visions of the others' deaths if the demon isn't stopped?"

The masked demon doesn't hesitate. "Yes. At the moment, the killer believes you may be one of these remaining girls on the target list. Regardless, with access to your soul, the killer is sending you into each victim. You are meant to suffer—and possibly die—with each target."

I can't go through that. Not again and again as each girl dies in my place. I don't care if I might somehow survive these visions. I just … can't face that again.

The masked demon shakes her head to correct me once more. "The visions are dangerous, yes. But what is more important is that with this connection to your soul, sooner or later the killer will *find you*. It is critical, therefore, that you understand why the killer is after you."

I'm a bit numb as she maneuvers me back to the couch. Then she turns on the TV and fast-forwards to my conversation with Duane in the guest room. Without any explanation, she presses play, and I relive it all again.

As I watch, she sits in the love seat beside the couch, again swinging her feet over the edge.

Although it's still strange to see my life from the outside, and although what Duane tells me is still terrible, it's somewhat easier to take it all in now. This time, I can really focus because I'm not overwhelmed with shock. I lean in toward the screen.

Once the scene is finished, she turns the TV off again. Again without a word, she looks over at me. She's waiting for me to say something. To realize something. I can see only her eyes from behind the mask, but they're dim, almost haunted.

I flop back on the couch in frustration. "What am I missing?" I ask.

She links her fingers over her stomach. "Seattle to Atlanta is a long distance for a baby to travel on its own."

Someone—mortal or otherwise—obviously brought me to Atlanta. All Duane said was that the others "found" me. Duane didn't know me until I showed up outside my parents' door in Atlanta, so one of the others must have brought me there. It had to be someone who wanted to help me. Someone who cared for me enough to take me across the states.

"Elizabeth," I say, voicing my thoughts. "She found me beside the car. She said she was about to cross over but was pulled back for some reason. She found me and must have followed as the rescue team brought me to the hospital. And then she must have moved me after the hospital caught fire."

Although I can't see her face, I get the sense the masked demon is smiling.

Questions pour out of my mouth all at once. "Is Elizabeth one of the 'others' Duane mentioned? Are they working together? What about Damien? She told me she brought Damien to me. And your master"—I nod toward the huge desk—"you said he's helping me too, right?"

Looking at the stone desk, suddenly I wonder about Damien. I know he's a demon and a powerful one. He could have demons working for him, such as the masked demon. Elizabeth, at least, believes he is trying to help me. Could Damien be her master?

I know she can hear my thoughts, but she doesn't reply. "Can I meet him, your master?" I ask out loud.

The masked demon stiffens. Her eyes flash to the door. Mine follow, expecting it to open. It doesn't.

"No. My master is next in line for the throne. He cannot get involved, which is why he charged me with watching over you."

It can't be Damien, then. Damien was trying to leave Hell, not take it over.

Sadness curls around me. I didn't realize it until just now, but I wanted it to be Damien. I wanted to believe he was helping me. If not for me, then for Elizabeth.

"Listen," she says, "you are doing well piecing things together. But you still have more to uncover."

I release my breath in a huff. *More?* What more could there possibly be?

"Something very important," she stresses.

I stand and pace by the TV, replaying in my mind everything Duane told me, searching for something left unsaid. The conversation begins to mix as if in a blender. The words spin round and round, but a few points stick out.

My mother's car accident. The twelve girls' parents dying the same day. And sacrifices.

"Are you sure it was an *accident*?" the masked demon asks, listening to my thoughts.

My gaze flashes to her. I'm unable to speak. Unable to think. It can't be true.

"The killer knew your parents," she says.

She stands and slowly moves toward me. Her eyes are distant. Even more haunted. Pained. She blinks.

"The killer caused your mother's death."

*No.*

My mother is not only dead but *murdered*.

I sway, and she places her hand on my shoulder to steady me. Her essence rushes in, filling my broken heart.

"Many beings are forbidden from taking a life themselves," she says, "so they use other means. The killer must have compelled the other driver to crash into your mother."

"*Why*?" It's all I can manage.

"The killer wanted your mother to die," she says. She tightens her grip on my shoulder. "The killer wanted you to die as well."

I sink to the floor. She lowers herself with me, never letting go.

"You were not meant to survive, but you did," she says. "It was in the news. You were called 'the miracle baby' who was somehow born during a car wreck."

Tears spill. A "miracle" is the last thing I'd ever call myself.

"The killer saw these reports and knew you had survived."

"Is that why he set the hospital on fire?" I ask.

The masked demon shakes her head. She takes a breath, though I feel it's more for me than for her.

"To protect you, the others working with Duane set the nursery on fire. They replaced you with another baby who would be identified as you so the killer would assume you had died.

"Elizabeth moved you to Georgia and set you at the Pages' door. You were placed in a foster home for three weeks while the Pages waited to adopt you. But the killer followed. As a precaution, a fire was started at the foster home to falsify your death again."

The fires were set to … *protect* me?

Sacrifices.

Her essence intensifies, soothing my shattered heart. Then it splits and enters my mind again.

"The pattern, Maddy," she says.

Car crash. Fire. Fire. The same pattern over and over in my mind.

She stands back and removes her hands.

It takes a moment for my thoughts to settle before I can speak. "Are you saying the pattern is some kind of test? The killer is murdering the other girls by car crash and fire just to see if any survive?"

"Perhaps. But more importantly, the pattern is a message: the killer might not know which girl you are, but it knows what the others did to protect you."

I look away, horrified. My hands shake. A tear slides down my cheek.

I begin to stand. I have to leave. Now. Somehow. I have to tell MJ. He has to stop the demon. Together, we have to stop the demon.

Before I can get to my feet, she grabs my shoulders and pulls me down again. Her essence rushes in, half going to my heart, the rest filling my head again.

It clouds my mind this time. Thoughts disappear. The room spins. I feel lighter—free of all the guilt and pain of the day.

"MJ suspects you are a target, possibly even who the killer is really after, but he is in denial. Tell MJ the killer is coming for you, but tell him you do not know why. Say you just know."

"I just know," I repeat.

"He may argue, saying the killer is targeting only adopted girls. Do not tell him you are adopted. Instead, tell him it does not matter. Say you do not know why, but it just does not."

"It just does not …"

"Tell him to trust you—if he does not trust you, then he will truly know what it is like to lose you, and it would be his fault."

"His fault …"

After a moment, she removes her hands.

The fog lifts, and the panic and trauma rush back. I tip backward and catch myself less than an inch from crashing into the TV. She stands and tries to help me, but I push her away.

"Stop it! You can't just compel me like that!"

"I have to. There is much to tell MJ and much to keep secret. If you tell him the full truth, he might take you away. We cannot have that."

I tense, recalling Duane's "promise." Is that everyone's big plan, to take me and hide? That's what Damien did with Elizabeth, and it didn't work out well. Screw that—if I'm going to die soon, it won't be while hiding.

The masked demon's eyes dart to the side. She's looking at the door again. "My master will not like what I have done, but I do not care."

Screw her master. Screw *her*. My stomach knots, hating the control she has over me. She wears the porcelain mask, but I'm the puppet.

My rage forces me to my feet. "I hate you! I hate all demons!"

She crosses her arms and tilts her head, waiting for me to finish.

"You say you're trying to help me, but my life has been a disaster since you demons showed up! You're ruining everything!"

She leans into me, inches from my face. Even though we're the same height, she seems to tower over me.

"The killer has known about you since birth. You have lived as long as you have only because beings on both sides are working together. For *you*, they have put aside a hatred that was forged the day man first walked on Mortal Ground. Think about that the next time you open your mouth." Her eyes burn brighter than the flames in the room.

"I …"

Words fail me. My body slumps. She's right. I probably would have died a long time ago if it weren't for

Duane, Damien, and Elizabeth, plus the masked demon and her master.

"I'm sorry," I say.

"That is a decent start." She relaxes her stance. "Demons are not the monsters you think they are. They were people at one point. Angels are not perfect either, but they get an unlimited supply of do-overs. Demons are sentenced to the City of the Damned for eternity. The punishment does not always fit the crime."

I hadn't put much thought into how or why people get sent down here. Seeing as it's quite possible I myself will die soon, I should probably have some idea about the afterlife other than the little bit MJ has told me. For all I know, I may not have much say about where I'll ultimately go.

The masked demon looks at me for a long moment before it dawns on me. I don't know what *she* did to end up here.

She sighs and turns away. "I was born."

I wait for her to continue, but she doesn't. "I don't understand."

"Me neither. But I have spent my entire life here, living vicariously through you."

Her hand runs through her hair, then she looks over at me. Her eyes are brighter again. Even through the mask, I can tell she's smiling.

"This will sound cruel, but I like when you are in danger. Being inside you, up there, it is better than I imagined."

We're both quiet for a long time.

"What's your name?" I finally ask. "I'd like to call you something better than 'the masked demon.'"

She laughs. "I like that. It is a mouthful, though."

"Exactly, so ..."

She shrugs. "I do not have a name, so it will do."

Not only has she grown up here, but she doesn't even have a name.

"What do you mean? What does your master call you?"

"'Girl,' if anything."

"Well, then, that settles it. We're giving you a name. What name do you like?"

Her scarlet eyes—vibrant now—look me over. She adjusts her body to mimic my posture.

"I like yours."

The atmosphere between us shifts, becoming heavy. My pulse quickens. Although she's a demon, I haven't been afraid of her since that first time. But this sudden shift has me wary.

She takes a step toward me. I take a step back.

Fear closes in. My breathing accelerates. Behind her, I see the archway of her bedroom. A bedroom exactly like mine. She's watched me my whole life ... She enjoys coming up to save me ... She's been inside me ...

She wants to *be* me.

"You cannot understand it now," she says, "but our fates are entwined. You get to live up there and experience everything, while I am stuck down here waiting and watching. Always watching. You are my only connection to the life *I* should have had."

She presses a button on the remote, but I can't take my eyes off her.

"I do not know how long this will work," she says, taking yet another step. "But even if it is only for a few minutes, I will cherish them always. Thank you for this, Madison."

"Wh-*what*?"

She advances while I keep backing up, putting as much distance between us as possible.

"When I help you in moments of danger, I cannot stay in you for long—your soul fights me. But if I send your soul somewhere else, I should be able to stay in you longer."

"No." I shake my head. "Please don't do this."

"Elizabeth showed you a past belonging to MJ," she continues, ignoring my pleas. "To keep things balanced, I will show you one from the other side."

I risk a peek over my shoulder, and the TV is pulsing in familiar waves. "No! I don't want to go through that again. Please don't—"

"I am sorry, but it is for the best. You need to see that demons are not all bad. There is hope, for some. Good luck, Madison."

She shoves me backward into the TV.

# CHAPTER 41

# MJ

I T'S NOT EVEN FIVE O'CLOCK IN THE MORNING WHEN
Alexander and I enter Maddy's room in the Veil of
Shadows. I'm filled with trepidation, and not just because
the night was so disastrous. I have no idea what awaits me
when she wakes. Are we still over? Does she hate me? Will
she send me away?

"I'm glad you're back," Tamitha whispers, even
though Maddy can't hear us. "I nearly called for you a
moment ago."

"Why? What happened?" I move to Maddy's bedside
with her and Alexander following. I scan over her, but she
seems to be sleeping peacefully.

"She was sweating again and had a mild fever,"
Tamitha says, "but otherwise I saw no signs of duress.
Then a few moments ago her heart raced. But then
it returned to normal. She rolled over, and now she
seems fine."

Tamitha looks at me with pleading eyes. "I don't
understand why she has these dreams, but we need to
make them stop. Even with a relatively 'mild' dream like

this, it can't be good for her body to go through so much in such a short time."

"I don't know how to stop it," I say with a resigned sigh. "Maddy believes the dreams will end soon—once she's seen everything the Dream Girl wants her to. I hope she's right."

"Did time away help you?" Tamitha asks.

Alexander cuts her a look before moving away.

My shoulders slump. "Not as much as I would have liked."

Tamitha nods, then moves over by Alexander as they give me some space alone with Maddy.

Of all the things that transpired during our time away, the Council's knowledge of my "psychic" perturbs me the most. They weren't happy with the vague answers I gave them, both verbally and mentally. They'll want her identification soon, and I may not be able to hide the truth from them. If they summon me again, I won't answer. I won't expose her. If they summon me again, we'll have no choice but to run.

Maddy nestles into her pillow. I crouch down, watching her. While the night wasn't a big success, it did allow me time to focus on what's really important—us.

My friends can help me keep her safe, but I'm the only one who can fix our relationship.

I think back to last night and the things she and I said. She told me she was done with all of this. She just wanted to be normal right now.

Suddenly an idea grows.

"Maddy wants to feel normal," I repeat, this time out loud as my thoughts come.

"She was angry," Alexander says.

"She didn't mean it," Tamitha adds.

"She did," I say. "And there's nothing wrong with that. Her whole world has been turned upside down. Maybe if I give her a normal day, it can help her find her footing."

I look between them, hoping they understand. It's risky, given everything going on. But she needs this. *We* need this.

They're silent—deep in thought.

Then Tamitha says, "That could work."

Alexander nods. "We'll help. What do you need from us?"

I take a deep breath. For the first time in days, I feel a sense of relief from it. "Take over my Protector duties. Just for the day. Alexander, be alert for the Influencer. Tamitha, keep a close eye on the Shadowwalker. Have Sissy continue protecting Amber. Give Maddy and me the day to just be a couple. Let me take her to school so she can be with her friends. She needs them as much as I need you. I'll figure the rest out as I go."

Maddy stirs.

"Go relieve Sissy and inform her of the plan," I say as I keep my eyes on Maddy. "I'll meet up with you all at school."

"Good luck," Tamitha says.

They disappear, leaving me to face the uncertainty of my relationship.

Standing here watching Maddy on the verge of waking feels awkward. She explicitly told me she didn't want me hovering over her in the Veil. I move into the hallway, do a quick check to make sure the rest of her family is still asleep, then step out of the Veil.

When I hear her yawn, I take a deep breath and knock.

"Who is it?" she asks on the downturn of another yawn.

I swallow my fears. "It's MJ," I answer in a voice as neutral as possible. I hope she won't send me away.

I wait.

And wait.

And wait for a response.

Finally, I hear footsteps coming toward the door. She opens it. She places one hand on the doorframe and the other on the door, blocking my entrance.

Everything inside me clenches.

I look up, expecting to see anger. But instead, wide green eyes slide up and down my body. Her lips twitch, fighting a smile. She pushes the door open and steps to the side.

"Might as well come in."

My lips part enough to release my breath. She's never quite looked at me like that. Angry or not, apparently she still likes what she sees.

I enter her room, and she shuts the door behind me. My essence jolts and my senses sharpen, feeding off the tension in the atmosphere. Even though I'm in her room and we're both safe, my body is reacting as if a demon were in here. I glance at her bracelet still on her dresser, just to be sure. No stones are black.

"I know you have called the shots lately," she says, "but today will be different."

I turn, startled by her assertiveness. She's still mad, but at least she's speaking to me.

"We'll do whatever you want," I reply.

She tilts her head, gazing at me for a moment, then she smiles. "I want to run and feel the wind on my skin. I want to watch the sunrise and hear the world awaken. I want to have breakfast with Dean, Marie, and Hannah. Then I wish to go to school and see the triplets, Luke and Mason, Shawn, and Kelli." She nods to herself. "Yes, that is it."

I blink, confused. That's what she's done every day, especially since I've been around. Why does she think that's any different? Then again, it's perfect. That's exactly what I had in mind for this "normal" day I want to give her.

Now isn't the time to argue or question her, however. "Consider it done," I say.

Her smile widens and her eyes sparkle, practically illuminating the dimly lit room.

Muscles inside me loosen as my fear, doubt, grief, and pain vanish. Her eyes are magnets pulling me toward her. She owns me, heart and soul. Inside my chest, I feel a thump that echoes through me. It does it again and again as my heart restarts.

I step toward her, my arms reaching out to hold her so she can feel the power she has over me. But her smile disappears, the light fades, and she steps back.

My heart falls silent once more. It's too soon. She's not ready.

"Maddy I ... I'm sorry. For last night. For everything. Please ... forgive me."

She stares at me a long while, her eyes moving all over me again. She bites her lip, then slowly slides her tongue over her teeth.

I inhale sharply as I feel movement hit me in the nether region. The room seems to be boiling. A bead of water runs down my neck. I'm sweating. Visions flash in my mind's eye of us together. This time we do more than kiss. My palms ache, wanting to caress her skin and act on my thoughts.

No.

Not yet.

I don't even know if we're still together. Nothing makes sense right now.

"We will discuss last night," she says, lifting a narrow brow. "But not now. The list of things I want to do is long, and I am unsure how long I have before something tragic happens."

Before I can say a word, she saunters past me into the bathroom.

THE FIRST THING ON THIS "LIST" OF HERS IS A RUN IN THE park at dawn. I barely take my eyes off her as we run side by side. She gazes over everything in wide wonder, as if she were memorizing it. She's lived here most of her life and seen this all before, but the way she's looking at everything ... I can't take it.

Back in her room, she spoke of something tragic happening. Was it related to her dream? I don't know. But she knows something I don't. Something is happening. Whatever's coming, it's my fault she's not ready. I should have been training her to fight, just like she said. I wanted to protect her, but I've left her vulnerable.

"How about we stop and work on your abilities for a bit?"

I know this goes against the "normal" day I wanted for her, but I have to do something.

"It would not do any good now," she says without slowing her stride. "Tomorrow, though, you should do that."

I fall back as both my mind and body slow with confusion. She's not herself this morning. She's overcome with joy—and passion—one moment, then full of doom the next.

She stops on the bridge as I catch up. She leans on the railing and stares at the treetops, eagerly awaiting the sunrise. I stand behind her, watching her face light up with the first few inches of bright golden rays.

A tear falls down her cheek.

I watch the sky for her echoed rain, but it doesn't come. Has Maddy figured out how to control that ability, or is this still a by-product of last night?

"It is so beautiful," she whispers. "Promise me, MJ, that you will never stop watching the sun rise and fall."

"I … I promise."

These are the words of someone who doesn't expect to survive today.

Once the sun has fully risen, she turns to me, wearing that same breathtaking smile from earlier. "Okay. Now I will return home to shower. Then I will have breakfast with my family."

Seeing her smile, I reach for her hand, but she pulls it back again. I feel a twinge of sadness—she hasn't let me touch her all morning. I would think that means she's still upset with me. She *seems* happy, though—the sky is clear. Either I'm missing something, or she's doing an amazing job masking her emotions. I shouldn't have taught her that.

I shove aside my own pain and instead focus on her. "Maddy, if something was going to happen to you, you'd tell me, right?"

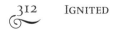

"I hope so. If anyone could stop it, it would be you." With that, she turns and casually strolls to her home. I follow, pondering her choice of words.

I watch her through breakfast. The room is packed with Maddy, me, Maddy's family, plus the Shadowwalker and his team.

Everyone eyes Maddy with curiosity. She's more affectionate, hugging and touching her family—though she still refuses to let me or the Shadowwalker touch her. Not only that, but she's wearing a dress—a tight, short dress. She looks good. Sexy, actually. I can't deny it. But it's just … not her.

I can hear her family's thoughts. There's some concern—especially from her father—about the dress. They think, of course, her wardrobe choice is meant to impress me, and they're not too happy about that. At the same time, they are happy about the positive change in her attitude. They're not sure if it's Maddy blossoming on her own or if it's a sign of her happiness with me. Either way, they like having "Old Maddy" back—the Maddy who existed prior to that trip with the Shadowwalker three years ago.

I glance in his direction.

*What's going on?* he asks. He's been frowning since Maddy bounded down the stairs to breakfast.

*I'm working on it,* I reply.

At school, I follow slowly behind as Maddy makes a mad dash for her friends as soon as we're through the doors. Still affectionate with everyone but me, she hugs each of them as she calls out their names. It's as if she hasn't seen them in a long time.

"Whoa," Kelli says. "Who the hell are you, and what have you done to my best friend?"

I believe she's joking. But as I listen to their thoughts and watch their incredulous faces, I can't help but worry. For them to sense it too …

Kelli does a circle around Maddy, her mouth open the whole time. "You look frickin' hot! I love your dress—I'm so jealous."

My mind is bombarded with the thoughts and images of Maddy in the other students' minds. She has the attention of everyone in here. Normally that would bother her, but she's basking in it.

Several of her male classmates are concentrating on Maddy's legs and what is beneath her dress. I don't need to be a mind reader to know what they're thinking. I shoot icy glares around the room to ward them off, but the bell rings before I stop even half of them.

I rub my forehead, fighting against a massive headache. Whatever I'm missing about Maddy, I feel it's just out of reach. Why can't I figure this out?

In her first two classes, Maddy's the star. She's the first to raise her hand when the chemistry teacher asks questions, and she gets them all right to his obvious surprise. In choir, she volunteers to do a solo to the cheers of her shocked choirmates.

This is Old Maddy again. At least, that's what everyone thinks. I'm so confused by it all. I've always known she's smart and talented, but I had no idea just how gifted. And I had no idea she could be so affectionate, full of hugs and warmth for those around her. *Almost* everyone around her, that is.

Just as her family did, everyone here wonders if it's because of me, if I'm the reason Old Maddy has come out of her shell. If it *is* because of me, that should be a good thing, right?

Then why are red flags still going off inside me?

I don't know why she's Old Maddy today. But more importantly, if this is "Old Maddy," I don't know why she ever changed into "New Maddy" in the first place. I don't understand what the Shadowwalker could have done or said that would make her change so much of herself.

# CHAPTER 42

## Maddy

**M**Y FALL INTO THE MASKED DEMON'S TV ENDS almost as quickly as it begins.

I blink, trying to orient myself, but all I can see is fabric with large flowers. It's at an odd angle—sideways. The more I stare at it, the more I realize I'm the one who's sideways. I think I'm lying down on a couch.

My ears buzz as a muffled sound filters in. It sounds like a small child whimpering.

I try to turn toward the sound, but my head won't move.

I can rest assured I'm not inside girl nine because the masked demon, not the demon serial killer, sent me here. But I still need to figure out who this is and how to disconnect at a moment's notice. Regardless of who this is, I can die in here if something goes bad.

Okay, whoever you are—apparently you have something to show me.

I relax and let my unknown host take over.

MY EARS PRICK WITH THE ALL-TOO-FAMILIAR SOUND OF sniffling.

*Again?*

No. I shouldn't be mad at her. It's not her fault. I roll off the couch, rub the sleep from my eyes, and yawn. A full day of school and band practice after helping at Uncle Don's farm is sure taking its toll. But I'm building strength. The next time *he* comes after me, he'll be in for a big surprise.

She sniffles again.

I stumble to the television and shut it off. I didn't want the sound on, but the picture helped lull me to sleep. I climb the orange and brown shag-carpeted stairs, leaning heavily on the banister as I try to shake off my exhaustion. Then I follow the narrow hallway to her bedroom.

Her dolls are on the floor. He'll hate that. I place them back on her shelf.

A sob sounds from her closet.

I sigh and open the door. The last bit of exhaustion evaporates as I take in the sight of her curled into a ball on the floor.

"What happened, Meg?"

I brush back her long brown hair, and tear-filled, green eyes stare up at me.

"I—I dumped it," she says through a sob. Her little body shakes.

I haven't seen her this upset since the funeral. A seven-year-old shouldn't have to deal with any of this. I sit and scoop her up into my arms. She sobs into my shirt.

"Come on, Meggles—tell me what happened."

She cries harder at my nickname for her. I miss the sound of her giggles. It's as if all the joy in the house died the night she flatlined.

"He's-gonna-be-so-mad-at-me, JayJay." The words almost stream together as one.

"Not you, little Meggles. Now tell your big brother what happened."

She raises her tiny fist and opens it. Mom's perfume bottle rests in her palm. Empty. Orchids and cherry blossoms linger on her wrist.

My heart stops.

Not her perfume.

"Oh, Megan. What did you do?"

Her fist tightens around the bottle, and she pulls it to her chest. She burrows into me, wiping tears and snot on my shirt.

"I couldn't remember what she smelled like. I just wanted to sniff it, b-but it fell off her dresser."

He *is* going to be furious. That was the last present he bought Mom before she got sick. He puts a little on her pillow every week. He thinks I don't notice, but I do. Otherwise, I wouldn't think he cared at all.

Tires crunch in the gravel driveway.

We stiffen.

*He's home.*

I run my fingers through her soft hair. She looks so much like Mom. Small, same brown hair and green eyes ... I can't stand the thought of him punishing her.

"I'll take care of it."

Her crying stops. She pulls away, horror in her eyes.

"No, JayJay. You can't take the belt for me. I did it. I deserve to be punished."

"It's not the first time I've gotten it," I tell her, "and it won't be the last. Besides, I'm stronger than you. I can take it, you can't. But I don't want you around. Go next door to Paul's. I'll come get you when it's safe."

She throws her arms around me and hugs me as tightly as she can.

I hug her tighter and rest my chin on top of her head. The apple scent of her shampoo fills my airways.

"I love you, Meggles."

"I love you too, JayJay."

The door downstairs bangs open. Loud thuds echo as he stomps through the living room and into the kitchen. Glass clinks as he grabs a bottle and glass.

*Whiskey.* He had a bad day at work.

This is gonna hurt.

I take the bottle from her hand, shift her off my lap, then stand. Without saying another word, I grab her hand and lead her down the stairs. I open the door, grab her Mary Janes, and hand them to her. She hugs me. After a moment, I peel her off me and send her to safety.

With the door shut, I close my eyes and rest my head against it. Please God, let him see it was an accident. Let him understand. Just—this—once.

"*Boy!*" he shouts from the kitchen. I jump. "Where's my dinner? Work my ass off to provide for you ungrateful brats, and you can't even make dinner on time. What kinda lazy bastard are you?"

Even without the perfume spill, I have a feeling my night would have ended with a sore backside. This will make farmwork unbearable tomorrow. But there's no point in delaying the inevitable. The more he drinks, the harder he hits.

I take a deep breath, square my shoulders, and turn to meet my maker.

He glares as I enter the kitchen, stroking his growing beard. He's sitting at the table—the bottle of whiskey is in front of him along with a nearly empty glass. As he finishes it, I head to the fridge, hoping he will be happier once he's fed.

"I thought we could have sandwiches for dinner."

"Sandwiches? *Sandwiches*! I didn't bust my ass all day to come home to a sandwich! Your momma wouldn't never—"

"Yeah, well, she ain't here now."

I duck as the whiskey bottle is lobbed at my head. It hits the cabinet and shatters. The kitchen fills with the pungent scent of cheap alcohol as it drips down the cabinets and onto the floor.

I resist the urge to groan, knowing I'll be the one cleaning it up later. I don't know how Mom put up with him. He's much worse now that she's gone, but he sure wasn't a saint before. He didn't hit her—he reserved that for me—but he never appreciated a thing she did. And he always put her down. It's times like this that I wonder if she was glad for death, even though I know she didn't want to leave Megan and me.

His chair squeaks against the floor as he rises. In two short strides he's standing in front of me. His blue eyes scowl into mine. I narrow my blue eyes right back.

My heart pounds in my chest. If it weren't for Meg, I would have left the day we laid her to rest. Maybe sooner. But I can't stand the thought of the welts that would show up on her fair skin if I weren't here to protect her.

Uncle Don gave me a job. I'm saving every last penny to get us both out of here. Between that and the few gigs the band's done, I have two months' rent stashed away. Once I get a few hundred more, we're gone.

He huffs in front of me like a mad bull.

Without a word, I raise my shaking hand, opening my fist to show him the empty bottle. His gaze slowly follows.

In a flash, his hands wrap around my throat, squeezing so tight I can't breathe.

I grab his wrists, fighting for air, but he only grips tighter.

Pushing me into the kitchen counter, he slams my head into the cabinet. Over and over again, he pounds me into it. My ears ring and my skull aches.

"*What did you do?*" he screams.

My chest burns. Darkness creeps along the edges of my vision.

"That's all I had left of her!" he shouts.

He lets go.

I collapse to the floor. My hands and arms sting with an unfamiliar pain. All I can do is cough—violently, desperately. No matter how much air I suck in, it's not enough.

Metal clangs as he undoes his belt.

I brace myself. This pain—this pain will be familiar.

Leather slashes through my shirt. The crack sounds through the kitchen. Tremendous fire rips through my body, but I know it'll only get worse. I don't scream. I won't let him win. I'll take my punishment. It's the only pain strong enough to block out the pain of losing Mom. It's the only thing real in this nightmare.

Again and again, the leather hits my back, tearing away first at my shirt and then at my flesh. He's never done this many before. I don't know how many more I can take.

I pound the floor. Those strange sharp pains ravage my hands and arms again. A small river of red flows from them. Shards of glass stick out of my hands and arms.

*The broken whiskey bottle.*

I concentrate on the burning in my arms, hoping that pain will be enough to get me through this. I have to. He will tire soon.

"It should have been you!" he screams as the belt opens and reopens my skin.

"*Jesus!*" I finally cry out.

My vision blurs as images of Meg flash in my mind. He would have killed her. I can't let him do this to her. Ever.

I can't let him kill me.

DEATH. IS IT HERE FOR HIM OR ME?

Fire tears apart my back, but I no longer feel the bite of each lash. I've managed to break away from JayJay, though I don't have the strength to leave his body.

I'm trapped. If I don't find a way to fully separate from JayJay, I will die. I'm slipping into a peaceful numbness I've felt before—moments before Lauren's death.

Images flash in my own mind. My family. My friends. MJ.

My heart constricts, tormented by the memory of what I said to him yesterday. I told him he should have killed me. Everything would be better that way.

My heart races. Blood pumps through my veins so fast it feels as if my heart will explode. Darkness lingers for me. I latch on to the pain, letting the grief and fear take hold.

No. I have to fight it. I can't die here.

Why did she send me here? I don't understand.

Death is coming. But he can't have me. I won't let him.

Through JayJay's eyes, I watch his father step away, leaning on the countertop in exhaustion. He runs a hand through his overgrown black hair. For a moment, the lashes cease, though the fire still burns.

Icy blue eyes stare down at me, though they only see JayJay. "Jesus? You're asking for Jesus, boy?"

I take a staggered breath and close my eyes, trying to block out the horrors around me. In the darkness, I think of MJ—of running into his arms and begging him to forgive me.

I open my eyes, praying to be home, but instead I'm still staring up at JayJay's father. It didn't work.

The numbness of death grows stronger. My eyelids droop. Thoughts jumble.

I fight the darkness. I fight the numbness. I can't die here. I focus on the only thing I see—JayJay's father.

The father pants, the red-stained belt hanging in his hands. "Haven't you figured out there is no God? If there were, he would've taken you off my hands instead of my Judith."

At the sound of his mother's name, the boy lets out a cry of anger and pain—and loss. He pushes up off the floor and lunges at his father. My body moves with him, still stuck inside him.

He grabs his father by the collar and slams his glass-and-blood-covered fist into his father's neck. A large shard pierces him, sinking into flesh and artery. At the same time, his father sends his fist into JayJay's stomach.

JayJay's abdomen tightens from the sharp shock. He lets go of his father and stumbles backward into the counter. He looks down.

The black handle of a kitchen knife sticks out of his gut.

He touches it, then pulls his hands away. They're covered in blood. His own. His father's.

I stare at JayJay's hands. The longer I do, the more they morph between his hands and mine.

The bloody hands, the knife, the bottle. All I can think of is Ben ...

"Why?" JayJay asks. His voice barely makes a sound. He collapses to his knees, slumping over. Darkness hovers over him, anxiously awaiting his final breath.

"He should have taken you, Justin," his father mutters. Blood drips from the side of his mouth and down his throat. He falls to the floor.

Justin.

I scream.

# CHAPTER 43

## MJ

DISAPPOINTMENT HITS ME THE MOMENT WE WALK into math. There's a new substitute. I was hoping Maddy's Guardian, Ms. Morgan, would be here. I wish I could ask her if I'm just being paranoid or if she too noticed anything off about Maddy. I haven't seen Ms. Morgan since we talked at the cabin outside Seattle. Come to think of it, other than the Shadowwalker, I haven't seen any of the beings that are supposedly helping Maddy. I could use their help.

Halfway through class, Maddy becomes restless, shifting in her seat. I wonder if it's because of Tom. He's been staring at her legs all morning, picturing her in his mind. Thinking of touching her and kissing her in ways I myself thought about this morning. If he doesn't stop, he's going to have a pair of black eyes.

Suddenly Maddy's hands curl into tight fists and she groans. It's quiet enough that her classmates don't hear it, but I do. She's in pain.

I lean across the aisle. "Maddy, what's wrong?"

She grimaces and slumps over in her seat. "I must speak with you in the hallway."

"Now?"

She nods.

I close my eyes, focusing on the sound of the clock in the front of the room, listening for its rhythmic tic. I block out everything else. Slowly, the ticking stops. I reopen my eyes, and everyone except Maddy and I is frozen.

Her face clenches in pain again, but she puts up her hands to block me from touching her before I even make a move.

"Did you stop the whole school or just this room?" she asks.

"I … how do you know that's what I did?" I've never told her I could do this. Did the others?

She doesn't answer. Instead, she releases a shaky breath. She looks at me for an answer.

"The whole school," I finally reply.

"That is good." She leaves her desk and slowly walks out the door.

I follow, my hands in tight fists as I fight the urge to reach out and help her, to let my essence discover where this pain is coming from.

"Maddy, what's wrong? Tell me what's happening."

She continues her slow pace as we walk down the hallway. Suddenly she stops, cries out in agony, and leans into a nearby locker as her body doubles over.

"Maddy, please!"

I wrap my arms around her, not caring if she tries to shove me off. As my essence enters her body, it's met with resistance, then it's shoved out of her. I stagger back; my hands and arms sting as if they were burned. The last time this happened …

"Help her!" she cries. "I did not mean for this to happen."

Her eyes open, pleading with me, but all I can see is that Maddy's beautiful emerald eyes are now scarlet.

Even though I stopped time, it still seems to slow as Sissy, Alexander, and Tamitha appear and surround us. All of us stare at the demon possessing Maddy.

"Who are you?" I growl.

She groans and falls to her knees as if something struck her. "I do not"—she gasps—"have a name."

"How long have you been inside her?"

She cries out again and can barely speak. "Today. Since waking. Yesterday, for a time too. I told her to lie then. You were not ready to know of me."

Maddy lied to me.

I have to blink just to clear my mind of the thought. Getting her back is all that matters. This demon has taken her twice now.

"What do you know about her?" I continue, my anger rising.

She spasms and shrinks lower to the ground. "I know everything. I am helping—"

"Don't you dare say you're helping her!"

"MJ, stop," Tamitha says. She points to Maddy's back. "Look!"

Maddy's red dress is darkening. Her body spasms again, and the demon holds back a scream. A gash appears on the bare skin at her shoulder blades.

The demon is hurting my Maddy.

"Get out of her now!" I shout. I stand over her, holding back the urge to grab her and shake her. She's holding Maddy captive.

I've lost count of how many times I've performed an exorcism, but I don't want to do that. This demon is powerful. I'm not willing to risk Maddy getting hurt any more than she already is.

"I cannot leave her. She is in a vision, and—" Another blow from something unseen rattles her body.

"A vision? Of who? Tell us!"

"Should I go as backup for Protector Steve?" Alexander says, looking at me for orders. Steve has been assigned to protect Teresa Adams, the next victim on the killer's list.

"Wait," I reply. Something tells me this isn't a vision of the next victim. According to the pattern, she will die by fire.

The demon grinds her teeth in torment. "I cannot tell you what she is seeing. Only Maddy can. But she will not come out unless you help her."

Several more blows come as I stare in silence at the demon asking for my help. She cries out again and pounds the floor.

I fall to my knees in front of the demon. I forget about the killer. If this is a vision of the next victim, the girl is likely nearly dead, anyway. I forget about everything but Maddy.

"I'll do whatever you want. Just tell me what to do."

"The line between sides is thinning," she says, panting for air. "We are ... running out of time. Touch me. I do not ... have the strength ... to fight you now. Call out to her. Compel her to come back."

I shake my head. "She can't be compelled."

Red eyes meet mine. "She is not … in control right now."

"I can't compel you eith—"

"The vision is killing her!" she cries. "I am slipping. I am losing my hold on her."

I hesitate, then place my hands on her shoulder. My essence flows into her slowly. I'm met with no resistance this time. I take a deep breath and push it forward.

She slumps into me as more blows hit her back. Then she raises Maddy's arms and turns them over. Tiny little cuts mar her beautiful skin from her elbows down to her fingers. Blood trickles like rivers.

I force my eyes up to the fluorescent lights on the ceiling, trying not to cry. Trying to keep it together. Maddy needs me.

As I look back down, I feel a small glimmer of hope. Alexander, Tamitha, and Sissy all have their hands on Maddy's body, healing her and trying to help me bring her back.

This time, even their essences flow freely.

"Tell her to come back," the demon whispers. "No matter where Maddy is … she hears you. Bring her home. I am trusting you, angel … with this knowledge."

I hold her closer, holding back my emotions as I reach out and connect with Maddy's mind. I push past the darkness, forcing her to open up to me. When my essence cycles back to me, I know I've gained control of her.

I've done this countless times before, but never with Maddy. I don't know if I should be relieved or upset that it's working now. All I know is that it adds another question to the very long list of things I do not know about the woman I love.

As my essence pours back in, I say in the calmest voice I can manage, "Maddy. Come back to me, *minn hvatvetna*. I *dare* you."

Even though the demon still writhes in pain, the creases in her face ease as a bit of tension leaves her.

"I meant what I said." Her voice is weak, barely above a whisper. She looks into my eyes. "You can save her. But you must start communicating. Train her. Love her. Trust her. Everything else will fall into place. She loves you too. She is just … afraid to say it. Do not give up on her. She almost said it yesterday."

A tear falls down my cheek as the demon closes her eyes. Maddy's body slumps in our arms. I hold her closer, burying my face in her hair.

Her heart suddenly races.

I pull back just as her eyes fly open and she gasps for air.

She looks at our stunned faces, then her eyes lock on me. They're back to her stunning shade of emerald green.

"MJ," she says, her voice wavering.

Without thinking, I kiss her. I kiss her through my pain of nearly losing her, my anger at the demon and the killer, my frustration with myself, and my joy that she's back.

One by one, the others remove their essences so the moment only belongs to Maddy and me. I hear them step away.

Maddy's arms wrap around me, and she deepens our kiss. Our passion could burn the school down around us, and we would be oblivious to it.

"I'm so sorry," I murmur against her lips.

"Me too," she answers back.

I wrap my arms tighter around her, trying in vain to keep her with me.

She screams, breaking our kiss. Her fingernails dig into me.

Her back.

I more gently pull her against me and inspect the damage. Her dress is soaked in blood, and countless lashes leave her skin open and raw. The pale skin of her arms and hands is lost under the river of blood.

I push my essence to her back, arms, and hands, fixing the damage.

"I am so sorry," I whisper over and over again.

The pain lessens. The scars are healing, but it will never be enough.

"Don't," she says, her voice weak and rough.

"Don't what?"

"Don't fix it all." Her eyes plead with mine. "Pain is what saved me. I need the scars. I need to remember what happened and how close I came to—"

She turns away. A tear clings to her lashes, but before it can fall, I wipe it away. My thumb strokes her cheek.

In that moment, I realize just how close I came to losing her.

# CHAPTER 44

# Maddy

S LOWLY, MJ LIFTS HIS HANDS FROM MY BODY. AS HIS essence withdraws, the pain returns, but it's not as bad as before. I examine my arms. The cuts are scabbed over, and the skin is only slightly pink. It looks as if the cuts happened days ago instead of five minutes ago.

I sit up as his team circles around us. They all gasp again at the sight of my back. I peek over my shoulder. Pink lines crisscross on my shoulder blades and dip below my dress. I shut my eyes, fighting the memories of the vision.

"Tell me what happened," MJ pleads. "Tell me everything."

How can I even begin? How can I tell him about the masked demon bringing me to Hell? How can I tell him about the vision of Justin? How can I tell him about the demon hunting me?

And exactly *what* can I tell him? The masked demon said there's much to tell MJ and much to not tell him.

MJ is looking at me, waiting for a reply. I lift my chin. No matter what happens from now on, I'm going to tell him everything I can.

I probably shouldn't while everyone else is here, though. The demon said I should talk to MJ, not his team. I glance at them.

MJ follows my gaze and understands. "Leave us," he tells them, "but don't go far."

Without a word, his team disappears.

"Thank you." I give him a small smile.

He offers a smile back. "You're welcome. Now, tell me everything, please. Somehow I need to stop this from happening to you."

My fingers play with the hem on my dress running across my thigh, and I look across the hall at the row of lockers. Suddenly it dawns on me.

I'm at school—not home. I'm in a dress. I'm in *this* dress.

"Tell me she didn't," I say as I exhale.

His brows narrow, and suspicion fills his eyes. "What, Maddy?"

"She said she would, but I didn't think she could."

"Could what?" he repeats.

"The demon put me in the vision so she could come up here and live my life. And it worked."

He stiffens. From the look on his face, I can tell he isn't surprised. Maybe he knew? Maybe that's why he and his team were surrounding me when I came out of the vision?

I look down the hall again, finding it empty. "Where is everyone else? She didn't … she didn't hurt anyone, did she?"

"Everyone is fine. So you *know* this demon?" His voice is clipped. "Who is she? Tell me so I can make her pay for hurting you."

I open my mouth and wait for that sensation of not being able to tell him the truth. But this time it doesn't come. I can tell him about her.

"I don't know her name. I only know what she looks like. She's the one who took me from the park Wednesday after Sissy tried to attack me. She pulled my soul to her again last night, then sent me into a vision of—of—"

Fear, pain, and unease send my nerves into a frenzy as I relive what I saw while inside Justin.

MJ's face softens with worry. "The vision really rattled you, didn't it?" he asks.

I sniffle as I nod. The shock and pain are too raw. I need MJ to get through this.

"Could you do something else for me, please?" I ask.

"Anything you want, consider it done."

"Can you hold me?" My lower lip trembles as tears creep up.

Immediately, MJ pulls me into his chest. At first, he holds his essence back, remembering that I asked him not to use it to take away all my pain.

I take a few deep breaths, safe and warm in his arms. I tell him about the vision—though I don't say Justin's name. While I speak, MJ's essence slowly begins flowing again. I don't think he even realizes it. I don't care. I just want to be in his arms. And I can only imagine the horrible thoughts running through his own head. Sending his essence no doubt makes this easier for him too.

As I tell him of the moment when Justin and his father stabbed each other, he sits up with determination. "Who was the boy?" he asks. "I might be able to save him if I get there in time."

I hesitate, giving myself a moment. "No. He's already dead. He's been dead a long time."

MJ's face clouds with confusion. "How do you know?"

If I tell him now or sixty years from now, he will never understand.

"Because it was Justin."

MJ pulls away. Crimson eyes stare at me. "That *monster*? You almost died inside *him*? I can't believe he almost took you away from me again! He'll pay for this!" His hands ball into fists.

"Stop!" I say. "Justin didn't do this to me. This was a vision of what was done *to* him. He's the victim here, not me."

MJ's body shakes with rage. "Don't you *dare* feel sorry for him! He threatened your friends and family. He killed Ben. He nearly killed you. He is a *demon*."

Loss and guilt ripple through me. "I hear what you're saying," I reply. "I know you're right. But after seeing where Justin came from, his life … I can't help thinking that maybe, somehow, things could have been different. Maybe Justin wouldn't have done what he did if he was given another chance. And why did he go to Hell, anyway? What he lived was Hell."

MJ's crimson eyes intensify, becoming a deep blood red. "He's where he belongs. What doesn't make sense is why that demon would possess you just to show you a vision of another demon that almost killed you two days ago."

"She said it was because I needed to understand both sides, but I think it goes deeper than that."

"What do you think it meant, then?"

I shake my head as so many ideas are swimming in there. "Maybe it's related to Justin—about how he wasn't always evil. Maybe demons as a whole. Maybe more demons were like him. Or maybe it's about me and my ability to restore their emotions. Or maybe it's some combination. I don't know yet. What I do know is that I'm sick and tired of almost dying for the truth."

MJ turns away, but not before I see guilt flash across his face. "I thought I was protecting you by not telling you everything. But you were right last night. I should have told you about Duane and the targets. I should have told you a lot of things. Starting now, I'm going to."

I don't want to talk about last night. Not yet. It's as much my fault as it is his.

"She watches me, MJ," I say, redirecting the conversation. "The demon."

His eyes widen with questions. Before he can say anything, I keep going.

"She and someone she calls her master watch my life from Hell. She's sent her soul into me a few times when I've been in trouble. She claims it's all for my protection. I want to believe her. But after what she did today and the things she told me last night … I'm not sure what to believe anymore."

MJ moves in front of me, taking my hands in his. Again he holds his essence back, allowing me to just feel him—his calloused, strong hands.

"Believe this," he says. "Believe in us."

I stare into his hazel eyes. There is still so much about him that's in the dark. He can say the same about me. But no matter what, we keep ending up here—together. And when we're like this, the insane world suddenly doesn't seem so crazy.

"I believe in us, MJ. I trust you." I inhale. "Which is why I have to tell you something else. Something that will change everything."

He leans closer and places a hand on my cheek. "There is nothing you can say that will change how I feel about you."

I grimace, knowing that's not true. I close my eyes, readying myself to tell MJ the truth. Suddenly her words pour out of me. "The killer is coming for me, but I do not know why. I just know."

"No." He wraps his arms around me gently, but his voice is firm. "I've checked. The targets are very specific, and while you have some things in common with them, you don't have … everything."

"It does not matter," I say, hating that it's not my voice, wishing I could stop this and tell him the full truth. But her words just keep coming. "I do not know why, but it just does not. Trust me. If you do not trust me, then you will truly know what it is like to lose me, and it would be your fault."

# CHAPTER 45

## MJ

I HOLD MADDY CLOSER, NOT READY TO LET HER GO. HER words sound strange, just as they did the last time this same demon took her. I suspect the demon is controlling her somehow. But whether the words are her own or the demon's, I cannot deny the truth of them.

The killer demon is coming for her, and if he gets her, it *would* be my fault.

I suspected she was a target the day I met her. Then I allowed myself to be misguided by the one thing Maddy didn't have in common with the other targets. But I was a fool. The fact that she's not adopted does not matter. Just as she said.

It's obvious now. I see that. Maddy manipulates the weather, controls at least two elements, has dreams or visions of demons and the mortals in danger from them, creates alternate worlds, time travels, resists all immortal abilities, restores emotions in immortals, and has even made my heart beat. And that's just the abilities I'm aware of. She could have more still. With her many abilities, why wouldn't the killer—and others—be after her?

I will stop this monster. I will stop him, and I will stop everyone else from ruining her chance at happiness. Even if it kills me.

But until then, I have to do something to keep her safe.

I stare into her emerald eyes. In them I see something that hurts me more than her words: fear. She knows what the demon killer is capable of—even more than I do.

I cup her chin, my thumb moving back and forth along her cheek. She leans in to my touch.

"Let me take you away," I beg.

I know she won't say yes. She won't leave her family and friends. Not until she has too. Still, I keep talking, hoping I can sway her. I'm desperate.

"Let me keep you safe. We can go somewhere remote, just the two of us. Like … a cabin in the mountains."

Her eyes widen. She looks a bit confused and yet a bit suspicious.

"Or Paris or Jamaica—or even the North Pole," I continue. "The location doesn't matter. All that matters is staying hidden from everyone. You would be safe, and you wouldn't have to pretend for anyone. We could do whatever we wanted."

She doesn't respond. Maybe she's considering it.

I place a soft, tender kiss on her lips. She gives in to the kiss, needing it as much as I need her. I hold my essence back, wanting to kiss her as a mortal. As a man who loves her.

She clings tighter to me. Having her here, touching her and tasting her with my lips, the need to protect her overwhelms me.

"Please," I beg again against her sweet lips. "Come away with me."

I move back, just enough to see her clearly. She stares at me, searching for something unknown. Then her lips shift into a small smile.

"If I have to leave," she begins, "I want to go with you—no one else. But I'd rather stay and fight."

I turn away, but she brings me back to her. She scoots closer, pressing her forehead to mine and placing a hand on each side of my face.

"They're dying for me," she says. "I can't just abandon the rest."

"I'll send more Protectors to guard the others. He will be stopped."

"Good. They need more help. But I'm still not hiding. Not yet."

"Maddy, I—"

Behind us, we suddenly hear a throat clear.

"I'm sorry to interrupt," Alexander says. He's staring down the hall. "Tamitha and Sissy are concerned with how long the Immotus has been intact. They're worried others will come if we keep it in place much longer."

I nod. They're right—we can't keep everyone frozen forever. We have to restart time and return everything to normal, just as it was before. I turn back to Maddy, seeing the dried blood on her skin and ruined dress. My own clothes are covered in her blood as well.

"I'm taking Maddy home to shower and change into a new outfit. Before we return, tell the others to compel everyone to not notice her outfit change. I'll—"

"Stop," Maddy says firmly. Her voice is sharp. "Tell me what's going on. What's the Immotus?"

I send my essence into her, trying to calm her. "It's one of our angelic abilities. With it, we alter time. Currently, time is at a standstill in Mankato. Once the Immotus lifts, time will move a bit faster to catch up to the rest of the world, though only those who are more sensitive will notice something off."

Maddy frowns. By now I know her well enough to realize she's bothered by this.

"We had no choice," I stress. "We needed to know what was happening to you without anyone else seeing or hearing."

She considers that a moment. "I understand that. But I still don't like it. It's still wrong."

"Maddy, it's fine. All over the world, at any given time, at least a dozen places are frozen. It's done to protect mortals. And afterward, they go on living as if nothing happened."

"It's not *fine*," Maddy says, jumping to her feet. The building rumbles.

Her reaction takes me by surprise. From the side, I see Alexander take a step back—caught off guard as well.

"We're not pawns!" Maddy shouts.

"Hey," I say, scrambling to my feet and standing before her. "It's okay. That's not—"

"It's not okay!" she says over more rumbles. "This is why it's so hard for me to accept what you do. You stop time, you compel mortals just as much as the demons do."

"What?" I say, stunned. "No, Maddy. They do those things to cause harm. We do it for good."

"Good?" she repeats, shaking her head. "How is compelling the *entire school* to forget what I was wearing good?"

I stiffen, then take a step closer to her. But she steps back.

"We're not pawns," she repeats.

All I can do is stare, not knowing how to comfort her.

I TAKE MADDY HOME SO SHE CAN SHOWER. WHILE SHE'S IN the bathroom, I pace in her bedroom.

How upset she is makes me wonder what else happened with the demon. Where was she taken? What was said to her? What else happened to her?

I've never stepped back to think about how often we compel mortals. With it not working on Maddy, I'm learning just how much I lean on it. What if she's right and we do use it just as often as demons? Granted, we use it for different reasons, but the effect is still the same. When it comes to the bigger picture, we all treat mortals as pawns.

I reach in the Veil for the bag of clothes I picked up from Immortal City and begin changing. I have to think of a way to bring Maddy back to school without compelling everyone. My reflection in her dresser mirror makes me pause. My gaze roams my assignment clothes—plain white shirt and blue jeans. I have several identical sets. If one set gets soiled or ruined battling a demon, I can change into a new set without anyone noticing. Maybe the same can be done for Maddy.

I reach out to Tamitha.

*Yes, MJ,* she says once we connect.

*I need you to find a dress identical to the one Maddy wore earlier,* I say.

I could have sent Sissy—she's been itching to get back in my good graces—but Tamitha's attention to detail will be best here.

*Consider it done,* Tamitha says.

We disconnect. I turn and stare at the bathroom door, then listen for Maddy's heartbeat.

It's quick, though it has been since she came back. This demon that possessed her has me more worried than the others. Maddy is powerful. Strong enough to fight off an Influencer with heightened abilities. So whoever this unknown demon is, she must be even stronger.

She's not a Morpher. They don't operate this way.

My gaze lands on the Segrego bracelet still sitting on Maddy's dresser. I suddenly remember that the stones didn't react to the demon this morning. They should have. I myself sensed a demon's presence. But I dismissed my instinct when the stones didn't react. That can mean only one thing—somehow this demon doesn't belong to the Caste.

As I'm staring at the bracelet, Maddy exits the bathroom.

I stand there, stunned by her appearance more so than I was this morning. She's in the same style of dress as this morning—Tamitha must have found it quickly. Now that I know it's really Maddy … the dress seems different.

My body tightens and the room feels warm against my skin.

But Maddy's arms are crossed, and she's looking away. Her eyes are distant. Is she lost in a memory, or deep in thought?

Her fingers tighten on her arms, holding herself even more.

Before I can move to comfort her, emerald eyes land on me. I'm stuck in place, rooted by the sadness in them.

"Last night," she says, "I saw how you looked at me after the tree fell … You were afraid of me. Of what I could do."

In a flash, I'm in front of her, holding her. My fingers run through her hair, and she leans into it.

"I was afraid *for* you. For us. I didn't know you had that much power, but I should have. That was my fault. We need to get a handle on your abilities. Let's do some training."

Immediately, I realize I'm still not sticking to the goal I originally set for the day—before everything went to hell. Today was supposed to be normal.

Or maybe my goal is all wrong. How can life be "normal" right now? For that matter, Maddy hasn't been "normal" since the incident with the Shadowwalker three years ago, when she pushed her family and friends away.

But ever since coming back from the Influencer's house, I've seen the desire in her eyes to repair those relationships. And Father knows she and I have some repairing to do.

Maybe what she really needs is a night of healing. A night where she can see just how much she is loved by her family, friends, and me.

My mind races through the information I obtained from reading hundreds of dating books in Immortal City. Within a second, I have the perfect date planned for her. Tonight is going to be—what is the word Amber said when she met me—*epic*.

I can't conceal a sly smile as I look at Maddy. "Never mind," I correct myself. "No training today. We have other plans."

Uncertainty flashes in her eyes. "But how can you want me after I tried to hurt you? That's why I took off your bracelet."

I calm her emotions while doing my best to control mine. "It was an accident. I'm fine. What hurt worse was that I thought I lost you. "

"Why?"

"Because of everything I kept from you. Because of how angry I made you. I'm … an idiot. But regardless of what you think of me, it's your bracelet. I want you to wear it."

"Do—" She stops and pauses. Her insides suddenly become a jumbled mess of knots and fear. "After last night and today I mean … do you still want to be with me?"

I place a hand under her chin, tilting her head up. "Nothing could make me stop loving you." My lips curve into a sly smile. "Not even *you*."

She rests her head on my chest, but not before I see her smile. "What would I do without you?"

I kiss her hair, inhaling the fruit scents of her shampoo. "Doesn't matter. You're never going to find out."

"Good." She wraps her arms around me, and I do the same.

"Maddy, before we go back, there's one thing I'd like you to do for me."

## CHAPTER 46

# Maddy

MY EYES LAND ON THE BRACELET, KNOWING WHAT MJ's going to ask.

Yesterday it felt like a heavy chain tightening its hold on me, marking me as his for the world to see. Today I want it on my wrist so I can feel his love for me and know I'm safe.

MJ steps in front of my dresser and picks up my bracelet. "Before I give this back to you," he says, "there's something about it you need to know."

He holds the bracelet out for me to see. "The gems aren't the kind you find in stores. They're used by Protectors. They represent the twelve types, or Castes, of demons. When they're near, the corresponding stone turns black."

I stare at the heavenly objects bound together by white-gold links. There's so much about him and his world that I don't know. I can't deny the depth of my feelings for him, but how can I be in love with him already?

I don't want to run. I want to learn everything I can about him—both his Protector life and his mortal one. And

I want this … this beautiful, otherworldly gift he created to not only show me how he feels but also to keep me safe.

Suddenly I'm reminded of Elizabeth and the necklace Damien gave her. It was far too beautiful and expensive to be worn every day—especially just around the cabin—yet Damien compelled her. Was her necklace special in the same way my bracelet is?

"Please," MJ whispers, moving closer to me.

His knuckles caress my cheek, and the movement echoes throughout my body. I lean closer to him, craving his touch, warmth, and security.

"They keep coming after you, trying to take you away … I can't lose you. I won't survive it."

The scene I saw on the TV in Hell—him holding my vacant body—comes barreling back. I need to fight them off. I need to stop letting the demons use me. It tortures him. I want a future with MJ. If the bracelet helps me—helps us—fight them …

I nod and hold my arm out for him. Cool metal wraps around my wrist, and MJ secures the clasp. As he pulls his hands away, the bracelet feels different this time. It's no longer a heavy, foreign object that causes everything in my body to go on alert. Now … I don't know. It just feels *right*. As if it's always been there.

"It's beautiful, MJ. Thank you."

He exhales, his shoulders lower, and muscles in his face loosen as he smiles. My wearing this means so much to him.

"This won't repel demons, but at least now we can have a heads-up of when they're coming." He wraps his arms around me. "It's time we head back to school. Remember, time will move faster as we catch up to the rest of the world. I'm glad time will go faster, because we have a special night ahead of us. That's all I'm going to say for now—it's a surprise." He grins.

I wrap my arms around him too and smile as I anticipate this surprise. No matter what happens from this point on, I must hold on to MJ.

WE NEED TO RETURN TO OUR SEATS IN MATH CLASS BEFORE MJ will lift the Immotus. Walking the halls is like walking in one of my dreams. Every room is silent. Everyone's frozen in the same position they were in when the Immotus was cast. A few students were in the process of grabbing things from their lockers. In the classrooms, teachers are motionless in front of stationary students. I'm used to this in my dreams from Elizabeth, but it's creepy knowing this is real life.

I move through the rows of statue-students in math, most of who are staring straight ahead.

"You're taking this better than I expected," MJ says.

"This is how my dreams used to begin—with everyone frozen. Before they went crazy, that is."

"Hmm … " he says, but doesn't question me further.

I wave a hand in front of Kelli's face, watching for a reaction, but there isn't one. "This doesn't affect them?"

"As I said before, people who are sensitive to the world around them may feel as if the day has dragged on, while others will feel nothing."

I still hate how easy it is for them to mess with our lives and not care. Somehow, if I survive all this, I need to put an end to them treating us like pawns. It's much more than this Immotus. I think about Duane and the others, putting those girls in harm's way to protect me. I think about how Sissy—and even MJ—nearly killed me. They sacrifice us when it suits them. Demons and angels are equally at fault here.

I notice Tom as I take my seat. He's staring under my desk at my legs. That's disgusting. I shift this way and that, trying to find the best way to sit in this damn dress. But it doesn't matter—he'll still see way too much of me.

MJ growls in his seat beside me, glaring at Tom too. "The sooner this day is over, the better. I'm running out of patience with him."

MJ's beautiful hazel eyes are narrow slits, and his perfectly kissable lips are pressed together in a thin line. Even angry, he still manages to captivate me.

"He's an idiot," I reply. "Don't waste your energy on him." I tug at the hem. "I just can't wait to get out of this dress she picked out."

MJ shakes his head, removing the angry expression. "I know it's not really your style—and I know it's definitely not what you want to wear to school." He leans across the aisle and places his hand on my bare knee. "But as your boyfriend, I must say you do look amazing in it."

My breath catches, and my heart skips a beat. He holds his essence back. I'm acutely aware of him, his skin on mine. The callouses on his hands from years of fighting, the warmth of his touch spreading out on my skin—heating me both inside and out.

Everything but MJ falls away. His gaze darkens, and his lips part. I reach out, placing my hand on his smooth cheek. His eyes close, and he relaxes into my touch.

"*Hvordan kom jeg så heldig?*" MJ asks.

"What does that mean?" I ask in breathless wonder.

His eyes reopen, and he stares into mine. "How did I get so lucky? You are many things to me, Madison. You are my life force—my reason for being. No matter what happens in the future, whether we stay here or have to leave, you will always be my home."

Then he shifts back into his chair, moving beyond my reach, and pulls his hand from my knee. "Ready?"

Oh, I'm ready. But not for school. I want to be anywhere else right now. I want to feel and taste him. I want to do more than we've done before. I want the world to feel the fire building inside me. I want to let it all burn.

I take a deep breath, trying to calm myself, but fail miserably.

"Are you ready?" he asks again.

I nod, not trusting my voice.

Instantly, life resumes. Everyone carries on as if nothing happened.

# CHAPTER 47

## Justin

I'M NO GOOD. NOT ANYMORE. THAT PART OF ME WAS lost during the Trials when I arrived in Hell. Maybe even before then.

In this lifetime, I've caused nothing but pain and suffering. Even when I tried to do good as a mortal, I still failed. I still hurt everyone. I'm good at that. Really good. I'm not meant to be the hero.

And yet here I stand—in a living room in Atlanta, Georgia, in a house that once belonged to Mads—trying to be just that.

She was an infant when they lived here. And she was only a few months old when they left. But still I had to see it. I have to know everything about her.

There is a mild hum in the air, similar to standing too close to power lines. It's the remnants of an essence—a powerful essence. Someone high up visited this space often. Most likely a member of the Fallen. Was it the Acquisitioner? Or Death?

Either way, it doesn't bode well.

I move farther into the room, bypassing the gray furniture and tables and coming to a stop in front of a bookcase. I pick up a picture frame. The photo is of a man and woman holding a curly, black-haired toddler. They're smiling—full of happiness. I put it down and look around again at how comfortable they've made themselves in Mads's home.

I clench my jaw as I move from room to room. More pictures of that family decorate the walls. It's as if Mads never lived here at all. There's no proof of her being here. They've just replaced her.

I return to the main floor, wishing the family were home so I could make them suffer. If I had time, I'd wait for them.

But the clock is ticking on Mads's life. The longer I draw this out, the greater the risk of losing her forever.

Even though I didn't find the answers I was looking for, I need to head back. Sudden relief floods me at the thought of seeing her again. I've been away from her for too long. I think I've figured out her weakness. The first chance she's alone, I'm going to test it out.

That contract will be signed by tomorrow—even if I have to use the blade on MJ and his team to accomplish it.

# CHAPTER 48

# Maddy

MJ WAS RIGHT ABOUT THE DAY MOVING FASTER. As the final bell rings, I'm relieved. I'm anxious and excited for the surprise MJ has planned after school.

His arm is around me as we walk to my locker. He's done this since math. I like this even better than holding hands. I feel closer to him, more cherished, more loved, more protected.

As we round the bend in the corridor, I see my girl-friends and my sister, Hannah, standing at my locker as well as Tamitha, Sissy, and Amber. Flashbacks of earlier in the week pop uninvited in my head. I tense up, hoping Justin's not here. Last time all my friends gathered like this, he was controlling them.

MJ places a kiss in my hair. "Don't worry. It's okay."

His ability to guess what I'm feeling by the slightest change in my body is becoming a comfort to me. Even with our secrets, he still knows me better than anyone. Even myself sometimes.

"Run along now, MJ," Tamitha says, bouncing up to greet us. "We're ready to take it from here."

I turn in the nook of his arm to stare up at him. "What is she talking about? Aren't we going to spend the afternoon together?"

He smiles. "Actually, spending time with your friends is part of the surprise. I know how important they are to you. Go shopping, do your nails or whatever you ladies do to get ready for a date."

"Date?"

He leans down so his lips are against my ear. "That's the other half of the surprise. Tonight I'm taking you out for dinner and dancing with all your friends. Pick out something special. That's a dare. I can't wait to feel you against me while we dance, like we did on the dock yesterday."

I feel weightless as a million troubles plummet from my shoulders to the linoleum floor. As much as I want to spend time with MJ, I want to be with my friends too—my time with them could be ending. How did he know I needed this?

He places a sweet, swift kiss on my lips. As he pulls away, I feel his essence lingering inside me. Even though he won't be with me physically this afternoon, at least I'll still have a part of him inside me.

"Enjoy your day, *minn hvatvetna*."

He lets go, and I'm completely, utterly lost in him. All I can do is watch as he turns and saunters down the hall with a little extra strut in his step.

I smile, knowing I'm responsible for his happiness.

Kelli comes up beside me, linking our arms together and resting her head on my shoulder. "Seriously, how often does Norway work out? 'Cuz *damn*."

Kayla, Maggie, and Hannah appear on my other side, murmuring in agreement as we all ogle my immortal boyfriend's behind.

"What did he call you?" Kayla asks in a breathy, distracted voice.

My smile widens. "I don't know what it means. It's his native language."

Our view is suddenly obstructed by Amber. Her hands are on her hips as she taps the toe of her stiletto.

"Yeah, yeah. MJ's a slice of heaven with the butt of a god. We get it. Now let's get this ridiculous afternoon over with so we can destroy whatever shreds I have left of my social life."

"I'm sorry," I say as sweetly as possible. "But MJ said I'll be hanging out with my *friends*. That doesn't include you."

Her lips twist into a grin resembling the Cheshire Cat's. "Take it up with them." She nods to Tamitha and Sissy.

My heart sinks. They're protecting me. But they're also protecting Amber. She has to come—it's a package deal.

Suddenly I remember my friends don't know Tamitha and Sissy. But as I look around, no one is questioning them. They've placed themselves in my group of friends. They compelled them.

Knowing there's no point in arguing, I leave with Hannah and my girlfriends flanking me while the Protectors and Amber follow close behind.

Hundreds of students are gathered on the sidewalk outside. Normally they would be peeling out of here with that joyous sense of freedom coursing through their veins. Especially with it being Friday.

Is something wrong? Is it a demon? I glance at my bracelet, twisting it around to ensure each stone is still its usual color.

"Where did you get that?" Sissy asks.

I look up, and her steely gaze is glued to my bracelet. I cover it, protecting it—protecting MJ's love for me. I turn to Tamitha. She's staring at Sissy too.

After a moment, Tamitha gives her head a little shake. She smiles at me. "Come on. You're going to love this."

The crowd splits as if an invisible ship were passing through. As the last students clear the way, they reveal a shiny black Hummer limo.

# CHAPTER 49

## MJ

I WATCH FROM THE VEIL AS MADDY AND HER FRIENDS drive off in the limo. I hope she enjoys her day of fun. I hope she's looking forward to our date tonight as much as I am. The way her eyes lit up with that elated sense of pure happiness assured me this is the right path for us.

But I know she's holding back. When we were getting to know each other, she told me she'd never fall in love. I just don't know why yet. I can't get her to open up to me about it, but hopefully my next surprise—waiting for her at the mall—can help with that.

"Don't tell me we're shopping too," Alexander says beside me.

He was joking, but in a way he was right. While Maddy's time will be spent relaxing, as she deserves, mine will be spent gearing up to keep her with me. After the events today with the demon possessing her, I know it's only a matter of time before someone or something comes after her again.

"We are going shopping," I reply. "Just not down here."

He arches a brow. "Okay. Lead the way."

"In a moment," I say as I turn to him.

Suddenly, my hands feel damp. I'm sweating. I've never been nervous around Alexander before. But then again, I've never done what I'm about to do either. I myself need to open up.

"There are things I need to tell you first."

Alexander tilts his head.

"Remember how I said I'd tell you why I've hidden my thoughts from the Council for so long?"

I start from the beginning, telling him about the day I died and the role the Acquisitioner played. Then I tell him about Lifa's thirty descendants I secretly protected—unsuccessfully, that is. I tell him how the Acquisitioner is responsible for their deaths as well.

As it pours out, I can't even look Alexander in the eye. "I've done all this without the Council's knowledge or approval. Without anyone's knowledge."

I know he would have helped me, had I only asked. Maybe we could have saved some of them together. But I never gave him that chance. I foolishly believed I alone had to carry that burden. I'm making the same mistake with Maddy.

"Well, what's done is done ... " Alexander begins. "So let's focus on what we can do now," he says. "I'll help you protect Maddy from the beings after her. Once she's safe, you and I will deal with the Acquisitioner together."

His support should lift my spirits, but the situation is much more complicated than he realizes. It's time to open up about everything.

"You were right all along," I admit. "There's no such thing as coincidence. Maddy is connected to everything." I hesitate. "She's the true target of the demon serial killer."

He staggers. "What? Have you … when did she tell you this?"

"Earlier today." I turn to him, my eyes beseeching his. "I'm going to lose her."

He straightens. "No, you won't. We'll help. We call more Protectors down if we have to. And Maddy—she's not defenseless either." He pauses, placing a hand on my shoulder. "You're not alone, brother. Together, we will stop this."

In his face, I see determination. I smile as my chest lightens. A sensation I haven't felt in days fills the air—hope.

I don't know much about the demon killer or the female demon who possessed Maddy, which means I don't know what chance I stand against them. And eight centuries of experience tells me I have zero chance against the Acquisitioner. But I'm going to battle him anyway. Battle them all. With help from Alexander and the others, there's a chance—albeit slim—the Acquisitioner won't get Maddy. None of them will.

"Thank you, my brother," I say.

Then together we step into the Great Divide.

WITH A RENEWED SENSE OF PURPOSE, I STRIDE THROUGH the gates of Immortal City with Alexander quick on my heels. The main streets are polluted with more angels than I have ever seen. They call out to me, but I ignore them. I'm on a mission.

I know what they want to talk about. There's a buzz in the air. They're filled with confidence, counting on me—

us—to stop the demon serial killer. They know we're close, especially now that there's news of my "psychic."

The Supplementum is crowded when we enter. I breeze past the desk, again ignoring the angel's protest, and open the double doors of the workshop. There are more angels than before immersed in projects.

"Whoa," Alexander says, taking in the massive number of weapons scattered across every available surface. "I've never noticed how overwhelming this room is."

I nod. There was a time when this place was run by one weapons master and a lone assistant. But as time went by, demon attacks increased, and so did the need for heavenly tools. Thus, more assistants were added. Yesterday John had eight assistants. Three more angels have been added since then. The space has grown to accommodate them.

My stomach tightens, knowing war is fast approaching.

With time no longer on our side, I rush to the back of the shop. As we walk, I reach out to Alexander using Cerebrallink.

*What happens here you are not allowed to repeat. Not even to Tamitha. Not yet.*

His eyes drill into me as I continue on to the last workbench cluttered with the weapons of the multi-tool pocketknife. John is where I saw him last, standing over a blade and bending it to his will. This one seems like a simple long sword, but knowing him, it's much more.

I clear my throat in between bangs.

"Yes. Yes. Just a minute," he says, waving the hand with the mallet in our general direction.

We back up to avoid being hit.

He bangs the orange blade several more times, then dunks it in a barrel of brilliant white light. He turns and removes his goggles.

"Ah, MJ. I was hoping you'd come back. I have something for you." He pulls out the sword he just made and hands it to me.

As before, fire dances along the blade once it's in my hand. I hear Alexander inhale. All breath leaves me too. Memories come rushing back.

The clang of metal on metal echoes so loudly, my bones brace for impact. The putrid stench of charred flesh fills my sinuses. And in my mind's eye, I see Nikolas and Lifa. She was brave, like Maddy. She kept trying to hide me and get me to safety, even though I was the king's warrior. And then there's *him*, the bastard Acquisitioner responsible for eight centuries of torment.

The memory fades, leaving his black gaze seared in my mind, as it has always been.

I turn my attention back to the sword. The hilt is shaped like a closed fist, the grip is wide enough for single-hand use, and the blade is long and double-edged. In the inlay, beside the fire insignia, is the inscription "Ulfberht." It's an exact replica of the sword from my mortal days.

"How did you come by this?" I ask in astonishment.

He taps his temple. "Knowing the how and why ruins the beauty of mystery."

Alexander's gaze is glued to the fiery sword still in my hand. "Is it true, then? Is the Holy War upon us?"

John rubs his chin while I grab a scabbard from the counter and sheath the sword, extinguishing the flames. I hold up a finger to John.

"Excuse us a moment, will you?"

Then I turn to Alexander and connect with Cerebrallink.

*I believe it is,* I reply. *And because of this, we must do whatever we can to keep the demons from getting Maddy.*

*If she's connected to everything, as you said … do you think she's somehow connected to the war too?* he asks.

I sigh. *Justin, Damien, the unknown demon killing the girls, the female demon from this morning, and the Acquisitioner are all after Maddy. Why do you think that is?*

*I don't know,* he replies.

*Think about what she can do. Then think about what would happen if they managed to get her right before the Holy War. The scales would be tipped in their favor. We would lose. There isn't a weapon in this room that could stop her abilities. And even if there were, I wouldn't allow anyone to use it on her. I will do whatever it takes to ensure I don't fail her. I cannot lose her. I can't ask you to help me with this, but I hope you will.*

He gives a small smile. *I'm with you until the end. So that's why we're here? To arm ourselves?*

*Just as a precaution,* I say.

He slowly exhales and takes a closer look at the weapons surrounding us. *All right. Grab whatever you think is necessary.*

I nod and turn my attention back to John, whose eyes have been flickering between us.

"What do you have to ward off entities?" I ask. "Demons, spirits, renegade angels, et cetera. All are dangerous at the moment."

"Hmm …" His bushy brows pull together. "Nothing like that exists that I am aware of, but I will work on it."

That's not what I wanted to hear, but I had suspected as much. If he had created something like that, we'd be using it already.

"For now, though, take this." John picks up the multitool pocketknife and holds it out for me.

"I thought you said it was a prototype."

"Someone has to test it out. Seems fitting it'd be you."

I shove it in my pocket. "What else?"

"Take whatever you think you'll need. Everything has been enhanced with the power of the Veil of Shadows as well as the Immortal Flame insignias."

We load up, both of us harboring dozens of weapons concealed on our bodies through the Veil of Shadows. Even Tamitha and Sissy will not detect them.

I think about Tamitha and Sissy, back there with Maddy and her friends. I hope, for all our sakes, tonight goes smoothly.

But if not … Alexander and I will be ready.

## CHAPTER 50

# Maddy

WE PASS DOZENS OF SHOPS IN THE MALL AND finally enter one with barely covered mannequins in heels that could cut down the height gap between MJ and me. It would make kissing him a lot easier, but I'd probably break my ankle.

I linger in the entrance while everyone scatters for different racks. Even though I'm smiling and even though this excursion has been fun, I feel this dark cloud forming in the distance, casting a shadow on everything. It just feels … strange. I've been dealing with angels and demons for so long—real life no longer makes me feel welcome.

"Are you okay?" Sissy asks, walking back to me.

"Sorry, it's just—"

I pause, debating whether I should confide in her. I look to Tamitha, and she's watching us with a hopeful yet cautious expression.

I turn back to Sissy and sigh. "This will sound crazy, but I feel like I'm dreaming, like this isn't real. I feel like I'm actually somewhere else—somewhere bad—and I created this happy scene to cope with it."

"Well," she begins, "I'm not an expert on you or anything. But I'm fairly certain that if you were going to create some alternate world to make yourself happy, it would not contain Amber. Or me."

I drop my eyes. She does have a point.

"You are having fun, though, right?" Sissy asks.

After a moment, I nod. Hanging out with my friends has been a nice change of pace from all the crazy.

"So why are you hesitating?"

"I can't help but feel something is going to come along and ruin all this."

She tilts her head and narrows her amber eyes. It's the same look my mom gives me when she's worried about me. "Why do you think that?"

I shrug. "Because I'm happy."

"So?"

"So, something bad always happens when I'm happy. At least this week, anyway."

She frowns. "Nothing bad will happen."

"You can't know that."

"True. But if something were about to happen, you have us and that." She points to my bracelet. "I'm not sure how much MJ told you about its powers, but if a demon were within five miles, we'd know about it. As you can see, we're fine."

My left hand rubs over my bracelet. It does help to know I have a warning, but it isn't enough to fully dissolve this sense of foreboding.

"This was optional for me—coming on this girls' day," Sissy adds in my silence. "I wanted to come, though." She looks me in the eyes. "I want to apologize for trying to kill you."

I stare back at her in shock. "Uhh … thanks," is all I can manage.

The other Protectors have told me she's sorry, but I never expected her to say it to my face. Actually, I never expected to be face-to-face with her like this. MJ didn't want her around me until he trusted her again. Her being here and talking with me must mean she's earned his trust again. He wouldn't put her—or me—in this position otherwise.

"He's important to you, isn't he?" I ask.

"Who?"

"MJ."

She nods. "He's important to us all. He's the first Protector, as well as the best. We all look to him for guidance."

My heart clenches. I didn't know he was the first. But then again, I've been avoiding finding out anything about that part of him.

She gives me a weak smile and motions to the store. "Shall we?"

I follow her, joining my friends.

WE'RE ALL GETTING NEW OUTFITS FOR TONIGHT. THEY ALL find what they want right away, then they band together on a mission to find me *the outfit*. I'm not exactly sure what *the outfit* even is. Tamitha said when I try it on, I'll know it's the perfect one. And she said that when MJ sees it later, it'll make him go stupid for me. I don't really want him to "go stupid." I don't know what that even means, but I'm curious.

I feel silly modeling each dress as they sit in a line outside the dressing rooms. Amber's disinterested with everything. Kayla and Maggie seem to disagree about each outfit I try. Sissy says she likes everything, though I think she's just trying to be nice.

The reactions I pay the most attention to are Kelli's, Tamitha's, and Hannah's. They've been the most animated. Kelli makes catcalls. I'm sure I'm the color of a boiled lobster.

I've been a little self-conscious about my scars from this morning and how much each dress shows. No one has commented on them, even though I know they must have seen them. Are they being compelled not to notice them? Probably.

As I walk out to show everyone the latest outfit, the chatter stops. The silence makes Amber look up from her phone. I'm wearing a white-lace, knee-length dress with a heart-shaped top. The skirt whooshes and fans out when I spin. It's perfect for dancing.

One by one, my friends smile. Amber even cracks a smile for a second. I smile too. They like it. I like it.

There's just one problem.

"I'm not sure what shoes I should wear …"

"Oh!" Tamitha says, jumping up. "I've already got that covered." She reaches behind the bench and grabs a backpack I hadn't noticed her carrying around before. She pulls out … my cowgirl boots.

Amber makes a disgusted noise and goes back to her phone.

I grab the boots from Tamitha. Tucked inside is a pair of my socks too.

She thinks of everything.

I slip on the socks and boots and stand in front of the full-length mirror. I twist and turn, trying to see from all angles. I think this is the one.

My smile widens, thinking of MJ's reaction. I hope he'll like it. He went through so much trouble for me today.

My smile falls.

Trouble he shouldn't have gone through. Girls are dying for me. And here I am getting ready for a date with a man who might be the only being who could save them.

I turn away, disgusted with myself. I open my mouth to tell everyone tonight is off, but I stop when I see the joy on Hannah's and my friends' faces.

Within the last week, I've almost lost them more times than I care to think about. It's very possible I could still lose them before my birthday next week. But they don't know that. They can *never* know that. They deserve to be happy, just as they are right now. I need this moment with them to carry me through whatever comes next.

I take a deep breath, bury my emotions, and force a smile.

I'M THE LAST IN LINE AT THE CHECKOUT COUNTER. THE sales clerk carefully packs the dress, then slides the bag to me without ringing me up.

"How much?" I ask.

Once I knew this was *the outfit*, I never even looked at the price tag. Now I chew my lip as I grab the emergency credit card from my purse. I'm supposed to use it only if something happens when Mom and Dad are gone.

The clerk just smiles. "Everything has been taken care of. Have a lovely day, Ms. Page."

I shake my head in confusion. "But I still need to pay."

Tamitha grabs my bag in one hand and my wrist in the other. "No, you don't. MJ took care of it—for everyone. Come on now. We're on a schedule."

I let her pull me along in the mall, but I'm lost in the thought of MJ buying all our clothes. Does he even have *money*? Or did he compel the woman to just write it all off?

My brooding stops when Kelli squeezes my arm while jumping up and down next to me. I follow her gaze to see not only that we are about to enter a beauty salon but also that my mom is here, smiling at me.

"What are you doing here?" I ask in a daze as Mom wraps her arms around me.

She pulls back, and tears pool in her eyes. "And miss you getting ready for your date? Not a chance."

Tears spring to my eyes as well. She's here. For me. Even though I know how busy she is. I want to hug her and tell her I love her, but I can't. It's too soon. Doing that could bring the Perfugae. I can't risk ruining this night. Not for my friends. Not for MJ. And not for me. MJ did all this for a reason. He knew I needed them.

I can't tell my mom, or my friends, how I feel about them yet. But maybe today can be the first step toward repairing our relationships. Maybe today I can start to heal.

WE'RE ALL DEPOSITED IN CHAIRS FOR PEDICURES. MOM takes a seat beside me, while Kelli takes the other. Even though I think it's ridiculous to get a pedicure—my cow-girl boots will hide it anyway—I don't say anything. I'm still too stunned at MJ's surprise of inviting my mom.

As my pedicure begins, my chair comes to life, giving me a massage. It digs into knots in my neck, back, and even my butt. I sigh as some of my tension evaporates.

Mom grabs my hand. "Are you nervous for tonight?"

"Yes," I reply in all honesty.

Her other hand pats the top of our linked hands. "I was too on my first date with your father. I know this isn't your first date with MJ, but still. It's a big night."

I sit up. "Really? You were nervous when dating Dad?"

She nods. "I couldn't eat all day. I tried on every outfit in my closet as well your aunt Deb's, trying to find *the outfit*."

I smile a little, realizing *the outfit* is a universal connection all girls and women have had for years.

"By the time I was ready, he'd been waiting downstairs with your grandfather for almost an hour."

I smile a lot at this, thinking about Grandpa and the hell he would have put Dad through. I'm glad MJ isn't going through that tonight with Dad. He's been through more than his fair share with Duane already.

My stomach rolls, thinking about Duane. It's yet another part of my life that's more surreal than real. Everything has changed.

"Where did you guys go?" I ask, distracting myself.

"Roller skating."

"Really?"

"Yes. I liked to roller skate, and your father knew that. Your great-aunt Jeanne—the one who played roller derby—taught me. On our date, I made several laps around the rink before noticing your father clinging to the wall. He's a very talented musician, but skating is not his forte."

"So why did he do it?"

"He was so nervous, he chose the first thing he knew I'd like."

"Huh." I sit back with my head swimming. Dad is always so calm and confident. Hearing he was nervous about dating Mom gives me hope.

"So tell me about MJ," Mom says.

I smile. "He's—"

"Perfect," Kelli says.

"And hot," Kayla and Maggie add.

"Have you kissed him?" Mom asks.

I can feel my cheeks heating. Part of me wants to say, Who doesn't know we kissed? The evidence is burned into Hiniker Bridge. Instead I opt for a simple, "Yes."

"So … tell me about it. Is he a good kisser?"

"*Mom*!"

"I've seen them kiss, Mrs. Page," Tamitha says, sitting several seats away.

I whip around to her.

"He's so good I can feel the heat of it." She winks at me, and my jaw drops.

"Really?" Mom asks, suddenly sounding concerned.

"She's kidding, Mom," I cut in. "We've kissed only a few times—and that's all we're going to do."

"I'm glad you're happy, honey. He seems really great"—her smile is tighter now—"but this is pretty fast for you. You're so different with him."

It is fast, in some ways. But in other ways, it feels just right. I don't want to voice that, though. It wouldn't make

laurie wetzel   371

sense to Mom or anyone. It barely makes sense to me. I just … feel it.

"Seriously, Mom," Hannah says when I haven't replied. "He's her person."

I look back and forth between my mom and sister, trying to figure out what that means. "What?"

My mother's smile grows into a sheepish grin, and she sits back, content.

"What?" I repeat.

Everyone else mimics my mother's grin of silence and rests back into their chairs. Apparently, they all get it.

I lean back too. It's not exactly easy to describe MJ. He's just everything I didn't know I needed. I guess that's what they mean.

Manicures follow the pedicures, then we're taken to salon chairs to have our hair and makeup done. The stylist doesn't ask me about a style. She just rambles on about dating advice as she works on my hair and touches up my makeup.

Eventually I just tune everything out and keep my eyes shut. Between the dress, nails, makeup, and now hair, I'll be a different person. I don't want to see another different version of me. I don't want to think about the remaining targets—especially when Amber is sitting five chairs away from me.

"Finished," the stylist sings.

I don't look in the mirror yet, but I know I have to. My stomach flips over as I roll my eyes up and finally lift my gaze.

# CHAPTER 51

# MJ

"RELAX, MJ. SHE'LL BE HERE IN TWO MINUTES," Alexander says.

We're standing outside the restaurant door, and he's making faces at the statue of a bear next to us. I roll my eyes.

Tamitha and Sissy have been giving me reports every fifteen minutes during their trip to the mall. Even though Maddy needed this time to reconnect with her friends and family, it's been torture leaving her again.

I've planned out every detail to ensure she'd be safe at the mall and here at the restaurant tonight. Even though I want tonight to be about healing and reconnecting, focused on us and having fun, I can't forget she's always in danger. The more variables I can eliminate, the safer she'll be from the forces targeting her.

It's because of them—the many demons, the Acquisitioner, Damien, and the unknown dream woman— that I no longer harbor any unease about using the instruments John created to destroy them. The next time something comes after her, that being will serve as an example to all others. She's off limits.

Tires crunch in the parking lot. There are other restaurants in town—we will eventually have dates there too—but Kodiak's is special. It's where we first ate together and I tasted food for the first time since dying. But most importantly, it's where I learned her name. I rented the whole restaurant just for our private group tonight.

"They're here!" Jake calls out.

Thanks to the second limo I rented especially for them, Maddy's guy friends are all here—even Tom, whom I brought to keep Amber civil. We're all wearing dress shirts, ties, and pants.

I stop my pacing and watch the Hummer limo pull up alongside us. The driver opens the door, and the girls climb out. Maddy's last.

Just as it did the first time I saw her, the world stops. I close the space between us. Her gorgeous emerald eyes stare up at me from underneath long lashes. I'm lost in her. My fingers run through her soft hair. The last of it falls from my fingertips, then I run my hands along the white lace of the short sleeves on her dress.

A moan slides up my throat, and I close my eyes, fighting the urge to kiss her. I don't know if I can contain myself right now, and there are too many witnesses.

When my eyes open and I see the shy smile on her pink lips that matches the glow on her cheeks, a twinge in my chest rattles through me as my heart beats twice.

Father, I love her. I want to tell her how beautiful she looks and how much I missed her, even though it was only a few hours. But all I can manage is one word.

"Hi."

"Hey."

"You look …"

"You too."

"Are you two always this articulate?" Amber asks behind us. Her annoying voice and even more infuriating thoughts break the spell.

Still desperate for some contact with Maddy, I kiss her forehead and breathe in as much of her as possible.

She presses her body against me, and I wrap my arms around her. Confirming she's safe and whole smashes the sensation of foreboding I've felt since our fight last night. We're going to be fine. We're together, and absolutely nothing or no one can stop that.

If anything even dares to try, Alexander and I are ready. Our many weapons are concealed in the Veil of Shadows.

With a great effort, I end our embrace and offer her my arm. "Shall we?"

She slides her arm through mine. "Yes."

I SIT BESIDE HER AT A TABLE SURROUNDED BY HER FRIENDS, my friends—*our* friends. The others laugh and talk animatedly about school, shows, sports, and various other topics, but I don't pay attention. I'm caught up in watching her. The longer we stay here, the more she allows herself to be happy. She doesn't have to force herself to smile or laugh at the appropriate times; it just comes naturally.

*Are you okay?* Tamitha speaks privately inside my mind.

I turn and meet her gaze. *Yes. Taking a break from it all and having a special night like this is exactly what she needed.*

*Good,* she says. *Now stop hovering, stop worrying, and enjoy yourself too. This night is as much for you as it is for her. We're supposed to be the Protectors for the night. You just focus on being a man in love.*

I smile, then kiss Maddy's hair.

Maddy turns, and those dazzling emerald eyes hit me and take my breath away.

"Thank you for today," she says. "I know you put a lot of thought into everything, and I … just thank you."

"You're worth it, *minn hvatvetna.*"

A loud smack suddenly hits the table, and we jolt toward the noise. Kelli's hand is on the table as she glares at us.

"All right, Norway. Spill it," she snaps. "What does that mean? What do you keep calling her?"

The light in Kelli's eyes says she's not really angry. I can hear her thoughts too. She's curious about the name and protective of Maddy. She wants to believe I'm Maddy's knight in shining armor and our love is real and ever-lasting. Gazing at the others gathered around us, I realize that's what they're all hoping. Except Tom. He's hoping I fail miserably so he can have his turn.

"It's a term of endearment from my home country. It means, 'my everything.'"

# CHAPTER 52

# Maddy

*M**y everything.*

My friends swoon, but I'm too caught up in MJ to care. I knew his nickname for me was something special from his heart, but I had no idea what it meant. Now I do, and it's my new favorite phrase in the world. No two words have ever made me feel so special, warm, and loved.

I am loved by him. No matter what I've learned about myself, no matter what I have or have not expressed to him, no matter what the world throws in our way at every turn … he loves me.

My heart swells, and I caress his smooth cheek. I hear a soft moan from him again as he relaxes into my touch. Butterflies rise to my throat. I can't speak.

If I could, I would tell him how wonderful he makes me feel and how nothing will ever come between us again. I want to let go of everything and tell him who I am. I want to say the words I've only ever said to my sister. *I love you.* But the butterflies won't budge. I can only hold him and hope my eyes convey everything in my heart.

AFTER DINNER, WE PILE INTO ONE LIMO. IT'S A LITTLE
crowded, but I'm glad we're taking one—I don't want to
choose between MJ and any of my friends. I don't want to
break this amazing circle of love, friendship, and support
we've all built tonight.

I've missed hanging out with my friends like this. I
shouldn't have stopped. Things would have been different
if I hadn't pulled away. But right now, I have a great life
full of amazing people—my friends, my family, MJ, and
his team. I don't want to lose any of it.

My heart feels full tonight.

I've found my new favorite position: sitting on his
lap with my head on his shoulder. His essence constantly
flows between us, not lingering anywhere, because there's
no place it needs to focus on and fix. I don't feel any
pain, even though the marks of Justin's death are still
on my body.

My thoughts hover on Justin. As crazy as it sounds, I'm
grateful the masked demon showed me that vision. At one
point in his life, Justin wasn't evil. Maybe there's still hope
for him? And if so, maybe there's still hope for me.

The limo stops, and the doors open. He and I stay
seated as everyone else climbs out. I think MJ doesn't want
to stop being this connected to me. I'm more than happy
for the added time. Alone.

"Tonight has been one of the best nights of my
life, MJ."

He kisses my temple, sending even more of his essence
into me, strengthening the protective coating his kisses
always create. "It isn't over yet. Come on."

He leads me outside, where our friends are waiting for us. Behind them is a small building with a neon sign flashing the name of the band playing inside. It's Dad's band. Not only has MJ surrounded me with my friends and family all day, but he brought us all to see my father play. This is perfect.

Almost perfect, that is.

"MJ, we can't go in there. That's a bar. We're not twenty-one."

"It doesn't matter tonight. I've taken care of it."

I'm pretty sure I know what that means, but I'm so excited about seeing Dad and his band, I let it slide for now.

MJ and I pass through a cloud of cigarette smoke from the few people lingering just outside the door. Inside, the bass from the speakers beside us pulsates through my body while we wait in line. The bouncer nods at MJ and waves us all through without checking our IDs.

The dance floor is packed, but it parts enough for MJ to lead me and my friends to the center. Hannah comes up to me so we can wave at Dad on the stage. He gives us a big smile.

"This is so awesome!" Hannah says, looking over the crowd.

I know exactly what she means. We've only ever seen Dad's band open for someone else. Tonight these people are here to see him and his band. The joy on their faces, the infectious laughter, and the packed dance floor are for him and his music. I can see why he loves this so much.

Song after song, I dance with MJ, Hannah, and our friends. During slow songs, MJ and I are as close as we can possibly get. He tugs my arms up to his neck. Once I lace my fingers behind it, he wraps his arms around my waist. During fast songs, my hands are in the air and I'm jumping around. There are no thoughts in my head other than the lyrics to the songs I've heard Dad practice in the basement.

No matter how many dates MJ takes me on in the future, this will always be my favorite.

After ten songs, Dad and the band take a break, and we all head to a large table in the back. A minute later, a waitress arrives with everyone's drinks. Most of us ordered virgin daiquiris. Everyone laughs as Mason gets a kiddie cocktail with a little umbrella.

I lean back into MJ and kiss his jaw. "Thank you."

"For what?"

"For being amazing."

Kelli gags. "Would you two just get a room already?" She waggles her brows at me, then sticks her tongue out before bursting into a fit of giggles.

One by one my friends join in.

MJ's body shakes with laughter too. I smile, tilting my head back to look up at him.

"What?" he asks.

"I like hearing you laugh."

His smile widens, and he gives me a gentle squeeze. "It's only possible because of you, *minn hvatvetna.*"

I snuggle closer to him. "Good."

Dad's band goes back on stage, and my friends rush back out to the dance floor.

"Shall we join them?" MJ asks.

I shake my head. "Not yet. I'm sick of sharing you."

His fingers link with mine across my belly. "I understand that. You did have fun at the mall, though, right?"

"Yes. More than I expected to, actually. What did you do today?"

"Missed you."

I snort. "That's not what I meant—but I missed you too."

We snuggle in content silence for several moments before he says, "I returned to Immortal City with Alexander to pick up a few things, I bothered Tamitha and Sissy relentlessly to make sure you were having a good time, and then I got all the guys ready."

"It sounds like you were very busy."

"Yes."

"You are having fun, though, right?" I pose the same question back to him.

"This is one of the best nights of my life. Seeing how stunning and happy you are ... Only a handful of nights compete with this one for the label of perfection—and they all involve you too."

I close my eyes and absorb the love in his essence and his words. My heart beats stronger, sending warmth radiating through me. I sit up and stare into his shining hazel eyes. The sound of my father's band and the hundreds of people around us disappear. We haven't left, but it feels as if we have.

The longer I gaze into his eyes, the more I feel this pull from him, urging me to say the words he's said time and time again. He deserves to hear them. I want to say them. It's the truth. I do love him. More than my next breath.

"MJ, I ..."

He leans forward.

"I ... I need to use the bathroom."

His eyes shut, and he frowns before slouching backward.

He's disappointed.

I am too.

Without even looking at him, I break away. Pushing through the crowd, I head to the bathroom. I slide the lock into place on my stall door, then lean against the wall for support.

What is *wrong* with me? Why can't I say it? He's not going to hurt me. He's my everything too. I want a future with him. So why am I hiding like a coward in the bathroom?

Maybe I need practice? The one and only time I've said those words was stolen from me—erased from Hannah's memory. That won't happen, though, if I say those words to him. MJ's mind can't be erased. He'll always remember the first time I say it, just as I'll always remember the first time he said it on the bridge last night.

I take a deep, trembling breath and leave my stall. I slowly wash my hands, then stare at my reflection in the mirror.

"I love you."

I wait and watch for something awful to happen.

Nothing does.

I say it again and again. After the fourth time, I add more.

"I love you, MJ."

A smile spreads across my face, and my heart skips a beat. I say it again, and a rush of relief flows through me. This is right. This is the perfect moment to tell him. I can do this.

As I reach out for a paper towel, my bracelet catches my eye. All the rainbow-colored stones have turned gray. MJ said a stone would turn black when a demon is near.

What does gray mean?

I have to find MJ. I turn to rush out the door, then stop in my tracks.

Standing between me and my way to MJ—staring at me with those piercing black eyes I hoped I'd never see again—is Justin.

# CHAPTER 53

# Justin

I COVER HER MOUTH, STOPPING HER SCREAM, AND GRAB her arm, careful not to touch the many scars that have marred her once-flawless skin. I push her up against the vanity—ignoring the pleasure growing inside me.

My essence rips through her, calming the storm brewing inside her, making sure she won't set the building on fire or do anything else to raise the alarm.

Touch. That's her weakness. The answer was right in front of me the whole time. She affects me—and I affect her—through touch. That's why I could compel her Tuesday. I was touching her and linked to her. The only reason it didn't take was that we were interrupted.

Emerald eyes flash to the door, waiting and watching for MJ to come rushing in.

I smirk. "He's not coming, Mads," I whisper, making sure even those with immortal abilities cannot hear me. "None of them are."

Her attention returns to me as she glares. My hand still covers her soft lips, but I can guess what she'd tell me if she could speak. My essence picks up a mix of defiance and fury inside her. There's a little fear, though not as much as I would have expected. Her eyes once again dart to the door. She doesn't believe me. She still thinks he's coming to rescue her. Her faith and trust in *him* has reduced what little power I had over her.

Pressing more of my body against her, I lift my hand, revealing my ring. "Do you see this?" I pause, waiting until she looks at it. "This ring is enchanted to hide my essence. The four Protectors have no idea I'm here."

Her eyes narrow, glaring at me again. She still doesn't believe me. The anger inside her swells. Actually, it's more like … annoyance.

I shake my head, both frustrated and awed. I'm here, moments away from finally stealing her, yet instead of being scared, she's pissed. Pissed I ruined her night. A night *he* created for her.

The thought of him makes rage bubble up inside me, but I hold it back, not wanting to hurt her. It's time she realizes that this—she and I together—was always going to happen.

"I've been waiting for the perfect moment to get you alone, all to myself. I've watched you almost nonstop since Wednesday morning. Remember the twigs snapping by the bridge that morning? Remember seeing me in the bathroom when you came out of the shower? Remember the 'wind' that pushed that worthless excuse of an angel over when she dared insult you?"

Her eyes widen. And in their depths, I can tell she does remember.

"I've hardly ever left your side for days. And none of them—including the legendary MJ himself—has known it. They can't sense me. They won't help you. They'll have no idea where I've taken you."

Her body shakes, and she closes her eyes. The fear I've been waiting for, hoping to feel, builds inside her.

She finally believes me.

A tear clings to her lashes, but before it can fall and summon rain outside, I wipe it away with my thumb.

As much as I want to relish this moment, I know I can't. Even with my enchanted ring and my control over her abilities, I'm not foolish enough to believe I have unlimited time here.

I push more of my essence into her. Her eyes pop open, questioning the change. I lock onto her gaze and connect to her mind, hoping this works.

My essence comes back to me. Unlike the time at my house, I'm ready for the darkness that exists with her. Even though I now have total control over Maddy, I still cannot access her memories.

I drop my hand from her mouth, confident she won't scream anymore. Not unless I want her to.

Mads's eyes dull, becoming dazed. I speak even softer to her—making sure no one outside this room can hear us.

"You and I are going on a little trip, Mads, but we need to make sure we're not followed. From now on, your emotions will be suppressed. No matter what you're feeling, you are not allowed to project it into the environment."

She nods. "Where are we going?" Her voice is flat, lacking her usual emotion.

It's working. I can't resist the urge to smile.

"The only place that makes sense: where it all began."

"Okay."

Again I smile at her flat tone.

After what feels like an eternity of waiting, she's mine.

# CHAPTER 54

# MJ

WITH A SMIRK, ALEXANDER PLOPS DOWN INTO THE chair beside me, causing the table to shake. "How can you be sulking in the corner while everyone else is having the time of their lives?"

I rub my neck, hating that he's right. "I know. But I thought she was going to say it. I could see it in her eyes, then she raced off to the bathroom."

His grin fades. "Look, you're putting too much pressure on her. And yourself. She'll say it when she's ready. She just said it for the first time ever a couple days ago, and that was during a life-threatening situation," he says, nodding toward Hannah on the dance floor. "You shouldn't expect her to say it so soon to you. Plus, you have to know she loves you, right?"

"I do, but—"

"Then let that be enough for now. This is new for both of you. Stop racing to get to the finish line. Live in the moment. You've gone eight hundred years without any emotions, and now you're demanding declarations of love from a girl you just met. You barely know each other.

Love means acceptance." He leans closer. "Have you truly accepted Maddy?"

"Of course I have," I reply immediately.

"Even everything that's still unexplainable about her? Or the secrets we know she's still keeping—whether she's compelled to keep them or not?"

I lift my chin with certainty. "There is nothing she can do or say that will make me love her any less than I do at this very moment."

"Good. Now, what about her? Does she accept all of *you*?"

My certainty wavers. While I know she loves me, there are parts of me she struggles with. All of them stem from my angelic side. There's still so much she doesn't know about me.

Some of it I'm intentionally holding back. It's not that I'm keeping it secret; I'm just waiting for the opportune moment. So far, I haven't found the right time to share my age and history with her. She's seen my death and even traveled back in time to my village, but I'm still nervous of her reaction when I explain it all.

Alexander is right. How can I expect her to say she loves me when I haven't given her a chance to truly know what loving me means?

I stand and move away from the table.

"Where are you going?" he asks.

"To talk to her."

"Last time I checked, you don't have the right equipment to enter a ladies' room."

That's right. She's in the bathroom. I curse under my breath.

*Tamitha,* I say using Cerebrallink. Even though the music is still blaring, I know she'll hear me.

*Hey, MJ!* she hollers back. *Grab Maddy, and get your butt out on the dance floor! Tell Alexander to get back out here too.*

She and Alexander have danced together most the night. With them both filled with new emotions, something is brewing between them. I'm glad they're happy. I'd love to join them, but grabbing Maddy is the part I need help with.

*She's in the bathroom,* I reply. *I think I upset her. Can you go get her?*

*What did you do?* she asks.

*Just go.*

*Fine.*

She discretely disappears from the group of dancers, using the Veil to travel the short distance to the bathroom. We take the traditional route and walk.

As we reach the door, it opens. Tamitha's brow is furrowed, and she's frowning.

"She's not in there."

Alarm pulsing through me, I push past her, searching the small room myself. Both stalls are open.

Maddy's gone.

Alexander places his hand on my shoulder. Standing there in shock, it takes me a few moments to realize he's asking me a question.

"I'm sorry—what?" I ask.

"When did she come in here?" he repeats.

Fear ripples through me. How am I supposed to think back? The only thought in my mind right now is that she's gone.

I close my eyes and shake my head. "I don't know," I say. "Maybe five minutes."

Was it really that long? Why didn't I think to check on her? Why didn't I follow her?

I take a breath, trying to calm myself enough to search for her heartbeat. The pounding mixture of music and hundreds of racing hearts fills my ears. But in my fear, I can't sort through them to find her.

"Could she have come back out without you noticing?" Tamitha asks. "Maybe she went back out on the dance floor. I used the Veil to get here, so our paths wouldn't have crossed."

I let her words sink in. Maybe. She could have come out of the bathroom and went to the dance floor while Alexander and I were talking.

"Okay, well, don't panic," Alexander says. "Let's go check—"

Before he can even finish, I race out of the bathroom. I cling to this explanation, willing it to be true. I speed through the crowds, searching the happy faces of her friends for her. She's not here.

Her friends keep dancing around me—their minds absorbed in the great night. They're all oblivious to my horror.

Tamitha and Alexander arrive next to me, and Sissy is with them as well.

"Did she go outside for air?" Sissy asks.

I look at the three of them, desperately searching for any other explanation—any reason other than something terrible. And in that moment, I realize exactly what happened.

My chest aches, my silent heart clenching in agony.

"We let our guard down," I begin.

I feel their eyes on me, but I don't stop.

"There were four of us here, and that filled me with a false sense of security. I let Maddy go off on her own. I didn't even think about the killer, the Acquisitioner, the female demon, Justin, the unknown spirit that's watching her—who knows what else. I gave any one of them the opportunity to snatch her away in a building full of Protectors."

My heart sinks further. So many things are after her. And I left her alone—I upset her and sent her running to the bathroom. I failed her.

Guilt and grief take hold of me, buckling my knees until I cave, unable to withstand the pressure any longer. I prepared for every scenario. I have dozens of weapons to keep her safe. And still I failed.

"No," Sissy says adamantly. "We were monitoring for essences. I didn't feel any."

Tamitha and Alexander nod in agreement. But all I can do is shake my head.

"I never felt an essence when I knew there was a being in the woods Wednesday morning," I say, voicing my thoughts. "None of us felt an essence when something attacked Sissy yesterday at school. And even though I sensed a demon this morning when Maddy was possessed, the Segrego stones didn't react, so I did nothing."

"MJ," Alexander says, shocked. "How can this be happening? Demons aren't that powerful."

"Maybe the rules are changing as we move closer to war," Tamitha says in a small voice.

I dig my nails into my skin as my fists close. "And because of my arrogance, I just handed the woman I love to our enemies. They'll use her to destroy everything we stand for. And in the process, they'll destroy her too."

The hopelessness I feel is reflected in them. I turn away.

No matter what happens next, no matter how long it takes, I will find Maddy.

# CHAPTER 55
# Maddy

A QUIET CRACKLE SOUNDS. IT'S FAMILIAR, LIKE LOGS popping in a fireplace. My other senses kick in as I listen to the muted sound. My back is pressed against a cool, smooth texture. It's cushiony. Like a leather couch.

I think I've been sleeping. My eyes are still closed as I contemplate waking. I could easily drift back to sleep here, but I feel as if I shouldn't. Why not?

*Justin.*

My eyes open, and I fly off the couch. My gaze darts around the room. Where is he? Where did he take me?

"You are awake!"

That's not Justin.

I follow the airy voice to the masked demon as she exits the bedroom that's an exact replica of mine. I'm in her living room. She must have brought my soul here and left my body behind with him.

"*I* did not bring your soul here," she says, responding to my thoughts. "My essence has to be inside you first, remember."

If she didn't bring me here, then who did? I need to know. The days of being kept in the dark are over.

"Good," she replies. "Your strength is very empowering."

I snort. Empowered is the last thing I feel right now. I look past her to the massive space belonging to her master. Did he bring me here? If so, where is he?

"Out," she replies again to my unspoken words. "But yes, he is responsible for you being here."

"He didn't"—I swallow a lump in my throat—"send his essence into me, did he?"

She shakes her head. "No. You would remember having that much power inside you. You are here because my master has gone to great lengths to keep you alive. The demon compelled you in the bathroom, then took you away through the Veil of Shadows. It is a dangerous space for you, as any being inside it would be pulled toward you. That is why my master cast a protection spell over you a long time ago. It ensured that if your soul ever entered the Veil, your soul would come here."

All this talk about what her master has done to keep me alive makes me think of the *sacrifices* Duane and the others in his group have done in my name too. My stomach curls, filled with revulsion.

But right now, I need to focus on one problem at a time, and my current problem is Justin. When he suddenly appeared in the bathroom, he must have compelled my abilities away. That's what he meant about suppressing my emotions to keep them from projecting into the environment.

The other things he said flood my mind as well. My hands grip my hair as I try not to cry.

Justin's been watching me. MJ *knew* someone was in the woods Wednesday morning—I even knew it. But we both allowed ourselves to be comforted by MJ's lie.

Still, how was he to know Justin has some stupid ring? It's not MJ's fault. It's mine.

I should have listened to my instincts. I should have done a lot of things differently since surviving that horrible night in Justin's house. Mainly, I shouldn't have been foolish enough to believe for one second that I was safe. I was naive to think Justin was nothing more than a nuisance. He's powerful and desperate. Both make him unstable and dangerous.

I lower my hands and glance at the masked demon.

"Do you know where he took me?" I ask, pointing to the TV.

She grabs the remote and turns the TV on. The scene is dark, but I can make out Justin carrying my unconscious body up a sidewalk to a two-story house. I don't recognize where we are. My stomach twists from thoughts of what he plans to do to me.

I tear my attention from the screen to meet her gaze. "How can you and now he compel me? I thought I was immune to that ability."

"It is more difficult to compel you than other mortals, but you are not immune to it. We have to touch you and send our essence into you in order for it to work. I am unsure if it would work for the beings whose essences do not flow freely through you—but that is a problem for another day. Today, we need to get you away from the demon."

I turn back to the TV and watch, numbly, as an elderly woman answers the door and lets Justin inside. He must have compelled her too. She leads him down a narrow hallway littered with knickknacks and photos of her loved ones to a bedroom at the end of the hall.

I hold my breath and watch him gently place me on the bed. He brushes several strands of hair from my face, then leans down, whispering something in my ear. If I didn't know better, I'd say it all looks tender and loving.

Memories of his horror house resurface. It belonged to an old woman too. Justin killed her and left her corpse on display for weeks. Ben died there. If it weren't for Elizabeth, the masked demon, and my own abilities, I would have died too. Or became Justin's *pet*.

I take a sharp breath. That's why he took me—it's another attempt to make me sign the contract. My arm stings, recalling the pain of Justin's previous attempt to make me sign it.

"What do I do?" I ask, my voice hollow. "I don't know if I can go through this again."

"You are still stronger than other mortals, though," she says, clinging to the hope I've lost. "His compulsion should wear off."

"How long?"

"I do not know."

Justin leaves me on the bed, then leads the old woman out of the room. I make a silent prayer, hoping he won't kill her too.

I can't believe I'm seeing this all unfold on the screen— let alone that it's really happening. My body is in some unknown place with an evil monster who wants to do God only knows what to me.

I take a step closer to her.

"Can I stay here until the compulsion wears off?" I ask.

She's silent for a moment.

My heart beats faster, hoping she'll say yes.

"As greatly as I want to keep you from him," she begins, "I do not think it would be wise to leave you in such a vulnerable state with him. His desire for you runs deep. I do not know what lengths he will go to keep you tethered to him."

I crumple to the floor—my sense of strength and security evaporates. "I can't fight him off like this. How can I? You're the one who's actually been fighting him all along."

"That is not true," she states. "I have merely helped you for a few minutes here and there. You have done the rest."

Her words give little comfort. The "rest" that I did came from the very abilities he compelled away. Now I'm powerless against him.

She kneels beside me. "I will go back with you. You must surrender control to me immediately. I will be inside you to help you get away. But because of what I did this morning, I am unsure of how long I can stay with you. It could be five minutes, or it could be five seconds. I will fight him and hopefully incapacitate him long enough for you to escape."

I give a weak nod.

"When you feel me leave, no matter when it is or what is happening, run. Run and do not stop until you have made it to safety. He—and everyone else—cannot feel your essence. He cannot find you if you hide."

I cringe, thinking of Elizabeth and Damien. Why does everyone think hiding is the answer?

"You do not know what happened between them," she replies. "He hid her to protect her. Hiding, sometimes, is the bravest thing you can do. It is the only way you will survive this night."

She's right. I don't know what happened between them. I haven't seen all the dreams. Someday, it'll be time for me to see the most important dream—Elizabeth's death. It's coming. I can feel it. As much as I don't want to know how she died, I need to know. I need to know what happened to her, and I need to know what happened to me that very same day.

The only way I can learn any of that is to get away from Justin. I have no other option but to run and hide.

My fear of Justin lessens as I embrace the masked demon's plan.

"Okay," I say. "I understand."

"The moment you are free from his compulsion, create a storm. I cannot contact MJ, but he will find your storm."

My heart aches as I think of MJ waiting for me in the bar. If I hadn't run away to hide in the bathroom—if I had only told him I loved him—this wouldn't have happened. If I don't escape, I will never be able to tell him how I feel. Him or anyone else I love.

The masked demon stands and clicks a button on the remote. "Once I am strong enough, I will come to you again."

She pauses and looks at me very carefully. "I am doing this without my master's approval or knowledge, so he will not be pleased, but I do not care. The Influencer has broken many rules tonight, and he will be severely punished— which will bring my master great satisfaction."

The screen pulsates. She holds her hand out to me. "Ready?"

I shake my head. "No. Not yet." My attention flits between her and the screen, recalling my last trip into it. "You showed me Justin's past. You wanted me to understand him—to see the good in him. Why are you against him now?"

"I am against anything that is a threat to you. Right now, he is just that. He is acting … in a way he should not be."

I continue staring at her, debating whether I can truly trust her. Fear and desperation shine through her crimson eyes. Whether she's afraid of what Justin will do to me, what her master will do to her, or a combination of both, it doesn't matter. What matters is that, despite her fear, she's still ready to charge into the unknown with me. And instead of sending my soul somewhere else to protect me, she wants to fight him *with* me.

In this moment, I know she's telling the truth.

I place my hand in hers, reveling in the wholeness that fills me the instant we touch.

She pulls me to my feet. "Remember, surrender to me right away."

"I will."

I take a deep breath, then enter the TV, placing my trust and fate in the pale hands of a demon.

# CHAPTER 56

# Maddy

DARKNESS DESCENDS ON ME. THE MASKED DEMON'S hand vanishes from mine, even though I was clutching it with everything I had.

Where did she go? I'm alone. Panic fills me. Justin will be able to make me do whatever he wants. He's going to make me sign that—

*Surrender, Maddy!*

At the sound of her voice in my mind, my panic fades. She's still with me, somehow inside me. A part of me.

I let go, just as I've done countless times in my dreams. This time, though, I don't fade completely into the background. It's more like being in the passenger seat.

My eyes open to the old woman's bedroom. Before I can absorb the surroundings, my body leaps from the bed. The masked demon is controlling me, just as she said.

The door opens. Justin enters, smiling as he shuts the door behind him. "You're awake."

"Maddy is awake, but she will not be staying with you," the masked demon replies.

Justin straightens as his smile falls. He stares at me, her, us for a moment, then his eyes blaze red. "You're the one that took her in the park. How dare you possess her again. She's *mine!*"

A blade suddenly appears in his hand—though it's unlike any I've seen before. Brutal. Ancient.

Inside me, I can feel fear coming from the masked demon. She recognizes the blade. She's afraid of it.

"Use that on me, and you kill Maddy," she warns. But there's something more in her voice. Something she's not saying. Something she and Justin both understand but I don't.

Justin's knuckles whiten as he clutches the blade. Veins appear in his neck as his jaw tightens. As suddenly as it appeared, the blade vanishes.

He crouches in front of the door. "I'm not letting you leave here with her," he says. "I've waited too long for this moment—for her."

More quickly than I've ever moved before, she clears the distance between the bed and door and stands in front of Justin. His eyes widen. A moment later, she lifts my hands, grabbing him by the collar, then tosses him across the room. He hits the wall and falls to the floor.

As my hand reaches for the handle, I feel her essence slipping from me, forcing me back into the driver's seat.

*Run, Maddy.*

The last of her essence leaves me.

I can do this. Even without my abilities, I'm not powerless. I *refuse* to be helpless. All I have to do is just get outside. Then I'm free.

*I can do this.*

I glance at Justin, still slumped on the floor, then yank the door and run through the hallway. As I race through the living room toward the front door, I hear something squeak behind me.

I turn and see the old woman sitting up in surprise in her recliner. Relief floods me. She's still alive.

I can't leave her here. No one else will die because of me.

I glance down the hall. I don't see Justin. With as hard as he hit the wall, he could be unconscious. Still, we have to hurry.

"Come with me," I say, helping her up from the chair.

"Just a moment, dearie," she says calmly as she reaches for something beside the chair.

I glance down the hallway again as my heart races. Justin still hasn't come out of the room. But then again, he could be hiding in the Veil. Either way, we need to leave—

Something pokes me in the stomach.

I turn back to the old woman. Her wrinkled features are tense with determination. Her arms twitch, pressing something against my stomach.

"We can't leave," she says. "That is what the young man said."

I look down to see the barrel of a shotgun aimed just below my ribcage.

I stare in disbelief, my once-racing heart now seized. "Please—"

Her finger squeezes the trigger.

The blast echoes in my ears. I fly backward, landing on my back in the hallway.

Intense, agonizing pain stems from my belly. Fire ravages every nerve ending. My hands touch the lace on my stomach. It's wet. I pull my hands away—they're covered in blood. My blood.

I stare up the barrel of the shotgun at the old woman, unable to move, unable to breathe as the world moves in slow motion. I tried to help her, tried to save both our lives, and she shot me.

I've come close to death multiple times in the last week. But this is no vision or dream. This is real. I'm really going to die.

Justin is suddenly standing beside the old woman. In one smooth motion, he places his hands in her gray hair and twists her head around—snapping her neck. Her limp body falls.

Before she hits the floor, he's kneeling beside me.

"Hold on, Mads," he begs. "I'm going to fix this!"

His hands press down on my abdomen. I try to scream, but I can't find the air to support it. Horrible gasping, gurgling fills my ears.

My head rolls to the side. My eyes land on the front door. Freedom was ten feet away. I reach out a bloody hand toward the door, wanting to be closer to my family, my friends, my MJ.

Justin's essence enters me. I hear him cry out, swearing as he feels my pain.

I grit my teeth as a metallic taste fills my mouth. A small sense of victory fills me. The more I succumb to the pain, the worse he feels.

Bursts of white light flutter in front of me. My eyelids drop for a second. Familiar darkness encircles me—Death here for me again. When I open them again, his panicked eyes meet mine as he hovers over me.

"No, Mads! Stay with me. You can't die!"

I don't want to go into the darkness, but I don't want to stay with him either. My eyelids fall again. This time, memories of MJ stream forward. I want to hold on to MJ for however long I can.

I let go of the fight.

# CHAPTER 57

# MJ

BEEPS SOUND THROUGH THE SPEAKERS FROM LAPTOPS set up on the Pages' kitchen table. Five FBI agents stare at the screens, their fingers dancing on the keys as they desperately help me search for Maddy. The Shadowwalker compelled them to search for her nonstop. It's been four hours since she disappeared.

I don't know who took Maddy, but I will find her. I *have* to believe I will see her again.

After the bar, my team took Maddy's friends home and I came here. I stood in her bedroom for I don't know how long, just wanting to feel connected to her. That's where the Shadowwalker found me. He took one look at me and knew she was gone.

From that moment, he took over—having already had a plan in place for a situation like this. He began by compelling Maddy's family to not think about her or notice she's missing. They've come through the kitchen several times, but in their minds, we're all working on an FBI case.

Next he got his team looking at weather all over the world. It's a two-pronged approach. First they're looking for any unusual weather fluctuation that could be a signal from Maddy. Unexpected rain, thunderstorms, tornados—they're even monitoring for sudden explosions and fires. Second, they're also checking on places where it's currently and consistently rainy. Whoever took her may be smart enough to hide her someplace where the weather would shield her emotions.

It's a long shot, but it's our best chance of finding her. Yet I feel so helpless sitting here, placing all my hopes on nothing more than weather reports.

We lock eyes for a moment across the kitchen. If it weren't for the Shadowwalker, I'd feel isolated in my despair. I don't need to tell him what's at stake if we don't find her—he knows. He's protected her her whole life. He kept her safe for almost seventeen years.

I didn't even last a week.

"It's raining in Dublin, Ireland," Travis, the tech-savvy FBI agent, says.

The Shadowwalker and I race over to Travis. "What was the forecast?" I ask.

"High of forty degrees with a fifty percent chance of rain," Travis replies.

I close my eyes and reach out to Alexander. *Have you finished with Vancouver?*

*Yes,* he says. *She's not here.*

*Check Dublin next.*

I sever the connection, rest my hands on the table, and let out a long exhale. Alexander, Sissy, and Tamitha have checked 103 locations since the Shadowwalker suggested this plan. To search for her, my team is doing what I did last week: listening for any signs of movement inside a building without a soul attached to it. They're scouring every inch of the cities I name. Each one has come up empty.

Why isn't she panicking? Is she unconscious, as she was for a while when Justin took her? Or is she possessed again—perhaps by the female demon? Is someone even more powerful affecting her?

I pound the table, rattling the computers. I never should have let her out of my sight. No matter how long it takes, I will not stop until she's safe in my arms again.

As for whoever took her, that being will get the privilege of assisting me in testing all of John's new weapons. By the time I'm finished, her attacker will know *exactly* how I feel about what it did tonight. I will force out an apology. Then, and only then, will I destroy its soul.

# CHAPTER 58

# Justin

I WAIT FOR HER PALE PINK–SHADED LIDS TO REOPEN, BUT they don't. Her heart stutters, and I send my essence there to keep it beating. Even though the pain is excruciating, I push through it.

This wasn't supposed to happen. That damn old woman was only supposed to keep Mads from leaving. I didn't mean *shoot her.*

Mads and I were supposed to talk. I was supposed to make her sign that contract.

The Acquisitioner's words float through my mind: *According to both Heaven and Hell, Madison does not exist. If she does not exist, neither side will claim her soul.*

If I fail ... if I can't save her ... I'll lose her forever.

I tilt my head to the ceiling, calling on the God I've ignored since my death.

"Spare her. I know you don't know who she is, but I promise you, she's important."

I pause, realizing just how true the words are. What she does goes beyond me. It affects all of us. I don't give a damn about them, though—only her and I. To keep her, I'll do whatever it takes.

I take a breath, and this time, I speak from my heart. "Do this for me, and I will change. I will fight for her. I will stop ignoring the way she makes me feel. I'll stop denying that she makes me—*a demon*—feel the wondrous emotions you gifted me when I was mortal. She doesn't deserve the curse I placed upon her. Please. Please help her."

I stare at Mads for what seems like an eternity. Relief finally fills me as the rhythm of her heart steadies. But she's far from safe. There's still a gaping hole in her stomach, and her blood pools around us.

If, by some miracle, I'm able to save her, I will spend eternity making it up to her.

HER BODY STABILIZES WHEN THE WOUNDS FINALLY CLOSE. I carry her back to the bedroom and gently place her on the bed. I lie down beside her, keeping my essence inside her. I hold my breath, both watching and feeling for any signs of duress.

There are none.

I don't know how she got those wounds on her arm and back, but they're gone now too. They must have happened while I was here in Georgia the first time, digging into her life. Those wounds looked painful, however she got them. For some reason, I'm more relieved they're gone than I am that the gunshot wound has closed.

I first noticed those scars when I was watching her at the clothing store. I wanted to immediately go find MJ and beat the crap out of him for failing to keep her safe. Then she stepped out in that lacey white dress, emerald eyes shining and a smile so full of joy … She looked more beautiful than I've ever seen her before.

The happiness on her face distracted me. It distracted me for so damn long, I nearly missed my opportunity to take her away tonight. I finally snapped out of it when she went to the bathroom at the bar and said *those three words* with *his* name at the end. I knew it was time to finally take her.

But this … this wasn't supposed to happen.

I didn't know she was unconscious until we arrived back in Atlanta. I thought maybe she used her ability and went to that bridge she took me to. I knew she couldn't stay away forever, so I waited. I never expected her to be possessed. Somehow the demon took her soul when we were in the Veil.

Who is this demon? How can she possess Mads? The demon knows about Mads—she knew what would happen if I touched Mads with the blade. How does she even know about the blade?

But most importantly, what *connection* does she have to Mads? There has to be something linking them for Mads to trust the demon enough to let her possess her.

The only surefire way to keep Mads away from that demon and all the others is to force her to sign the contract. But if I do that, then I hand her—and myself—over to someone who is as bad as all the demons combined.

I don't know what to do anymore.

I tuck a strand of hair behind Mads's ear. She came so close to death… to slipping away forever. She's unconscious again. It will take her some time to return to me.

I wish she were merely sleeping. I love watching her sleep. It's the only time when she's content and I'm free to admire her. Watching her now … it's easy to forget the peril we're in and allow myself to fantasize that we're together in all the ways I want. Maybe, if I save her, we can still have that.

I push more of my essence into her, searching for whatever is preventing her from waking and coming back to me. No matter what I find, I'm not letting go. I'm never giving up on her. I will hold her until I see her magnificent eyes open again.

My essence returns to me with no explanation. It's as if Mads is *choosing* to remain where she is—wherever she may be.

I crack a smile. Even unconscious she's stubborn.

She'll wake at some point. I'll wait. She's gonna be pissed—to say the least. I can only imagine what her emotions would have stirred up if I hadn't compelled that ability away. She would have given away our position for sure.

I look down at her and frown. I don't like compelling her. Part of me wishes I had never figured out that touch is the key. From this moment on, I will compel her only to keep her safe.

Before her, life was just easier when I compelled everyone around me. No one could stop me from getting what I wanted—girls, money, liquor. It didn't matter. It was all mine. More importantly, compelling everyone was my way of making sure no one got too close. Even as a demon without feelings, I guess I've always been that scared, pissed-off kid.

But Mads called me on it. Last Saturday over the phone, she said I've made my life a lie. She was right. Deep down, I've always known my life was shallow. I like that she challenges me—a demon—to be a better person.

If we're going to have a future together, it can't be one built on manipulation and lies. When she wakes, I'll tell her everything. I'll give her the truth *he* won't. Maybe then, finally, she'll understand I love her more than he does.

## CHAPTER 59

# Maddy

"I LOVE YOU, MJ."

I see a smile spread across my face as I look at my reflection in the bathroom mirror. For some reason, it's such a relief to say those words.

I have this strange feeling I missed my chance to tell him I love him. But I haven't. MJ's waiting for me at the table. I can go tell him right now.

I turn to dry my hands, and there, standing behind me, is MJ.

"MJ," I say with a nervous laugh, "what are you doing? This is the ladies' room."

But he just stares at me, his eyes wide and his mouth open. He must have heard me—he heard me say I love him. We gaze at each other for a moment, then he smiles and wraps his arms around me.

My heart swells. I feel this sudden, overwhelming desire to hold him closer. I don't know why, but it feels like an eternity since I've seen him.

"Let's go dance," I say.

MJ leans back, smiling down at me, looking at me with so much love that I never want this night to end.

"We are dancing," he says.

We're suddenly on the dance floor. Music fills my ears, and we're swaying.

Everything is covered in fog. It's hard to see through it, but we seem to be the only ones here. I don't even see Dad's band. But then where is that music coming from? "Where are my friends? My father and his band?"

"I sent them all home. I didn't want to share you anymore."

I smile and rest my head on his chest, grateful to be alone with him.

But with each revolution, this odd feeling grows inside me—like I'm missing something. Something important. I hold MJ tighter and try to ignore it, but I can't.

I break away from MJ, shaking my head. "This is wrong. I shouldn't be here."

But MJ just wraps his arms around me again, continuing our dance. "Nothing is wrong, Maddy."

I close my eyes and lean into him, wishing I could just lose myself in this moment. But from somewhere deep in my mind, I hear words I said earlier today to Sissy in the mall: *I feel like I'm dreaming, like this isn't real. I feel like I'm actually somewhere else—somewhere bad—and I created this happy scene to cope with it.*

Again, I push away and stop dancing. Panic fills me. "No. I mean it. Something is *wrong.*"

MJ touches my face. "We're together. I love you, and I know you love me too. Stay here. Stay where I can keep you safe."

"No."

I start marching back to our table, but the dance floor never ends. I stop and spin around. Every direction is dark.

"Where are we, MJ?"

"We're together," he says, pulling me back to him. "That's all that matters."

His essence picks up inside me, working to calm my rising panic. Once again, we begin to move, dancing to a song no one is playing.

This isn't real. It can't be.

This is a dream.

I did this. Something happened to me—something bad—and I created this to cope.

My heart aches so deeply that tears stream down my face. MJ wipes them away.

"Don't cry, Maddy," he begs. "Please."

I stare into his hazel eyes, memorizing his face, feeling as if this is the last time I'll see him. The tears fall harder.

"I'm sorry, MJ. I have to go. *I love you.*"

"No, Maddy. Just stay. I can't keep you safe if you leave. I can here. I can love you. And you can love me. But only if you stay."

"I want to stay," I say. "I do. I don't know what's happened to me, and I feel like … if I leave, I might never see you again. But I can't stay here. Staying here is giving up. I can't do that."

"Living isn't giving up," he pleads.

Tears pool in his hazel eyes as he stares at me with such despair that I step away.

"I'm sorry," I say. "This isn't real. *You're* not real."

Then I close my eyes, ignoring his desperate pleas. I have to concentrate and wake myself up.

I can do this.

As the fog lifts and I feel myself awakening, I hear someone take a breath beside me.

"Are you okay?" A familiar male voice cuts through the darkness.

I blink, adjusting to the light. Although it's dim, it's still a harsh contrast. A room begins to take shape, and foggy memories stream forward of being someplace new. Someplace dangerous.

I turn, and Justin's lying beside me in bed.

# CHAPTER 60

# Maddy

I JUMP UP, PUTTING THE BED BETWEEN ME AND JUSTIN. With the quick movement, my head sways. I grab the mattress for support.

Slowly, Justin gets out of bed on the other side, surprisingly giving me space.

As my head clears, so do my memories. I begin to piece them together. Justin took me from the bathroom at the bar. My soul went to Hell, and the masked demon came back with me to help me escape. I remember her fighting Justin and knocking him out. She left and I ran. I made it all the way to the living room, but the old woman shot me.

Oh, God. She *shot* me.

My hands fly to my abdomen. There's a gaping hole in the center of my dress, and the lace is stained with dried blood. There's dried blood all over my skin too. But I don't see the wound.

"I healed you," he says softly. "You're fine now."

I collapse, sitting on the bed. Nothing is fine.

Part of me wants to go back to wherever I was with MJ. But I can't. I can't go back to that dream, and I can't escape this reality.

There's no point in running now. In the best-case scenario, the masked demon will perhaps return and help me escape again. In the worst, I'm on my own until his compulsion wears off, if at all. MJ, the other Protectors, Elizabeth—they have no way of helping me.

Tears well up, and my vision blurs, but the tears won't fall. I can't cry. The house should be quaking from a storm matching what I feel inside me. But he's taken that from me. My emotions are prisoners, just as I am.

Suddenly Justin's standing in front of me. I flinch as he moves to touch me. He stops.

"I'm not going to hurt you, Mads. Never again."

In a flash, his words ignite a fire inside me that I wish could burn around me.

"You expect me to believe that?" I hiss. "You do nothing *but* hurt me. You are a cold, cruel monster. I remember every single horrible thing you've put me through!"

"Do you want me to erase those memories from you?" He doesn't even hesitate. And he says it so plainly, as if asking whether I'd like some ice cream.

A shiver runs through me as I answer him with silence.

"Thought as much," he replies. "But don't worry. I won't do that—not unless you force me to. Your memories are part of what makes you, you. As infuriating as you can be sometimes, I've grown accustomed to you."

I hold back the desire to laugh. He thinks he knows me. I don't even know me. Every day, I slip farther away from who I was as I become someone unrecognizable.

But as I look into his soulless eyes, I see how sure he is of himself—and me.

"When I heard the gun go off and saw you lying there, covered in your own blood, I thought I was too late. I thought I'd lost you."

My stomach quenches as phantom pains fill me. I try to ignore it.

"Yeah, well, don't act like you did me any favors by healing me."

"You don't get it, Mads," he says, shaking his head. "I thought I *lost* you. I took you to save you, and in the first couple hours, I nearly lost you. Forever."

His voice carries that same something the masked demon's voice carried when she told him not to use the blade on me.

"You're unclaimed, Mads," he says, his words heavy. "Neither Heaven nor Hell know of you. If you die, there is no peace, no afterlife, waiting for you. Just eternal nothingness. If even that."

He reaches out, running his fingers through my hair, but I'm too stunned to even feel it inside or outside of me. Of all the things I've learned about myself.

Unclaimed.

Nothingness.

"That's why there's a contract—it's a claim on you. It gives me the rights to your soul. I took you because I planned on making you sign it," he says, still caressing my hair.

This is it, then. I can't move. I can't breathe. I'm powerless to stop him this time. My blood drains from me as if he has already pierced me with the feather pen.

"But I don't want you to sign it. Not anymore."

I stare at him in disbelief. He stares back with an expression I've never seen on his face before.

Silence lingers between us.

"Why not?" I finally whisper.

He bends down so we're eye to eye. "Have you ever been to the circus, Mads?"

My eyes widen in surprise.

I don't know if he actually expects an answer, but I cautiously nod. I've gone twice—once with my family, another time as a school trip. Both were happy memories. I cling to thoughts of my family and friends, doubting I'll ever see them again.

"My mother took me to the circus when I was young," he says. "There was excitement. Danger. And everyone was happy. It was a rush I'd never felt before. My favorite part was the lion tamer—seeing the most feared jungle animal be tamed by nothing more than a whip and a chair. As I watched on, I envisioned joining the circus myself." His mouth forms a small smile, but there's also a hardness to it.

I can't stop myself from thinking of Justin as a little, innocent blue-eyed boy. As JayJay. But was his father already hitting him at that young age? Is that why he wanted to run away and join the circus?

"When the show was done, I snuck away from my mother and found my way backstage, to part of the circus the public isn't supposed to see. I came across the ringmaster, lion tamer, and the lion in its cage. I was hiding behind some props, and I wanted to rush up to them, ready to join the circus right then and there. But I stopped when the ringmaster picked up the whip and slashed the lion tamer across the back."

I wince, not expecting this turn in the story. I feel a memory of a sting on my back that I know he feels too. I look down at my arms and suddenly notice the scars are gone.

I kept them to remember. He took them back.

Justin grimaces. "The lion apparently hadn't performed to the ringmaster's standards. It didn't act ferocious enough. The crowd wasn't as scared as he wanted them to be. He threw the whip down to the tamer and ordered him to whip the lion. Whip him until he roared. Whip him until he bled. Whip him until he learned who was boss. And he did. I saw every lash."

My heart sinks, thinking of that scared little boy witnessing such horror—not unlike what he himself endured at the hands of his father.

"After, the ringmaster left," Justin continues. "I couldn't believe it, but the lion tamer reentered the lion's cage. I expected the lion would eat him—tear him to shreds for what he did. But he didn't. Instead, the tamer held the bleeding, broken lion and cried.

"So I got out of my hiding spot, walked up to the cage, and just stood there in silence. He looked up at me and said, 'To love someone, sometimes you have to hurt them to save them from being hurt by others.' You see, neither the lion nor the tamer had any control over their fate. Only the ringmaster." He pauses. "I never understood what he meant until now."

His eyes bore so deeply into mine that I can't help but lean away.

"I know I've hurt you, Mads. And I know I'm supposed to make you sign the contract. But if you do, then you'll be the lion and I'll be the tamer."

My lips quiver. Terror builds inside.

"Wh-who is the ringmaster?"

Justin gently places his hand on my cheek. I cringe as his essence enters me again.

"He's known as the Acquisitioner—he acquires souls for the Devil. He's the leader of the Fallen. He wants to use your abilities to assure himself as the new ruler of Hell.

But I will do everything I can to stop that from happening. I want us to be together—see the world. I want to make you happy."

His thumb strokes my cheek. "I need to know, is there even a remote possibility you could ever love me like you love *him*?"

Instantly I think of MJ and how I'll never get to tell him I love him. I whimper. I don't mean to—it just happens.

Justin places his forehead to mine. "Please, Mads, don't fight me. Let me love you, and love me back. That's all I want. Can't you feel how right we are for each other?"

I can't reply.

Justin pulls back. He stares at me, willing me to answer him. But I just can't.

"Tell me there's a chance, Mads," he begs. "Maybe not right away—I can understand that. But once I save you ... and we're free to be together, can you try to love me?"

Fear and heartache swell inside me, making it so I can't answer him.

He sighs.

Then in one motion, he lifts me and slams me against the wall. He leans his body into mine and grabs my wrists, pinning my hands beside my ears. His eyes are deep crimson.

"No! Let me go!" I shout, clamping my eyes as tight as they will go.

"Answer me, Mads! Could you love me?"

"You're a liar and a murderer! I'm not giving you what you want. *Ever*!"

"As you wish, Mads."

His essence picks up—more of it flows into my head. For a moment, I struggle and fight against him, trying desperately to free myself. But then my eyelids start to open. I can feel myself losing the battle even to keep my own eyes shut.

My eyes now open, I try to turn away, but my head is still. I try to shove him off, but I can't move my arms. His essence feels like lead inside me.

He leans over me, peering into me with his cold, black eyes. "You've left me no choice. From now until midnight next Friday, October thirty-first, whenever I ask you a question, you will answer it without delay. You cannot lie to me. You will learn to appreciate me and the things I do for you."

He smiles. "You're mine, Mads. Willingly or not. *Do you understand?*"

I want to scream and tell him to go to hell.

Instead I reply, "Yes."

## CHAPTER 61
# Elizabeth

I TURN AWAY, NOT WANTING TO WATCH HER REHEAT the poker in the flames of her elaborate fireplace.

My gaze lands on the bruised and bloody face of Chris Morgan. She's chained to a metal platform beside mine. Our capture has been harder on her—she's been in and out of consciousness for the last three days. That monster is using Chris's screams as another device to torture me.

Chris's pain and suffering is my fault. I'm the one who convinced her so many years ago to help us with Madison. I'm the one who talked her into staying on Mortal Ground to protect Madison in a way Guardians never have before. I'm the one who chose the cabin I shared with Damien as the meeting place should Madison ever be in trouble.

And I'm the one who led Reina, the Gatekeeper, to us both.

The poker sizzles, ready for the next round of questioning. With Chris unconscious, this round is for me. I should be used to the pain by now—we've been at this almost nonstop since Wednesday morning. No matter what she does to me, I will not give her the information she wants.

I concentrate on the candelabra dangling twenty feet above me. Over a hundred black candles, with flames reaching higher than any natural candle's flame, blaze in an eerie glow against bone holders. Human bone. I try not to grimace in horror. Instead, I pretend it's just an oddly beautiful candelabra and the curved and broken bones belong to some animal.

Maybe that's all I am to her.

My breath catches as the red-hot poker touches the skin under my right ribcage. I try not to scream as layers of my flesh burn away, creating a foul smell.

"Come on, Elizabeth," Reina coos, "let it out. That has to hurt."

Reina's onyx eyes gleam with firelight, and her plum-colored lips smile as she towers over me. She looks just as wild and brazen as the day I met her. I suppose she'd have to be, being the only surviving female Archangel. Black locks, tightly curled, frame her oval face and extend down to her red-leather corset that matches her leather pants. Behind her, black-feathered wings extend high above her head and flow down to meet the ground.

"Just a little scream?" she pleads, running the poker over more of my skin.

It sizzles like bacon on a skillet. I bite my cheeks against the pain.

"Your screams are my favorite part. You can actually *feel*, which makes this even sweeter. Do you still think it is worth it—the pain, years of lies, death, and exile—all for that abomination?"

For a moment the heat is gone. I release my breath, hoping she's gotten bored again.

"Yes," I pant. "And I'd do it all over again—"

Reina jabs the end of the poker into my abdomen, burning me from the inside out. I finally scream and wither against my restraints. The red glowing shackles peel away more skin on my ankles and wrists, causing my scream to deepen.

If I could, I would enter the Great Divide and leave this godless place. I can't, though. The horrible devices holding me to the metal slab are enchanted so the dead can't escape from them.

She pulls out the poker again. "You are a fool, Elizabeth." She smirks. "It will be all the more enjoyable when I finally break you."

I turn away again and close my eyes, sending out a prayer that Madison is safe.

I wanted to stay long enough to make sure she woke after MJ pulled her from the fire, but then I felt the Gatekeeper's presence on Mortal Ground. I knew if I lingered, I would only lead Reina to her—after seventeen years of great lengths and sacrifices to keep her safe. So I left her unconscious in MJ's arms, recovering from the Influencer's attack, and I fled to our cabin to meet Chris.

I open my eyes. Reina turns her back on me, reheating the poker. Everything inside tightens, anticipating the pain. I will withstand whatever Reina does to me. I must in order to keep Madison safe.

She will save us all.

I turn and stare at Chris again. Her lids flutter as she begins to regain consciousness. That was the longest stretch she's been unconscious. Her wounds are barely healing anymore. She can't take this much longer.

Her eyes suddenly open and lock on mine.

I wish Cerebrallink worked in here so I could tell her to stay still and quiet. She needs more time to heal before Reina tortures her again. Instead, I tilt my head toward her, my eyes searching hers, then pretend to sleep for a moment. I hope she will understand I want her to rest and recover her strength.

After a moment, her chin drops slightly in a nod before she closes her eyes again. I take a breath, then return my attention to Reina.

The flames dancing around the poker reflect in her onyx eyes. "I killed you because I thought it would free *him*," she says. "I thought it would bring Damien back to me. Of all my lovers, he is my favorite."

At the sound of his name, hope blossoms in my chest. My gaze flashes to the enormous set of doors on the other side of the room, watching for him to come rushing in to save me.

She tilts her head back and laughs. "That is right. I can say 'Damien' as many times as I want, and he will not hear it. My chambers are protected. You can say it too. Give it a try. Cry out for your lover to save you. Your faith in him is pathetic."

"What's pathetic," I spit back, "is lusting after—"

She slaps me with such force, my head smacks against the slab. Her lips curl, and deep loathing pours out of her eyes.

"I was supposed to be rid of you. But then you had to save that damn *abomination*. It had so much power in its puny body and no way of controlling it."

Right after Reina killed me in that car accident, I saw Madison. Oh, the things she could do. Her very breath, even as a newborn, defied the rules of both Heaven and

Hell. I brought Damien to her. We both knew she would never be safe if anyone found out about her. They would either kill her—as Reina has tried to do—or use her abilities to bring great devastation.

Of all the Fallen, he feared Reina the most. Because of her, he has always protected Madison from a distance. He couldn't get involved unless it is absolutely necessary.

"I followed him, letting him lead me to the child in Seattle. I admit I thought he killed it—he killed so many in that hospital. But then you resurfaced with it in Georgia. Again, I thought he killed it when he burned the foster home. It took me sixteen years to figure out he lied to me."

In one swift motion she clears the distance between us and shoves the poker into my abdomen again. I bend forward, cringing in pain, unable to scream from how badly it hurts. Tears stream forward, blurring my vision.

"So which one of the remaining four girls is she?"

She twists the poker inside me, trying to draw out my answer.

Through the intense pain, all I can think is, thank God she doesn't know who Maddy is. Her list only includes the decoys. They were Damien's idea. I never approved—up until this year.

Slowly, Reina inches the poker out, allowing me to breathe and answer her.

"I don't … know what … you're talking about."

She shoves the poker back in and leans over me, coming so close I can feel the heat from her skin.

"I will find the abomination." Each word is felt against my cheek. "And I will destroy her."

Reina withdraws the poker and points it at Chris—my blood drips off the end. "Who else besides this Guardian is helping you hide her?"

Chris stiffens in fear at the reference. I pray Reina doesn't notice.

Her eyes narrow at me.

"No one," I reply.

"Liar!" she growls. "I know you and Damien have others hiding her. That is how you were able to guard the child without leading me to her again. Is there another traitor among us? Or perhaps it is another from your side?"

"There's no one," I lie again.

I wasn't able to send word to Duane the Shadowwalker before Reina caught us. I don't know if he's aware of what Maddy went through at the demon's house. I hope he is. I hope he and the Protector are working together to save her.

"What about the two Protectors who showed up just after the eighth girl died? Are they working with you too?"

I hold my tongue.

She clucks, disappointed, and sets the poker back in its holder. "Well, no matter. I will find out who they are soon enough. Whoever is protecting the abomination, I will end them. I will end them all."

At that, a blade suddenly appears in her hand. It's made of bone, curved and broken. Red leather wraps around the handle. She raises it to my cheek. Power—evil power—radiates from it.

Everything inside me tightens.

"This," she says, "is a present I had created for myself. It destroys lesser beings like you. It cannot kill an Archangel, however—a girl can never be too careful."

She marches over to Chris—and stabs her in the heart.

Chris's eyes fly open in horror, and her mouth drops. Before I can scream, she's gone. Her body vanishes. Forever.

Violent sobs rack my body. This too is my doing. I may not have held the blade myself, but her permanent death is on my hands.

Reina inspects the blade, holding it up for us both to see. There isn't even any blood on it—no proof she just destroyed Chris. She smiles, satisfied with what she's done, then the blade disappears.

"I know about your Time Keeper," she says.

My grief vanishes. "What?"

She points to the right. I strain my neck. Beside her plush velvet couch, I see the white edge of what looks like a fountain.

"How thoughtful of you to create that for me." She grins.

Fear grips my heart until it's so small I feel hollow. "What are you going to do with my fountain?" My voice is as empty as my heart.

"Dearest Elizabeth, I have already done it. I used the fountain to link to your pet and suck her soul into the body of the last girl I killed. She felt the flames of death as if it were her own. I will do the same with the remaining girls. For her sake, you should hope she is the next girl." Her grin widens. "Personally, I hope she is the last."

She grabs my chin, her long fingernails piercing my skin as she forces me to stare into her soulless onyx eyes.

"I will destroy the abomination—and with it, her ability to make the dead feel. *I* will be crowned the new ruler of the City of the Damned. Damien will be mine again. And I will spend *eternity* torturing you for your sins."

She gives my face a hard shove, then spins away. "Good-bye, Elizabeth. I am off to kill your precious savior."

"*No!*" I scream, struggling to break free as she walks away. "Reina, please don't—"

A massive door slides shut behind me. The motion blows the flames out on the candelabra.

Maddy has no idea what's coming for her. Damien can't help her—not yet.

Her life rests in the hands of the Original Protector—though if he knew who and what she really is, he would destroy her too.

# Acknowledgments

THANK YOU SO MUCH TO ALISHA BJORKLUND, SARA Campbell, Sharon Lenz, and my husband, Mike Wetzel, for helping me not only continue Maddy and MJ's story but also make it a story worth reading.

I would also like to thank all my family and friends who have been gracious enough to allow me to use their names and or likenesses for characters in my story—especially my friends whose names I use for the victims of my killer. It takes a peculiar sort of person to be okay with someone killing you in a book. And it takes an even odder sort of person to read her downfall and offer suggestions on how to make it more gruesome. That is just one more reason why I love you all.

To my friends and family whom I haven't yet included in my books—I'm getting to you. Have patience. There are many more books in this series as well as other stories in the works. If you want to be in a story sooner . . . send one of the following: gummi worms, ice cream, or caffeine. Or watch the boys. That works too.

To my editor, Angela Wiechmann—I am grateful and blown away by your dedication to your craft. Together we create amazing things, and I can't wait for our next adventure. To my designer, Tiffany Daniels—your ability to create such wonderful covers based on nothing more than my words astounds me. Thank you again making my story look so beautiful.

Finally, I want to thank Amy Quale, Dara Beevas, and Laura Zats at Wise Ink Creative Publishing for continuing to believe in me. Your unwavering trust, faith, and support are the greatest gifts of all, and I do not take them lightly. I look forward to many more books and many more years of working with such talented, remarkable women.

L AURIE WETZEL HAS always had a passion for writing, but it wasn't until a New Year's resolution in 2011 that she finally shared with her husband her lifelong dream of being an author. He read the very first draft of *Unclaimed* and gave her the words she needed to hear: "This is what you need to be doing." Three years later, her dream became reality when the first book in the Unclaimed Series was published.

Laurie lives in Mankato, Minnesota, with her husband and two young sons. She became a thyroid cancer survivor in 2014 and has since helped raise awareness and donations for research through events held in person and online. When she's not writing, working, or spending time with her family, she's reading, working out, or catching up on her favorite shows.

For updates on *Unclaimed* and *Ignited* as well as other works in progress, feel free to check her out online.

 /LaurieRWetzel

 @Laurie_Wetzel

 lauriewetzel.com